Uncharted Territory

Uncharted Territory

Hadley Hoover

To Laura:
Happy Reading!
Hadley Hoover

Writers Club Press
San Jose New York Lincoln Shanghai

Uncharted Territory

Writers Club Press
an imprint of iUniverse.com, Inc.

For information address:
iUniverse.com, Inc.
5220 S 16th, Ste. 200
Lincoln, NE 68512
www.iuniverse.com

ISBN: 0-595-19367-6

Printed in the United States of America

To my own two-legged and four-legged guys
—both of whom love me unconditionally.

ACKNOWLEDGEMENTS

Distinct gratitude to Rose Howard, my "real" North Dakota friend: Thanks for a lifelong friendship no matter how far apart we've lived.

Special thanks to all from around the country and closer at hand who read *Miles Apart* and then wrote, e-mailed, or stopped me on the street to ask, "When's the next one coming out?" You hold the answer in your hands.

CHAPTER ONE

Block letters on the front window informed the curious that CATE'S CAFÉ was OPEN MONDAY—SATURDAY 6:00 AM—7:00 PM, but neglected to mention one pertinent detail: the woman who shared her name with her business was also cook, wait-staff, baker, cashier, and daily entertainment. The aroma of this morning's coffee cake gained steadily on the lingering wisps from last night's dinner special as Cate swooped from the kitchen with four plates lining one arm, each reaching its destination with nary a mishap. From a corner table, Victoria Dahlmann watched Cate juggle banter and breakfast with equal ease.

"How long has this place been called *Cate's* Café?" Victoria asked idly as the woman swooped from kitchen-to-table with four plates lining one arm. As usual, Victoria had followed her nose's recommendation and now chased the last crumbs of pecan coffee cake with her fork.

It was more than Cate's considerable culinary skills that made her business flourish in a struggling North Dakota town. Every day, the guarantee of news and gossip pulled a steady stream of regular customers past the cold coffee pots on their own kitchen counters. Victoria eyed the remnants of the cinnamon-streusel topping on the plate as she waited for the answer to her question from the man who shared her table.

"Her dad opened the café and named it after her before she could even walk," responded Luke Larson. "Why do you ask?"

She shrugged. "Just trying to catch up on the town history I've missed out on by moving here so late in the game," she said and chased a crumb with her fork.

"Prairie Rose believes in keeping its business names plain and honest. Who owns it, what it is. No grandiose promises, no bragging. Just the facts."

"And that's why we have Ed's Garage, Cate's Café to cover the who-owns it, and Wilson's Clip and Curl to satisfy the what-it-is!"

"You're on to us. Oops, since my name is above the entrance to Larson's Grocery, I had better go run it."

It was easy for Victoria to understand why *eligible* ran a close second to *nice guy* in anyone's description of Luke. The plain and simple reason: Luke—compared to most other single men in Prairie Rose—still had his own teeth and hair, and he had a visible means of support. He owned Larson's Grocery. That covered *eligible*. And *nice* was equally obvious: his eyes said *You are important enough to me to have my full attention* when he talked with anyone and his actions matched.

In the short time—just since June—since Victoria had moved from Minneapolis to Prairie Rose, she had learned the facts about Prairie Rose. Before she had even flipped a single calendar page she realized that a much revered triad sustained physical life in this town: dozens of backyard gardens, this very café, and the grocery store at the opposite end of the block.

"I need to meet the dairy truck. See you at church tomorrow." Luke stood beside the table, digging around in his pocket for coins to pay for coffee.

"Nah, we'll meet up before then. I'll be in to the store later today, Luke. It looks like Old Mother Hubbard's cupboard at my house." Victoria flicked a wandering bronze curl back from her face and conducted her own assessment of the unsuspecting man as he moved away. *Hmmm. Good-looking in a PG-rated movie kind of way. Not sure what*

PG-rated kind of things he'd do, but, hey! She watched Luke move confidently between the crowded tables.

"Any good sales today at Larson's Grocery?" The query rose as he passed one group of four men.

"Always!" Luke shot back with a wide smile. "Of course, an avowed tightwad like you doesn't admit anything is a 'good sale' unless it's free, right, Harry?" Knowing that Harry would lead the spontaneous laughter at his own expense, Luke made his exit with a chuckle that robbed his words of any maliciousness.

"Well, you set yourself up for that one, Harry," Cate teased. "You better spring for coffee today for your friends here to counter the tightwad label!" Good-natured and accustomed to the ribbing, Harry pulled out his wallet and obliged, but not without the obligatory deep sigh.

During the four months since she had backed the rental truck between the wrought-iron gate posts that marked her driveway, Victoria had slipped easily into the comfortable routines of a small town. Just like the locals, she now paused to chat with friends and acquaintances pushing carts along the grocery store aisles, or stopped to shoot the breeze with neighbors enjoying the evening air from their front porches.

What a perfect place to launch my career! No endless staff meetings that accomplish little. Lots of freedom to try new things. She leaned back in her chair and grinned for no particular reason other than sheer euphoria. *And some of the nicest people on God's green earth.*

Just then, a supposedly red pickup truck—held together more by its coat of rust than by Detroit's ingenuity—pulled up to the curb with much grinding and rattling. Victoria pushed back two chairs in readiness for their next occupants. But before Oscar and Jean had even slammed the truck's doors, Victoria's gaze shifted, snagged by a split-second reflection of sunlight on a door that opened across the street.

A man stepped outside the brick-fronted building and stretched to his full height. Arching his back beneath a polo shirt tucked into jeans that might well have been spackled on his body, he tilted his head toward the sky.

Good Lord. That looks exactly like…It can't be…Tell me it isn't true! Oh dear God.

It wasn't prayer, it was panic. It should have been prayer, when the Reverend Victoria Dahlmann's mind skidded to a stop, but it was panic. Sheer, stressful, heart-pounding panic. A dreaded tornado cutting a swath through Prairie Rose right then would have created less havoc in her life than the sight of that one man soaking up the morning sunshine across the street.

Around her, townsfolk chattered and laughed. Inside her, life as she now knew and loved it screeched to a halt.

"Mind if we join you?"

"Huh?" She looked up into the pleasant faces of Oscar and Jean who had every reason to believe that the chairs she had pushed back just seconds earlier were intended for them.

"Mind if we join you?" Jean repeated sweetly.

"No, not at all," Victoria said, and pushed herself back from the table and stood. "In fact, the table is all yours; I have to leave." She jammed her hand into a jeans pocket to pull out a couple of crumpled bills and tossed them on the table. Oscar and Jean looked quizzically at Victoria, then at each other, and shrugged as they sat down cautiously, wondering if they had misinterpreted the unspoken invitation of two chairs pushed away from the table.

Unwilling to look, but incapable of stopping herself, Victoria stole one last desperate glance out the window.

No longer standing and stretching.

He was moving!

In fact he was half-way across the street, homing in on Cate's Café.

Victoria emitted a small wordless sound and made a beeline for Cate at one end of the U-shaped counter. "Cate, I'm heading out your back door, okay?"

Cate's "No problem" hung in the air; her questioner was long gone. Before she could even wonder about that odd retreat, the front door to her café opened again, and she sent a greeting to her latest patron wafting over the din. "Hey, Doc! Here's a spot for you with these old reprobates at this table. Shove around, Gus. Make room for Doctor Alex."

"Two coffees over here, Cate, when you get a minute," Oscar drawled from the corner of the room, and Saturday moved back on track for all the inhabitants of Prairie Rose except one.

Victoria reached her backyard in less than two minutes. She opened the back gate and hung on it until she could catch her breath. The last time she remembered racing like that, she had earned a blue ribbon from her girl scout leader. No one lurked nearby handing out any awards today. *Where is my dog?* "Cino?" she called, adding the familiar two-tone whistle.

No response from the galloping bundle of fur that usually would have been in action at the first squeak of the gate. A laugh and the smell of pipe tobacco pulled Victoria to the side of her house. "Unless Cino's taken up smoking, something fishy is going on," she sputtered as she strode across the lawn.

Seated two-to-a-side at her picnic table, four gray-haired men—only one of whom she knew by name—stared back at her like deer caught in the headlights. A box of doughnuts, a margarine tub containing what looked like powdered sugar, and a thermos formed a line on a green plastic tablecloth. Each man held a steaming coffee mug.

Cino sat with head cocked to one side and with ears at attention, his chin propped on the far end of the table. He allowed his tail to recognize Victoria's presence, clearly torn between unabashed love for his mistress and the enchanting visitors to his domain. "Excuse me?" The words were polite, but Victoria's tone meant business. "Bryce, did I miss an appointment with you and your friends?"

"Hello, Pastor Victoria! You're back earlier than usual, aren't you?" Bryce side-stepped her question while he finished swirling his dough-nut in the margarine tub. *Yup, powdered sugar.*

The man seated next to Bryce stood up, his legs still between the bench and the table which gave him less than perfect points for posture. "We had planned to be gone before you returned, but you've changed your schedule this morning. We're the ROMEOs. You know Bryce—he picked your back yard—and I'm Richard, and this is Lewis," a bald man saluted her, "and that talkative fellow is Mitchell." The pipe smoker nod-ded in response to his name and puffed without comment.

Have I been dragged down a hole with a small girl named Alice? Should I be calling 911 right about now?

"You must not know about us, being fairly new to town like you are. ROMEO stands for Retired Old Men Eating Out," Richard offered in explanation. "We're very sorry to have disturbed you. Usually we meet earlier, but some of us had scheduling problems today. We'll be out of here in no time."

His words were a bugle-call to action to the other three men. The tub of powdered sugar disappeared into the nearly empty carton of dough-nuts. Bryce whisked away the thermos, cups and tablecloth into a box beside him. Each leaving friendly pats on Cino's head, the men headed for the gate. Victoria stood alone with her now disconsolate dog in her own backyard.

She stared at the picnic table incredulously, wondering for a moment if she could possibly have imagined the whole scene. Bewildered and tense, she headed for the back porch swing. "*What* was *that* about, Cino? You broke about six rules as far as I can tell," she said and flicked a tell-tale clump of powdered sugar off his muzzle. He flopped down beside her, sighing loudly.

Then she noticed a Mason jar of mums beside her back door—out of the way of traffic, but strategically placed where she was sure to see them. This was curious, but coming after the shock of seeing *him* on

Main Street followed by finding a geriatric men's group in her back yard, a jar of flowers on her back porch hardly registered on her scale of strange events.

* * *

"Champion dog, indeed," Victoria muttered under her breath. Her mood was anything but Sunday-best. The mental image of her dog at full alert with his front legs hooked on the top rung of the wrought iron fence was all too vivid as she strode across the lawn. Despite his obstinate oblivion to her explicit commands, she had run out of time to discipline him properly in the few minutes she had grabbed at home between comings and goings on the busiest morning of her week.

The church bell beckoned her with more authority than she possessed in dealing with Cino. A minister couldn't keep an entire congregation waiting just because her canine housemate had turned unexpectedly and inexplicably willful. "Yesterday he welcomes total strangers into our yard, and today he decides he's top dog," she moaned.

Part of Victoria's problem was that she was exhausted. She had not slept well. Why not admit it? She hadn't done much of anything well all day Saturday. From the time she hit the alley behind the café and zeroed in on her own back door, she hadn't known a minute's peace. And now she was more than a little jittery from consuming twice as much coffee as usual in a futile attempt to counter very little sleep.

Hang it all, anyway.

Throughout the opening rituals of the service order, she could hear muted excited barks dulled by the thick walls and she grimaced, wishing she'd had the time and energy to drag those 125 independent fur-clad pounds across the lawn and lock each and every stubborn one of them securely behind the kitchen door with the dog-door blocked off. Her jutting chin was the only clue that the confrontation was not over as she began her pastoral duties before her stoic North Dakota parish.

The organ's majestic notes caressed the arches of the sanctuary and subtly began to stroke her frazzled nerves. Victoria smoothed the ministerial robe that whispered around her ankles, and forced a few measured breaths to relax her body. She then rose from the high-backed platform chair.

As she ascended the four carpeted steps leading to an intricately carved oak pulpit, thoughts of the rebellious dog and her sleepless night were replaced by the needs of her congregation and the purpose for them all being there. She whispered a quick prayer for all, like herself, whose private worlds distracted them today.

An uncommon restless tension hummed during the final seating of latecomers and now continued with craned necks and whispered confidences. Victoria had been so preoccupied initially that she had only subconsciously noticed the people's agitated state. Looking out over the normally unflappable crowd, she was propelled up to full speed with them.

He was here.

Victoria bit her lip and wished she could go home. *Ho-boy, this caps the weekend. Two males royally messing up my life—one canine, one human. And that's not counting the four trespassers!* Swallowing hard, she turned pages in the oversized pulpit Bible and reverted to her old grade school habit of marking the spot with her index finger.

This was her second run of today's sermon. Two hours earlier, eighteen miles away, the smaller Indian Hills congregation had heard it first. That was Victoria's only hope of making sense now with such a visitor's eyes riveted on her face.

The final piece in the summer's puzzle fell firmly into place and filled in the rest of the picture. No doubt about it: The man who had stretched in Saturday's sunshine was the same man who had been the topic of endless morning discussions up and down Main Street for the past four months.

His flesh-and-blood identity confirmed the reason Victoria's heart beat so erratically just when she needed to be calm and professional.

Walking down the aisle, he staked a claim on the aisle next to Widow O'Dell who didn't shift her ancient bones so much as an inch in the fifth row on the left when her seatmate smiled at her. If anything, she moved a fraction closer on the pew she had guarded like a homesteader for over forty years of Sunday mornings.

Amazingly enough, the look on Sadie O'Dell's age-lined face wasn't one of tight-lipped vengeance against the squatter. While she would have withered any other interloper into fearful retreat with one piercing glance, she appeared to admire this man's nerve in usurping her site.

Despite the widow's widespread fame as seamstress, she made no effort to limit her undisguised approval to his wardrobe selections for his first religious excursion in Prairie Rose. He actually looked quite comfortable in the tailored tan suit, a crisp mauve linen shirt without a visible wrinkle, and wonder-of-wonders: a diagonally striped burgundy and blue tie. For someone whose coloring practically shouted "Scandinavian!" the entire gentlemanly ensemble certainly boasted appropriate choices for his occupation despite a physique that prompted thoughts of basketball courts and cheering fans.

Behind Victoria, the choir's rustling robes snatched her back to the present; she managed a jagged breath. "Our special thanks to this morning's readers from the youth group. It is especially fitting to have young voices read today's text. Peter, one of Jesus' disciples, is a grown man with a dangerous job, fishing on that unpredictable Sea of Galilee. But in Matthew's Gospel, we see him respond to life with an enthusiasm that is all too often characteristic only of the young..."

The brick walls of the century-old church held the mid-September morning's warmth at bay, but trickles of perspiration threatened to betray Victoria's placid demeanor. It was bad enough to have arrived back in Prairie Rose late Friday night after eight days away, and be counting on Saturday to regain all her energy in anticipation of Sunday.

And it sure didn't help to discover her pride and joy, Cino, barking at God-only-knows-what beyond the fence when she rolled back into town this morning after the first service at Indian Hills.

But the more disconcerting realization came each time during the flawless eighteen-minute homily that her eyes swept to the West side of the sanctuary, the unfaltering gaze of Prairie Rose's other newcomer rocked her trusted reserve. He had arrived during her absence. Even before that, he had released a whirling frenzy of joy in town when he announced his impending arrival with a tasteful quarter-page advertisement in the weekly newspaper.

At least a Doctor Alexander Johanson had done so in early July.

She didn't know any Doctor Alexander Johanson.

She knew Zan Johanson. Oh Lordy, did she ever know him. And Zan Johanson knew her in ways altogether too familiar for the woman in clerical robes to even think about, especially when standing in the pulpit with a task at-hand.

Yesterday, the sight of him through the café window had knocked the wind plumb out of her sails, but his appearance on Victoria's turf this morning sank the whole wretched boat. Somehow during her Saturday ruminations she had doubted—no, she never even suspected—that he would bother with church. *No-no-no, not the Zan Johanson I knew.*

Finally, she completed the last point on her sermon outline and sank into the chair out of the congregation's view. The choir rose behind her to lead the closing anthem.

"Oh God, our help in ages past, our hope for years to come, be Thou our guide while life shall last, and our eternal home," they sang. *Ain't that the truth.* The lines of that centuries-old hymn were suddenly more than words on a page—they were a crucial lifeline for Victoria.

Familiar routines pulled her through the next quarter hour: the walk to the back of the sanctuary, pausing there to pronounce the benediction; the flurry of greetings from these kind and amiable people who had taken a chance on her, their first woman minister.

Then, like the Red Sea parted for Moses, the wall of people split in two and all lanky six-feet-one-inch of him moved toward her with out-stretched hand. "Thank you, Reverend Dahlmann, for the sermon. You've given me a challenge for the week."

It didn't take one nickel's worth of that costly knowledge gained in three years of Seminary classes for Victoria to interpret his seemingly innocuous murmuring. She knew that this visitor whose left-cheek dimple sign-posted every smile was not referring to her exhortation to step out in faith like Peter. It was all she could do to hold back an unpro-fessional snort. Instead, she lifted her hand to meet his and said evenly, "Thank you, Doctor Johanson."

Voices formed a humming cocoon around them. "Just Alex." *Straight blonde spun-silk hair. Strong, confident hands.* Coming from lips she found impossible to ignore, his next words jolted her. "May I invite you for brunch? My place. Across the street. End of the block."

Victoria dropped her eyes to their still-clasped hands and moistened her chalk-dry lips. "Uh…" *No, say no, Victoria.* "Yes, I could do that." *You idiot. You certifiable idiot.*

"Great! I'll let you finish here," he glanced at the people milling around them, "and see you soon." He released her hand with a lingering and possibly imagined squeeze. Sunlight enveloped him as he passed through the church door. There was not one drop of saliva left in her mouth when she turned to the next person in line.

"We certainly can add that to our leadership meeting agenda this week, Luke. Good idea." *Why did I say yes to his invitation?*

"Yes, I had a great time in the mountains, but it's good to be back." *Why? Why me? Why now?*

"Thank you, Mrs. Martin. I'm glad you're enjoying this series of ser-mons." *As soon as I get home, I'll call and excuse myself, plead a headache.*

"Have a great first year of college, Sherry! Will we see you at Thanksgiving? Wonderful!" *Yeah, right! Like a doctor's going to buy that hackneyed excuse!*

"The christening for the newest Guddman is coming up quickly! Isn't she growing fast?" *If I don't go, he'll back off and life will be able to regain...Dream on, Kiddo; it's unlikely your life will ever be normal again.* Groaning inwardly, she bent to admire a child's Sunday School artwork.

Finally. She closed the door behind the last parishioner and leaned against the wall in the back of the now-quiet sanctuary. *What an hour! Actually, what a whollop the last twenty-four hours have aimed straight at me.* Gravitating to the fifth pew, she lowered herself to the very spot where today's visitor had sat.

What had he seen? The pulpit gleaming from years of tender care? *Yeah, right.* The light streaming through the stained glass window of The Good Shepherd? *Not likely, since his eyes stayed glued on me.*

Why had he come? Out of curiosity? *Step right up, folks! Come see a clergywoman in action!* Or more likely, to win points with townsfolk by attending services of worship? *I, for one, am not buying this religious camouflage donned by the new doctor.*

Victoria pursed her lips and scratched a senseless pattern on the pew cushion with a peach-tipped fingernail. Two congregations, the Prairie Rose Community Church and the rural Indian Hills United Church, had called her at the beginning of the summer as their shared minister. Seminary and her internships had prepared her well for the demands of such a position in an isolated place.

Prepared? Sure, except for forward young doctor's invitations—that disruptive man whose eyes said more than his lips.

Cino's voice was again heard throughout the land. Victoria sighed as reality yanked her world back into focus. The squeak of the opening church door brought to life the waiting hunk of tri-colored fur. Victoria grinned at her three-year-old Bernese Mountain Dog who waited all a-twitter by the fence near the church's back entrance. "Hold on, Buddy!" She quickly covered the space between them. "Yes, yes, I've missed you, too." Opening the gate, she gave the hand signal that brought Cino from his air-borne-with-delight leap to a heel position; they moved back toward the church together. "I'm not quite done over here, yet, but you can come visit. Is that what you wanted?"

As she opened the door again, and Cino padded in beside her and claimed his favorite spot on the rug, she unzipped the robe and let it shimmer farther down her arms. In the small attached restroom, Victoria tugged a comb through her burnished copper hair and assessed her reflection in the mirror.

The peach linen dress showed seat-belt wrinkles added during the trip back from Indian Hills. Her makeup subtly attempted to offset the ungovernable curly bronze frame her hair formed for her face. And, despite her faithful care to wear a straw hat all summer, a few stray freckles were now stubborn reminders of her first gardening experience. She wrinkled her nose playfully at her reflection and turned off the light.

Back in the office, she quickly filed away her sermon notes, jotted several calendar notations from conversations of the morning, and puttered around watering the plants. Soon there was nothing left to do but go.

Victoria squinted in the bright sun, facing her home. Cino flopped next to her, one huge paw affectionately pinning her foot in place as they surveyed their house together.

Surrounded by a vast lawn with stately old cottonwood, elm, and pine trees, the residence usually overwhelmed her. Two stories high with a full rough-finished basement, impressive dormer windows on both front and back sides of the roof, five bedrooms, two bathrooms, and a family-sized kitchen complete with a walk-in pantry were daunting enough. But when you added a formal dining room, the old-fashioned parlor, and an enchanting screened porch that wrapped around three sides, it provided far too much dwelling for a single minister and her four-legged friend. Locals called it The Rectory, even though decades had passed since anyone living beneath the ten-foot ceilings had answered to such a formal title as "Rector."

Several minutes of exposure to the noon heat ended her reverie and she moved to open the gate into the yard. "Go inside, Cino. It's too hot for you out here." She pulled a thistle out of his white vest before bending to give him a hug and savor his responding nuzzle. "Take care of the house until I get back. And no more barking, you hear?"

With a sigh, the dog sat at her feet offering his best depressed-pooch impression. She shook her head ruefully, pointing toward the house. "Your pity-me efforts are in vain. Sorry." Cino dragged his feet toward his dog-door, mirroring his mistress' reluctance in crossing the street to the waiting Doctor Alexander Johanson.

CHAPTER TWO

Pancakes?

The front door was open and the unmistakable smell of pancakes drifted out, mingling oddly with a heady scent of recently watered marigolds in window boxes on either side of the screen door. A tell-tale garden hose draped over the porch railing, dripping into a puddle below.

The creaking porch signaled her approach even before she touched the door. This alerted a four-legged doorbell who skidded to a stop just shy of the door and growled ominously. All the while, a white-tipped tail threatened to wag itself right off.

"Good grief, he's got a Berner!" The words erupted in a shocked gulp. She had no idea if the outburst had carried to her host; she instantly hoped the old house had walls thick enough to preserve her rapidly dwindling reserve of dignity.

From inside, the familiar voice called out, "Come on in! Either follow my official greeter, or trust your nose. Just head through the living room, then hang a right."

Victoria opened the door and stepped inside and let the dog sniff her up and down. "You're a beauty," she whispered, trailing her fingers across her alert and furry escort's perfectly shaped body as they moved toward the kitchen. She felt light-headed, but incapable of taking deep breaths to remedy the condition.

Gone were the suit, tie, and dignity of the morning. Long muscular legs burst forth from faded cutoffs, disappearing into much-worn leather sandals. A bibbed tarp-like apron attempted to cover his chest. A bare chest. The knotted strap around his neck pulled it up only mid-way.

Victoria smiled resolutely, yanked her eyes away from that well-toned body to say heartily, "It sure smells good in here."

He gave his attention to flipping the eight pancakes puffing up on the stove's griddle. "Yup. Nothing tops the smell of hundreds of pancakes bubbling' away."

"Your count is probably not too far off." Victoria stared unabashedly at the steaming piles on the kitchen table. "Expecting an army to drop by?"

"Not today! It's such a mess to make 'em that I cook up a double recipe at a time. When those on the table are cool, I'll freeze them. Having just arrived in town, I've got a freezer that needs filling!" He shifted his shoulder to hitch up the wandering apron strap. "Hard to imagine that they'll cool down much, hot as it is in here," he added. For a woman who earned her living using words, Victoria was speechless.

Beads of perspiration shone on his shoulder blades. "You'll have to excuse my attire for this auspicious occasion. The hotter the kitchen gets, the less I wear." He jutted a leg in her direction, an unnecessary illustration of this unnerving detail.

"No problem." *Unless you consider my erratic non-ministerial pulse a problem, Doctor.* Long sheets of waxed paper lined the table, with rows and rows of pancakes spaced inches apart; he showed no signs of easing up on the mass production. "It looks like you're gearing up for the Feeding of the 5,000, if you'll allow a Biblical allusion." *Yikes, I sound like every minister ever invented for late-night movies: stuffy, prudish, phony, sickening.*

He laughed easily. "Well, it's more like we're feeding me 5,000 times, Reverend Dahlmann!"

Suddenly, she had never felt less like Reverend anything. "First names will be fine—okay, Alex?" She clipped the words off, forcing herself to keep a casual tone, despite the flare of temper that fueled the retort.

"You got it, Tori!"

Victoria's jaw tightened. "*That* name was left behind years ago. In high school. I go by Victoria now, as I'm sure you've figured out. I'll appreciate it if you remember that. I'm happy to call you Alex and leave 'Zan' in the past for you, too."

Alex dramatically slapped his hand in the general location of his heart. "You'll only ever be Tori for me." Enchanting chuckles rumbled in his throat. "Must say, I just couldn't believe it when I saw you standing up there! You looked so, uh, regal. In a, dare-I-say-it, sexy way." He whistled reverently.

Her knees wobbled. "When I, uh, saw you in the congregation this morning, I found it a bit difficult to absorb, too. That's the last place I ever imagined to find you." Outside, the strident call of a grackle punctuated a lazy afternoon for the rest of the world. She spoke in a rush, "I read in the local paper a few months ago that a Doctor Alexander Johanson was coming to town to revive his grandfather's practice."

In the brick building across the street from Cate's Café. Yesterday's shock nearly took her breath away a second time.

"I'd called you Zan for so long that I'd actually forgotten it was 'Alexander' abridged to just one syllable. And 'Johanson' isn't exactly an uncommon name, at least in the Midwest. It never dawned on me that the doctor the whole town has been waiting for would be you. Besides, what with your carefree attitude toward life, I would never have imagined…"

He finished for her, "…that your ole Zan Johanson would surface, all grown up with a real-life career as Doctor Alexander Johanson. But here I am—the guy who shared that memorable senior prom night with you, to say nothing of fourteen pretty intense months leading up to it. Same fellow, remember?"

Victoria nodded like a marionette controlled by strings only he held. She gripped the vinyl padded back of a kitchen chair. "I didn't even know you had gone to medical school. You were one of several 'lost' members at our official class reunion." She felt the familiar comforting warmth a dog provides so well settle in around her ankles, and bent automatically to stroke the soft fur.

"Yeah, I never was much good at keeping in touch; and once Mom and Dad moved away from the old neighborhood in Duluth, I didn't go back. I just never got motivated enough to send back that questionnaire even though it got forwarded several times until it eventually reached me. Besides, I was in Alaska over the reunion. Had to answer the call of the wild just one last time before I entered the forever-and-always-grown-up world." His grin was lopsided and much-too-familiar.

Victoria managed a weak smile in return.

Undaunted, Alex continued, "You, however, missed the weekend in June when I made my pre-move visit to Prairie Rose. Just think how exciting that could have been! I didn't make it to church that Sunday, though; I was checking out the hospital connections in Minot."

"Uh, I was at a Friday-Saturday conference. I heard all about how the new doctor had been in town, though, believe me."

"And then," he wagged the pancake turner at her, "you missed the welcome party for me last weekend. My parents came up for the whole week and helped me get settled, and Prairie Rose rolled out the prover-bial red carpet. Very impressive! But you were nowhere in sight. Gone." His shoulders sagged in mock depression.

She nodded. "I was in California. Yosemite. Just got back last Friday evening."

"What a gad-fly you are! Conferences, trips—pretty early in your tenure here for a vacation, isn't it?" he teased. "Haven't you been around for only a few months?"

"Yes, about four," she agreed, wondering who had been on the other side of that informative conversation, and just who and how many others now knew a few more of the juicy details of her life than made for comfortable small-town living. "The church leaders who interviewed me had agreed to that time away before I accepted the call. An old friend got married, and she had asked months ago if I would perform the ceremony. You probably know her; do you remember Molly? Molly Winstead."

Batter sizzled on the hot griddle as Alex expertly poured new portions. "Sure do. Who could forget your old high school sidekick? Who'd she marry, anyone I'd know?"

"A Californian, Jordan Kendall. He's a pro golfer."

Sputters drew his attention back to the stove. "Whoa! Things are starting to pile up on me here. Shake a pretty foot, Tori, and wrap those guys cooling on the table to make room for more while I finish here. How many will it be for you? Place your order!"

She looked at the griddle where batter formed six-inch golden circles. "Uh, one will be plenty." She moved toward the sink to rinse her hands. *Please, please call me Victoria. "Tori" brings back too many memories that are best left in the past, just like "Zan" should for you.*

"One?" The disbelief in his voice was genuine. "Good grief, woman, I'll fix you three, because you're bound to change your mind after you taste them. They're sensational, if I do say so myself."

She stared at the steaming rows on the table. "I'd never be able to eat three that size." Blatantly ignoring her protests, his mid-air pouring drama created six creamy lakes of bubbling batter. She sighed. "Do I need any wrapping instructions?"

"Fold the long side of the waxed paper over the whole row and then just accordion-fold them." He beamed approval as she followed his instructions. "What a team! I always knew…"

Enough! "Alex." Her sharp tone sliced the word off cleanly. "I'd rather that our past, uh, relationship, be kept between us. There's nothing to be gained by people around here knowing all about us back in high school."

He grinned. "Ah, I see. A professional secret! We'll just sweep all our wickedness under the rug!"

All too aware that Prairie Rose was suddenly shaping up to be the longest chapter of her life, Victoria frowned, straightened her spine, and slammed a mental door closed on that conversation. "So, blueberry pancakes?"

"Some are. Halfway through, I tossed in fruit. I'm a simple man with simple tastes. Very loyal to what I love."

Victoria skirted his comments with the only casual remark she could produce, "You must eat lots of pancakes."

"Well," he confessed, "it's one of the few recipes I'm any good at making. For future meals," he nodded toward the microwave, "I just zap 'em with my Aunt Edna's home-grown maple syrup drizzled between them. I brought a couple dozen jars of it with me."

"To think we both passed Miss Torgerson's Home Economics class! For me, it's tossed taco salad. I've gotten good at that over the years."

"Taco salad; the recipe with your Mom's green salsa dressing?"

"Ummhmm. And this summer—with home-grown tomatoes from my own garden."

"Wow. That brings back memories."

"It has its disadvantages, though. You can't freeze it, and the recipe is hard to reduce, so it pretty much becomes the main course for the week, and it gets less enchanting every day."

"But, you could invite a crowd the first time you serve it, or even a hungry neighbor the next day."

"Right, but people tend to remember taco salad so I can't do that too often."

"Kinda like pancakes!"

They laughed together for the first time and Victoria looked around the kitchen. "Can I help you with anything else?"

"There's not much else to do. All we're having is pancakes. Not even any bacon or sausage. Sorry. I need to hit Larson's Grocery tomorrow." He hunched his shoulders and looked sheepishly over his shoulder at her.

"No apology required. I must admit I was surprised at your invitation."

"No more so than I. But once I saw that familiar head of mahogany curls up there, and knew that it really was you, my old heart-throb, under that sedate black robe, it was destiny. Wild horses couldn't have kept me from asking you for lunch, Tori. And that's no cliché."

"So, are you enjoying Prairie Rose?" she asked, wishing for sudden darkness to hide her flushed cheeks. As soon as the words left her lips, she knew he saw right through this feeble ministerial chitchat.

"Yup. And a great thing just shot off the charts."

Grimly determined to take control of this steadily deteriorating situation, Victoria gave voice to one topic that had been overshadowing their entire conversation. "I see now why I came home from my trip to discover my male Bernese ready to climb the fence." She smiled into the shining eyes of Alex's dog. "Looks like we both followed through on that teenagers' dream of ours."

Alex arched an eyebrow and bent down to flip the dog's dainty ear back in place. "I'm guessing' you like my little gal, huh?"

"I know what her name is, too, don't I, Alex?" She dropped down beside the gentle dog, and pulled back as if burned when her fingers met Alex's hand stroking the animal's angora-soft snowy vest.

"I'm sure you do." He gave a final pat to one slender paw before he rose and washed with a doctor's care at the kitchen sink.

"Hello, Cali. You're like a princess," Victoria whispered. The tail thumping rhythmically affirmed her guess. *Oh God, why would You allow my past to follow me—to threaten me like this?*

"Cali's almost always right with me wherever I am, in the house or out and about, but right now she's ending her first heat, so she's been living with different rules," he said. "Very confusing to her. Especially since we haven't been here long enough for anything in the house or the yard to be familiar to her yet."

Victoria nodded and said, "Poor Cino. I finally know what his problem has been. He's been right across the street from a potential mate, and has been separated by wrought iron and rules."

"Cino, huh? Yup, looks like we've both remembered, Tori," Alex said quietly. "As I recall, after we saw our first-ever Berner loping along the shore, we vowed to get a male we would name Cino for Mendocino and a female we would call Cali for California. The fact that we haven't been together for years didn't alter that promise, did it?" Victoria's breathing turned ragged when he reached to run a knuckle down her cheek. "What did you do with Cino during your trip to Yosemite?"

"A fellow who works at the grocery store, Dave, stayed at my place and took care of him for me. They get along great."

"Sure, I know Dave. Okay, that explains it. Cali went absolutely crazy about the time the store would have been closing each evening. Dave must have been walking Cino then."

"Poor dogs! They'll love each other, I know."

"I take it ole Cino is an intact male?"

"Intact, and ready to act on it," Victoria said. "Didn't you hear him woofing in my yard during church this morning?"

"I had other things on my mind," Alex said with a sly wink. "Who would ever think that a little burg like Prairie Rose could be so, uh, stimulating?"

Victoria answered evenly, "It's a great place to start out. Many ministers' first churches are dismal experiences. Many of my fellow seminary graduates are already counting the days until they can make a graceful exit from their first pulpits." Cali's insistent nose nudged her arm to resume the lagging attention paid her.

"That's unfortunate. Personally, I think that Prairie Rose is not only a great place to start out, but also a perfect place to stay. This whole county is without any established medical services closer than Minot and Williston. Talk about job security! Even in this uncertain age of medical care, I'm digging in here. This kind of practice is what I've dreamed of ever since I started thinking about going to medical school."

Balling up the apron and aiming it at a kitchen chair, he pulled a shirt out of a belt loop that the apron had hidden. "Besides, with the Internet and every doc's lifeline—Medline, and cell phones, beepers, e-mail and all, I'm as connected to my patients, my colleagues and medical experts I can consult as I would be in the heart of any city, just with fewer meetings! And, a big plus: I can take my dog to work with me when it's my own clinic! Cali's a dandy receptionist—she has quite the calming effect on anyone in the waiting room."

Swallowing became a forgotten skill as Victoria's eyes zeroed in on a faint scar across Alex's taut mid-section, the scar from the night when he fell off the high school bleachers clowning around with her. *Oh boy. Oh-boy-oh-boy-oh-boy.* Cali's tail wagged with a beat not unlike Victoria's pulse. *I'm going to develop cardiovascular problems in this seemingly stress-free town, I just know it. It was bad enough when I thought it was just Zan—oh, Lord! I mean Alex—but now it's also his beautiful little Cali, another part of the circle of dreams that two high school romantics chased.*

Alex's words were muffled until he had tugged the shirt over his head and shoulders, "I really love Prairie Rose. Dad and Mom and I worked like beavers to get the Clinic fixed up after being vacant for almost ten years," the scar disappeared from sight, "and several ladies from town helped us get this house ship-shape again. I tell you, it's a heady experience to be so welcomed." he added, stuffing shirttails in along his waistband. Victoria's last chance at normal respiration vanished as his hand moved up and down, back and front.

"That's good." She spun back to face the table and added yet another packet to the growing stack of wrapped pancakes. *Get a grip, Victoria. You're an ordained clergywoman, not a love-starved teenager anymore.*

"So far, I've felt that they're coming more out of curiosity than real medical needs, but that's fine with me. It's not every doctor who sees patients in their healthy condition before a serious health need develops. The rate I'm going, I'll soon have medical histories on almost everyone around here. Maybe it's because I announced no charge for the first visit!"

"Our two professions are a lot alike in that respect. We often don't see people until they're desperate." She relaxed a bit as the conversation veered to a safer topic.

"Din-nah is served in the dine-nah," he intoned as he turned off the griddle heat. "Lead on, Cali-girl."

With the final six steaming pancakes piled on a platter that he carried aloft like a veteran waiter and with his free hand pasted against her back, Alex guided Victoria through the door into the dining room. His hand stayed in place an extra minute, warm and alive. Victoria shivered while clear memories of countless other touches rushed in, unbidden and unwelcome.

Lace curtains fluttered in the open windows. Two placemats graced opposite sides of a round oak table. Alex positioned the platter on a quilted runner and then pulled out a captain's chair, bowing at the waist. She could have sworn he murmured, "For you, Love" but with canine jaws working diligently on a rediscovered hunk of rawhide in one corner of the dining room furnishing the background music, it was difficult to be certain.

Victoria slid into place; Alex rounded the table to his own chair as she stared, dumbfounded. Ornate silver, heirloom china, linen napkins delicately edged in handmade lace marked their places. From Alex's attire, she would have expected mismatched dishes and a sticky syrup bottle plopped in the center of the bare kitchen table. He smiled knowingly as she met his eyes. "Pretty cool, huh? I doubt that Grandma ever served pancakes on these dishes, but in honor of the event, the minister coming over and all, I thought she would approve."

"So this is your grandparents' home?" Victoria made frantic jabs at a normal conversation, letting only the fringes of her mind wonder why this domestic scene caught her so off-guard.

He nodded. "When Grandpa closed his practice, they stayed in Prairie Rose for a while and he worked only when emergencies demanded it, but eventually the long, tough winters got to them. They bought a condominium close to Mom and Dad several years ago. Grandma passed away a few months later, but Grandpa still lives there. So, now I wake up each morning in their house and work all day under Grandpa Johanson's shingle."

Victoria leaned back in her chair, and let her head fall back on her shoulders briefly. When she met his eyes again, Alex's gaze released a flood of memories. "What are you thinking, Tori? Ten words or less." His voice was tender as he challenged her in their old familiar way.

Victoria paused, then held up her hands and ticked off each word, "This isn't going to work. You and I together. Again."

"Technically, I recall, our old rules said contractions count for two words. And I don't agree; our being together again is…"

"…dangerous," she interrupted. "Be serious. What're we doing here?" He opened his mouth to answer. "And I don't mean sitting in your Grandma and Grandpa Johanson's house, eating pancakes," she added; he snapped his jaw shut. "We may live on two sides of the same street, but we're *not* 'together' again."

In the quietness of the step-back-in-time dining room with fading flowered wallpaper and worn but still exquisite carpet, Victoria wrapped her ankles around the legs of her chair and stared across lace and china at Alex. Cali sighed and took a rest from rawhide, moving to a spot beneath the table where she could doze and still keep track of their two sets of feet.

Victoria felt her anger dissipate as a cool, wet nose searched out her toes; her laugh erupted. Cali answered with an approving, active tail thumping approval of the mood shift. A responsive smile flitted across Alex's face as Victoria's sputters of amusement grew to contagious proportions.

"I'm sorry, Alex. Cali must sense I need to lighten up. Do you realize the ridiculous odds that have come into play here?" She dabbed her eyes with the corner of Grandma Johanson's time-softened napkins. "Who ever would have thought that Tori Dahlmann's first church would be in the same remote North Dakota town where Zan Johanson would begin a medical practice?"

"Pffft," he expelled a puff of air, "I can go you one better than that! Who would have dreamed that sexy Tori Dahlmann would even *attend* church once she left her parents' rules and regulations behind, let alone pastor one? Or that goofy Zan Johanson could possibly ever settle down long enough to choose medical school over fast cars and the call of the wild?" He lifted the platter and held it for her.

After she had taken the top pancake, he continued, "We were going to move to Mendocino, raise and breed our Bernese Mountain Dogs, and never, ever choose careers that had dress codes, and we agreed that a Volkswagen Rabbit would be the perfect car, remember? That was after we saw that 'way-cool artist dude' driving one, the guy who set up his easel on the beach every morning. Remember?"

"Northern California's rocky coast was much too romantic for us, and it sure didn't help that we spotted the first Berners either of us had ever seen romping on the shore in that idyllic setting. And I'll just bet we also didn't notice that the sea air had probably rusted out that artist's car, did we?" She poured maple syrup on the steaming cake. "Thank goodness we got realistic and realized that some things are just dreams. That's what growing up is all about."

Alex's voice was soft. "We're a long way from the coast, but someday I'll roll all the windows down and take you for a ride in my Volkswagen Rabbit. It's guaranteed to get your juices bubbling' again."

Victoria felt a flush cross her cheeks, fully aware none of her juices needed any help with bubbling right now and very glad her own garage door blocked the view of her VW Rabbit. "We need to establish a new foundation because Prairie Rose isn't Duluth or Mendocino. And we're no longer the teenagers who nearly wrecked our own lives, and definitely caused our parents so much grief and so many sleepless nights, either."

"Ah, yes. We're now The Minister and The Doctor, is that what you're trying to say? Two professionals, each solving humanity's problems in our own way." His arms punctuated the words with dramatic swoops, and Cali stiffened warily in her spot on the floor. "You might say we have this place all wrapped up. Body and soul."

"That's a rather flippant way of looking at our purposes here, Alex. At least my purpose."

He raised his eyebrows, "Well, I've got to tell you, Reverend Dahlmann," her name slid across his tongue with taunting irony, "that when I saw you standing up there on the platform, I felt something that certainly wasn't very holy, and I found it difficult to flip into analyzing it from a medical standpoint. It was genuine male-female electricity moving between my pew and your pulpit this morning. Remember 'The Film' in fifth grade?"

She sucked in her breath sharply. "Alex. Listen. We are now thirty years old and finally getting launched in the careers that have cost us bunches of time and effort and piles of money. I don't know about you, but I have no desire to get run out of this town on the rails of any sordid rumors or even shocking truths. When I leave, it will be with my reputation intact. Got that? We are no longer teenagers with busy little hormones coursing through our veins." She sank back against the chair, her flash of anger having run its course. "But we could make the best of it and be mature responsible friends," she ended pleadingly.

"I think I've already identified what's coursing through my veins," he said. Amused cornflower-blue eyes taunted her as he lounged in his chair and let a deep breath ripple through his chest. "But I must say, you've become quite a spokesperson for purity!"

"You aren't listening at all to what I'm saying, are you?" she protested, futile in her effort to block out the rhythmic movement each breath made beneath his form-fitting shirt. *Why should I remember his muscle structure so exactly that if I were blindfolded now, I could still identify his body by touch even after all these years?*

He rocked back on his chair. She knew, as surely as if she had ducked beneath the table to check, that his toes held the chair's front legs off the floor. *He always did that to chairs, to his mother's horror; and he always wrecked havoc with my emotions.*

"I'm trying, yes," he nodded resolutely, "I'm listening. In my head I know you're probably right. In my heart, I'm a bucking bronco."

Her tongue unconsciously mimicked his when he moistened those lips she was dismayed to discover she could still taste in her memory.

"But Tori," he said, lowering his voice until it tugged at everything feminine in her being, "this morning, those feelings weren't covered with over ten-plus years' dust. They were very, very current." Her heart was trapped in quicksand. "And when they hit me, I said to myself, 'Hey, Doc! Welcome back to the human race. After more than a decade of dogged scholarly pursuits, it's good to know that your body is still in good form.'"

She silently bemoaned her red-headed fate to produce undeniable blushes. "I'm sure it is," she said dryly. They sat in silence, assessing each other across cooling dinner plates. He reached over—as naturally as when they had lived in sweatshirts and jeans and eaten mushroom-sausage-double-cheese pizza after every football game—tracing the curvature of her hand with his strong, slender fingers.

A gentle breeze tapped the branches of a bush against the window screen. "Alex, I think it's best if we don't meet again like this. Alone, I mean," she whispered.

"What? You've got to be kidding." He jerked his hand back from hers and slapped the table; water sloshed in the goblets. "Don't ministers have friends?" Stunned disbelief tightened the lines of his face. "Come on, Tori, lighten up! I have no intention of ignoring the one woman in this town I know can reach my soul." Frustration tightened his jaw line.

She eyed him shrewdly. "I'm positive you don't mean that in any religious sense," she said, and instantly rebuked herself. *Prude!*

"Bingo. Give the lady her prize." He erupted from his chair like a volcano, throwing his mangled napkin down. "Tori, I can't believe you can honestly say you want to be, what was it? 'Mature, responsible friends.' Every time we meet, you'll have your robe zipped up to your chin, and I'll have my stethoscope draped around my neck—our professional chastity belts." He snorted; the chair rocked precariously as he shoved it aside.

"Alex, we can't pick up our relationship on the same level we left it. We've changed. And I think it's a change for the better for both of us." Her mouth was dry, her eyes moist. "I'd like to be friends. But on a new level. Can't you understand that? And an even bigger question: can we achieve that? This is uncharted territory for both of us." Her palms hurt where her nails dug half-moons into their skin.

"You probably don't remember the promise that I made to you one pivotal night in our relationship: you were scared to death, but I vowed that you would always be my one true love. As I recall, you promised the same."

A pivotal night, for sure. "I remember. But a lot of years have come and gone—I have never expected you to stand by a vow made under such circumstances."

His voice was so soft she could barely hear it. "But I have." He released a pent-up breath of air that set his blonde hair fluttering wildly across his forehead. She stared, remembering all the times she had wound baby-fine strands of his hair around her finger. On beaches. On the cold school bus coming home from away-games. On their front lawns. In his ancient rust-laden Plymouth Valiant with the sometimes-muffler.

As if pulling away from her imagined caress, he spun on his heel and strode to the window. He flung the curtains aside and braced himself against the frame, his muscles taut, his head bowed. The grandfather clock ticking in the corner was a steady metronome against his jagged breathing. Cali padded to a spot beside her master. Leaning against his leg, she sat and watched Victoria with eyes that were warning and cautious.

"Do you remember Mendocino? Really remember it?" he asked hoarsely.

Do I remember? Our families, spending the best week of each summer at the beach. The two of us, young and aching with love, walking barefoot on the soggy sand in search of rocky hide-a-ways. Do I remember? Obviously we both do, as evidenced by our dogs' names and what's parked in our garages. Victoria jabbed an unsteady hand through her hair.

It was a standoff; two hearts on guard.

His voice was low. "I went back there in May for the first time in many years. Remember early mornings? The mist comes in off the ocean and hovers like a cloud of emerald, or sometimes purple, or even a golden haze about two feet above those meadows that are always full of wild flowers. Remember?"

Victoria nodded as Alex continued. "It was as if I were iron filings flying to a magnet when I came around that bend in the road and saw the town on the horizon just like it has been for over a hundred years. It's a powerful scene. I parked at the far end of Main Street and walked down the foot-path like we always did. Then, I climbed up on that big old scarred redwood bench—it's still there—and sat there with Cali beside me, looking out over the ocean. I tried to figure out what it was about the place that's so arousing and still captivating, even after all this time."

Victoria could have sworn she felt the cool sea-breeze against her hot cheeks.

Abruptly, he turned back and leaned on the end of the table. His eyes were coals at flame-point, his voice smoky, "After this morning, I know the answer. Mendocino's three-colored mist is like your eyes and both are etched permanently on my subconscious."

Even all these years haven't been enough to forget what we had, huh, Zan? She shifted uncomfortably in her chair, aware of a tidal wave roaring toward her inner shore. She was helpless against its power. "This scares me something fierce."

"We're here together, Tori."

"That's what's scary." She tried desperately for a light-hearted tone.

"Please know that I'll give you friendship. God knows it's going to kill me, but I'd be the loser if I said no to that request. But you've got to give in on one thing for me." A flash of the old teenage heart-breaker shot through the doctor's eyes.

She smiled cautiously, "This promises to be good. What's my point of surrender?"

"I cannot, no, I *will* not call you Victoria. Please be Tori for me."

Her mouth twitched. "Okay," she assented slowly, "but only on the condition that in public you manage to dredge up some deeply buried dignity in your actions toward me."

"Fair enough. Hey, you said 'in public'—that would imply we'll have some not-in-public times!" His eyebrows raised expectantly above jewel-blue eyes.

"Maybe I spoke too quickly," she protested weakly.

He was beside her in an instant, pulling her to her feet. He tipped her chin until she looked directly in his eyes.

That old male-female thing is apparently alive and well in me, too.

His hand was a smoking iron, imprinting her with his brand. "Hey, that's okay because I lied about one thing: I do want something more from you." His lips pressed against hers, igniting a smoldering passion.

Never mind what year the calendar says—it is high school all over again.

His left hand formed a familiar support for her neck while his fingers wandered through her curls. She leaned into him, molding her body against his, finding that her curves and his long lines still sculpted the work of art she had locked up safely in her gallery of memories. Her hands moved instinctively to their forever spot, splayed open across his shoulder blades. His right hand shifted easily to her lower back, drawing her closer to him and sending her senses to dizzily dangerous heights.

Young Zan had been heaps of trouble for young Tori. Now, Doctor Alex Johanson spelled dilemma and disaster for the Reverend Victoria Dahlmann. *How does one respond to resurrected, risky love? With fear and a slammed door, or with joy and out-stretched arms?*

Her eyes closed slowly, her lips opened in welcome; his slow-dancing breath seduced her. Two bodies that had once moved to ocean songs now swayed like wheat moving in a prairie wind. Finally, with a determination that went against her heart, Victoria pulled back from his lips. Her head found the long-remembered spot on his shoulder where a tell-tale drum roll of his heart pounded beneath her ear.

Cali reared up and pinned Alex's arm in place behind her with two front paws; they formed a tripod, two humans under the watchful protection of one canine.

"Well," Alex said huskily, "now we know what we're dealing with as we start over on our new adult relationship."

Her hair tumbled around her neck again as she slowly inched away from him. "I can tell I'm going to have to bring my own four-legged chaperone if I'm going to be around you!"

Despite her desperate attempt at light-hearted teasing, she knew the last few minutes had told Doctor Alexander Johanson all he wanted to know: Tori's youthful desires still burned inside the mature Victoria.

The score in the game of love might as well have been in neon lights on the roof of Alex's house—Hormones: 1; Sensibility: 0.

CHAPTER THREE

"So, Victoria, I hear you and our new doctor had dinner together yesterday."

"My goodness, where would you hear that?" Victoria's hand jerked as she positioned her cup for a refill of freshly brewed coffee.

Cate Jones grinned and leaned one elbow on the cash register, cupping her chin in the palm of her hand. "When you gonna figure out that the only damned, 'scuse me, thing that spreads faster than a hot story in this small town is a grass fire?"

Victoria blew needlessly across the surface of her coffee before she spoke. "Well, your wild-fire story is correct." She put the cup down and pulled a check out of her pocket. "Let me settle up last week's tab, okay?"

Cate made short work of giving her a tally and asked casually, "I presume you met Cali?"

"*I* presume that the whole town thinks it's a hoot that the two newcomers have virtually matching dogs, huh?"

"You got that right! But everyone pretty much decided it was just one of the things you'd enjoy finding out yourselves. That little town in Iowa that kept those seven babies a secret for so long has nothing on us! So, I gather you were surprised?"

"It was one of the more interesting aspects of the day," Victoria agreed dryly.

"Have you seen the car Alex drives?"

Victoria groaned. "I've heard it from the man himself—it's a Volkswagen Rabbit."

"Sure got tongues wagging, you two together and all yesterday. Who cooked?" Cate moved a steaming muffin to a plate and slid it along the counter. "Here, try this and tell me what you think."

Victoria had not liked the direction of this conversation and gladly latched on to the proffered detour. "Mmmm, fresh and hot. Terrific! Peach?"

"Yup. Who cooked?" Cate persisted.

"He did." A cautious smile crossed Victoria's face.

Cate hooted. "He did, did he? Hell, 'scuse me, that must have been one interesting meal! Doctor Alex doesn't strike me as much competition in the food prep' arena here in Prairie Rose."

"Now, Cate, I don't think…"

The proprietress of Prairie Rose's sole café moved along the counter, wiping stray crumbs into one hand. "Lord knows I don't mean to judge, but when a fellow asks me how Lucy makes such a good salad, and all it has in it is a couple kinds of lettuce, some tomato hunks, a few slices of cucumber, and one damned, 'scuse me, little green onion chopped up, it's safe to figure I'm not talking to any big-time chef!"

Only two other customers were in the café during the lull that came mid-mornings when Al Jenkins put out the day's mail. Both now smiled from across the room at the sound of Cate's contagious laughter. "To be honest with you, he and I are on the same level in the kitchen," Victoria confessed morosely.

"Tell me something I don't know! If anything else were true, would the two of you be hitting my counter for at least one meal every day, Monday through Saturday? Sometimes I wonder how you survive Sundays. Speaking of Sundays, tell me, what did God's gift to Prairie Rose feed you?"

Victoria cleared her throat and shifted her position on the stool. "Pancakes," she muttered around a bite of muffin.

Speechless at last, Cate patted her short-cropped stunning white hair and studied a spot on the wall beyond Victoria's head. Tears sprouted in the corners of her eyes; she chomped her bottom lip and spun on her heel, moving at top speed through the swinging kitchen door. As it closed behind her, one word echoed back. "Pancakes!"

Victoria smiled feebly at the couple by the window, hoping against hope that they had not overheard enough of the preceding conversation to fuel the day's gossip. She fiddled with the salt and pepper shakers on the counter. Salt on the left, salt on the right, pepper in front, pepper behind. Lucy's inimitable laugh echoed from the kitchen and verified that Cate hadn't missed the opportunity to share the news with her long-time employee.

Cate returned bearing two steaming Dutch apple pies, fresh from the oven and begging for takers. "Sorry, but that one caught me by surprise. I suppose someone in my business shouldn't complain when newcomers can't either of 'em cook worth a damn, 'scuse me."

Noticing a signal from a table of four women, Cate rounded the end of the counter, coffee pot in hand. Adeptly pouring streams of coffee from an alarming distance above each cup, she hit her mark every time even while laughing along with something said at the table.

Later, after Cate finished ringing up a sale and chatted briefly with the exiting customers, she came back to Victoria. "So he eats here quite often?" Victoria asked with studied casualness. Except for Lucy rattling pans in the kitchen, they were alone for an unpredictable chunk of time.

"Like clockwork. It's only been little more than a week or so since he got here to stay, but when you were in California, he hardly missed a meal here once his folks left. I swear, he already knows my menu better than I do! He comes in for coffee first thing when I open, and takes it with him across the street. Couple of days I sent a bag lunch over to him if the special was getting low and he hadn't shown up on schedule. I pretty much feed the guy."

"I'd say that shows he's a man of good taste."

"And single! If I could chop off a couple years, and hadn't been lick-ing the spoon so long," without an ounce of self-consciousness, she perched her hand on a trim hip that surely needed no apology, "I might give you some real tough competition. Don't let this hair fool you; I started turning white in my senior year of high school, but that's another story." Absentmindedly, she rewiped the already-clean counter and looked expectantly at the opening door.

Victoria wrinkled her nose playfully. "Yeah, like you're hard to look at, Cate!" She spun around on the stool. "Do me a favor; send the word around, ahead of any rampaging stories, that I'm here to pastor two churches, not chase the doctor, okay?"

Cate's vigorous nod set the pencil bobbing over her ear, "It may be like locking the barn after the horse got loose, but hell, 'scuse me, Lucy and I will do our best."

Victoria grinned. "Start a new tab for me with the coffee and don't forget to add that muffin, okay? Catch you later." She pulled down sun-glasses from their perch atop her head, settled them on her nose and left the café.

With face upturned to catch the sun's warmth, Victoria paused on the bottom step. The weathered shingle—most possibly the Senior Doctor Alexander Johanson's—swung above the entrance to his grand-son's office, welcoming patients to a dignified building. A blue bicycle leaned against the newly sandblasted brick front. The double doors and trim around the windows shone with fresh hunter-green paint. Geraniums thrived in whiskey-barrel planters beneath the windows. Inviting redwood benches flanked the entrance. The scene could have been a Norman Rockwell painting titled, "Here to stay."

How can the guy have such limited goals that he would burrow into a struggling little town? Just how does he plan to pay off his medical school bills? Victoria ran a hand around her collar, flinging her hair back in an auburn cloud behind her, and headed off toward her office to begin studying for Sunday's sermon. Her goals were firmly placed in the future, carefully tended, and polished to a high sheen. On this step of her career ladder, she had a job to do. For her time in Prairie Rose, ministerial duties were the top priority, not the new man in town.

The message light on the answering machine was flashing, so she punched necessary buttons, listened and jotted down a request for a bulletin announcement. As usual, once she had the Biblical commentaries spread around her on the huge desk, she was eager to begin. She turned on her computer, selected the sermon file, searched the Internet for the exact wording on the introductory quote she planned for the next message in the series, and felt the outside world retreat.

Cino, her faithful study partner, flopped over on his back to catch any stray cool breeze across his belly, and promptly dozed off in his watchdog place between her and the door. His occasional snorts and snores were music to her ears as she studied.

The hum of the box fan in the window and the distant shouts of children a block away on the school playground were pleasant background noises, not disruptive at all as the computer keys clicked away beneath her racing fingers. However, every so often she would realize her hands had slipped off the keyboard and her mind had wandered; she found herself aimlessly thumbing pages and sketching senseless designs on a tablet. Victoria flung her pen down on the desk and clicked *save* on the computer toolbar.

Releasing an ear-popping yawn, she frowned at the scribbled pages where a sketched replica of a doctor's shingle had appeared. "Get out of town, Alexander Johanson! You're messing up my head."

The best way to clear the cobwebs of fuzzy thinking, according to her old friend, Molly Kendall, was to make a list of Pros and Cons. "That's exactly what needs to be done," Victoria muttered and drew a line down the middle of a page on her tablet. Cons—always on the right side of the page—flew out of her pen:

1) I don't agree with his goals.
2) Is he husband-material for a minister?

3) Too much negative history. We'd always have our past hanging over our heads—especially with our families.

4) He thinks we can just pick up where we left off—maybe he can; I can't.

5) What would happen if the whole truth and nothing but the truth were told? Picking up with him again would require total honesty on my part.

The Pros list took a little longer and filled one less line on the left column:

1) No surprises with his personality—no getting-to-know-you time required

2) There's lots to like about him—he's fun, good with people, loves adventure. He's got a Berner!

3) He can handle my having a career—and our careers are compatible

4) I used to love him, so falling in love again wouldn't take much

"Well, there you have it. The Cons win. So sorry, Dr Johanson. The you-and-me thing won't be happening." She chose a stick of cinnamon gum from a tin on the desk and roamed around straightening her framed diplomas on the wall, plucking a dead leaf off the ivy on the end table, plumping up a pillow on the couch, and touching her toes ten times.

She informed a puzzled Cino, "Sorry, pal, but this deviation in behavior on my part does not constitute an invitation for a walk on your part." He dropped his head between his front legs and continued to watch his mistress' every move.

Digging deep into her reservoir of discipline, Victoria dropped back into the desk chair, slipped off her sandals and dug her toes into the carpet. After blowing a prize-winning bubble, she refocused intently on her work.

Several hours later, though, when she stopped to let Cino out to answer nature's call, she totally lost her powers of concentration. Groaning when familiar cramping claimed her body, she counted off the days on a mental calendar. She leaned her head against the cool rest-room wall in frustration.

Once again, her own body had side-swiped her. Indexed under "E" for endometriosis in medical textbooks, it was under "D" for day-in, day-out in the story of her life. She would never forget the first time she read and reread the litany of symptoms described in an article:

Pelvic pain? *You betcha.*

Exhaustion? *Check.*

Lower backache? *Oh, yeah.*

Stomach and bowel problems during menstruation? *Been there, done that.*

Bloating, swelling? *Got that right.*

Heavy, irregular periods? *Bingo.*

The fact that such a list even existed had given her hope: it wasn't all in her head, and it wasn't "just part of being a woman" which some would have her to believe. Today, they were "fighting a war in the South," as she and her mom had called their mutual symptoms all these years. And even though thousands of women shared her diagnosis, she felt alone in her personal and secret combat zone.

Battle-worn already, she returned to the office to let Cino back in and ripped the doodling page from the tablet. Labeling a new folder with a tentative sermon title, she hit *print* on the computer. What she collected from the printer was an alarmingly short stack of pages. "This puny output is ridiculous for as long as I've worked," she said, expelling a puff of frustration.

Cino loudly enjoyed a drink of water from his bowl, flopped down in anticipation of yet another nap and stretched his legs contentedly. Victoria stuck the sad excuse for sermon notes into the waiting file folder, turned off the computer and headed, barefoot, through the door opening into the sanctuary.

The baby grand piano waited beneath a heavy velvety form-shaped cover that she removed. She raised the lid to the height of the longest prop and slid across the bench, repositioning it for her long legs to rest easily on the pedals. Wrapping her toes resolutely around the cool metal, she slowly relaxed their grip as the pedals warmed.

Middle C floated out into the vast room. Caressing the keys, she searched out random, disjointed chords. The keys felt dusty despite her daily playing; she filled her lungs and blew across them like black and white candles on a birthday cake.

Her hands moved automatically to capture the notes floating in her mind and transform them into audible music. A haunting melody swept across the empty pews; she could almost sense it wafting up into hidden crevices of carved woodwork around arched windows, floating like fragrant winds across the prairie.

Beneath her experienced touch, the piano sang softly to her, gliding from spiritual to love song, from hymn to blues, each a mirror of her soul. Sometimes it seemed she hummed along, but she often couldn't tell the difference between the music in her mind and that coming from her fingertips.

Returning again to her office where Cino chased rabbits in his sleep, she selected a heavy volume from the bookshelf, turned off the fan, curled up in the overstuffed chair by the open window and began to read with unbroken concentration. Birds, sheltered in the plumage of the trees, twittered outside unheeded. Except for letting Cino out when sounds of children returning home from school announced the hour and called him to fence-duty, she was fully engaged in the task before her.

At last, she closed up the office and whistled to Cino who was posted in his regular afternoon spot in the corner of the yard closest to the school—the spot guaranteed to have most hands reaching through the bars of the fence to give him loving pats. The two of them headed into the house. She refilled the dog's food dish, freshened his water, and willed her body to keep moving.

Soon she was walking on the shady side of the street toward Rachel Lindquist's home. As she stood on the porch, movements from within told her a second knock wasn't necessary. "The best part of Mondays is seeing you! Come on in, Victoria!"

"Hello, Rachel. Guess I don't need to tell you that I've brought the cassette of Sunday's service."

"Come in, dear, out of the heat." Rachel beamed over her shoulder and Victoria took hold of the handles to turn the woman's wheelchair around in the hallway. "I've got lemonade ready in the kitchen. Hard to believe iced drinks still taste so good this late in the season. Can I tempt you?" In answer, Victoria rolled her friend's chair toward the kitchen. "Please reach two of those glasses from the top shelf in the china closet."

"These are beautiful, Rachel!" Victoria said, admiring the gold-rimmed stemware.

"They are, aren't they? They were a Christmas gift one year from the school board to Randolph and me. Tell me, was yesterday the christening for the Guddman baby?" Rachel asked eagerly.

"No, that will be next week. Yesterday we used several young readers for the Scripture. It was a fine addition to the service. We'll definitely use them again. I think you'll especially enjoy that part on the tape." She placed the cassette on the coffee table amidst a crossword puzzle book, a leather-bound volume of Browning's poetry, and a stack of current issues of several news magazines. Rachel might not leave her house often, but her mind took untold journeys.

While Rachel chatted, Victoria sank into the cushions on the long couch, pressing her forearm against the now throbbing pain in her abdomen. She nodded at appropriate times and sipped lemonade, until a casual remark nudged her out of her reverie. "When Dave brought my groceries from Larson's Grocery this morning he said the new doctor attended services yesterday."

Victoria refrained from smiling. "Yes. Doctor Johanson was there."

"You must have made quite an impression on him." Rachel's laugh was crystal clear. "I also heard he invited you to dinner."

"It strikes me from time to time," Victoria said wryly, "that telephones are a wasted commodity in small towns, what with word of mouth and all!" She sighed melodramatically. "Yes, Rachel. He invited me to dinner." Her cheek twitched.

"Isn't that nice? I'm glad he's living in his grandparents' home. That's such a lovely place. Randolph and I visited there so often." Memories brightened her eyes as she smoothed silvery hair.

"You did?" Victoria asked, and then shook her head ruefully. "Sometimes I forget that in a town of 300 everyone pretty much knows everyone."

"Yes, we knew each other quite well. We veteran townsfolk are pleased to see Old Doctor Johanson's shingle hanging up again. It adds a sense of continuity to life." She smiled gently at her guest, and concern lined her face. "You look tired, my dear. I hope you're not forgetting to take time off from your duties. You need it and deserve it. Your job is never completely done, so don't even try to do it all at once."

Victoria forced a brightness to her voice. "Good advice. Say, I want to ask you something. Do you know anything about four men who call themselves the ROMEOs?"

"Oh! Did the ROMEOs visit your backyard?" Rachel asked with a wide smile. "Well, of course they would—you have a picnic table!"

"And that connects in some way to them being in my back yard?"

Rachel shifted herself up in her chair, her whole body twitching with delight. "Oh my, yes! Last year, Bryce and Irene Butler visited Bruce's brother in South Carolina. Bryce came back all a-twitter about something his brother is part of down there. ROMEO simply stands for Retired Old Men Eating Out. Isn't that delightful?" The dignified woman giggled.

Victoria arched an eyebrow. "So they said, but it still doesn't make much sense."

"Well, I am sure the idea works a lot easier where there's a broader assortment of places to eat! The way I understand the original regulations, each week one fellow in the group selects a place to eat breakfast. It has to be where a waitress takes the order and serves the food—no fast-food joints. That's where it gets a bit tricky in Prairie Rose. They don't want to eat at Cate's Café every week."

Victoria joined in Rachel's laughter. "So, they've improvised!"

"That's not all. Each man is expected to find—which I gather is read as *steal*—a flower from a garden in his neighborhood—buying flowers is not allowed—which he presents to the waitress. They always leave a nice tip, too—the flowers are to be chivalrous! The waitresses love it, Bruce says, and beg the ROMEOs to come back!"

"I can imagine they would! So we now have Prairie Rose ROMEOs."

"Our guys were forced to become quite inventive. Rumor has it that they have waiting lists—men who want to join, and women who want to get picked! They are very secretive about who is next on their visitation list and when it will happen. The key is a picnic table because it makes it all a lot easier. I've heard that women are actually asking at the General Store about how much a picnic table costs!"

"Maybe the high school shop class could build them!"

"That's an idea! Anyway, the ROMEOs pack up a picnic basket with breakfast or snacks and a thermos of coffee and sneak into some woman's backyard in the early morning to enjoy their club meeting! How did you know they picked your backyard?"

"I found them—actually, Cino welcomed them in my absence. When I came home after coffee at the café on Saturday, there they were—doughnuts, powdered sugar, and all."

"They must have been so disappointed about getting caught! They are very quiet, they never leave a mess. All in all, they have managed to cause quite a stir—some women brag about being picked, others wonder why they haven't been, and all summer long, backyards have been kept mowed and picnic tables cleaned off, ready in anticipation. I'll have to admit—I paid a high school boy to drag my old picnic table out of the garage and repaint it!"

The sparkle in Rachel's eyes made Victoria smile. *The power of romantic gestures!* "Oh, one other thing: do our ROMEOs bring flowers like their South Carolina counterparts?"

"Oh my yes! Usually from another unsuspecting woman's garden! Even *that* has become something of a status symbol! Didn't they leave you a note?"

"I got mums, but no note."

"I'd wager they are Mildred's mums. The ROMEOs risked their lives cutting those—she guards them like a hawk—but actually, she's probably quite proud to have been robbed. Too bad you don't have a note—that's usually the proof they've visited you. Something to show around and brag about!"

"Maybe I'll get a belated "We were there" note! My abrupt appearance did seem to discombobulate them a bit! Have they 'borrowed' any of your flowers?" Victoria asked with a grin.

"I'm not sure, but I had thought my marigolds looked a little more thinned out than usual—not that those stinky things would make any lady happy!"

Victoria arched her back as a spasm moved through her abdomen, and then allowed herself to hunch over in an attempt to recover without drawing attention to herself.

"Tell me, is there anything left in your garden these days for the ROMEOs to steal?" Ever a lady, Rachel often sensed Victoria's discomfort and respected Victoria's privacy enough not to pry.

"Not much. One of these mornings we'll get together in my back yard and you can direct me in tilling it all under."

Rachel's eyes shone. "Some people hate that part, but I have always found it to be rather therapeutic. Life is cyclic, like a garden."

Ain't that the truth? I wish you could you also help me till the good doctor under a heap of dirt! "We had quite the garden, didn't we, Rachel?"

"*You* did a good job."

Victoria laughed, "How could I miss with you on the sidelines coaching me each step of the way? Everyone told me you're Prairie Rose's finest green thumb, and they were right. I'm honored to have you as my mentor. If the ROMEOs steal anything blooming from my garden, the compliment is all yours!"

"I must say, I enjoyed our backyard talks." Rachel leaned back in her chair and said wistfully, "It makes me hope the winter goes quickly so we can get out in the garden again next spring."

"If winter drags on too long, we can always repot a root-bound Swedish Ivy from my office and chatter away!" Victoria offered and rose, forcing herself to stand tall despite another jab of pain that nearly crumpled her.

Masking her disappointment that the visit must end, Rachel turned her wheelchair to escort Victoria to the door. "Thanks for coming by. You're so good about bringing sermon tapes when I don't get out to church."

"It's always a pleasure," Victoria responded through the screen door. They had agreed early on in their friendship to discuss the multiple sclerosis that had altered Rachel's life so dramatically only when there were changes in her condition. Rachel's plea for "one friend who doesn't act as if I were a medical condition first, and a person second," was easy for Victoria to understand and respect. "See you again soon."

Half a mile away at the edge of town, she came to mailbox marked "Harker" at the end of a long driveway leading to a house that seemed painted against the backdrop of wheat fields. She heard a door slam and saw a child leap down three steps and race toward her. "River-ant Victoria, Hi! Where's Cino?" The preschooler's voice bounced with each pounding step.

Victoria bent to the child's level and hugged her close. She buried her face in the sun-streaked hair, reveling in the special child-in-summer smells. "Hi, Jillie. You sure ran fast! Cino stayed home today. It's too hot for him to run too much."

Jillie's ponytail bobbed with each nod. "Want to see me run to the house? It's not too hot for me!"

"Okay, little girl!" Victoria said and traced a starting line in the dirt with the toe of her shoe. "On your mark, get set..."

"Gooooo!" Jillie sang out as she sprinted off; Victoria followed the whirlwind of dust. When she reached the yard, she swooped up a kitten rubbing against her ankle and smiled down at Jillie who lay panting dramatically on the grass. "Tell Cino I wudda beat him!"

Victoria nuzzled her face in the kitten's fur until, sensing they weren't alone, she looked up and saw a woman in the shadows of the porch. "Hello, Gail."

"Mommy, River-ant Victoria came to see me run to the house!"

Gail closed the screen door behind her. "Reverend Victoria may have had a different reason for coming than just to see you run like a rabbit," she said tiredly as her eyes queried, *Why did you come?* Jillie looked up, confusion written in her eyes, but beamed happily when Victoria winked reassuringly. "Come in, Pastor." The screen door squeaked in protest when she opened it wider.

"Thanks, Gail. Aren't these hot Indian summer days something?"

"I'd do better if the nights cooled down more. I can't find a comfortable position," Gail ran her hands down across the rounded, straining apron front. "I don't know that I'll make it until Thanksgiving." Her lethargic expression kept the words from sounding like a litany of complaints.

Jillie tugged a child-sized chair up next to Victoria at the kitchen table and listened quietly as the two women talked. "How will you get to the hospital when you do go into labor, Gail?" She wasn't an expert on pregnant women, but she had to agree that Gail didn't look as if she would last another eight to ten weeks.

"Buzz's folks will take me. They've been good about checking on us. The neighbors, too." Her lifeless eyes scanned the stack of dirty dishes lining the counter, the floor with hints of several meals, and hamburger thawing on the drain-board. "I get my steam up after supper when it turns a little cooler, and I get all sorts of work done. Usually." Her body language, even more than her tone, told of her dejection.

Victoria pushed back her chair. "How about if you stretch out in your bedroom and aim this fan right at you to help you get more comfortable? I'll let Jillie entertain me while you nap, or at least rest a bit." Her last words were muffled as she bent to unplug the fan.

Gail stared blankly at Victoria. "You'll baby-sit?"

"I'm not a baby," protested Jillie, squirming in her chair.

Victoria reassured the child with a hug, "Jillie and I will be fine, don't worry about us. Shoo, go get some rest. Besides, time with Jillie is so special for me."

Gail left with weak protests, the fan cord dragging along behind her. Once the bedroom door had closed, Victoria whispered conspiratorially to Jillie, "Okay, now. We're going to have fun. I'll wash up these dishes and you get to help me rinse."

"Can I stand on a chair?" Jillie asked in awe.

Solemnly, Victoria nodded. "Just this once."

Elbow-deep in soapsuds, Victoria tackled the piles of dishes. Jillie seriously dunked each dish and held it high to let the water drip off. While they worked, Jillie rambled on about why kittens have whiskers, and where the sun slept every night, and about the little bump under her chin that wiggled when she talked. Her shirt got progressively wetter with each dish she rinsed.

Counters wiped off, Victoria asked, "Do you know where your Mom keeps the mop?"

Strutting importantly, Jillie led the way to a closet in the hallway. "Shhh! We don't want to wake her up," Victoria said as she tied rags from a bag in the closet to Jillie's feet.

"What are these for?" Jillie asked with a giggle.

"When I wash the kitchen floor, you get to skate around and help me get the suds everywhere, okay?"

The chore was more like a game than work for the two of them; after fifteen minutes of washing and rinsing, they left a gleaming floor to dry. "Will you read to me?" Jillie asked, tugging on Victoria's willing hand.

"I sure will, but first we've got to get you into a dry shirt. Can you help me find something in your bedroom?"

Holding hands, they tiptoed past Gail's closed door and down the hall. Victoria halted in silent admiration at the door. Exquisite drawings of acrobatic girls illustrated a banner taped to the door. The contortions of their bodies formed each letter of *Jillie's Room* with hats tossed into the air to dot each *i*. "Honey, who drew this for you?"

"Mommy did. She's got colored pencils. Even a purple one." Obviously, to the artist's child, the possession of purple pencils out-weighed any appreciation for prize-winning talents. Jillie dug into a drawer, leaving a typical little-girl mess in her wake.

Victoria voted for a shirt that looked like one Gail would approve for playwear, and then helped Jillie pull off the wet one. "*Now* will you read to me?" the little girl asked impatiently.

"Which stories are your favorites?"

The child picked several well-worn books off the low shelf and, hand-in-hand again, they headed back to the living room. As they settled in on the couch together, Jillie wedged herself up against Victoria and listened intently, adding a remembered word from time to time.

Victoria read about bears that talked and rabbits that lived in castles, reveling in the magic of a child's carefree world while her abdomen ached with the verity of a woman's pains.

The bedroom door opened during the third story; four eyes from the couch watched Gail waddle into the living room. She smiled faintly and plopped down in the rocking chair. "Oooh, that was pure heaven. I dozed off right away and stayed asleep. I can't believe how refreshed I feel." She set herself rocking with the push of one foot.

"Mommy, River-ant Victoria let me *Stand On A Chair*," announced Jillie proudly.

"Hope I didn't break any house rules!" Victoria said meekly.

Gail yawned, "Not likely. Rules have gotten a little thin lately with me pregnant and Buzz gone. So, Jillie, what did you do when you stood on the chair?"

"River-ant Victoria put soap on all the dishes and I took it off. Then I skated on the kitchen floor."

Victoria laughed and said, "No secrets with her around, are there?" She plucked the sleeve of Jillie's shirt. "The shirt she was wearing is hanging over the hamper in her bedroom. I'm afraid it got pretty wet with our escapades in the kitchen. We picked out a dry one."

Gail shrugged and hefted herself out of the chair. "You could have floated the place down the road for all I noticed. I really conked out. Oh! You didn't have to do my dishes," she protested from the doorway to the kitchen. "Good grief, did you wash the floor, too? The place looks great. I sure didn't expect this."

"After all the water we got on it, it seemed appropriate to clean up after ourselves," Victoria said to hedge the embarrassment she could see shading Gail's face.

Out on the porch, as the two women watched Jillie chasing the kitten, Victoria chose the words that seemed most casual of all that tumbled around in her head, "Gail, you're doing a terrific job helping Jillie cope with Buzz's death, but how are *you* doing? Is there anything I can be doing to help you more through this hard time?"

"Nothing I can think of."

"Are you sure? Would you be willing to loan Jillie to me once in a while? It would give you time for a nap, or allow you to read uninterrupted or just be alone without care-giving responsibilities for a few hours. Cino would be delighted to have a child to play with *inside* the fence!"

Gail jabbed a stray curl behind one ear. "Oh, that's asking a lot of you, busy as I know you must be. I'm pretty tough. A lot more so than I ever thought possible. I guess a person does what they have to." Victoria respected the brief silence before Gail continued, "After the baby gets here, I know I'll have to start working to make ends meet, but until then, Buzz's folks are helping as much as they can. My folks, too, but Iowa's so far away."

"You're carrying a lot on your shoulders. I want you to know that I care." Victoria said, lightly touching Gail's shoulder. "Not just as your pastor, but as your friend. Okay?"

Gail nodded and leaned over the railing to pluck a dead rose from a bush. "I wish you could have had the funeral for Buzz." She flung the flower out beyond the porch. "The minister we got from Williston was okay, but…" She let her words fade away.

Victoria stared at the faded crimson petals on the ground. "I wish I could have known Buzz. He must have been a special guy." She noted a round cedar table out by the clothesline. Dolls and teddy bears sat in heavy metal lawn chairs painted rainbow colors. Play dishes set for a tea party told the rest of the story. *If the ROMEOs want to brighten some-one's life, this is the place they ought to come.*

"Buzz was so wonderful. Our love just got better every year. We were married just over eight years. He was so good when I was expecting Jillie, always coming in from the fields or barn to check on me. He was really happy about this child. It's hard being pregnant and a widow," the word caught in her throat, "but I'm glad that I'll have a real memory of Buzz in the baby. It will be good for Jillie, too."

Victoria squeezed Gail's hand and said, "I'd better head back home. Thanks for sharing your daughter with me. Think about my offer, okay?"

"Thank *you* for everything. I can't believe the minister did my dishes and all…" her voice trailed off to silence.

"Someday you can pass the favor along to someone else, okay?" Victoria suggested as she stepped off the porch. "Gail, I want you to call me if you need anything, or if you just want some adult company. Anytime at all, okay?" Gail nodded and squared her shoulders in an unconscious gesture of taking control again.

Jillie skipped beside Victoria down the driveway. They turned and Victoria waved back at Gail who stood watching them from the porch. "Bye for now, Jillie. See you again soon."

"Bye." The child hopped unsteadily on one foot back to her mother while Victoria walked toward home. Weighed down by her thoughts, she was oblivious to smells of roasts, simmering spaghetti sauce, and all the other family dinners along the way.

When she reached the Rectory, the pain attacking her reserves made it difficult to focus on what she wanted to suggest at the evening's church leaders' meeting. Finally, two aspirins kicked in and she relaxed at the kitchen table over a tuna salad sandwich with an open notebook in front of her. For the next hour she gave undivided attention to jotting down ideas until she had filled both sides of several pages. She headed back over to church to create a computer document from her notes and print out sufficient copies for the meeting's anticipated attendees.

In the brief time remaining, she subjected Cino to a rapid grooming session. "If you're going to be around this crowd, you had better look good, fella! Most of these people think a dog your size belongs outside, so we've got to spiffy you up, or they'll tell me you have to live in the garage. And they can do that, you know—this is their house! We're just the current tenants." Cino shuffled in place, tolerating her hasty ministrations to his coat. "There. What a handsome boy you are! And stay clean—no rolling in the grass!" she called after him as he escaped through the dog door.

The sun inching toward the horizon made the evening sky an artist's delight. When the doorbell rang, Cino greeted each arrival effusively. Victoria directed the five men and three women representatives of the two churches to the living room. Dancing streaks of colors through the windows highlighted the polished floor.

Everyone helped themselves from a selection of hot and cold drinks on the oak buffet, and clustered in twos and threes to catch up on each other's lives. One of Victoria's first suggestions as their new pastor had been to move the monthly leaders' meetings from the sterile environment of either church to the Rectory. The church leaders seemed to enjoy the change, and the meetings had been well attended.

Business began promptly under Luke Larson's leadership. As this year's elected president for the joint congregations, he followed a written agenda and kept the meeting moving along at a steady but unhurried pace. From her spot at one end of the couch, Victoria nodded mentally in approval of his leadership and took part in the lively discussions at his request.

The vote passed to host a Harvest Dinner as a combined event for both churches. They tabled the final decisions on the Christmas program until a later meeting. As an item of new business, they gave attentive consideration to Victoria's proposal for a six-week trial program of something she tentatively called "Mom's Morning Out." They followed along closely as she led them through the points on her hand-out.

"Where would you have these meetings?" asked Sally, a young mother herself.

"I just jotted down these ideas late this afternoon, but I'd thought the children's activities could be in the Prairie Rose Fellowship Hall, with the mothers meeting at a home. Someone like Rachel Lindquist is sure to extend an invitation. I'd like to try the experiment in Prairie Rose first," she said, directing her attention toward the Indian Hills church representatives, "since I'd try to work with the Home Economics teacher here to have high school girls care for the children. I know Ms. Otto teaches a childcare unit and perhaps she would approve of this as a hands-on project. If the program flies, we could begin one at the Indian Hills church, too."

Several towns maintained local grade schools with their consolidated high school in Prairie Rose. The silence in the room indicated the tension this decision from fifteen years ago still generated for the villages represented in the Indian Hills country church. Victoria tried, whenever possible, to keep things balanced between the two churches, or at least present valid reasons for choosing one over the other.

"Quite an interesting idea, but how does it fit in with your ministry and our church's vision statement?" asked Wilbert, the most confrontive one of the group.

Victoria nodded thoughtfully. "That's an important question, Wilbert. Young mothers may well be the most neglected members of our community. They are each unique, but do share common needs. A mother can feel trapped by her young children, or tired of them, or lonely, or guilty over such feelings." Victoria paused, allowing her words time to sink in.

She continued, "These feelings, if not understood or eased, can lead to all sorts of problems." *Like depression, in Gail's case, when coupled with other weighty issues like the death of a young, loving husband.*

"I commend you, Pastor," said Luke, after several moments passed. "As a show of my support, I'd like to donate the refreshments for the trial period, if the vote passes."

"Thanks, Luke." Victoria warmed under his smile of approval. After a few more minutes of discussion, a vote was taken and passed unanimously.

"Did Larson's Grocery happen to send any of those refreshments for this evening?" teased Bob, a farmer whose lean build belied his non-stop appetite. "You know, it would help us recommend certain doughnuts or evaluate cookies more wisely if we could sample them." Laughter adjourned the meeting, extending into the friendly visiting over refilled cups and glasses.

Luke lingered at the end to help Victoria clean up after the meeting and stopped to admire a painting on her living room wall. "You sure have added a lot of your personality to the Rectory—I like what you've done around here. Tell me about this picture."

"This is Mendocino, a coastal town in Northern California, and is one of my favorites. My family spent many summer vacations there so it's always been a special place for me. An artist friend sketched it from a photograph and then gave me the oil painting when I graduated from seminary." She gazed thoughtfully at the sun-kissed beach with the picturesque town perched above it like a lighthouse drawing one toward the shore.

"It looks enchanting."

Seconds passed with Luke standing quietly beside her. "It is. Have you ever been to Northern California, Luke?" She ran her fingers through her hair as if to shake loose the memories. "It's so much different than the Southern part."

Luke's eyes followed her actions; like dozens of men before him, he found it difficult to corral his thoughts after watching the vibrant curls tumble down around Victoria's face. "No, I've had to stick pretty close to Prairie Rose, what with the store and all." A smile illuminated brown eyes. "Unless you count the trips back and forth to North Dakota State University over four years while I got my degree, and then one evening each week for several more years when I went back to NDSU for graduate courses, I haven't done much traveling." There was no self-consciousness or defensiveness in his statement, and this pleased Victoria.

They walked to the screened porch together. Beneath a harvest moon glowing over treetops, he adjusted his collar, cleared his throat and said, "Pastor, as the chairman of the church leaders, I've been remiss in my manners. I would like to invite you to dinner." He dipped his head and examined his shoes intently.

Victoria's eyebrows shot up; thankfully, the darkness covered her utter astonishment at his invitation and his discomfiture. "Why, Luke, you haven't been remiss at all. I'd love to come. May I bring anything?" *Ice cubes? I can usually produce them without mishap.*

"Not this time; it will be simple. Is tomorrow evening open for you?" Victoria nodded as he turned her way. "Good. Come earlier if you would like, but we'll eat about seven o'clock."

"I'll look forward to it. And thanks, too, for the offer of refreshments for Mom's Morning Out. I appreciate your support."

"It's good to have you in town, Pastor. Even after just the few months you're been here, I can tell you've got lots of fresh ideas. That's what this town and our church need."

"Perhaps you could call me Victoria. 'Pastor' seems much too formal, especially across a dinner table," she suggested gently.

He smiled awkwardly. "Yes. Goodnight, Victoria." He said each syllable distinctly, giving her name a majestic lilt. She watched until he turned the corner.

Within minutes she downed more aspirins at the bathroom sink, thankful she had made it through this much of the evening before the most intense pain began. She filled the bathtub and lowered her body into it until her hair floated on the surface like a veil. Propping her head against the rim with a rolled towel for a pillow, she massaged her taut stomach muscles and gave up the last vestige of pretense that all was well. Cino stood guard at the bathroom door, willingly suffering the steam to be near his mistress in her obvious distress.

"This womanhood stuff isn't all it's cracked up to be, Cino," she moaned in the steamy room after half an hour. "You men have it so easy." Her fingers now resembled raisins; she stretched out a slender leg, pointing her toe to push the lever that would send the water spinning away.

After crawling between cool, flowered sheets, she began a ritual instigated years ago during frequent sleepless nights. Focusing on each room she'd spent time in during the day, she summoned pleasant memories of each place. This day's accounting ended with Luke Larson on the

screened porch. Technically, a porch was not a room, but the invitation
for dinner provided a happy ending to the day, so she allowed the
images to send her into sleep's embrace while the night breeze billowed
the curtains like a young girl's hair.

CHAPTER FOUR

"Rev'rend loves the Doctor, and he loves her!
   Will they marry? That's for sure!
   After the wedding, what do you see?
   How many children will there be?"
Victoria's eyes shot wide open in the sun-brightened bedroom. Young voices in a sing-song cadence marked the beat of feet hitting the pavement. She leaped over Cino's body beside the bed and bounded to the open window.

Three little girls and one jump rope in the church parking lot. The rope whipped beneath the flying feet of the lone jumper while the rope twirlers counted, "...eight, nine, ten, 'leven, twelve..." *Twelve kids for the Rev'rend and the Doctor? I don't think so!*

A bell signaled the beginning of the school day and Victoria watched the children meander off, trailing the jump-rope behind them. She drove her fingers through her hair, forcing it into a pile high on her head, and stared at the tousled bed-sheets where just moments before she had slept so blissfully. *It's not even forty-eight hours since I was in Alex's house, and there's already a jump-rope rhyme about us?*

Face down, she flopped on the bed, clutching a pillow against her wildly beating heart. Had an adolescent window peeper watched while she acquiesced with such abandon in Alex's arms? She pounded the bed in frustration. "This, Zan, is precisely why we have to behave," she yelled into the pillow. Cino crept toward the door, tail between his legs, uncertain as to what major crime he had committed that brought on the angry muffled voice.

"I'm not yelling at you, Cino," Victoria promised, watching his exit. Dejectedly, emotions spent, she pushed up off the bed and moved to the closet where she strummed her fingers along the dangling sleeves. The chanting children's verse echoed in her mind, "...*she loves the doctor and he loves her...*" as she stared at her clothes.

After pulling on a pair of faded jeans and rolling up the sleeves of a favorite cotton blouse, she made a bathroom stop, and then stalked down the steps. She poured a glass of orange juice and headed for the backyard with the latest weekly edition of the *Prairie Rose Chronicle* tucked beneath her arm. In a frenzy of revived frustration, she attacked the leaf-speckled picnic table as if it were the enemy. Using the rolled-up paper still encased in its brown-paper wrapper like a whisk broom, she sent debris flying. Cino dashed for safety beneath the porch.

"Leave a little paint on that table, woman!" Startled, she turned to see Alex coming up the driveway on a black bicycle with saddle baskets flanking the rear tire.

"G'morning." Victoria bit her lip as she stared, slack-jawed, at the one person in all of humanity who she didn't want to see in her backyard. "What are you doing here?" she asked curtly. Cino came to life with a bear-like rumble emanating from his barrel chest the instant Alex touched the gate. He moved protectively toward his mistress and took his place between her and this unknown intruder.

"Well! Lookit here." Alex stared at Cino. "He is absolutely stunning, Tori." He secured the bike's kick stand and stood motionless. "Hey, fella. Good job taking care of your lady." He held out the back of his hand, and waited as Cino moved toward him. Pretty soon the tail began to wag, then the sniffing moved from hand to pants leg, to shoes, and back to hand. Apologetically, Cino looked back at Victoria as if to say, *Sorry,*

*but he's obviously got a female Berner at his house. Can you top that? I
don't think so.*

"Traitor," Victoria muttered to her dog, and turned to her gate-
crasher. "What, I repeat, are you doing here?"

"Had to detour on my way to work to save the innocent table! What's
its crime?" Escorted by a now entranced Cino, Alex walked toward the
table, thigh muscles rolling beneath the tan slacks with each movement.

Well, he's not exactly deteriorating with age, is he? She frowned.
"Nothing, compared to the hideous damage done to my reputation."
She slapped the table one last time.

"What's got you heated up so early in the morning?" He shrugged off
a navy blazer and draped it across the end of the table. "Offer me orange
juice, and you can explain that thinly-veiled accusation! And over toast,
I'd listen to your song-and-dance about how you came to own that
ancient Volkswagen Rabbit I see hiding out in your garage!"

"Thought you always ate at, uh, never mind. What about your office?"

Alex patted a beeper attached to one side of his belt and the cell
phone on the other and said, "No sweat. I'm a modern doctor, you
know. Small town, big tech!" He rolled up the sleeves of his pale blue
button-down shirt, loosened his knotted tie one notch, and nestled into
place at the picnic table. "Until I find a receptionist, I've let the word out
that my hours may be a little irregular, but I'm always reachable."

Victoria huffed off to the kitchen; when she returned, Alex had
spread open the single section newspaper on the table and practically
bubbled with mirth over the front page. "Have you read this yet?"

"No. What's the big story?"

"You. Front and center."

"Give me that!" She impatiently offered him a brimming glass in
exchange for the paper. No toast. She wasn't ready for that challenge at
this hour of the day.

He accepted the juice, but pinned the paper to the table with one forearm. "No way, Tori! This story is just begging to be read aloud. But first, you need to talk to me. What's wrong?"

She plopped down dejectedly on the bench opposite him and squinted in the sun. "This morning I woke up to a jump-rope rhyme about us. You and me."

"Really? Let's hear it."

"That's not necessary, and quit grinning; this is not good news. Suffice it to say, I can't believe that after so little time in town together, we're already a gossip item."

He nodded solemnly and stroked his clean-shaven chin. "Wow," he said in a monotone.

"Try not to be so upset, Doctor," Victoria snapped with sharp sarcasm as she jumped up again and stomped a grasshopper who had dared to venture too near the table. "Cino, don't just sit there worshipping your new hero. Chase bugs, or something."

Alex sighed and shook his head, clicking his tongue in gentle rebuke until she glared at him. "Sit. Listen. This will take your mind off slanderous rope-jumpers, I guarantee." Dramatically, he flicked the newspaper flat and took a satisfying gulp of orange juice. Without waiting for her retort, he began to read aloud.

"'Local Pastor Performs Wedding in Yosemite Chapel. The Reverend Victoria Dahlmann,'" he dipped his head respectfully toward her, "'left Prairie Rose a week ago Wednesday to catch the flight from the Williston airport which connected first to Denver, Colorado, and then on to San Francisco, California. She was driven to Williston by Mr. and Mrs. John Thomas who spent the day with their married daughter, Mrs. Ronald (Cathy) Herbert, who has lived in Williston for seven years since her marriage.'" Alex's cheek twitched with restrained merriment.

"Paragraph two," he intoned. "'Arriving in San Francisco in the late afternoon, Reverend Victoria secured an airport rental car.'" A reverberating chuckle interrupted his monologue.

"No detail too small, huh?" Victoria grudgingly let amusement tweak at her frustration.

"Shhh! '…and drove to Yosemite National Park. She spent several days exploring nature's monumental beauty, during which time she conducted a wedding rehearsal and attended the rehearsal dinner hosted by the groom's parents. Friday evening she performed the wedding ceremony at The Yosemite Chapel. The bride and Pastor Dahlmann are childhood friends.'"

"Small town journalism at its finest, huh, Alex?" Victoria grinned.

"You'll have to send a copy of this to the bride, whose name, incidentally, is omitted from the account of her own wedding! Molly should frame this!"

"Go on, I'm sure there's more. Did our heroine ever return to North Dakota's rolling wheat fields from Yosemite's wonders?" She batted her eyelashes coquettishly.

"What an insightful question! Yes, dear listener, there is more." Alex shifted on his side of the picnic table. His shoe hit the ground with a thud and he stretched his leg out beneath the table until his foot rested on Victoria's thigh.

Just like old times. Under the trees along any lake, during long talks on the football grandstand. His foot on my lap, my head on his lap—anything, just so we could be touching.

He read on, and she automatically extended her hand flat along his ankle. "'Mr. and Mrs. Thomas drove back to Williston Saturday evening to return their grandson, Billy, to his home after his visit with them in Prairie Rose. They picked up Pastor Dahlmann at the airport at that time.'"

Yikes! Here I am, sitting in the backyard of the Rectory caressing Alex's ankle. Right in plain view of anyone who walks past and looks through the fence, or spots us through a window! Instantly, her hand slid to a safer zone in her lap.

"'Reverend Dahlmann will show slides of her trip to Yosemite at the fall meeting of the Garden Club.'" He folded the paper and tipped his head for the last swallow of juice; Victoria shifted, easing him off her leg. "Whoops, guess I forgot physical contact is taboo, huh?" His foot dropped to search for the shoe.

"Stay tuned for updates on the continuing saga of Our Lady Minister!" Victoria said giddily, watching one stray blonde hair that a gentle breeze set fluttering down to his shoulder.

"Think what they could do with our wedding..."

"Excuse me? May I remind you, Alex, our relationship is purely and simply platonic? No weddings, no wooings." Her lap felt empty.

"I've been giving your ultimatum some thought. But all I come up with is questions. Why do we have to set rules? Why can't we just wait and see what happens?"

"Long ago I made my decisions about romance and marriage. I came to a crucial point in decision-making about my profession, and I weighed the options and set the goals for my life."

"Did you talk over these goal-things with anyone?"

"Of course."

A frown tugged at Alex's mouth. "Well, it's my opinion that if anyone told you that ministers should ignore their sexuality, you got rotten advice."

"No one coached me for or against marriage and a family. I just realized I'm very happy being single."

"Oh. Did you go out with guys in Seminary?"

"Not that it's any of your business, but yes, I did."

"And?"

"And what?"

"Did any of them propose?"

"Alex!"

"Just answer me."

A loose curl wafted across her face; she tucked it back in place before she spoke. "Yes, one did. I turned him down. I knew if I married another minister it would become difficult to maintain a professional identify of my own, and even more of a challenge to give a marriage the care it deserves. Some can do it; I can't."

"Well, lucky for us, I'm just a doctor!"

"Alex," she said gently, "coming to Prairie Rose has crystallized for me that my profession is my life. I love my work enough to sidestep what seems the new standard path for women, career plus marriage. For me, career is enough."

Alex played with the stem of a leaf that had drifted down on the table. "I'm stumped. Unless you took some secret vows, Tori, I can't believe that the church or God would expect a beautiful woman like you to spend your life alone."

"Don't blame the church or God. If you were to ask ten women ministers, you would likely hear ten different reasons why they are either single, or married. It's a personal decision."

Alex's gaze captured hers as he said softly, "Sometime I'll tell you about my personal decision. I made it over ten years ago and reaffirmed it sitting in the pew at Prairie Rose Community Church this past Sunday morning." He reached across to capture her hand.

"Aren't you going to get to work awfully late, fancy buzz box or not?" Her breathing was shallow, her heart pounding as she slid her hand free of his firm grasp.

"Hey, I'm well into my workday, Lazybones! I was up with the birds, checking on some false labor pains at one house, and then pacifying the wife of a man who couldn't keep food down. She was more upset than he was, probably because she'd fed him Mexican food when all he wanted was soup last night!"

"What's this, a doctor who makes house calls? Oh! Was it Gail Harker with false labor pains?"

Alex shook his index finger playfully, "Confidentiality, Tori, confidentiality! I'm seriously shocked that a woman of the cloth wouldn't respect…"

"Pffft!" she interrupted, "In a town this size, there aren't many pregnant women at any one time. Gail's been looking pretty miserable."

"This is a hard time to be pregnant, especially with the heat lingering so long into fall." He readjusted the knot of the tie that perfectly matched his robin's-egg-blue eyes. "Does Gail attend your church?"

"Their family name is on the membership lists, Buzz's funeral was in the church, so I'd say yes. Jillie comes to Sunday School, even though Gail hasn't attended much. Alex, did she seem more depressed to you today than before?" She looked up from pushing another drifting leaf in and out of a space between table boards. "When I stopped out there yesterday afternoon—well, I'm worried about her. It's rough enough to be a widow at her age, but with pregnancy added to the situation, it's extra tough."

"This morning was the first time I've seen her. She said very little, but I'd already heard that her husband had been killed in a farm accident a few months ago." Deep furrows creased his brow.

Victoria described the young mother's listlessness and lack of energy, noting gratefully that Alex didn't brush off her concern.

"Depression is normal for someone in her present situation, but I trust your assessment of there being a change in her. I'll make a note of it and keep tabs."

Victoria nodded, "I really like her. She's doing a bang-up job of raising Jillie. It's only been a few months since Buzz's death, it happened just before I got here, but this isn't like just another trip out with the combine crew for him; this time he's not coming back. It must be awful for her, facing the impending birth and knowing she'll be raising two kids alone. I just hate to see her retreat into grief without help."

Alex rubbed his cheek with his knuckles, the automatic gesture Victoria knew so well from the past that signaled his concentration.

"In a larger town there would be support groups and grief classes, and such. In Prairie Rose, anyone who has lost a mate is old enough to be Gail's grandparent. That's hardly the ideal support network for a young mother."

Victoria smiled without humor, "If only my fellow seminarians could eavesdrop on this conversation. They were so worried I would lose my pastoral skills here. They thought I'd rot away on little old ladies' porches, drinking endless cups of tea and then going home to develop yet another homily for my growing file of funeral sermons. They didn't see how Prairie Rose could prepare me for a big-city ministry in the future."

Alex's face was expressionless. "Ah, yes. The future. That's when we rip off those sticky letters that spell your name on the church sign. Then you move on to bigger and better things while the next pastor comes to town for another short stint and yet another name goes up on the sign in new sticky letters. That future."

Her temper flared. "Isn't it a little unrealistic, in this time of struggling farm economies and all, to expect that I would stay here forever? In a few years when it's time for me to leave, it will be an ideal parish for a retired minister. It has been before, and it will be again."

"Ideal for whom? You? The congregation? The old guy?"

"Alex, you're making a much bigger deal of this than it needs to be. Professional people move around. That's the way it is. Shouldn't you, for that matter, move on someday, too? Your head's in the clouds if you think you'll build a medical practice here that can support you, challenge you, and pay your bills."

"Hey, my heritage and my future are practically burned in place on my wooden shingle. And if you read the small print on the bottom, so is Prairie Rose, North Dakota."

Resolutely, Victoria took command of the moment. "That's all very touching, I'm sure, but it's not only your grandpa's name on the sign, it's his generation's thinking. Why would someone like you who has had the finest medical education and training stay in a small town beyond a few years? It's a waste of your preparation, experience and ability."

"Oh, I get it. Prairie Rose is good enough for people like us to practice on, but it becomes a 'waste' if we are willing to stay here once we've got our skills honed, is that it?"

"You always did plop yourself firmly on the opposite side of every argument, didn't you? Well, that trick drove our teachers crazy, but it doesn't work with me. Don't purposely misread me, Alex," she said sharply. "I think it's admirable that you are here. Not many doctors are willing to turn away from a chance for a more lucrative practice. I'm glad you had other motivations. I just wish you had goals that reached a little higher."

"I'm sure you've got high enough goals for both of us," he said with gentle irony. "Why are you here?"

"I'm in Prairie Rose because I liked the way they were willing to take a chance on a rookie. In any larger church, I doubt if I would have been hired as senior pastor without experience. I wanted a chance to go solo, not just be part of a staff. I'll learn more this way, and that will make a difference later on."

"So, what you want notched next on your professional belt is a larger church? Or is it that you like being number one?"

She flinched. "You make me sound like a heartless ladder-climber. Hey, we both want to help people. Prairie Rose is where we're both starting out. Don't accuse me of unsavory motives just because I won't retire here."

"Okay. Truce. You promise not to accuse me of sloppy goals and gross negligence of my professional standards if I do retire here, and I'll drop my tirade on your plans. Just don't ask me to applaud you as you drive away."

The clock in the Catholic church steeple tolled the half hour. "Truce." Victoria eyed her backyard guest coolly. "Well, Alex, take good care of Gail's baby. He or she may be the beginning of your future."

Alex nodded seriously. "I plan to. I was surprised Gail called me this morning, since I assumed she had a doctor caring for her in Minot or wherever by this stage of her pregnancy. It's gratifying to realize the town needs me."

"I'm sure money is tight for her."

He nodded and stood beside the table. "Whether she knows it or not, Gail has given me freedom to keep an eye on her advancing pregnancy and her emotions. That ought to help you rest better. From the dark circles under your jade eyes, I'd wager you didn't sleep much last night." With a finger under her chin, he tilted her face upwards. "Take it easy today."

"Yes, Doctor. I'd planned on it. Besides, it's my day off. On Tuesdays I can do what I want."

"Must be nice. Until I get my practice better established, I'll only have hours, not days, off. Cali is lucky to get walked these days when she can't be with me." He swung the still-folded jacket into the bike basket and released the kickstand.

Victoria looked from his legs poised, ready for motion, to the gleaming metal wheel frame. "I could have sworn I saw a blue bike parked outside your office yesterday."

Alex grinned and shrugged, "I'm a chameleon! Thanks for the juice. Stop by the office sometime and you can make a copy of the newspaper article to send to Molly." Gravel crunched as he bore down on the pedal. Blonde hairs on his forearm glistened in the sunlight. "And take a nap!" he called back over his shoulder.

Alone again in the quiet morning, a smile lingered while she scanned the rest of the paper. Feeling strangely content, she ambled over to survey the garden plot and pulled one last stray carrot still buried in the earth. After washing it beneath the outdoor spigot, she devoured it and surveyed the row of pumpkins. She had gone overboard on the size of the garden she had planted, but had enjoyed sharing her home-grown veggies with some of the elderly in her congregation who no longer had their own gardens.

She tossed the green stem back into the garden and hooked her thumbs in the back pockets of her jeans, whistling back at a crow that scolded Cino from the top of the bird feeder. Even with the harsh words that had erupted between them just minutes ago, talking with Alex again after all these years got her blood pumping like an oil rig.

Mid-morning, she headed across the lawn toward Main Street. Even before she opened the door to Cate's Café, the enticing smell of fresh baked goods beckoned her.

"Morning, Reverend," the town barber greeted her, pushing back a chair in welcome. "Join us."

She slid into it with an encompassing smile for the two men hunched over steaming mugs.

"Thanks, Frank." She nodded to her left and right, "Good morning, Al."

Cate reached around her shoulder and slid a filled cup in front of her. "Hi, Victoria. Wondered when we'd see you this morning."

"Cate knows our schedules better than we do, doesn't she?" laughed Al Jenkins, the postmaster.

Victoria grinned. "I think my Tuesdays get her goofed up. On my day off, my arrival time is pretty unpredictable."

Frank chuckled, "Kinda like those airplanes, I guess. You never know about them. Did your plane leave Williston on time?"

Victoria spooned an ice cube from her water glass into the coffee. "No problems coming or going. But you're right, you never know," she said, taking a first cautious sip.

"Read all about your big trip in the last *Prairie Rose Chronicle*. That was really something. Sounds like you did it all, Pastor," Al said.

"Yeah," Frank added, inviting a full report with his expectant look. "Quite an interesting story Fred wrote up."

"It was a good trip, but I'm glad to be back home." *Home, is it? Then maybe Alex is right to accuse; why isn't your name written in paint on the church sign instead of those easily-removed letters?* She dismissed her own accusing question with a toss of her head.

A meaningful glance crossed the table between the two men. "We're glad to hear you're happy here," Al said and winked at Cate who was working close to their table.

The door swung open, letting the Café's occupancy level shift and resettle as several entered and others left. Al and Frank bantered back and forth with folks they had known since childhood while Victoria watched and listened.

Bits and pieces of conversation from other tables filtered through the room; one sentence lodged in Victoria's mind. When there was a lull in the conversation at her table she said, "I just overheard someone comment that the state centennial was Prairie Rose's last hurrah. That's pretty pessimistic, isn't it?"

Frank carefully buttered the last bite of muffin before he answered, "Aw, we're not much for big events around here. We couldn't even agree on if the millennium started in 2000 or 2001, so the parties for that kinda flopped." He ruminated on this for a moment before continuing, "The big doings we put on over the Fourth of July each year last us a long time."

Al nodded, chewing on a toothpick, "With only 300 people left here, we're lucky to get strangers in town three times a year, let alone have anybody move here to stay. We're not likely to attract many tourists, with no motels or such. Besides, the people who come to town are probably visiting relatives and staying in the same bedrooms they grew up in."

"Time was," Frank interjected, "when Prairie Rose had a lot more life. Back when I was a kid, there were a couple of hotels. Now they're gone. And there were a few more cafés than Cate's here which has always been in her family; and we had two banks, now there's just the one branch-bank and it's not even open every day. The bar even closed when Myron died last year. But back in the late '20's, this area was pretty well known for its flour mills, 'n' poultry plants, 'n' creameries..."

Al interjected, "Yup, we won awards for best ice cream and butter several years running when my folks were newly-weds." He licked his lips unconsciously. "But that's small towns, for ya. Time marches on, and the young'uns head for big cities that offer more opportunities than this little burg ever has seen or will see again."

"I think our celebrations for the state centennial were great," Frank defended staunchly.

"That's because of the hype," Cate chimed in from behind the counter where she frosted a three-layer spice cake. "The whole state celebrated 100 years with great enthusiasm. But 109 or 117 years don't call for much hoopla. The next big one is light-years away."

Victoria listened and felt incredibly sad.

Frank reached into his back pocket for a worn leather wallet. "Don't take it to heart, Pastor. You can't turn the tide around. Prairie Rose is just real glad you're here. And the new doctor. Two newcomers at once are more than we ever expected."

"Thanks to Cate," Al said. Frank and Cate glowered at him and he coughed nervously. He shoved his chair away from the table with a noisy clatter and thrust a wrinkled bill into Cate's hand. "Gotta get back to the Post Office and figure out how to send a package to Venezuela. That durned Harvey Thompson keeps sending little boxes to the craziest places." The door slammed on his hasty exit.

"That Harvey ain't the only durned fool around here," muttered Frank, slapping his money on the table; he jammed on his hat and followed the postmaster to the street. Victoria watched through the window as the two men battered each other with verbal ammunition for several seconds and then parted.

She carried her cup to a stool at the counter. "Did I miss something there?" she quizzed Cate who had discovered a sudden need to polish the dairy case with the corner of her apron.

Cate mumbled an indelicacy and swiped invisible dust off the domed glass covering a stack of plump oatmeal raisin cookies. "I can't believe this town managed to keep its damned, 'scuse me, mouth shut this long." She topped off her own coffee cup from the pot, adding an extra spoonful of instant crystals from a jar under the counter to create a muddy brew.

Mechanical sounds of the dishwasher in the kitchen balanced Cate's silence as she came around the counter and slid onto a stool. She took several sips before she looked Victoria squarely in the eye. "When the church called you, talk was pretty busy around the Café, I can tell you. You surprised the hell, 'scuse me, out of us, Catholics and Protestants alike, when you accepted the call. The most we had ever figured for was a retired fellow. Like you heard," she tipped her head toward the tables, "people don't have much faith in Prairie Rose's ability to entice newcomers."

Victoria ran her finger around the rim of her cup as Cate continued, "Despite its quirks and failings—and believe me, I've seen them all—I still love this old town. It hurts to hear people run Prairie Rose into the ground just because it doesn't have higher numbers on the population sign." She yanked a napkin from the holder on the counter and grimly shredded it, wadding the pieces into a tight ball.

"I understand how you feel. This is a special place."

Cate nodded and picked up her story again, "Anyway, once you agreed to come, it was like a shot in the arm for people. But then they started to worry that you wouldn't want to stay once you discovered how everything is shrinking around here. To make a long story short, they figured that the only way to keep you here was if you fell in love and put down roots with a family."

Anger rose like bile in Victoria's throat and her eyes narrowed. "So they somehow convinced Alex Johanson to come…"

Cate grinned with undisguised amusement. "Nope! Believe it or not, that one fell into our laps. Fred Becker came a-flying in here one morning—I think it was in March—anyway, he was about ten feet off the ground. Seems he'd just gotten a letter from a Doctor Alex Johanson who was just finishing up his residency in Rochester, Minnesota, who was asking about rates for a quarter-page ad in the paper." She slid off the stool to deliver a coffee refill across the room. Within minutes, she was back. "First time that kind of new business had come Fred's way since his Dad died and he became the editor!" she added with a chuckle.

"I can imagine," Victoria said weakly.

"Well, one day back in May, Doctor Alex shows up in town. You were due to arrive the next week or so, and the Rectory was humming with activity, painting, cleaning, raking and such, which put lots of people front-and-center when the handsome young doctor and his parents walked around old Doc Johanson's house. And there was even more excitement when everyone realized that he was old Doc's grandson."

Victoria laughed, "When I got to town, I assumed all the excitement was about the upcoming Fourth of July parade!"

Cate scowled in mock seriousness and headed back behind the counter, "Whoa, now. Prairie Rose is a very patriotic town!"

"Right. Match-makers, is more to the point! But, there's another detail that you left out of your story. How did Alex end up here? There's got to be a reason he chose this town, despite his grandfather's practice having been here, and all."

Cate pursed her lips with an inculpable look. "Oh, from time to time I've dropped a line to Old Doc at his condominium. He has always been a friend to me. And he writes back, real newsy letters. He talked about his grandson graduating from Mayo Medical School and how proud he was that his namesake was following his footsteps with a residency at the Clinic. I could almost see the buttons popping off Old Doc's vest when that outstanding young man was invited to go on staff at Mayo Clinic."

He threw over that prestigious offer to come here? What's with this guy?

"Old Doc explained how the young doctor is a most unusual fellow who sincerely likes research and yet hopes to practice general medicine in a small town. That pleased him, too, because he knew the struggle his grandson was going through to buck the trends—much like he had years and years ago when he made the same journey here."

Victoria swallowed hard. *He does have goals, but they are so far removed from my own that they're hard to recognize as such.*

Cate continued, "Maybe I commented to Old Doc how we missed having a doctor close by, and how the slower pace in Prairie Rose would leave ample time for research." Her words were lost when she ducked to heft a basket of dirty dishes to her hip.

Victoria stared at her in amazement. "Cate Jones, you are someone to be reckoned with. I must remember that." Cate shrugged nonchalantly and disappeared into the back room, dishes rattling with each step.

Victoria pulled her tab out of the box by the cash register, added her morning coffee to the list and left the café with much to think about. Cino came to life from his shady spot by the café steps and padded along beside her.

Instead of the black bicycle that Alex had ridden earlier, there was a red one parked in the rack now. Victoria stopped short, rolled her eyes and muttered under her breath, "I'd love to see in his garage. He must collect bikes like Dad collects hammers. All lined up in nice little rows. Blue ones, red ones, black ones. All different sizes. He's crazy."

The bell on the door clanged when she walked into the grocery store. "Whistle when you're ready," a voice called from a side aisle.

"Okay," Victoria responded and grabbed a can of pop from the refrigerated case and then selected an apple and a banana from an attractive display. She trilled a whistle on her way back to the counter and soon heard the predictable shuffle.

Al Jenkins' son, Dave, came around the corner, sticking a dust rag into a hip pocket, "Good Morning, Queen Victoria. Where's Cino?"

"Hello, Davey Crockett! Cino's waiting for me outside. I see Luke is keeping you busy this morning." The young man beamed and nodded. "I'm ready to pay up," she said.

"Sure." Dave, now in his early twenties, had been working at the grocery store for several years. Rachel had told Victoria about the uproar in town when Luke had chosen to hire Dave, the town's only citizen with a mental disability, rather than one of several nondisabled teenagers who had applied for one of the few possible positions in Prairie Rose. But, that episode was in the past. Dave had worked out well; Luke had earned everyone's respect for the diplomacy with which he had handled the potentially volatile situation.

She watched as Dave carefully punched cash register numbers and then hit the correct change key. He slowly counted out coins into her out-stretched hand and then shook open a bag to hold her purchases. "Thanks, Davey C!"

"You're welcome, Queen V!" He smiled happily at their private joke and then scurried around the counter to open the door for her.

Fifteen minutes later, Victoria was walking along an unpaved road leading out of town. Her backpack held a light blanket, a thick paperback novel, sunglasses, a jug of water and bowl for Cino, and the brown bag from Larson's Grocery. Cino dashed ahead, sniffing out rabbits, sticking his nose down gopher holes, and raising dust. They headed for a spot they had claimed as a special getaway since the first week Victoria had been in town. She hated to think of losing it to winter snows.

The deserted house had a wonderful lawn; no one mowed it, but her blanket flattened out an oasis in the tall grasses each time she came to this hide-away whose crumbling brick wall marked its boundaries. Someday she would ask someone about the house's history, but for now she wanted to keep it her special place.

She spread the blanket under an oak tree, filled Cino's bowl with water, leaned up against the rough bark beneath the overhanging branches, and was soon lost in her novel. Flies were getting lazy this late in the season; crickets weren't, and their concert provided a pleasant background. Cino, finally tired of his fruitless pursuit of wildlife, panted his way back to the water dish, and then plopped down beside her while she read. Eventually, the captivating call of an unseen bird pulled her attention away from the book.

The sky was lacy with clouds above her; she stretched out on the blanket with her backpack for a pillow and crunched into the apple. A narrow section of the long grass around her parted; she lay motionless while a rabbit stared at her and then darted back into safety. A gopher popped in and out of his hole just yards away, but Cino slept on. "As long as you stay out of my yard, have fun, fella," Victoria called to the busy animal, causing Cino to stir and sniff the air. "Stay, Big Boy." He obeyed, but his look said volumes.

So Cate writes to Zan's grandpa, huh? She flung her apple core near the gopher's tunnel; he darted out to retrieve this free meal. *And Prairie Rose figures that the only way they'll keep me is to find me a husband.* She pressed her forearm over her eyes and sighed. *Well, this is one woman who won't put her career goals on permanent hold in a spineless response to that predictable incentive. Especially if their prime candidate is the distracting doctor who just moved to town. The surest way to kill my career would be to get hooked up with Zan again.*

Crows called to one another, occasionally swooping down from their flight paths across her blanket in curiosity before heading off to the bog beyond the empty house. From beneath heavy eyelids she saw a grasshopper on the blanket and tried to remember any time in her pre—Prairie Rose life that she had ever taken time for such simple pleasures.

Dinner with Luke tonight will be nice. Maybe once the back-fence gossips get wind of it, it will help to convince Alex I have a fulfilling life of my own. She smiled. Wind fanned the cattails and field grasses whispered soothingly as she rubbed Cino's belly until he fairly hummed with joy.

Luke must be about 35 or so. I wonder if he's self-conscious about his graying hair. It actually looks quite distinguished. I wonder what Alex will

*look like when he turns gray? Or do blondes become white-headed? What
was it Cate said about her white hair?*

She dozed off and on for an hour, roused to read some more, and
then nodded off again. Walking back home with Cino energized and
strutting beside her, she sighed contentedly to herself. She could now
report, if asked, that she had followed doctor's orders and taken a nap.
Now, if he would follow suit and keep his feet off her lap and his kisses
off her mind.

The afternoon passed quickly. She pulled weeds around the yard,
swept out the garage, and wrote an actual postage-required letter to
her parents who periodically complained that e-mails weren't the
same as "real" mail. Using the picnic table as an improvised desk, and
with pen poised mid-air, she stared at the spot where Alex had sat just
hours earlier.

Both sides of two sheets of stationery were filled with details of the
upcoming christening, highlights of the church leaders' approval for the
Mom's Morning Out trial period, a report on the ROMEO's visit which
she knew would give her dad a chuckle, and a quick sketch of the living
room to show the new locations of furniture she had shifted around
since they had helped her move in. It was jam-packed with news.

But not a word about a certain Doctor Johanson…Zan Johanson,
first love…Alex Johanson, neighbor who dropped in for orange juice
and ankle massages…Doctor Johanson, her parents' biggest worry from
the past who had just moved right into the present…with his lovely
female Bernese, Cali.

She frowned at her letter; it didn't lend itself to dropping a bomb at
the end. *PS. By the way, there's a new doctor in town. His name is Alex
Johanson. Yeah, isn't it a small world? We're both so busy, though, that I
doubt if we'll see much of each other. Oh, his dog's name is Cali, which I'm
sure calls to your minds the magic of California and Mendocino.*

Her parents would read her letter aloud over breakfast; she could see
the scene as clearly as if curtains rose on a stage beneath the cottonwood

tree. Blue willow dishes, fresh-cut flowers in a milk glass vase, the fringed tablecloth, Dad's reading glasses sliding down his nose, Mom listening, absent-mindedly twisting her wedding ring.

Listen to this, Maggie...Alexander Johanson...could it be Zan? Mom would purse her lips and flick imaginary crumbs off the tablecloth. Dad would stoutly insist that "the kids" had grown up now. Mom's eyes would cloud over; Dad would retreat in silence. *Is that all she says, Mort? Read it again.*

The few lines of such a postscript would spawn countless hours of speculation, forcing the bulk of her letter to be read once and forgotten. Victoria signed off and sealed the envelope quickly without including the troublesome postscript.

* * *

Strains of classical music from inside Luke's house piqued her interest when she rang his doorbell that evening. The front door swung open; Luke smiled a welcome that included approval of her full-skirted khaki-colored shirtwaist cinched at the middle with a rope belt. "Come in!"

They moved beneath the high-ceilings in the hallway to the living room. After a few minutes of small talk, Luke excused himself to finish in the kitchen, declining Victoria's offer to help. Choosing an inviting leather recliner, she lost herself in the riveting music. She surveyed the room with interest: rich browns and blues, masculine textures and solid furniture.

"Care for something to drink?" Luke appeared in the doorway with two glasses on a teak wood tray. "It's a new frozen tropical juice I just got in the store. I hope you like it."

"Thanks. What a beautiful room, Luke! Have I usurped your special chair?"

A slight smile showed his pleasure as he sat opposite her in a high-backed rocker. "No, don't get up. You're in the perfect place to listen to music. I'm glad you like the room; this was my parents' home, but they've retired out on the family farm after dad's brother died and left the place empty."

"Do they do any farming now?"

"No, they just wanted to keep the place in the family. I offered to live out there when I was ready to get my own place, but they missed the country. Both of them grew up on farms. And being in town is easier for me since I have the store."

She nodded. They listened in companionable silence until the last haunting notes of a violin disappeared in a whisper. "That's one of my favorite pieces," Luke confided. "There are speakers in the dining room, so we can enjoy the music during dinner."

"It smells wonderful!" Accepting her compliment with a gentle smile befitting the person who lived in this home with its aura of quiet solitude, he led the way to the dining room door.

The meal was a feast for the senses. Heavy stoneware and smooth brown goblets, crisp grill marks on the tantalizing steaks, steaming potatoes in their skins garnished with parsley-butter, vivid garden-fresh tomatoes with herbs and slivered roasted almonds sprinkled like jewels, and crusty garlic bread.

Victoria silently received each offered dish from Luke and gazed in amazement at her plate. "How did you accomplish all this since getting home from work?" *And how did you learn to cook like this is the more important question?*

A laugh rumbled in his chest, "That's one advantage to owning the store. I can leave Dave in charge and steal away to start the grill."

The evening was relaxing, the perfect end to the day. Luke was the ideal host, at ease at his own table. Talk flowed easily with no artifice or self-consciousness on either side.

"Tell me about your family, Luke. I've met your parents. Any brothers or sisters, or are you an only child?"

A hint of buried sorrow shaded Luke's face. "I'm never sure how to answer that. I had an older brother, Thomas, but he died in a car accident quite some time ago. So that makes me an only child now, but…"

Victoria said gently, "Your family has had its share of suffering, I can tell."

"We've learned a lot from it all," he responded and then smiled resolutely at his guest. "How 'bout yourself? I've met your parents, as well, during your first week in town. They're very nice—friendly, out-going."

"Yes, they are. And I've had them all to myself for all these years."

Allowing the conversation to shift to more neutral topics, Luke recounted Helen Wilson's latest dilemma: the junior and senior high school girls who came to the joint barber and beauty shop that Frank and Helen operate demanding to look just like Victoria. "Frank says if anyone could do it, it's Helen, but she says that while the Wilson's Clip and Curl does a fair job at keeping people happy, it's pretty hard to give anyone the same finesse our new resident wears so easily." His deep-set eyes personalized the compliment.

"I'm fortunate to have lots of hair; that I owe to my Mom. The color comes from Dad's side of the family tree, or maybe it's a sumac bush, in my case!"

"I dare say if we were to walk through Prairie Rose tonight, in full view of everyone peeking out from behind the drapes, every girl would show up in school tomorrow with her hair pulled up like yours, with a shell clip holding it in place above her left ear!"

Victoria smiled and adeptly changed the subject.

"One of my dreams," Luke confided at her gentle questioning over cheesecake with raspberries, "is to create a haven for people who need a quiet spot to escape city-madness. Prairie Rose is close enough to Minot, or even Williston, to draw from them. City people need a chance to relax in today's fast-paced society. If we could just get them here and make it special, I know they'd be back!"

"Prairie Rose definitely has small town charm," Victoria concurred. "Just this afternoon I reflected on how refreshing it is here. What ideas do you have for attracting visitors?"

Luke paused, scanning her face carefully before he said, "I've tossed around the idea of creating a jogging path or historical walking tour of the town and eventually opening a bed-and-breakfast inn. How's that for a pie-in-the-sky dream?"

Victoria's eyes glowed, "I like a man with goals! This has definite possibilities." She paused thoughtfully. "The streets are flat, which make it perfect for a walking or jogging path. If we produced a map with distances marked out…and purposely routed it past the historical buildings, we could combine your two ideas…"

Luke held up a cautionary hand, "Hold it, you said 'we.'"

Victoria paused, head tipped to one side. "Looks like I got a little carried away, jumping on your wagon like that!"

"I won't push you off. It's just a shock to have someone's support; so many seem resigned to Prairie Rose fading away."

Victoria took a hasty sip of water and dropped her napkin on the table. "Do you have a big piece of paper?"

Luke promptly left the room, returning with two grocery bags, masking tape, scissors, and two markers. "Like any good grocer, I have a healthy supply of brown paper bags! If I had known ahead of time, I could have brought home butcher paper!"

"Bags are perfect. Where can we work?" Soon they sat cross-legged on the hardwood living room floor, perched over an expanse of paper bags sliced open at the seams. Victoria's skirt dropped around her legs like a gown on the pillow Luke had provided and she felt like a kid again—playing princess-on-a-throne and coloring.

Luke drew quickly. "Okay, here's the town." He grinned ruefully. "It sure doesn't take long to sketch out the streets."

"What could be some sort of Trail Center, with restrooms?"

Luke tapped a spot with the tip of his marker, "This building was a furniture store; it's empty now like so many others. The floor space is wide open. There's already one restroom, so adding more isn't impossible."

They stared at each other across the brown-paper dream and spontaneously gave each other high-fives. Soon, bold arrows marked directions on walking paths, X's showed spots for benches, drinking spigots, and information signs. They even sketched out ideas for brochures to advertise the plan. Victoria learned that Luke, despite his calm, collected persona, had a dry sense of humor and was a clear thinker who had a fully developed ability to communicate well.

"Got any ideas for a name, Luke?"

"How does 'Meadowlark Trail' sound?"

"Perfect!"

Victoria was amazed at how quickly the evening passed. Luke walked Victoria back to the Rectory; the night air was cool. Very few lights were on in the houses they passed as they ambled quietly down the tree-lined street. "That was fun! Thanks for a great evening, Luke. I really enjoyed our planning and that meal: you're a fabulous cook!"

"Glad you could come. Thanks for sharing my dreams. We'll do this again sometime?" he asked shyly.

"Sometime? I'd say, soon! If we keep planning, we could see this idea come together in time for next spring. We need to get our plans constructed carefully before we take it to the town council or whoever needs to approve all this. Plus, we need to recruit others."

Luke's step was almost jaunty as he left; she lingered on the screen porch to savor the evening and watched Luke disappear around the corner. That's when the idea popped into her mind: it was the perfect way to solve the messy little detail that had niggled in the back of her mind for days: telling her parents about Alex.

She booted up her laptop computer and sent a cryptic e-mail that Mort and Maggie would see in the morning: *Had a wonderful evening—*

remember the grocer, Luke? He invited me for dinner at his place and we really clicked. We came up with a great idea for a project in town—more later on that. Oh, there's someone here you know: Alex Johanson went to med school and now has reopened his grandpa's clinic here. Luke will probably recruit him to help with our project. Well, off to bed—your daughter is happy and tired tonight. :)

Tonight, her thoughts were a jumble of Alex and Luke, one of whom resurrected memories of passion and desire, the other who offered a pleasant relationship in a new dimension. Small wonder that her dreams that night left her sheets in a knotted mess around her.

Walking out to her car Wednesday morning for an office day at the Indian Hills church, she grinned. *So, Victoria, you've suddenly got two men in your life. Alex with his pancakes and perverse passion, and Luke with his steaks and sensible serenity.*

CHAPTER FIVE

The baby's satin christening gown hung over Victoria's arm as she cuddled the infant. The stillness in the sanctuary was like a soothing lullaby. "Rusty and June Guddman, you bring joy to this congregation, the same way in which your daughter brings joy to your house, when you share this time of public celebration and personal commitment with us, your extended family."

Dozens of eyes watched her trace the delicate outlines of the baby's face with her fingertips. Victoria's face lit up with delight when two little arms waved wildly, close enough to brush her face. She shifted the baby to face the audience. "We welcome our newest child, Jenny Jenae Guddman."

As Victoria closed the brief ceremony with the traditional prayer, the lapel microphone she wore magnified the infant's gentle cooing. The tears in Rusty and June's eyes caught her off guard when, after tenderly kissing their child on the forehead, she placed the baby back in the father's waiting arms.

Church services over, she had just changed clothes when Cino barked once and dashed from the bedroom. Pausing, Victoria heard a knock on the Rectory's back door. She grabbed up deck shoes and raced barefoot down the stairs and peeked through the window before flinging open the door. *Alex.*

He held a giant jug of sun tea beneath a jaw-cracking grin. "Does iced tea sound good with taco salad?" The belated thud of her shoes hitting the floor matched her heartbeat.

"What makes you think I'm having taco salad for lunch?" she asked innocently. She signaled Cino into a reluctant sit-stay, and yanked her eyes off the taut, tempting body in blue jeans.

He waited expectantly on her back porch while she concentrated on wiggling each foot into its shoe. "Ha! Why else would the Taco Salad Queen of Prairie Rose be buying all the crucial ingredients on a late Saturday afternoon? Aren't you going to invite me in?"

"Uh, sure. Come in," she offered belatedly, stepping back to allow him entrance into her kitchen. "What are you, a grocery store spy?" she grumbled lamely and released her quivering dog with a "You're free, Cino."

Alex's retort froze as he crossed the threshold. "Wow, look at these high ceilings!" He absorbed Cino's typical Berner welcome with the ease of someone who gets an identical greeting every time he comes home. Scratching the ecstatic dog behind his ears, Alex's eyes took in the four walls in silence.

"Pretty impressive, huh? Would you like a tour?"

"You bet. Lead on." They deposited the iced tea in the refrigerator, and Cino padded along with them.

Every room fascinated Alex. The bay windows in each bedroom, the wainscoting in the dining room, the French doors between the living room and the parlor which was now Victoria's den, the original glass doorknobs on every six-panel door, the intricate woodwork throughout the house, and even the dusty attic with its steep, drop-down stairway. They explored together, pausing to caress the wood, admire the delicate designs in the wallpaper, and enjoy the vast four-direction views.

"Hey, you can see my house from this room. We can have a signal. One light flashing means 'I love you'. Two lights mean 'I want you.'"

"I thought it was one-if-by-land, two-if-by-sea," Victoria said dryly.

Alex shook his head solemnly, "No, I'm afraid that's just an edited version in schoolbooks. Impressionable children, you know; can't get them thinking about S-E-X when they're supposed to be learning history."

Victoria rolled her eyes and pulled him away from the window he had now guaranteed would continually remind her of him.

Alex voted to eat in the cozy kitchen rather than at the sits-ten-comfortably table in the chandeliered dining room. Victoria snapped her fingers and pointed at the corner and Cino ambled over to plop down facing them. "How do you do that?" Alex asked, amazed.

"Discipline."

"You should give classes."

"Cali seems pretty obedient."

"I only put her through the stuff in public that I know she'll obey!" Alex admitted.

"I'll have to give *you* classes," Victoria teased, "then you'll be able to control your dog. Dog training is wonderful education for *people!*" They smiled easily and then concentrated on food for the next few minutes.

"Did the church furnish this place, or is it all this old stuff yours? You've got some wonderful furniture." He scooped a generous spoonful of her homemade salsa over his taco salad.

"Much of it goes with the house, I guess, at least it was here when I arrived. Some of the pieces I brought down from the attic. Over the years I've collected what furniture I do have from country auctions and great sales. Good thing, too, otherwise, we'd be sitting out at the picnic table because, as you know, paying off school bills and buying furniture don't work well on the same budget!"

"Ain't that the truth?"

It was disconcerting to have Zan Johanson move from his safe, designated spot in her locked-up memories right into the Rectory kitchen with his faded denim eyes Victoria could not forget. Even more unnerving was how well he fit right in.

"The service was beautiful this morning, Tori. I know I wasn't the only person with wet eyes and a touched heart."

She jerked her head, prepared to rebuke his jesting, but saw sincerity instead. "Thanks. I felt it, too," she admitted softly.

"Old John Caston was standing on the church steps when I came out and he said something about, 'Can't recall the christenings with the men-Reverends, in fact I can barely remember my own son's, but this one with the new lady minister is gonna stick with me, I reckon.'" Alex's imitative drawl lingered and his steady gaze was like a caress.

"He's a nice old fellow; used to be a railroad man."

It was as if he hadn't heard her. "When I saw you with that baby in your arms, I thought, Tori's where she belongs. If anyone has any lingering doubts about calling a clergywoman, those qualms flew out the window today."

"What makes you so sure of that?"

He paused a moment to form his thoughts. "This morning, we saw one advantage you have as a woman in ministry. And I don't believe one of those 'men Reverends' that John Caston mentioned would have thought to wash Gail's dishes."

Startled, Victoria met Alex's eyes. "How...?"

Alex halted her question with a raised hand. "At crisis points in our lives, most people tend to gravitate toward the givers of those emotions that society has all too conveniently labeled as 'feminine.' I know *I* want mothering when *I'm* sick, and we all crave understanding and compassion during sorrowful times. Unfortunately, we men can come up with the right words, but we can't always express ourselves beyond that. I guess it's the true difference between caretakers and caregivers."

She listened, amazed, as his words opened a hidden door to her scrutiny.

He continued, almost as if talking to himself, "This morning, Tori, you changed one of the church's traditions—a christening—from a predictable, formal event into something vibrant and memorable. And we were changed, too."

Victoria was moved by his honesty, and even more so by his fervor. Her eyes glistened above a shaky smile. She rose from the table to refill not only their glasses but also her reservoir of composure.

While Victoria's back was turned, Alex asked casually, "Are you having any physical problems, Tori?"

She stiffened as if fending off an attack. *Wow, you have a doctor for lunch and look what you get!* "What do you mean?" she asked defensively.

Alex shrugged, "Well, we haven't been in town together for all that long, but on Monday, I'm buying milk at Larson's Grocery and I see you in the personal products aisle. Then when I bought deodorant a couple of days later, you were at the counter with more of those rather telling purchases. Two days ago, I walked you home and peeked in the bag I carried for you: off-the-shelf pain medication on top of the familiar boxes. Hence, my question."

She jabbed a piece of lettuce. "Isn't that rather personal, Alex, even for a doctor? And, since we're on the subject of invasion of privacy, do you always snoop at what people are buying?"

He nodded amiably, "Yup. To both questions."

They chewed in silence for several long, weighted minutes.

"Well? The doctor is waiting, Reverend Dahlmann."

"Nothing is any different or worse than I'm used to, *Doctor*," she said with heavy sarcasm coating his title.

He sighed. "Will you give me a straight answer if I clutch my diploma across my chest when I talk to you? It's not like I'm waiting for your menstrual cycle to end so I can ravage your body. As a doctor, I'm concerned, professionally because you live in my jurisdiction should an emergency arise. And, okay—maybe a little bit personally." His eyes sparked like blue coals.

Good grief, he's right. If I ever need a doctor fast, he's it. "Can we drop the subject?"

"Nope; not yet. Here are my observations. If I'm miles off, we'll drop the subject and I head back to medical school to retake Diagnosis 101. If I'm right, you give me straight answers. Deal?"

Sensing the tension in the room, Cino crept over to a spot close to his mistress. Victoria slipped a shoe off and rubbed her bare toes in his soft fur. Silence crowded the room until it felt stifling. She chased a piece of tomato around her plate, her veins pounding a percussion accompaniment.

Alex spoke at last, giving voice to his concerns, "From the dark circles under your eyes, I assume you don't always sleep well, which could indicate frequent trips to the bathroom during the night or persistent pain that robs you of sleep. From time to time, even today, I've noticed brief flashes of pain flitting across your face, usually followed by steeled posture. All that, coupled with the fact that I know your age, and having seen your recent rash of purchases of a personal nature—spread over a much longer time than what is normal—all this leads me to ask: Are you having any physical problems, Tori?"

The faucet dripped in the cavernous silence. Her response was a whispered, "Yes."

"Have you ever been diagnosed?"

He took her silence for assent.

"Let me hazard a guess. Endometriosis?"

She swallowed hard and looked squarely into his gentle, sky-blue eyes. "You must have gotten an 'A' in that Diagnosis 101 class. You're right on target: I'm just a typical case of the disease." Her smile was a mere shadow.

"You're hardly a typical anything, but you do fit the profile, Love. Are you taking any prescribed medication for it? Or are you just using that over-the-counter stuff I saw in your grocery bag?"

She grimaced, "Alex, I don't want to talk about this. I'm a private person; I don't like—or have a need—to blab all my woes and ailments to the world. This something I have learned to live with."

"Anything you say goes no farther than this room. You can trust me, Tori."

She inhaled deeply, forcing herself to relax with the release of the pent-up air. "I know, but it sure would be easier if you weren't someone who I…it's just hard to talk about something this personal with…what was the question?"

"Medication."

She chewed on her bottom lip. "You name it, I've probably taken it. The last one I just couldn't tolerate, even though it was touted as the new 'treatment of choice.' My last prescription ran out a couple of weeks ago, so right now I'm not on anything. What's the use? The next stage is surgery, I guess."

"Are you interested in having surgery?"

She frowned. "A hysterectomy seems so, oh, I don't know…drastic…and final."

Alex pressed his knuckles into his cheek and Victoria sipped iced tea; their thoughts hovered. "You know, surgery doesn't necessarily mean a hysterectomy. If anyone has let you think that's the case, you have not gotten the full story. Let me do some checking; I wouldn't presume to advise you off the top of my head since gynecology isn't my specialty, and it doesn't seem likely or appropriate that you would come to my office for a regular exam as my patient." He shot her Zan's own wicked grin.

"Ain't that the truth?" She softened her words with a shy smile.

"I'm quite sure you'd benefit from some of the newer research. I don't know how long you've suffered with this, but there are amazing treatments these days. Meanwhile, you call me if there's anything I *can* do to help make life a bit easier for you. Okay? Doctor's orders. "

"*Okay,*" she said ungraciously, "you're both bossy and nosey. Anything else, doctor?"

"One last question: do your parents know I'm in Prairie Rose?"

"Whew, now *that's* a leap without a segue! Well, I didn't tell them right off, but I finally realized that was silly. They could show up anytime, and here you would be." The clock ticked several seconds into history before she continued, "I gave them the barest of details, knowing how hard even that much would be. I know their imaginations and worries are running wild." She pushed her chair back from the table to begin clearing the dishes.

"So, I'm on their hit list, huh? I should have gathered as much when you disappeared right after high school graduation without a word."

"Well, you were on a very short list of people they didn't want to see around their daughter any time soon. I figure your life is safe as long as they don't think you're after me again," Victoria teased.

"Hmmm, that's a quandary, isn't it? My life or my passion!" He helped clean up the kitchen, whistling bits and pieces of crazy songs as they worked side-by-side. She was grateful that he sensed her need to digest all he had said to her.

"We'll have to introduce our dogs to each other, Tori," he said as he added detergent to the dishwasher. "The two of them will get along famously. Cali is almost ready to be back in circulation again. I'm sure getting tired of lonesome midnight walks with her just to keep the male dogs in town quiet."

I'm not sure I want Cino to discover puppy love with Cali. She got away with a nondescript mumble that signified nothing, hoping to buy time before what she knew was an inevitable event.

In the living room, Victoria challenged Alex to a game of Scrabble, each squatting beside the coffee table. He won by 52 points, much to his glee. "Winner takes the couch!" He let his shoes drop to the floor and stretched out his long legs. *You never could make your eyes behave when Zan Johanson wore jeans, Tori.*

Victoria remembered a conversation she had overheard at the Post Office, and knew this was the perfect chance to verify her suspicions.

"You wouldn't happen to know anything about the radio antennae going up on the grain elevator at the edge of town, would you?"

Alex raised one eyelid and offered a lazy, "Hmmm?"

"It wouldn't have anything to do with that eye-catching additional hardware on the roof of your Clinic, would it?"

"Well, I might have mentioned to Zeke—who I discovered is the proud manager of the Prairie Rose Grain Elevators—that I would be able to get faster Internet access if I wasn't limited to the painfully slow, dial-up connection that has been all Prairie Rose could offer. And it appears that the newspaper, and school, and a surprising number of citizens are also quite interested."

Victoria stared at him. "So how did the grain elevator get involved?"

"Well, I put a call in to NoDak Technologies—found 'em in the phone book—and asked a few questions, and then made some visits and calls around town. Turns out, since Zeke lets them put a special antenna on the grain elevator, he gets a rent-check in the mail from NoDak Technologies every month, and lots of people in these parts can benefit from Internet access without reliance on phone lines if they are so inclined to pursue it."

"Add me to your list of interested citizens. Oh, Alex, that check every month will be a real help to Zeke. I know he is still trying to see his way clear from some pretty hefty medical bills due to his heart condition, and I heard about his house fire last winter. It's been a rough year for him."

"Aw, I just wanted wireless Internet access."

"Yeah, right." Victoria felt a tug at her heart. "You're still one of a kind, Zan, 'way-back-when and right here-and-now," she said softly.

"Hey," he said changing subjects adeptly, "here's something to toss around on a lazy afternoon. How can you and I make a difference in Prairie Rose? And I don't mean the expected activities that go with our professions."

Victoria snagged a footstool with her toes and pulled it up to her chair while she pondered. "Luke and I talked about something similar the other night over dinner."

Alex frowned, "You and Luke? Dinner?" His eyebrows furrowed ominously. "Is that guy crowding in on my turf? Hey, Cino, I thought you were my friend! Did you let down your guard, boy?" Cino's tail swished at the sound of his name.

"Your turf? Excuse me, Alex, but the only male with any claim to this turf is four-legged!" She thumped her big boy's furry chest as he lolled on his back beside her and he sighed with joy.

"Yeah, but I didn't know you were having dinner with Luke, for crying out loud. I mean, he's the only other eligible bachelor in town."

"Oh, I don't know, old John Caston is single again since his wife died! I know, I know, not funny." She ducked in anticipation of a well-aimed pillow. "Luke and I had dinner. What's the big deal?"

"The big deal is that after your little speech to me about our new adult relationship, I don't like the idea that I'm the only one who got that song and dance."

"What makes you so sure Luke didn't hear my little speech?"

"He held your hand at the football game last Friday."

"Who appointed you my chaperone? And he did not *hold* my hand—that's called keeping me from tripping on the bleachers," she retorted defensively.

"Just keeping things fair and square. After all, the names that are permanently etched in a heart on the sidewalk outside your parents' house in Duluth aren't Luke and Victoria, they're Tori and Zan. Remember? 'True love. Forever.'" Just the faintest tinge of sorrow circled his eyes.

"Getting back to your question," Victoria prompted gently, reading between the lines of Alex's effort to mask his emotions, "what's dying in Prairie Rose is a sense of pride. When anyone moves away, those still here feel it again: Prairie Rose has nothing to offer anyone." *And that,*

Tori, is just what will happen when you pack up and leave. She waited, wondering if he would bring it up again.

Instead, he stared at the wall where she had hung a painting of a field of proud sunflowers. "I asked a farmer who was in my office the other day why they grow wheat and sunflowers in the same field. Do you know why?" Victoria shook her head as she followed his gaze. "Bands of sunflowers between fields of spring wheat protect the grain crop from the wind that could otherwise destroy it."

They sat in comfortable silence, each lost in their own ruminations.

"Hmm. The youth could be as important as sunflowers, couldn't they, if they stuck around?" she mused, picking up on his line of thought.

"Unless it hails. Then both crops are lost."

"Don't mess up the analogy! Not only have you suggested a plan for instilling pride in Prairie Rose, you might have given me the illustration I've been looking for; watch for it in my sermon next week!"

"Glad to be of help, Tori," he drawled. "Imagine how much help I'd be if we were married, supplying you with illustrations, and sensuous interludes from studying…"

She groaned, "You, Zan Johanson, have a one-track mind! Getting back to the topic, we need to get to know the kids. The plan has to start with them, don't you think?"

"Now who has a one-track mind? Okay, if we tried to cultivate pride in Prairie Rose with the older crowd, we could lose a whole crop of kids meanwhile."

"Good grief, you're starting to sound like the locals with this agricultural vocabulary! Next thing I know you'll be telling me about no-till techniques or nestings in the potholes…"

"And how did a big-city gal like you learn about that stuff?"

Victoria chalked up one point in the air with a tongue-licked fingertip, "I hear about all the latest farming methods when I'm at the feed store getting dog food. I haven't got a clue what it all means, but I know all the words!"

"Sneaky!"

"Back to business; how 'bout a pancake breakfast that the kids could put on for the older folks. I'm sure Cate wouldn't mind the competition for one morning."

Alex studied the ceiling thoughtfully while laughter played around his eyes. "Gee, who do we know who makes vast quantities of incredibly delicious pancakes quite regularly and could help these mentor these kids?"

Victoria fired the pillow full speed back across the room at Alex. He snared it mid-air, rescuing the lamp behind him. "I don't know," she said, "especially if that person has to be humble! An even better question is how do we get the kids together to propose this plan?"

"Did you say 'propose'? That brings to mind my...whoops! I assume that withering stare means no. Okay, we go to them. Where's one place they will all be at once?" he asked, jerking his head toward the front window.

She stared at him. "At Henderson's house?"

"No," he said with a withering look of his own, "one block down the street."

"The school? Alex, we can't go trotting into the school, or even hang out on the school grounds to solicit!"

"I bet we could if we were invited. And if the minister and the doctor can't wrangle an invitation, who can?"

Alex crossed one leg over the other knee, letting his foot dangle; Victoria flung her hair over the back of her chair; they let their thoughts roam again.

"Okay, how's this: we run a contest," Alex said presently, "and get permission to present it to the kids."

She picked up on his train of thought, "And when this yet-to-be-determined contest is over, winners are announced at the pancake breakfast. How's that?"

"So, what kind of contest?" he challenged.

"Hey, don't suggest 'contest' if you don't have something in mind," Victoria complained mildly. "What about submitting designs for a town banner to hang from the light poles on Main Street?"

"Is that something you and Luke thought up?" He lifted his head to eye her suspiciously above his knee.

"Get a grip, Zan!" She rolled her eyes.

In retaliation, he stuck out his tongue at her before he continued, "I've seen those banner dealies before. Dozens of places around the country have 'em for every season. There's probably a whole business built around making and selling 'em."

"Would it get out of hand if we opened the contest up to the whole school?"

"Probably. But we could have a second contest for the younger kids so they don't get left out. And for this one I do have an idea. It's not something that I announce on a megaphone on Main Street, but I received a grant to do research on pediatric farm accidents. People will find out about it soon enough, but right now I don't want the community thinking my only interest in seeing them is for research. Meanwhile, the elementary school kids could sure help with, oh, maybe a sketching contest, or something about safety."

"If we charged a small amount for the breakfast, we'd have money to pay for supplies, even though we would probably need to pay for them initially out of our own pockets."

"All right!" Alex gave her a thumbs-up. "I think we're on to something here, Tori. Now let's…" The sudden buzz of his cell phone jarred them and put Cino on full alert. Victoria calmed her dog and Alex swung his feet to the floor. "Doctor Alex speaking."

She handed him the pencil and notepad they had used for Scrabble and waited, half listening, half watching. *Interesting to see him in action. He's a dangerous combination of professional and sensual.*

"Where is he now? Good. You've done the right things so far. Keep him as quiet as possible and I'll be there within a few minutes." He disconnected and filled Victoria in succinctly while he reclaimed his shoes. "Marie Waters just found Don slumped over. They're at home."

"I'll go along to be with her. They are long-time members of my church. Do you need directions to their house?"

"No, I know the place. I'll grab my bag from home and meet you there." The door slammed behind him.

Five minutes later Victoria turned a corner and saw the bike already leaning against a tree. The Water's front door stood open, so she let herself in and called out from the entryway, "Marie? It's Victoria Dahlmann." She got no answer, but could hear voices from the back of the house and moved in that direction.

Alex had managed to get Don Waters stretched out on the bed in the bedroom; he now knelt, moving his stethoscope around the quadrants of Don's chest. Pale with fright, Marie watched from the foot of the bed. She looked up when Victoria stepped through the doorway and moved toward her minister like a sleepwalker.

Victoria pulled the older woman into a close embrace, guiding her from the room as Marie's voice lurked close to hysteria, "Oh, Pastor, he was all slumped over." Her shoulders shuddered; she sat for a split second and then bounced up, pacing restlessly.

Victoria waited for a moment before asking, "Marie, do I smell coffee?"

Marie stopped short, "Coffee? Yes, there's a fresh pot."

"I wonder if I could have a cup?" Victoria suggested gently.

Marie relaxed a bit, as Victoria had hoped. The familiar rituals of hospitality completed, the older woman sank back into her chair and took a deep breath. "We've been married for fifty years come next month; this is the first time…" Her quivering lip halted her words.

Victoria eased into a soft question, "How did you meet Don?"

Memories slowly eased the tension from Marie's age-lined face. "He came with a thrashing crew to the home place when I was sixteen; he was nineteen. I kept busy cooking for the men, but I found time to notice the powerful-strong and handsome new fella." Gnarled hands smoothed salt-and-pepper hair under a wispy hairnet. A sound from the bedroom drew her eyes back to the present.

"I'm sure he noticed you, too!" Victoria prompted to divert her once again.

Marie smiled shyly. "He came back to see me after harvest was over, and courted me all winter. Then one day in the spring I made a coconut layer cake and on his second piece, he said, 'Would you be willing to put your little white shoes under my bed for the rest of our lives?' Lordy, I had no choice but to say yes!" A blush painted her face like a young girl's again.

Victoria closed her eyes, envisioning a nervous suitor and the beautiful young girl inside the seasoned older woman beside her today. She could almost taste the coconut cake.

"My pa made us wait a full year since I was so young. But from the time I first set eyes on him, no other man could send life rushing through me like my Don could." Self-consciously, she folded pleats in her white apron. "I knew it was love. And it has been, fifty years of it," she whispered and chased a tear with a lacy handkerchief. She cried quietly. Sensing the healing tears would do their necessary work, Victoria said nothing.

Sitting in the sunlit kitchen, a rush of warmth heated the core of Victoria's body. The man who could send life tingling through her body was also in the next room, the man it was far too dangerous for the Reverend Victoria Dahlmann to love.

"He's resting now," Alex said quietly, stepping into the room, "I've told him that I will come back this evening to check on him."

"What's Don's problem, Doctor?" Marie asked, concern shading her voice. "Will this happen again?"

"I will know more after an examination in my office tomorrow. For now, he's in no danger. If he gets hungry, just feed him something light, like gelatin or broth for today. I'll call you in a couple of hours to see how he's doing and be back before bedtime. Meanwhile, encourage him to rest. It's the best thing."

"Thank you, thank you, Doctor. I'm so glad you're here in Prairie Rose." She clutched Alex's hand, but turned to Victoria. "And you, Pastor. You've both been wonderful." She walked them to the front porch, her arms lacing them together for a few moments.

Victoria and Alex headed home, the bicycle rolling beside them on the sidewalk. "Marie really appreciated you coming, Alex. It dawned on me while I was talking with her how unusual a housecall is these days, but how comforting it is, too."

He merely nodded; they walked along in companionable silence until he spoke suddenly. "They could call 911, but since I'm here and can serve as a quicker response than an ambulance that must come a great distance, then I'll make housecalls. I'm not trying for heroics, just hoping to provide the best care for my patients." They walked for half a block, each with their own thoughts. "We make a good team, Tori." Her lips parted for a ready retort; he halted it with a conciliatory grin. "Let me update Don's file and then I'll walk you home."

Since it was Victoria's first trip to his turf, Alex gave her a proud tour. "All that's missing is a receptionist. Cali's good, but she isn't much for medical records, electronic or otherwise!"

"You've made amazing progress, Alex. The exam room is set up very professionally, and this room is equipped just like hospital quarters," Victoria said when the last door swung open before them, "Very nice." Her glance took in a serviceable hospital bed and night stand along with a folding screen and a well-stocked closet of medical supplies.

"Grandpa had left all his equipment and furniture in place, and when I found the bed and screen and all, I realized how practical it is to have a room like this. Sometime there might not be time to send a patient to the hospital in Minot, or someone who doesn't live here could get hurt in town and need a place to wait for the ambulance, so I'm very grateful for his foresight to save it all. It's more than I'd have been able to start out with otherwise. Come on, I've saved my office for last."

He led the way to a room they had bypassed just behind the front door. "I chose this room for my office so I can watch people on the street when I'm in here doing office work. That way I won't forget that doctoring is all about people."

Victoria studied him thoughtfully and exhaled slowly, turning back to view the room. Floor-to-ceiling bookshelves hid two walls. Instead of a predictable still-life by one of the Old Masters, the picture Alex had chosen to hang where he could see if from his desk was a print of the classic featuring two young overall-clad boys looking out across a field. The caption read, *Been farmin' long?*

Alex pulled up Don Waters' computer record and carefully tapped out notes on his computer while Victoria thumbed idly through a magazine from the waiting room, and then they headed toward the Rectory. When they were within sight of the house, Alex cleared his throat and said in a strange voice, "Tori, if Luke weren't the only grocer in town, I believe I'd run him out of town. But I need a local source for pancake supplies." His grin was limp.

"Alex, it's not Luke versus you for my heart. We're friends. All of us."

"Okay, but remember, I'm the one who learned long ago how to kiss you until you begged for mercy." He pulled her close, so close she felt his uneven breath against her cheek. "Don't you be sharing those lips with anyone else." If his tone only half-convinced her that he was teasing, the stolen kiss banished every doubt. "After all, back at your house this afternoon, you *did* call me Zan, you know. So I'm taking that as a positive sign."

Victoria watched him swagger down the street and sighed.

The house seemed bigger than ever without Alex's presence. She headed upstairs to one of the bedrooms and sat for a long time beside the steamer trunk that had belonged to her grandparents. Sifting through books and papers from her three years of seminary, she realized it had been a long time since she'd looked through the collection.

Late afternoon shadows flitted across the hardwood floor by the time she finally found the paper she sought. She settled back in the wicker rocker, clicked on the floor lamp and folded back the cover of a paper entitled "High Heels and The High Calling."

Her paper had earned a coveted *"A+ Fine-tuned research and clean reasoning."* Coming from the professor known by the moniker "Arnie, the Ax," because of his merciless critiques of seminarians' papers, she had reveled in the commendation, knowing she had done a good job with a difficult topic. The ideas and theories that had been strictly future-tense at the time of writing were present-tense now. She let her eyes pick out the salient points as she quickly thumbed through the pages.

Traumatic choices. Overwhelmed by loneliness. Dilemma of supporting husband's career. Deep personal needs versus professional demands.

The paper lay forgotten on Victoria's lap; the rocker creaked beneath her. This assignment had been almost therapeutic to write, coming as it did during her struggle with the decision to remain single. It all paralleled her first acknowledgement of the brick wall that endometriosis could put up between her and future relationships. Knowing there were seldom easy solutions to life's tough questions, she closed up the trunk and headed out for an evening walk with a restless Cino.

As she passed the school principal's house on her return, Bob and Trudie Marshall called from their porch swing, "Hey, neighbor!"

"Hello, there!" She welcomed the disruption of her troubling thoughts.

"Come, join us, both you and your mistress, Cino!" Bob invited with a grin. Trudie nodded in agreement.

Victoria laughed, "Cino gets me some great invites! No, no, stay in the swing. I'll just perch on your step for a few minutes. I sure enjoy the swing on my porch."

"The shop class built them both," Trudie said. "It's always nice to be able to suggest constructive—if you'll pardon the pun—projects!"

"It's interesting you would mention projects," Victoria said. "I was just talking with Alex Johanson about that very thing today." She leaned back against a porch pillar and let the breeze search out her face. With the Marshall's encouragement, she shared the skeletal contest idea while Cino staked a claim on Trudie's willing affection.

"And you say Doctor Alex has another idea?" prompted Bob.

Victoria laughed, "Yeah, but he can tell it better than I can. You'll have to nab him and get him talking."

"Can you come Tuesday and present the idea to the kids?" asked Bob. "You could have half an hour at the end of the day. The kids and teachers will love shortened classes so early in the year!"

Victoria nodded, "Sounds like I'd better do my homework and get this idea out of the clouds and down on paper."

Monday's office hours went by quickly. The excitement of a project always energized Victoria; as a result, she also made great progress in her regular studies. With a successful day's work behind her, Monday evening she eagerly began the notes for her talk at the school.

When Alex pedaled up her driveway Tuesday morning, she was at the picnic table again but with the *Prairie Rose Chronicle* nowhere in sight. "Talk about undivided attention!" Alex teased, tugging on a stray curl that had escaped her wood-and-leather barrette.

"Guess what! I'm talking to the school kids this afternoon about our contest idea!" Her fingers paused on the keys of her laptop.

Alex whistled as he straddled the bench and moved up close to her. "The lady's a mover and a shaker!" He peered over her shoulder at the screen.

She tapped his nose with her index finger and said briskly, "You're next on the program. Just stop by Marshall's."

"Whoa. Slow down, woman! Bob Marshall, the principal?"

"Yeah," Victoria grinned wickedly, "and for once, a school principal wants to see Zan Johanson about something besides his, uh, questionable activities with Tori Dahlmann! Will wonders never cease?" She arched her eyebrows.

Alex grasped her wrist and kissed his way from her fingertips to her shoulder where he perched his chin at the latitude where her lips would be if she turned her head. "And what activities would those be?" Watching out of the corner of her eye, she saw his blonde eyelashes batting furiously.

With a hummingbird's light touch, she turned and dropped a quick kiss on his nose and shrugged his chin off her shoulder. "This very kind."

"I'll never wash my nose again," Alex intoned dramatically as he swung off the bench and firmly positioned himself on top of her tablet on the table. This put his knee exactly where it would be ever so easy to rest her elbow and let her hand dangle and move up and down his calf.

From her place on the picnic bench beside his feet, she had a provocative view of the very part of the doctor's anatomy that the single female minister in town really shouldn't spend too much time looking at and thinking about—or not looking at, but still thinking about.

"I present our contest idea this afternoon at an assembly," she said and looked him squarely in his knowing eyes.

"I love it when that pretty little blush comes sneaking up!" he said in a stage whisper and then continued in his normal voice as if nothing unusual had transpired, "Just so you don't get the idea that I'm letting grass grow under my feet, I'll make a phone call to the good man, Mr. Marshall, today. Knock 'em dead, schweet-hot!" He left, aiming kissing noises over her head. With commendable discipline, Victoria dragged her mind back from the all-too physical Zan Johanson to her presentation.

Her talk was a big hit with the high-school crowd; they milled around her with excited questions after the assembly. As she gathered her papers together, she nodded across their heads at the beaming principal. Even though she knew full well that any interruption to the seeming agony of school's routines was welcome to kids of any age, she felt good about the reception she received.

Victoria walked over to Alex's that night with Cino at her side. "Hey, Alex, are you and your housemate interested in having visitors?" she called from the step.

Cali reached the screen door ahead of him, skidded to a brief stop as Alex opened the door, and then leaped across space to land in a heap at Cino's feet. Victoria reached down and released an eager Cino's leash. Alex and Victoria watched their matching dogs play chase, perform show-off doggy acrobatics, present themselves in play bows, nibble at each other's ears, and fall hopelessly in love with each other.

With the sun setting in a blaze of autumn beauty, Alex whistled for Cali and grabbed Victoria's hand and ambled down the street, their two dogs running circles around them. At the edge of town, Victoria whistled a low note and indicated a left turn to Cino. He headed off with Cali following close at his heals.

Alex chuckled, "Maybe I'll just let the girl learn by example. He's got her wrapped around his paw!"

They ambled in companionable silence along the well-packed gravel road. Soon, the dogs tired and came back to their sides. Victoria smiled in the dusk, happier than the proverbial lark. When they returned to the Rectory, Cino nuzzled Cali, and looked up at Victoria as if to say, "Can she stay with us?"

Alex chuckled, "Cino's got the right idea, Tori." Victoria didn't need to ask what he meant as she stifled a wanton and unwise desire to embrace Cali's master with as much abandon as Cino had exhibited with the new love of his life.

The next edition of the *Prairie Rose Chronicle* touted stories of an upcoming PTA meeting at which "Doctor Alexander Johanson will speak about parents' roles in preventing adolescent farm accidents."

Two columns over, a boxed-in invitation to the elementary school's health fair stated that "Doctor Alexander Johanson and Mrs. Joanna Frame, the school librarian, are working with the children to gather and present accurate information."

✶ ✶ ✶

One evening that week, Luke telephone Victoria. "Would you have time to pace off the path? I borrowed a pedometer from the school. And I picked up the key to the vacant furniture store from Milt Browning today so we can look it over, too."

"Sure! Give me ten minutes, and Cino and I will meet you by the Post Office." Luke was waiting beneath the first hints of a hazy moon. He had brought their brown bag sketches, rolled up in a tube. After several hilarious attempts to adjust the unfamiliar pedometer to their pace, they set off following the directional arrows on their crude map, stopping frequently to make notations and corrections.

Their jaunt ended at the empty store where the steady beam of the powerful flashlight Luke produced from his hip pocket searched out dark corners. Excitement grew as they realized that with dedicated volunteers and minimal expenses the building could be ready for a spring opening of the walking path. Luke's one-armed hug seemed as natural as breathing.

From that point on, Victoria's days began earlier than usual and ended much later. She pushed physical pain into a box marked "Private" and kept herself too busy to feel sorry for herself.

Rituals changed or expanded to include new activities within their framework. On her morning walks with Cino she now sometimes met Luke on his way to open the grocery store. They compared notes on either continuing developments in the town project or church business. Impromptu conversations at the gas station pumps or in the aisles of the General Store usually led to exchanges of ideas that served to strengthen her friendships with the townsfolk.

"Gee, Tori, if I didn't know better, I'd say you're letting those roots dig down pretty deep in this North Dakota soil, considering that you'll have to yank them up in a few years," Alex teased one evening as they headed home after a planning meeting.

"No one can say I didn't get involved in the town, huh?" she said, flinching inwardly as she ignored the truth of what he said.

Propping his wrists lightly on her shoulders, he faced her in the shadows beneath a street light. "Tori, I fell for you when we were sixteen and I like what you've become over the intervening years. But think about where you're heading. Sometime you might want to take a new look at those goals of yours and see if you are happy with where they end up. And while you're doing all that introspection, make sure you're not hiding behind either a profession or a physical condition to avoid love." He brushed his lips across her forehead.

She pulled away from him and they walked the rest of the way in silence, parting with thin smiles and sparse words even though her thoughts were racing at a furious pace.

Solid mornings of studying in preparation for well-attended Sunday services remained a focal point in her life. A couple days each week in Indian Hills visiting those from the other half of her congregation provided balance to Victoria's hectic pace in Prairie Rose. With the cooler temperatures, she had begun to take Cino with her to Indian Hills and he was a good companion on the trip, as well as a welcome guest in the homes of lonely, elderly people.

One day an official-looking envelope showed up in her mailbox. She read it as she walked home. One of the larger parishes in the Midwest had come courting her via the United States Postal Service. It was definitely premature, given her short tenure in Prairie Rose, but flattering nonetheless. She tried to imagine Cino visiting anyone in a high-rise apartment, complete with elevator. "I don't think you'd like that, buddy," she told her office-mate. Strangely not enticed, she sent off a thoughtful reply and saved a copy in a new computer folder she named, "The Future."

With steady regularity, Tuesday mornings continued with Alex in the Rectory yard at the picnic table, or talking and raking the vast back yard together, or leaning against each other on the Rectory's porch steps with coffee mugs in hand. They talked endlessly with the ease of long-time friends while Cali and Cino romped together with doggy delight.

The pace was exhilarating. October had brought the switch from early services at Indian Hills back to Prairie Rose. Luke stopped by her office at the church one morning. "I keep hearing positive things from both congregations about your good sermons, Victoria. No wonder, with such concentration. I almost wore my knuckles out knocking!"

"Sorry, Luke. I was reading a new commentator and got so interested in his approach to the section for Sunday's message I guess I tuned out the rest of the world. Come on in."

"Well, I won't keep you. Just wanted to drop off this leadership meeting agenda. Also, my parents have invited us for dinner."

That event introduced Victoria not only to Luke's family but revealed his background. He came from hard-working, wholesome Norwegian stock and had a proud heritage. While his finely chiseled good looks came from his father, without a doubt, he had his mother's warm reserve.

Tyler and Amber Larson were somewhat awed by the presence of the "new lady minister" in their son's church and life and now at their table. They hastened to assure Victoria that the reason they seldom attended church was due solely to their advanced rheumatism and other sundry medical problems.

Luke unobtrusively directed the conversation to cover all the wonderful things about Victoria being in Prairie Rose. "Attendance is at an all-time high since she came." and "She has taken a vital interest in the children in town, Mom." All of which led his parents to ask if she would like children one day.

Victoria dusted off her traditional response to the question, "I enjoy children, but as a single person, I appreciate being able to just borrow them and then send them home!" Luke and his parents laughed, as had countless others before.

Seeing a stack of beginner's piano books on the gleaming upright piano in the living room prompted Victoria to ask about them. She was delighted to learn that Amber had ten piano students, each of whom came for weekly lessons in the sunny room. "There's time for two each day between school and suppertime, so it works out well. The school bus drops them off, and the parents have worked out a schedule for getting them home again. Usually, it's two from a family each day anyway. While one child has the lesson, the other does schoolwork or finds something to do quietly," Amber said, pointing to a child-sized desk in the corner next to a bookcase and collection of puzzles and toys.

"Do the children have recitals?" Victoria asked.

"Yes, twice a year. You'll be hearing from me when it's time to set them up, since we traditionally use the church's Fellowship Hall."

On the drive home, Luke commented, "It appeared that my father was flirting with you throughout the evening! I guess the Larson men, whatever our age, uh, enjoy your company."

"The feeling is mutual. Your parents are delightful people. Tell me, did your mother give you piano lessons, too?"

"Yes, but I'm pretty much married to the notes on the page—I'm not gifted with the ability to wander up and down the keyboard like you are!"

Victoria asked, "When have you heard me play?"

"Oh, I go walking in the evenings, and after checking out the source of beautiful music one night, I've known it could only be you at the keyboard each time. Any reason you didn't mention that you play when you were talking with my mother?"

"Well, she's a teacher—piano teachers and I have done battle over the years because I'd rather play the music in my head than the music on the page."

"Not a bad thing from my perspective. If you ever feel comfortable playing for my mother, she'll be enchanted. You've got what she wishes all her students, including me, had: music in your soul." He reached for her hand. His tight grip revealed a depth of feeling that his veiled expression hid. Surprised, Victoria looked at him as if seeing him for the first time.

Scattered gray strands throughout his dark hair highlighted charcoal eyes that now watched her carefully. At this hour of the night, hints of tomorrow's beard outlined his strong jawline.

"I admire you, Victoria. Very much."

"Thank you, Luke. I appreciate you, too."

His Adam's apple bobbed above the neckline of his blue cotton sweater like a buoy in deep water. "I like your sincere friendliness, your commitment to the ministry, and the way you've become a vital part of Prairie Rose." His chest lifted and fell in a quick exchange of air. "You're a very beautiful woman, inside and outside."

They went inside the parsonage.

"Lately, I've found myself thinking of you as more than my minister. To be honest with you, I don't know how to handle those feelings." His hands tightened in a bone-crushing grip and he finished in a rush of words, "How do you feel about me?"

The room spun crazily as the impact of his words hit her. "How...? Oh, Luke, I..." She, the professional who could capture an audience with words and hold them spellbound, could not formulate a simple response for the man just inches away.

"Have I, uh, do you, um, is there someone else who..."

Love Past, Love Present, Love Future all stood—like Scrooge's Christmas visitors—waiting her answer. "No, Luke, there's no one else.

But I don't want to lead you on with promises of more than a friendship between us. I am just at the beginning of my career."

He breathed like fireplace bellows. "Victoria, will you be willing to give affection a chance to grow between us—not rushing anything, but just taking it one day at a time and seeing what happens?" He touched her cheek with one finger.

Victoria's head pounded and she suddenly understood the problem of vertigo.

"God made men and women to need each other, to share love." Luke broke off his own words and laughed harshly, "Listen to me, telling a minister about God like I'm a great theologian instead of just a small-town grocer."

Tears fogged Victoria's vision and she struggled to her feet. The lamp's light formed a blurry halo around Luke's head. He stood and clasped his hands behind her back, his arms resting on her hips; a full awkward minute dragged itself off into history. She steeled herself against further tears. Slowly, gently she moved out of his embrace.

For a moment frozen in time, Luke's arms still formed the shape of the now-broken empty circle she had filled until he dropped them woodenly to his sides. "That was way out of line, and I apologize." He was the epitome of dejection.

"No, Luke, don't persecute yourself. You have caught me off-guard, but there is nothing shameful about anything you have done or said tonight. I am honored by your feelings toward me." She let her hand rest on his forearm for a split second. "I, too, enjoy our times together. Very much. And," she waited until he met her eyes, "I don't see any cracks in our friendship, Luke. And I cherish that friendship."

The evening seemed as much over as if an unseen hand had scrawled *The End* across its page. It would have been futile to try for normal conversation at that point.

At the front door, Luke hesitated briefly; then, kissing his fingertips, he pressed them lightly on her lips before stepping across the threshold. "Good night, Victoria." His eyes trumpeted his inner torment.

"Good night, my friend."

Alone, she turned off the living room lights and followed a stream of moonlight to the staircase. In the darkness she dropped to the bottom step, where she sat, head buried in her arms. Cino nudged his nose up next to her face and leaned into her embrace with a contented sigh.

Luke's openness had added another dimension to the issue she thought had been settled years ago. It reared up like the wild horses that once roamed the prairies, untamed and fearfully enticing. Cino leaned against her in a solid mass of comfort. "Oh, Cino, I'm so messed up. Sometimes I wonder why even you put up with me."

In a bed that again seemed all too lonely, her dreams that night were of a giant daisy that flung its petals around her as it chanted, *Alex loves you, Luke loves you, Alex loves you, Luke loves you.*

CHAPTER SIX

Throughout Prairie Rose, residents gathered summer gardens' final harvests, leaf-raking emerged as man's seasonal struggle against nature, and competition intensified for the street banner contest. The teens' ideas for the banner design had ranged from clever cartoons to intricately designed artwork. Alex, Luke and Victoria served with two teachers as part of the five-member panel of judges that reviewed the entries.

Finally, the selections were limited to two. When the last votes were cast, the unanimous decision was the simple pattern submitted by Lauren, a shy tenth-grade girl. A vertical band of blue for the background; gentle golden curves forming the lines of the prairie against the horizon; centered in the foreground, a single rose in silhouette—a pure image that communicated perfectly.

The flash of Fred Becker's official newsman's camera and the wild applause at the high school assembly assured Lauren of a claim to fame for many days. Soon rough replicas of the design began to appear in notebook doodles, as chalk-art on the sidewalks, and adults' rough sketches left on napkins at the Café.

A front-page photograph in the next edition of the newspaper showed several volunteer painters on scaffolding against the silos by the grain elevator. In four-feet high script, each of seven silos bore a letter of P-R-A-I-R-I-E. Silos two through six proclaimed R-O-S-E-! on a second line with the unadorned rose from Lauren's banner design painted on the silo on either side of the word. Foot traffic grew heavy and road traffic slowed past the elevators for days while people gawked at this visual welcome to all who entered town from the North.

The Associated Press releases about annual celebrations of North Dakota's admission to the Union now seemed inconsequential compared to the buzz along the streets. The citizens of Prairie Rose had aimed their attention straight at the future.

"You know what we should do, Tori?" Alex asked as they walked home having worked at the school for the past few hours painting a billboard that would go up South of town.

"Sleep?" suggested Victoria hopefully, unable to hide a yawn.

"Hold that thought! Until next week. What-say we invite the teen planning committee to our homes for a sleep-over? The girls could stay with you at the Rectory, and the guys could bunk down at my place. We could feed them supper and breakfast."

Victoria skidded to a stop mid-stride and stared at Alex with slack-jawed astonishment. "You, Alex Johanson, are crazy."

"…over you…" he crooned and then spun around, spanning her waist with his hands, "What do you think?"

"Sleep-overs are pretty tame these days, Alex. We're showing our age, though I'll admit you do a pretty impressive moon-walk." She covered his hands with her own in a futile effort to pry them off her body. "Hey," she hissed, "we're in public!"

"Say 'yes' to the sleep-over, and you'll go free."

She groaned. "Yes."

He dropped his hands. "Okay, now I'll get the kids' vote."

She watched his seductive strut and remembered that her swooning girlfriends had declared Zan "the best drum major ever" and knew that even now high school girls would fall in with whatever Alex Johanson suggested. Anyone knew that the guys were only too happy to be wherever the girls were. She called after him, "No campaign talks, Alex! Let their answers be *their* answers."

Two days later she learned the results of his campaign. "So, you're being invaded, eh, Victoria?" Al Jenkins chuckled and slid a book of stamps under the old-fashioned postal window grill for Victoria. "Joy said this morning at breakfast that she sure wouldn't trade places with you and Doctor Alex, but she admires you for opening your homes like you have."

"You may have to prop me up in the pulpit Sunday morning," Victoria responded with a crooked grin, "especially if I'm correct in predicting the amount of sleep I'm likely to get Friday night! Oh, can I get a couple of postcards, too?"

The door opened and Harvey Thompson came in with a flat box neatly wrapped in brown paper tucked under his arm. "Morning, Rev'rend."

Victoria stepped away from the window. "Hi, Harvey."

"'lo, Harvey." Al echoed, eyeing the package warily." Where's this one going?"

"Brazil." He added proudly, "South 'merica."

Al pulled a thick book from the shelf and thumbed through the pages, muttering all the while, "Brazil, Brazil. Dang it, Harvey, why can't you mail packages to Fargo like normal North Dakotans do?"

At the side counter, Victoria jotted a quick note on one of the postcards and eavesdropped shamelessly to the two men jawing back and forth. She dropped the card in the out-going mail slot and followed Harvey out into the brisk morning. "Who do you know in Brazil, Harvey?"

"Nobody." The man looked warily over his shoulders, "I don't know nobody in none of the places I send stuff."

"May I ask what kind of 'stuff' you send?"

"Caps." He toed a circle in the dirt lining the curb.

"Caps?"

"Seed caps." He tapped his vivid green hat's visor.

"Who do you send them to?" *And what do they do with caps that advertise fertilizers?*

"Kings, and such."

Kings? "Oh." *Is Harvey living just West of reality, or what?* "Why do you send the caps?" she asked casually, hoping she wouldn't scare him away from finishing this bizarre conversation.

She need not have worried; presented as he now was with an interested, noncondemning audience, only a funnel cloud could have stopped him. He shuffled off to the bench outside the Post Office. Gallantly, he flicked the bench clean of leaves and dust with his cap, motioned her to sit beside him and balanced the cap on his knee. "I send caps because that's something I got lots of. Caps, they's all over the place." He motioned as if one could float by any minute.

Okay, Victoria, you started it, now finish it. "Harvey, why do you do it? What do you get out of it?"

He reached into his vest pocket and pulled out an empty pipe that he stuck in the gap formed by missing teeth. He chewed on the stem and sucked in air with a faintly melodic sound. "Mail. They send me stuff back. I get lotsa mail."

The two of them sat quietly on the bench, one sorting through this surprising revelation, the other lost in contemplation of an empty pipe. "You must have quite a collection of…whatever, Harvey. I'd like to see it," Victoria said.

His eyebrows arrowed with surprise. "Eh? Well, I'll be doggoned." His neck disappeared into his jacket as he digested this new information. "Wanna come today?" Her nod was all the reinforcement he needed and they headed off, Harvey in the lead.

No more than ten words passed between them on the three-block walk. When he swung open the door to the spare room at his house, Victoria gaped. Bookshelves, tables, walls—all covered with splendid displays of headgear of the world. The mental gymnastics required to believe she was still in Prairie Rose left her speechless as she moved around the room. Harvey followed several paces behind, nervously twisting his cap. Each object on display was flanked by a framed personal letter from the sender and a map of the country of origin.

"You've gotten incredible gifts of caftans, turbans, helmets, and head-gear I don't begin to know the names for! And world leaders sent these in exchange for your *seed caps*?"

Harvey nodded and beamed.

"Does anyone know about this amazing collection?" Victoria asked, fingering a fez from the Near East.

Harvey's expression quickly changed from pride to dismay and he stammered, "Nope. Nobody. Well, Bertha knows, of course, but it all embarrasses her. Al fusses about the foreign mail coming and going, but it's my own bid-ness." He snapped his jaw shut and crossed his arms. Every inch of his body indicated that the discussion was closed.

Way to go, kid. You blew it. You just couldn't shut up, huh? Victoria offered what she hoped was a placating, unpatronizing smile and moved quietly among the displays.

"I'm the one who pays the postage," Harvey said in a last-ditch effort to defend himself.

"You can be very proud of your collection, Harvey. Tell me, how do you get the king's names?"

"I go to the library in Minot every time I take Bertha to see her mother in the rest home. They've got books that tell the names and addresses, you know."

Victoria was thoughtful when she closed the door to the Thompson home a few minutes later. As she passed St. Michael's Catholic church, Father Donovan signaled her with a cheerful "Good Morning, Victoria!"

"Hello, Casey!" she came out of her reverie to greet her only local col-league. "Got a busy day?"

"I'm off to visit parishioners in the country. Yourself?"

"Today is a day I have Indian Hills office hours."

The priest's face brightened. "Could I offer you a ride? I have several hours worth of calls to make out that way myself. I'd enjoy your com-pany if you'd care to drive along with me."

Victoria ran through her mental list of appointments. "That would work out fine, Casey. All my visits today are within walking distance of the church, so I wouldn't need my own set of wheels. I gather you're leaving now?"

"In about ten minutes. I'll swing by your place."

Their talk on the drive was refreshing as two kindred spirits talked shop and shared Casey's thermos of coffee. Victoria asked, "I suppose you know about the ROMEOs?"

"Oh, my, yes! It's amazing how much zest for living those four fellows have sparked in little old ladies around town!" Casey said with an infectious chuckle.

"Sounds like I should be insulted that they showed up at my picnic table!" Victoria responded with a raised eyebrow.

Casey's laugh echoed in the car, "Do tell!"

And so she did. By the time they reached their destination, they had also covered the complexities of church life, told light-hearted stories, pondered the mysteries of a Biblical quotation, and discovered that they shared a common friend in town: Rachel Lindquist.

When they drove back into Prairie Rose midafternoon, each had gained a healthy appreciation for the other that could have taken years to develop had they continued to meet only at civic events or on Main Street. "Let me drive next time," Victoria offered, and Casey accepted with alacrity.

* * *

Dave Jenkins was washing windows at Larson's Grocery when Victoria stopped in Friday morning to stock up for the upcoming invasion of young appetites. "Luke's inside, Queen V!"

"Thanks, Davey C!" Victoria chatted for a few minutes with him and then went inside to begin filling a grocery cart.

"Need any help getting these home?" Luke asked as he shook open a second bag. "You've got a bigger load than usual to carry."

"No, I can manage fine, thanks anyway, Luke."

"That was strictly a rhetorical question, Victoria! Dave's here, and I haven't seen much of you for the last couple of days." He picked up both bags and propped open the door with his hip. "Be back soon, Dave. You're the man in charge!" Victoria winked at the clerk; he blinked back with his version of a wink.

Leaves crackled underfoot as they matched strides. "How 'bout dinner next week?" Luke tossed out off-handedly.

Victoria smiled happily at this first suggestion of a private meeting since Luke's strained declaration in her living room. Though she wasn't seeking romance, she cherished friendship on the level he could offer. *Alex could sure take lessons from Luke on how two adults can be friends, good friends, without...* She spoke quickly to erase the memory of Alex's lips brushing across her temples the last time they had been alone. "It's my turn to invite you."

"I've got a ham in my freezer. Come to my place."

Can it be that Protestants have a patron saint of miserable cooks? "I'd be a fool to say no!"

"Good. Give me a call if you run out of food tonight, and I'll provide curb service for you."

"Thanks, I have no idea what to expect. I just know that kids always eat more than believed humanly possible!"

By dusk, the Rectory rocked with energy. Eight teenagers and the two adults manned work stations in the Rectory kitchen stirring the sloppy joes, buttering rolls, eating one potato chip for each one that stayed in the bowl, slicing dill pickles, baking fudge brownies, and howling when the two boys assigned to onion detail succumbed melodramatically to the tears streaming down their faces.

While the food disappeared at the dining room table, lively conversation blew like leaves across the prairie. Victoria found it quite enlightening;

she finally discovered the answer to the mystery of Alex's changing bicycle colors. From his first week in town with "the hottest wheels ever," he had made a deal with the Prairie Rose kids that, providing they left him with something to ride in case he got a call, they could try out his bike whenever it was parked in front of his office.

"Sometimes I wonder how far I'd make it on any call with the buckets of bolts you leave for me!" Alex complained good-naturedly. "Who belongs to the little purple job with the white wicker baskets that was left for me Wednesday noon?"

Eight voices erupted in laughter, "It's Terry's little sister's bike. You're lucky he took the training wheels off for you!"

"That bike of yours can stop on a dime, Doc!"

"Wish I could say the same for your wheels, Jeff; I almost killed myself the day you tied your beast up to my hitching post! Have you ever thought of oiling the chain? Or fixing second gear?"

"That's not Jeff's bike," tattled Jody with a glint in her eye. "It's his mom's! All Jeff has is a wreck of a Jeep!"

"Which never has any gas in it," Jeff moaned. The teasing was endless; Victoria met Alex's eyes often. She didn't doubt that he, too, was thinking back across the years to their days on the threshold of life and love.

Alex followed Victoria to the kitchen to replenish the food supply. "Fun, huh, Tori?" he asked, giving her the first bite of the last pickle. Shouts reverberated from the dining room.

"You bet. I'd have hosted this evening long ago if I would have realized I could solve the bike mystery! Call you 'the chameleon,' indeed!" She scraped the last spoonfuls of meat mixture from the pan. "Can you believe how much food those skinny guys can put away?"

"Maybe we should starve them for the rest of the night. Food creates energy, you know! Don't plan on getting any sleep once all this food changes over," he moaned and propped open the swinging door to the dining room for her.

What with brownies, popcorn, peanuts, pretzels, and pop, no one starved during the remaining hours of the evening. Alex and Victoria watched each other across the room; each time she looked his way, he met her eyes, tenderness bridging the space between them.

She knew he saw her in each girl; he knew she saw him in each boy. Watching the teenagers around them was bittersweet and each was glad for the din.

"Doc, we found a way to get a discount on banner supplies! Mr. Harstead is going to give us a 20-percent discount off whatever we buy at the General Store if we paint his storeroom and put all the stuff back neatly."

"That's terrific, Todd! Bartering skills like that can really pay off."

"And the rest of us have got a deal with Mr. Larson. We build him a new window display case," Jody chimed in from her perch on an over-sized pillow, "and he'll give us a good price on supplies for the pancake breakfast."

The teens spotted Victoria's compact disk collection and soon were arguing amiably over which CDs to play. They programmed the player to skip a few songs they deemed too schmaltzy and chose partners. After a fraction of hesitation on her part, Victoria and Alex joined the four younger couples on the hardwood floor.

Michael Bolton's bluesy voice always sent tingles roaming on Victoria's spine with his rendition of "Georgia On My Mind," but tonight the haunting melody had an added dimension. Alex floated his chin on her sea of curls like a surfer alone with the waves.

She forgot everything around her as he held her gently in his arms and whispered each word of the song into her ear; his voice was all she heard. The music became his breath, her heartbeat. At the song's end she looked up, unnerved by the message in his eyes; she quickly hid what she knew was a like response.

Choosing chairs a safe distance from each other, they sat out the next few songs, their eyes flitting from one teen couple to another, and then back to each other. To the casual observer, their dance was finished; for each other, the dance was still in full-swing. Sitting motionless in a chair across the room from Alex, Victoria was suddenly breathless.

Alex leaned back in his chair, knees falling open, shoulders straight. *Memories.*

He dropped his arm across the back of the empty chair beside him. *More memories.*

He dropped one ankle across his knee and she wiped damp hands on her slacks. *Doggoned memories all over the place.*

Face hot, she fled, clutching the empty popcorn bowl. In the kitchen she pasted her body against the refrigerator's cool surface willing her normal pulse and temperature to return. When she returned to the living room, she evaded Alex's eyes and the entire space around him. He exercised none of the same control and she finished the evening with a mercilessly flushed face.

When the steeple clock on the Catholic church chimed midnight, the boys thanked Victoria profusely and shouldered their sleeping bags. No sooner had they headed out for Alex's house than the girls began rehashing their evening, reliving each word, each look of the four guys who had paired off with them, and moaning over the stupid jokes.

Victoria watched and listened, recalling similar conversations with her girlfriends after high school football games, at slumber parties, in school hallways. She imagined that, as she had at their age, these girls showed an entirely different side to themselves at home, but she hoped their parents caught glimpses of their daughters' burgeoning womanhood that she was enjoying tonight and realized how very special their girls were. Eventually, someone noticed Victoria stifling yawns and soon all headed upstairs for what remained of the night.

Victoria closed up the house, smiling over special moments of the evening. Cino raced around between bedrooms, thoroughly excited about all his new charges to guard. Finally, he claimed a spot at the top of the stairs as the place where he could monitor all the action and know if anyone left the floor.

In the now-darkened living room, Victoria paused to look up at the ceiling which still creaked beneath the girls' movements upstairs. Plugging in a pair of headphones and nesting them in her curls, she muted the speakers. After programming the CD player to repeat "Georgia" three times, she slipped off her shoes and hugged her knees, letting the music melt every cell in her body into one pile of non-ministerial mush.

Even the sound of her morning shower didn't rouse the girls, so she tapped on their doors and eventually led them and Cino off for breakfast with Alex, Cali, and the boys. This time Victoria actually tasted the famous pancakes. Their thoughts colliding, Alex asked coyly, "Good pancakes, Victoria?"

"Good for body and soul," she said, batting her eyelashes. His lips shaped a silent O beneath eyebrows arched in mock surprise and he proceeded to whistle disjointed snatches of "Georgia" while refilling milk and juice glasses. She felt her cheeks redden and wished she could muzzle him when she caught the girls trading meaningful glances. She sipped hot chocolate and initiated spirited conversations until the group regretfully disbanded mid-morning.

The rest of the day was a wash; she gave Cino an extra walk, rattled around the echoing house, called a house-bound widow who needed a little extra tender care, and finally headed over to the church office to tie together loose ends for the next day's sermon. All was quiet, except the music that played endlessly in her mind and left her limp.

During Sunday's drive to Indian Hills, she admitted to herself that the sleep-over had been a good idea, even if it was getting harder to keep Alex at a mental or physical distance. *Why can't he be like Luke? Since that one awkward evening, my friendship with Luke has settled into a wonderful mixture of being co-workers and friends. With Zan…*Victoria shut the car door firmly and strode toward the church. *With him, nothing ever gets easier.*

* * *

The Harvest Dinner, held in the Prairie Rose Community Church Fellowship Hall, was well attended by both congregations. From her place beside Luke at the church leaders' table, she waved to Gail and Jillie across the room and made a mental note to talk with them before the evening was over.

She couldn't help noticing Jillie peering over her shoulder at Alex throughout the meal and his kid-pleasing exaggerated facial expressions that dissolved her in giggles much to her unsuspecting mother's embarrassment. Not surprising that when Jillie had a plate of pumpkin pie in hand, she asked and gained permission to join Alex at his table.

But, during the brief program following the meal, Victoria saw Gail scan the room and, unobtrusively, make her way over to where Alex sat with a happy Jillie cuddled on his lap. Bending over his shoulder, Gail whispered close to his ear; he pushed back his chair instantly, spoke softly to Jillie and they all made their way to the door.

Something with bristles turned inside Victoria's chest as she watched the threesome head out into the night. *Jealous? Come on, Victoria! You can't push him away, and then expect him to hang around forever. Besides, it's not like Gail is pursuing him. She's nine months pregnant, he's the doctor. And who wouldn't fall in love with Jillie?*

It suddenly seemed that the turkey and program had dragged on endlessly. She fidgeted in her chair despite her best intentions. There was much speculation regarding Gail as the evening finally drew to a close. Victoria went home to the waiting Cino, and sat in the dark living room for close to an hour, causing her poor dog no end of confusion. Alex called at midnight to tell her they were at the Minot hospital. "We stopped by the house to pick up her suitcase. Looks like it's baby time!"

"She's in good hands. Where's Jillie?"

"Gail had arranged with Brandson's. Isn't Cindy about Jillie's age? Well, I'd better get back. Just wanted to keep you posted."

"Thanks. I'll be thinking about you and Gail." She lay awake, trying to imagine Gail's feelings, wondering how it would feel to have a child delivered by Alex's gentle, competent hands. She resolutely dismissed tears. The night stretched long and lonely ahead of her.

When the bedside clock read 1:30, she finally gave up trying to sleep. After pulling on jeans and a heavy sweater, she crossed the lawn and let herself in the side door to the now-quiet church building. The faint aroma of roasted turkey lingered as Victoria made her way to the sanctuary. Following the bands of moonlight streaming through the windows, she found her way to the piano.

In the pearl-tinged darkness she let her tears flow; haunting music floated from the piano and gently eased a pain far worse than physical: the pain of love that can no longer be denied.

Emotions and melodies blended beneath her touch as she became both audience and performer. Finally, the dam of self control broke. With one finger, she let herself play "Georgia on My Mind," the song held back from the flood of music that had spilled over the dam tonight. Each solitary note plucked the air with poignant harp-like reverberations. When the song ended, she let the music die like the sob in her throat.

From the back of the church, a shuffling in a dimly lit corner preceded a slight cough and told her she wasn't alone. Before she could panic, a familiar voice said, "Thanks; I needed this tonight."

Father Donovan moved quickly toward the front of the sanctuary and leaned his elbows on the piano. "Casey? I didn't know anyone was here," Victoria said quietly.

"I guess I should have mentioned the other day that over the years, whenever I have needed to pray somewhere besides at my own altar, I have found my way into the peace and solitude of your church. Tonight was one of those nights for me. When you first came in, I almost called out to you, but I didn't want to startle you. And when you started to play, I knew I didn't want the music to stop." Shards of dim light played across his face. "I meant to slip out quietly, but I never expected to hear the 'William Tell Overture' and 'Nobody Knows the Trouble I've Seen' from the same artist—at least not in Prairie Rose. I couldn't leave. You have a gift, Victoria. Your music preaches a fine sermon of encouragement. Thank you."

She smiled ruefully. "If that's the case, I was preaching at myself. I felt like I needed a musical hug tonight."

"Hard day?"

She lifted tear-filled eyes, thankful the light was behind her, "Sometimes I just get lonely for things that will never be—does that make any sense?"

He nodded slowly. "The holiday season is especially hard for me." He fell silent in the aftermath of this personal confession, and then said. "That's a fairly shocking revelation from a Man-of-the-Cloth, eh?"

"I don't think so, but if so, it goes for this Woman-of-the-Cloth, too. Maybe that's what my problem is: holidays." Her voice trailed off. "Do we need to crank out a few sermons on loneliness, Casey?" She kept her tone light despite her heavy heart.

"Not a bad idea. If we're feeling it, others might be, too." He stood and arched his back, pressing his thumbs against his spine. "I will leave you now. Thanks again for the therapy, my friend." He ran his hand lightly along the lines of the piano to reach her, squeezed her shoulder gently, and headed out into the wintry night.

"Goodnight, Casey," Victoria whispered to the empty room. "And goodnight to you, too, Victoria," she replied, imitating Casey's rippling brogue in the stillness.

Alex called just after she had crept into bed. "It's a boy! Gail will want to make the formal announcement, but I wanted you to know all is well." He sounded jubilant.

"Any idea what she'll name him?"

"I'd thought she would call him whatever Buzz's real name was, but she said she's going to name the little fellow Alex. My first namesake!" The rest of the conversation was a blur for Victoria.

* * *

Invitations to Victoria for Thanksgiving dinner had sprung up from many directions at the Harvest Dinner. Victoria had hedged on giving an immediate answer to anyone and confessed to Cate the next morning, "I wish my parents were back from their cruise. I'm tempted to leave town and eat Thanksgiving dinner at a truck stop. Otherwise, whatever I decide will be rude to someone else."

Cate chuckled and expertly sliced three of her famous mile-high lemon pies as she said, "Sounds dreadful, I mean the truck stop part! Tell you what, run through the list for me and I'll fill you in on the town politics involved in your 'yes' or 'no' responses."

Victoria nodded appreciatively. "Good; keep me from playing musical chairs between Guddman's and Waters' and Luke's parents and Rachel and last-but-not-least, the Marshall's." She frowned at a perfectly good cup of coffee. "Solve that dilemma!"

The lemon pies joined a lone piece of apple cobbler in the pie case. Cate whistled. "Damn, 'scuse me, those are tough choices," and moved to ring up a sale. "Let's see," she said on her turn. "The Guddman's put on an impressive spread, but you've got to consider there will be more christenings coming up, and all *those* parents would then feel it necessary to invite you for Christmas or New Year's or Easter dinner, to keep up with the Guddman's. It could get to be more fancy chicken dinners than anyone should face in a lifetime. And heaven forbid you should be unable to make to each and every one!"

"Point well made. How 'bout the Waters?"

"Marie makes dynamite chutney. Almost good enough to outweigh your endlessly being called 'the new lady minister'! That could make for one hellacious, 'scuse me, long day." Cate grinned wickedly and lined up a dozen napkin holders to refill.

Victoria wrinkled her nose and gave the two-thumb's-down sign. Cate nodded, "Now the Marshall's. If you'll pardon my saying so, they're no doubt inviting you as a neighborly act. All their kids and dozens of grandkids will be home, and while you'd be welcomed..." Her words floated over her waggling hand in the classic so-so sign.

"Gotcha," Victoria said with a nod. "Go on."

"I'd vote for Rachel's. She always enjoys Thanksgiving. Years ago, she and Randolph began the practice of inviting others in town without local family to their home for holidays. People understand her system; she often has Father Donovan and, in the past, she frequently had old Doc and Mrs. Johanson, so you certainly fit the pattern. Besides, she sets a classy table and puts on a magnificent feed. And, her combinations of guests always guarantee entertaining conversation."

Victoria nodded. "Terrific idea. She helped with my garden, so I can share some of our harvest with her—like a pumpkin in hopes she'll make a pie! But you skipped the Larson's. I'm curious about the politics, as you say, with them."

"Amber and Tyler would love to have you." Her jaw tightened almost imperceptibly. "Maybe you don't mind this, but it could, uh, let's say, encourage their hopes that someday you'll be sitting at their table on a more permanent basis, if you get my drift."

Victoria stared at Cate in acute dismay. Their eyes met and held. "Whoa, Cate, my relationship with Luke is purely friendship. We've been working a lot together on the Meadowlark Trail, and I know we're billed as a regular duo at High School home games, but that's it. Friendship. Pure and simple."

"That's your side of it. He, on the other hand, is aiming for much more. Trust me on this one."

The weight of Victoria's chin anchored her arm in place on the spotless counter." Luke's a very nice guy. I could like him on a romantic level, *if* I were looking for more than a friend. Tell me, has he ever loved anyone from around Prairie Rose?"

A box of toothpicks slid from Cate's hand, contents scattering across the floor. She stared at Victoria and said softly, "I'll be damned." For the first time the habitual apology did not follow. "I'm amazed you lived here this long and haven't heard this downright juicy gossip." She stared into space, and then stepped over the miniature log jam on the floor to straddle an empty stool. "Yup. Fifteen years ago Luke Larson did indeed love someone: Me. Cate Jones. We were quite an item. Isn't that a hoot?" Her lips formed a mute circle.

Victoria's voice came from a deep cave, "I had no idea, Cate."

"Hey, no big deal." She slapped the palm of her hand resoundingly on the counter. "I was much too wild for him. You, now, represent everything I was not, make that am not. If I were Luke Larson and his family, I'd consider you the most perfect woman, too. Religious, sedate, a wholesome influence." She twisted the apron tie around her index finger.

Suddenly, Victoria heard Cate say in a long-ago conversation, "...*but that's another story.*" She knew Cate was now mentally turning the pages of that other story, whatever it was.

"Do you still love him?" she asked softly.

"Huh? Hell no, 'scuse me, Victoria." The familiar Cate was back; the curtains of mystery once again dropped into place. "There's too much water under that bridge for love to have survived these years, besides, it was just puppy love." She looked past Victoria as the door opened and several fellows from the grain elevator entered.

Cate waited on the men as Victoria tried to resurrect any memory of Luke and Cate in close proximity to each other, or involved in a conversation that would indicate a special relationship. She tried to imagine

Luke's arms around Cate, or picture Cate at Tyler and Amber's table. It was mind-boggling.

Conversation grew loud and boisterous around the men's table. "That truck of yours is making death rattles, Willie. You better be saving up for a new engine," one man said. Cate poured coffee with a steady rhythm and joined in the laughter and teasing.

"That blinkin' truck has cost me more dough than I care to tell. This is my third engine in that heap of trouble." Cate slid generous servings of German chocolate cake in front of each man.

"That should teach you to buy local and stop running to Williston for new wheels!" chided Eddie, waving his fork at his friend.

Cate tapped Willie on the shoulder and, when he looked up, licked one finger and marked a six-inch stroke in the air. "That's one for his side, big guy!" she chortled over the men's laughter. "Next time you need wheels, buy one of Eddie's tractors. He conveniently forgets the only other vehicles that he's got on the lot are trade-ins that nobody wanted anymore! That's what he calls 'buying local,' you know!"

Victoria watched Cate and the men's response to her. Cate exuded sexuality, but in a non-threatening, non-personalized way that put the men at ease with her while offering no invitations. *That's one foxy lady, with enough vitality to set some man's world spinning. But Luke? Good grief, I can't believe it.* Victoria watched Cate dodge customers who abruptly pushed chairs back into her walking space with the grace of an in-line skater on city sidewalks.

She caught Cate's eye across the room. "See you later." Cate nodded; her face gave no evidence of her recent revelations. Victoria hunched her shoulders and headed into the gusts that November brought to North Dakota as a preview of winds to come.

It was so cold by the next Tuesday that Victoria knew she had to put the picnic table away for the season and quit pretending it would be nice again in just a day or two. She was dragging it toward the garage when Alex came pedaling up the driveway with Cali running along beside. Amazed, she asked, "How on earth can you ride a bike in this weather?"

"Easy. Balance. And keep pedaling!"

"Wiseguy," she retorted. "Your brain is obviously frozen."

"Halt! What are you doing with our picnic table?"

Our? "Stowing it in the garage, Sir!" She clicked her heels and saluted. "Winter's coming, Sir. Anything left outside, Sir, will be the shape of a major snowbank, Sir, if all the reports of North Dakota winters are accurate, Sir."

"At ease, soldier! I was hoping for an excuse to keep you warm. Come on, I'll help you haul the table away, and then I'll 'stoke your furnace'" he wiggled his eyebrows suggestively, "with a cup of cocoa at Cate's, instead."

Tucked away at a corner table at the café, Victoria looked up and saw Luke watching them from the doorway. She waved; he nodded, but left without ever sitting down. Her gaze darted to Cate who was taking an order from two ladies fresh from Helen's beauty shop. Over the women's pert coiffeurs, Cate watched Luke leave. The look that froze her features tore at Victoria's heart and made her wonder if she really had been so blind for the past six months.

"Come across to my office," Alex said, dragging her attention back to their table, "and see some entries for the Farm Injuries Poster Contest." The wind whipped at their heels, blew them into the office and rattled windows as the door slammed behind them.

Victoria dropped into a chair and eagerly leafed through the tag-board creations. "You must have done a good job presenting your topic, Alex. These posters are priceless!" The wild colors, childish stick figures, and ragged penmanship on some and the computer-generated art-work on a few others made for an eclectic collection. "How did your talk go at the PTA? Were the parents receptive?"

He nodded. "I'm pleased with their response. Now if they'll just remember what they heard when it counts, back on the farm." He leaned over her shoulder while she finished thumbing through the remaining sketches. "Incidentally, I haven't forgotten your concern about Gail. Her delivery has been our main topic, but I've had a few chances to just talk. I think as we get to know each other better, she'll open up more."

"Good. Rachel says that Gail seemed to really enjoy the couple of Mom's Morning Out sessions she attended. They've planned a baby shower for her this week."

"That's wonderful—she needs all that loving. Oh, by the way, can I drop Cali off tomorrow? If Cino wouldn't mind being invaded, she needs to remember she's a dog."

Victoria nodded and admitted, "As far as he's concerned, she could move in!"

A buzzer sounded, triggered by someone at the front door, and Alex's office hours began again.

Victoria let herself out and headed over to Rachel's. They played a game of cribbage, chatted companionably about friends and families, and talked over the older woman's ideas for the historical project. "I'm having great fun with this, Victoria! Researching the history of old buildings and houses in town has become quite a passion for me. There's so much I didn't know!"

"I must tell Luke that we sure got the right person working on this, then!" Victoria promised with a hug for her friend.

"Are you and Luke keeping company these days?"

Victoria bit back a grin at the quaint phrase. "The Meadowlark Trail with all its tendrils into other activities keeps us busy. He's comfortable to be around. "

Rachel smiled and nodded. "Yes, Randolph was the same. Serious, but not stuffy, that's how I describe them both."

* * *

Thanksgiving Day arrived with a crisp wind that threatened the few remaining leaves on trees. Victoria heard her name carried along on the gusts behind her as she scurried along. "Wait up," Alex called out as he jogged to her side. "Where are you going at such a clip?"

"Rachel's."

"All right! Now *that's* something to be thankful for!"

"According to Cate, she invites people like us who don't have close-by families." Alex had one arm draped along her shoulders and they bumped along—together, apart, together, apart—with each step. "Now you behave in front of her; she's pretty shrewd!"

Alex smiled beatifically. "I'll be a saint. No kissing, no clutching you to my heart, no dropping to my knees with proposals."

"Now *that* is something I will definitely be thankful for."

Cate's prediction as to Rachel's hospitality proved correct: gleaming china and crystal, a delectable traditional menu, and spirited table conversation. Father Donovan rounded out the foursome and they lingered around the table long after the last crumbs of mincemeat pie disappeared.

"How 'bout a story, Rachel?" asked Alex. "You must have some good ones with all the historical work you've been doing on Prairie Rose."

"I've got one," Rachel said with a quick meaningful glance in Casey's direction, "that I won't be using on the historical tour posters, but I think it deserves to be told at least once. Perhaps these young people are the perfect audience?" Casey nodded thoughtfully in response to her suggestion.

Rachel folded her napkin and relaxed against the back of her chair. "Close to fifty years ago in Prairie Rose, a young teacher met a handsome doctor. One spring day, when the air was as sweet as only prairies can make it, they walked to a secret spot on a country estate where they had come often before. However, on this day they created a special moment in time that would shape them forever."

Times-past came alive on Rachel's face, and her three guests witnessed a gentle transformation.

"From then on, she knew that love had a name. For a reason she kept to herself, she never allowed that moment to be repeated. She told herself it was a matter of propriety, that their brief liaison had been much too dangerous." Rachel captured a stray crumb on the tablecloth with her fingertip while her spellbound audience waited.

"Time after time the doctor wooed the teacher. His ardent passion melted her heart, but not her will. About the time she was struggling hardest to persevere, the school hired a new principal. He was a striking man, quiet and strong. He took an interest in the young teacher and soon they were seen together frequently around town."

She paused. Casey nodded encouragingly and she continued. "Whereas the doctor had looked at the teacher with burning desire, the principal looked at her with respectable admiration. When he held her in his arms, she felt safe. When the doctor had held her close, she faced the constant danger of slipping over the edge of control. She chose safety over sensuality."

"How did the doctor respond to the teacher's growing romance with the principal?" asked Alex softly.

"Outwardly, he handled it like the gentleman he was. They saw each other around town, but never alone again. When the principal asked the teacher to marry him, she said yes."

"And the doctor?" asked Victoria in a strained voice.

"Five months after the principal and teacher's wedding, he married a girl from his home town who was lovely; they had a very good marriage, as did the principal and the teacher. Both marriages were strong and caring and lasted for many years. And neither the teacher nor the doctor ever told their respective mates about that spring day many years earlier. The two couples became friends as is often the case in small towns where it is difficult to avoid others without undue attention."

"What a sad ending, Rachel," Victoria said.

"Perhaps; wasted love is always sad. But there were many good times, too, for all four involved. One can't help but wonder how different life would have been if that young teacher had not chosen a safe relationship rather than marry the one whose name is love. But, both marriages were happy, no doubt about that. Love can grow if given a chance—and for these two couples, it blossomed and all felt blessed."

Each person around the table listened with breathless silence as Rachel finished quietly, "But I'm getting ahead of my story. That spring day when love had a name, for the teacher love's name was Doctor Alexander Johanson. For him, its name was Rachel Stone."

Victoria could feel her heart beating. It throbbed in her temple, hurt in her chest.

Rachel continued, "Eventually, Randolph Lindquist married Rachel and gave her his name and wonderful romance. Even though Randolph and Rachel's love was a thing of quiet beauty and very satisfying, Rachel knew it never repeated the depths and heights of passion she had experienced that special day with Alexander."

"I do not tell you this to belittle the marriages that made four people very happy. I grew to love your grandmother like a sister, Alex, and please know that I mean no disrespect to my husband's memory, but some things only come once."

Victoria lifted her water goblet with a trembling hand. Her thoughts, like a torrent of water, drowned out her surroundings for a brief moment. She nearly choked on the first swallow and quickly replaced the glass on the table.

"…not for any lack of effort, but because that's the nature of love. Alexander truly cherished his Charlotte until the day she died. And that, my dears, is one story that won't be told on any historical tour of Prairie Rose."

Silence hung around the table like a fog.

"You are a delightful reminder of your grandfather, Alex," said Rachel, face flushed above her lace-collared jersey dress. "You've got his eyes. I always told him that they rivaled Lake Superior for their many shades of blue."

"Thank you, Rachel, for the kind compliment. I treasure any comparison to that great man. Now I understand why you have said you knew my grandparents so well."

"Alex, I don't tell the story to diminish your respect or memories of your grandparents. In fact, I wrote to your grandfather several weeks ago and asked if you knew. He wrote back and said I was free to tell you. The friendship Randolph and I developed with your grandparents was a continuing highlight, truly a four-way friendship. Even now that both Alexander and I are alone, we honor the memories of our mates."

"I'm glad you told us, Rachel. It helps me understand, at last, why my grandfather spoke out so strongly in my favor when I was in high school and I fell in love with…someone. The two sets of parents thought we were too young, but it was as if he knew something about love that no one else…" His words faded for a moment; when he lifted his eyes again, they met and locked with Victoria's. She heard love's ocean roar.

Rachel led the way to the living room in her wheelchair, diverting their offers to help with dishes, and played a stunning game of chess with Casey while the younger couple poured over picture albums showing the early days of Prairie Rose. "You've got a superb history of the town in these albums, Rachel," Alex said. "Tori, we should elect her the official town historian in honor of all her work!"

Rachel smiled, not only at the compliment, but as she noted both the special name and the young doctor's arm slung easily across the back of the couch behind her beloved pastor.

Then, stilling Rachel's protests once and for all, they made quick work of the dishes, prolonging the pleasant afternoon as they restored order to the kitchen. Armed with turkey sandwiches for their suppers, Alex and Victoria left Rachel and Casey when the second chess game began. The wind had died down and a light snow was falling. "Let's go for a walk."

"Don't tell our dogs, but sure! I had better counteract the calories from Rachel's superb dinner," Victoria said, puffing out her cheeks in imitation of the family of squirrels that darted across the lawn. *We both need time to digest Rachel's story, too.* "Let me show you my favorite place to get away."

Alex stuffed their sandwiches into the hood of his jacket, letting it ride on his back. He tucked her hand inside his pocket and held it there firmly as they set off. Maybe it was the first snow's magic, or perhaps a lingering effect of Rachel's revelation in light of their own shared past, but when they sat close together on a brick wall that marked the entrance to the long-deserted farm that she had discovered that summer, Victoria did not move away when Alex's arm circled her waist. Nor did she reject his kisses. Each touch of his lips was a flame banishing the chill and she sought his warmth.

When the sun was a tree-shrouded reflection low in the sky, they meandered back to town. It was slow progress stopping as often as they did for caresses and soft private words.

They cut across behind the church to the Rectory's back door. "Oh, shoot; our sandwiches are still out on the wall," Alex said with a sigh.

"Want to go back and get them?"

"That's not how I'd choose to end a perfect Thanksgiving Day, Tori." The undisguised desire in his eyes required no elaboration.

Cino bounded through the dog door and gave them a welcome due soldiers returning from a war. Victoria sank down on the top step, pulling her eyes away from Alex's eloquent expression, "You know I can't. I'm sorry if my kisses have led you to believe otherwise," she said sadly.

"Tori, I've honored your wishes since September," his voice was ragged; he dropped close beside her on the step. "Can't we renegotiate? This new 'mature, adult' level is destroying me. You wouldn't be any less of a minister if you loved me again, would you?"

"It's not a matter of loving you or not loving you, Alex."

"Then what is it?" He pushed off the step and towered above her. "Is it Luke? No, don't open those Mendocino sea-green eyes at me in mock surprise. I'm not blind; everyone has noticed that he's giving me some pretty stiff competition. What kind of fool do you think I am? How much more do you think I can take?" The pain in his voice mirrored the wretchedness in his eyes.

"No, Alex! I...it's not..."

"Then what is it? Can you look me in the eye and honestly say you don't love me?" He reached down and tilted her chin, his arm rested on his knee, his foot pressed against her hip, pinning her in place against the pillar.

She stared at him until his anguished look cut deep inside her. As if in sympathy with the wretchedness in her soul, hot stabs of pains erupted in her body leaving devastation in their wake; the physical havoc mirrored her emotional upheaval. She jerked her chin off his finger and leaned her forehead on his knee. Wracking sobs distorted her words and pent-up emotions cracked her carefully-constructed dam and burst across the dry field of her heart.

Alex waited in stunned silence as the first rush of tears soaked his pants leg. Gently he smoothed her tawny curls, lifting strands of them, letting them fall back into place.

Lift and fall, like his hope and my despair. Lift and fall. Sadness shuddered through her hand-in-hand with the reality of her life.

With soothing murmurs, Alex released Victoria's hold on his leg, leaned down and lifted her up, guiding her to the sheltered porch swing. He pulled her down to his lap, her head nestled in the sweet spot on his shoulder, her legs dangling beside his.

"Hey, kid, you can't keep crying out here or your tears will freeze on your cheeks. Do you need a windshield wiper?" Her head bumped against his chest with answering nods; he cupped her face with one hand and flicked his thumb back and forth across her cheek; his tongue clicked like blades on a car window with each swipe he made.

He felt a brief smile move her cheek beneath his hand. While the snow fell quietly beyond them in the quiet dusk, he sang "Itsy, Bitsy Spider," his fingers walking up and down her sleeve. When Itsy, Bitsy headed up the spout again, Alex's fingers slowly walked their way to her hair to twist a curl by her ear.

Without missing a beat, the song transitioned to "Tori, Tori, all day through…just an old sweet song, keeps Tori on my mind…" He breathed the words to the rhythm of the creaking swing as it moaned an accompaniment to the song he edited for her alone.

"I thought it was 'Georgia all day through'" Victoria whispered.

"That's the other guy's song. For this man, it will always and only be Tori on my mind." He held her close.

Just held her.

The rushing response through Victoria's body was intense; her shoulders heaved as a left-over sob rumbled out. "What can I do for you, Tori?" he begged, his lips warm on her cheek.

"You're doing it; just hold me, like a man holds a woman."

He moaned softly, "Trust me, Love, you are very much a woman. As God is my witness, I am responding like a man."

The tears started again. "I'm sorry, Alex. I usually manage to curb such hormonal outbursts. But lately, I cry every time I realize all that will never be possible on the physical level."

His embrace tightened. "Endometriosis has too many letters to be a four-letter word, but I nominate it for special consideration. It's about as foul a word as anything Mom ever soaped my mouth for saying." His grip on her arm tightened unconsciously.

She tucked her hand inside his jacket and snuggled closer.

"How long has this disease called the shots for you, Tori?"

"Since I was fourteen. New symptoms have been added over the years, just to keep me guessing how much worse it could possibly get."

"And back when the waves slapped against the rocks along the coast of Mendocino and we romped in the sand, how was it then, Love?"

The question hung on the air for a moment before she could answer, "Bittersweet."

"Damn. Damn, damn, damn." He set them rocking vigorously with the shove of one foot against the porch floor.

"Aren't you at least going to say 'scuse me, like Cate does?" Victoria teased in a feeble attempt to lighten the moment. She pulled her hand out of the warmth she had found inside his jacket and followed the path of his frown across his eyebrows with the tip of one finger. *Rachel, I wish you could have told me the secret to holding firm against these Johanson men. How did you make it stick all those years ago?*

Alex shook his head, rubbing her hair with his chin. "Someday, my love, someday, I promise it will be sweet, not bittersweet," he vowed fiercely.

CHAPTER SEVEN

Flour hung in the air of the Rectory kitchen like an out-of-season North Dakota dust storm. Wearily, Victoria mopped up oil, egg whites, and dribbles of milk from the counter and floor. "The Twelve Days of Christmas" trilled out across the room for the third time that day and prompted her scowl at the radio and the snarled "Oh, shut up."

Three bowls lined the counter below three recipes she had taped to the cupboard doors. Wooden spoons rose like empty flagpoles from the mounds of dough. "What's next?" Victoria muttered as she pushed a wisp of hair out of her eyes with her forearm and peered at the card on the left. "Let's see: 'Batter will be lumpy.' I'll be jiggered; something's worked out just right. We have an Olympic-class example of lumps here."

She was jarred from her momentary self-congratulations by Luke's call to see if she had run out of any supplies; she snapped at him like a caged animal. No sooner did she hang up than the phone rang again. "'lo!" she barked.

"Whoa! Must not be a good time to ask if I could come by for a Christmas cookie." Alex's voice showed no respect for her crisis.

"If you want cookies, go see Cate. I'm sure she's managed to rustle up a few dozen just since lunch. Or try Gail. She's a bona fide little Susie homemaker," Victoria snapped.

Her sarcasm inflicted no damage. "Just thought I'd call and check on your progress with this ambitious project. After all, Ms. Taco Salad Queen, you're alone and the mission is dangerous."

Despite her frustration, his words softened her response, "As long as the Secretary won't disavow all knowledge of my activities if I blow up. Which isn't far from the realm of possibility here." Even her best resolutions couldn't keep the edge from her voice.

"Trouble in the Rectory kitchen?"

"Gee, you be the judge. The round cookies all spread out and got square; I had to hack them into pieces just to get them off the pan. The bars resemble volcanic lava, which isn't what the picture shows at all. Even worse, the sugar cookies are a dirty gray, and the chocolate cookies are white from flour. Oh, Alex, it's awful! Whatever possessed me to try to bake anything for my open house?" she wailed.

"It's the Christmas spirit. If it weren't for all the sleigh-bells ringing and chestnuts roasting, you'd never even have thought about Christmas cookies. But I'll bet they taste great."

"That sounds like something the Pancake King would say," she said morosely. "I should know better than to expect sound culinary advice from you."

"My pancakes, I must remind you, were a hit at the breakfast! People still talk about them."

Victoria sniffed the air suspiciously. "Well, your pancakes will be history in the gossip mill after they crack a few molars on my cookies. Gotta go. Horrible things are happening at 350-degrees here." The smoke alarm blared overhead in full support.

Half an hour later, Luke stopped by with a bag under his arm. After surveying the kitchen, he said casually, "A while back, I had ordered a few tins of imported butter cookies that I stuck back in the storeroom; I would like you to have them as a back-up supply. You never know how many people will show up for an open house."

Victoria stared at him through a flour-speckled gaze and said curtly. "Thanks."

"Anything I can do to help?"

Victoria took a deep breath and forced herself to answer civilly, "There are some folding chairs in the basement that could come up." Luke nodded and headed down. In his absence, Victoria muttered, "No way I'm gonna let him save the day in my kitchen. I've got my pride, scorched though it is." She heard him coming up the stairs, and directed him to the hallway where he leaned several stacks of chairs against the wall.

Luke stayed for cocoa and nobly consumed a bar and a cookie. "I couldn't help noticing, Victoria, you've got quite a supply of cardboard boxes down in the basement."

She nodded, "They're my packing boxes. Some are from a professional moving company and cost me an arm and a leg. Others are so perfect for books, that I'd be a fool to toss them. I'll never find such perfect ones again. Especially if I moved in the winter. All the boxes in town get set out in the snow and would never hold books once they've been wet."

"They're rather a fire hazard, aren't they?"

"I've tried to store them as safely as possible." *Lordy, after a day like I've put in, those boxes are my hold on sanity, my ticket out of here!*

Luke frowned, whether at her baking skills or her boxes, Victoria wasn't sure. For the first time since they had met, Victoria was glad when the door closed behind him. With a frustrated sigh, she set about cleaning up the kitchen. "Dang it, why does he have to be so confounded nice, and such a great cook, too?" Banging a few cupboard doors was good therapy until she slammed one on the tip of a finger and gave in to a little therapeutic cry.

When she came back in from taking the garbage out, cumulative smells from her baking escapades assailed her. Frantically, she chased odors out the back door with a wildly waving dishtowel, and then wandered through the house carrying a lighted bayberry candle. But even when she was dressed and ready to greet her first guests, her house smelled like a fire sale.

Near tears, she answered the doorbell's first chime. It was Alex and Rachel, fully three-quarters of an hour early, each bearing several bags and boxes. Alex theatrically carried Rachel up the steps, and made a dash back to the sidewalk for her wheelchair.

They made no comment on the air, but Victoria noticed Alex left the front door ajar, with only the storm-door warding off winter. To Rachel's delight, he spun Victoria up and down the hall in a frenzied dance, crooning "Havva yo-seff ah murry litta Crizz-amus!" Her hair fanned out as he dipped her low and grinned into her face. "You look lovely! Ministers with gorgeous red hair should always wear rustling jade dresses for their Christmas parties! But enough wanton levity; it's time for our splendid surprise." He added in a stage whisper, "It's why we're early."

He hoisted the mysterious packages from where he had dropped them just inside the door to Rachel's lap in her wheelchair and moved his army of three to the kitchen. "Bring on the cookies!"

Victoria gestured toward the tin Luke had brought and a plate of the not-as-bad-as-the-rest cookies and bars, salvaged from her six-hour disaster. "There they are. When those are gone, I'll bring out the rest. Maybe. I just couldn't face them yet. I've got lots of punch and hot cider, though. Maybe no one will think about cookies."

Alex nodded sagely and opened a large tin of gourmet popcorn. "My hostess gift tonight is shipped straight from Carroll's Corn. It's Chicago Mix: guaranteed to show up regularly in a medical school student's diet! Take a whiff of this marvelous stuff." He playfully slapped Victoria's hand away. "A whiff, not a sample!"

The irresistible aroma pushed aside the dismal memories of her day. "Thank goodness you ordered a big tin!"

With her wheelchair rolled up to the table, Rachel unwrapped treasures they had brought. A gleaming cut-glass bowl and several matching trays emerged from tissue paper. Rachel pushed up the sleeves on her red velvet dress and began to work magic, humming along with Alex's contagious whistling.

The doorbell startled all three of them when it announced the beginning of the gala evening. While Alex caroled a jumble of Santa Claus songs, Victoria welcomed her guests. After the next wave of people arrived, she dashed back to the kitchen where amazing things had transpired.

Rachel had cut Victoria's rejected cookies into bite-sized pieces and arranged them on a special tray with sprigs of holly. The burned parts had vanished. She had sliced the bars into tempting slivers forming three-layer delicacies with frosting shaping them into mouth-watering morsels. A dusting of powdered sugar and a sprinkling of glazed nuts over the whole assortment added seasonal festivity.

The popcorn sent out its tantalizing smells from cut-glass splendor, doubtless, the first such use for the heirloom bowls in their long lives. Alex filled small bowls he had commandeered from the built-in corner china cabinet and now directed an amazed Victoria, "Put a little bowl of popcorn close to every place people will congregate. The big bowl is for the main table."

Coats were piled high on the coat racks and hung in layers in the hall closet; the rooms soon echoed with laughter. Unobtrusively, Rachel rolled herself close to the door and directed the guests, red-cheeked from the cold, to the dining room where an array of holiday treats tempted one and all. Several had brought hostess gifts of homemade fudge, divinity, and special family recipes, all of which were added to the table.

Cino worked the crowd, watching the floor for possible morsels to claim, weaving his way through the rooms with majestic joy. After spending the day with his crabby lady, he wallowed in the attention of all these friendly visitors, and kept an eye on his now much-happier housemate as she, too, responded to the mood of the evening.

A piece of mistletoe mysteriously appeared above the arched doorway between the living and dining rooms and added greatly to the entertainment of the evening. Victoria was in the midst of a happy group when she heard Alex's voice, "…Yes, it's an old recipe from coal mining towns. They call them Miracle Christmas Cookies. Favorite recipe…during seminary days…someone from the farms of Pennsylvania…" Moving among the small clusters, he encouraged guests to make selections from a festive tray of the bite-sized cookies and transformed bars, paving his way with lies so brazen they were almost believable.

"Delicious! I hope Pastor Victoria will share the recipe."

"Mmmm! Slow down and let me snatch another one of those. The pieces are much too small for a man my size!"

"Never tasted anything so delectable; they're like French pastry!"

Victoria bit her lip to stifle a giggle. *Coal miner cookies, indeed! Burned to a crisp is more like it. Dear, sweet Zan.* Following his pilgrimage around the room, she melted at her core. *Whoops, watch it, Tori; you know what happens when you get drawn by his magnetism.*

Before Alex's rounds were completed, the tray was empty. Like clockwork, another rolled into the room on Rachel's lap. "Good thing you have replacements," Alex called out, "or I'd be attacked!"

Luke's familiar frame filled the doorway. Instantly, Alex was at his side. "Have some special holiday treats, Luke! Victoria made them, and they're the hit of the party."

Luke looked her way curiously; she shrugged and arched her eyebrows innocently. He chose a sample from the tray and stared at it. All around him, verbal ovations rose for what just hours earlier he had managed to swallow only by drowning them with gulps of cocoa. He was understandably puzzled.

Her skirt swishing, Victoria moved to his side, oblivious to the stares of admiration following her. "Beautiful, Victoria," he murmured, all too conscious of the crowded room but helpless in his response to the evening's hostess.

"Thank you, Luke." They made small talk that neither would recall minutes later. "May I bring you a glass of punch?" She excused herself and fled to the kitchen where, for the moment, she could be alone and give way to the giggles she had held back all evening. She was wiping tears away with a dishtowel when Alex burst through the door.

"Everything okay, Tori?" he asked, dropping the tray on the table and moving to her side. His arms linked around her and rested on her hips.

She nodded happily. Within seconds she knew it would take all her will power to slide away from him if she didn't act quickly. "Our public awaits the Miracle Christmas Cookies!" She bit her cheeks to keep from laughing.

"I just hope you can remember how you made them; you're bound to get recipe requests! Isn't this a great party?"

"Yes, thanks to friends." She smiled at him tremulously. Throwing caution to the winds, she pinned his face between her hands and gave him a straight-on tongue-teasing kiss. Cino chose that moment to charge into the kitchen and skidded to a stop beside Victoria on full-alert as if to say, *Am I needed here, or can I get back to the party?* "Everything's cool, Cino. Go have fun," Victoria said.

Unbridled joy in the shape of a kiss romped through the room, bumping from ceilings to walls, lips to hearts, finally lodging firmly in both souls. Alex grinned, "Wow! I may never leave this kitchen."

Cate arrived to a house throbbing with merriment. She wiggled her way through the crowd to greet her friend. "What a party, Victoria! There are cars lined up like it was Sunday. I see Fred Becker's here with his reporter's eye on your crowd. You'll make front-page news tonight!"

Victoria laughed deliriously, "No matter what may show up in the *Prairie Rose Chronicle*, I'll have to tell you the full story someday. It's priceless! Have you had punch yet?"

"Just got here. Point me to the food!"

"No need at this party, it comes to you!" Victoria laughed just as Alex, balancing the tray above his head, shouldered his way toward them. "Merry Christmas, Cate! You simply must try one of these before they're gone. But don't ask for the recipe, it's a secret!" he said with an exaggerated wink for Victoria.

Victoria shook her head in mock despair, noting from the corner of her eye that Luke was watching them from across the room. She waved and he smiled across the noisy room. *I hope Annabelle Adams isn't telling Luke anything he really needs to know; I don't think he's paying much attention to her!*

After nearly four din-filled hours and scores of visitors, the Rectory emptied, spilling its guests out into the crisp, starry night. Soon only Luke, Cate, Rachel, Alex, Victoria, one stray leather glove and an exhausted Bernese Mountain Dog remained. Alex turned on the CD player and soon speakers reverberated with carols; they sang along lustily while they restored order to the house.

Then they gravitated to the kitchen table with the few remaining goodies. "This party reminds me of the ones Randolph and I used to give. Alex, your grandparents usually helped us," Rachel said dreamily.

Victoria blew out a contented puff of air, "I don't know how I would have managed if you and Alex wouldn't have come when you did, Rachel." She hesitated, and then blurted out an unedited story of her day until all were helpless with laughter.

"The moral of that story," Luke chuckled, "is 'Frosting Can Fix It'!"

"Frosting helps," Rachel agreed, patting Victoria on the arm, "but personally, I hold with pretty dishes, lots of gumption like our Victoria showed, and a sprig of mistletoe here and there…"

"…and plenty of tall tales to accompany the disguised disasters," Victoria interjected. Whistling tunelessly, Alex concentrated on the ceiling, his curling eyelashes adding convincingly to his disarming innocence.

Cate laughed and pushed back her chair, "What a crazy night. I loved every minute of it, but the last half hour is the best! However, tomorrow is another day, or should I say, today already is?" She tapped her wrist-watch and led the way to the front hall.

* * *

Victoria's parents arrived the next day to spend the holidays with her. "Your house is beautiful, Honey! I recognize some of them of course, but where did you find all these other lovely old decorations?" her mother exclaimed, moving through the house in the perfumed essence that reminded Victoria blissfully of her childhood.

"Last Sunday I issued an invitation for the teens to come help decorate. Half a dozen came, and they found intriguing boxes that previous occupants of the Rectory had left stored up in the attic. Obviously, they couldn't bear to leave an inch undecorated! Even Cino's food dish got a sprig of mistletoe hung overhead because the kids are hoping Cino and Cali will make puppies for the whole town to fight over! Cali is Alex's dog, you know. She's a gorgeous Berner who had her first heat a few months ago." Mort and Maggie Dahlmann exchanged a guarded glance behind their daughter's back.

Their days were full. The three of them navigated the planned route for the Meadowlark Trail and picked up the key to check progress at the furniture store being renovated to serve as the Trail Center. Then, at Mort's suggestion, they all joined the crew on a bitingly cold evening, working together to build and varnish frames for lockable baskets to hold trail-users' personal belongings.

One afternoon when school was over for the day, Victoria met with the elementary children who would serve as shepherd- and angel-clad ushers for Sunday's service. She acted as prompter, and often needed to hide a grin behind her script as she noticed shepherds keeping anything but watchful care over their sheep, and pint-sized versions of heavenly hosts acting in less than angelic ways of peace and goodwill toward men.

Maggie managed to sew life back into the swaddling clothes so crucial to the Christmas story, and then lengthened a cape here and shortened a gown there, mended a ripped angel's wing and reattached a sleeve for a wiseman's robe. Since Widow O'Dell was swamped with special orders for her regular customers at this busy season, everyone appreciated Maggie's willingness to take over the nitty-gritty details of fitting costumes to actors.

Adults and children from the congregation were eagerly awaiting their roles in a live outdoor nativity scene. Mort, armed with tools and gadgets he produced from the trunk of his car, whistled cheerfully while he and Gary who owned the hardware store strung floodlights around the spot designated as Bethlehem on the church lawn.

By their third day in Prairie Rose, Mort and Maggie Dahlmann were known to all but the housebound. With the arrival of the week's *Prairie Rose Chronicle* with its articles and photographs, even those folks had no doubts that Victoria's parents had landed in town.

The fourth day, they came face to face with Doctor Alexander Johanson when they landed at Cate's Café for a mid-morning break. Victoria had casually broken the news to Mort and Maggie via that late-night e-mail that Alex was in town with their daughter, and allowed several mentions of his name in a few phone calls since then, but suddenly long-distance ideas were close-by reality.

Alex's face lit up when he saw Victoria beside her parents and crossed the room quickly. "May I join you? Merry Christmas! And welcome to Prairie Rose!" he said, grinning infectiously, giving no clues to the emotions Victoria knew raged deep inside. "I must be the only resident you haven't met up with since you arrived! Everyone who has come to see me lately has some Mort-and-Maggie story to tell, it seems."

Mort Dahlmann half rose out of his seat as the two men shook hands. Alex turned to Maggie with a bewitching smile, "I'm glad to catch you before more of your visit vanishes. I'd like to invite you to my home for a dinner during your time here. Your daughter says you'll be in town until after New Year's."

Victoria grinned behind her hand. *Can't quite decide what to call me, can you? Call me Tori, and you know you'll give Mom and Dad too much to remember. If you call me Victoria, it will kill you to bow to propriety. I love it!*

"How nice! Mort, isn't that nice?"

"It sure is," he agreed and smiled questioningly at Victoria.

"Uh, Alex, that's too much work for you."

"Nonsense. Just say when, and we're set."

Minus a vote from Victoria, they settled on the next evening and resumed a light-hearted conversation. Mort and Maggie surreptitiously watched Alex. Victoria noted with alarm that they did not appear to see the boy who had stolen their daughter's heart and innocence years earlier, but instead saw only a respectable, fascinating doctor who now unequivocally replaced their fears with delight.

You're not making this easy, any of you. Zan, knock it off! Quit dazzling my parents with how enchanting you are, okay? Mom and Dad, I am delighted that you no longer assume that Alex and I living in the same town means Disaster-with-a-capital-D, but do you have to accept him with such abandon? Have all your memories changed in just this one encounter? She was a puddle of glumness beside a sea of charisma.

Finally, Alex excused himself and the Dahlmann-threesome made the rounds of the stores up and down Main Street, stopping in, at Mort's insistence, to see Alex's office as well. When they opened the front door, Victoria stopped as if hit by a brick. There, at the reception desk—looking like part-and-parcel with the new desk—sat Gail. It was a mental war-zone as facts bombarded Victoria's mind.

Bang! A crib is set up in the back corner.

Bang! Bang! Gail is here. In his office.

Bang! Little Alex is sleeping soundly.

Bang! He's hired her. He said he needed a receptionist. *Bang! Bang!*

Bang! Jillie is playing with all those wonderful toys in the kid's area.

Why Gail? Why not a elderly gray-haired lady who was not so…appealing?

Instantly, Victoria rebuked herself. *What happened to "Rejoice with those who rejoice," or is that something you preach, rather than practice?* Her head ached, suddenly and with blinding intensity. Gail looked up then and smiled happily. "Come in! I'll tell Doctor Alex that you're here. He's in his office between patients."

She flew off, their protests falling around them like the pieces of Victoria's life crumbling inside her. In a daze, she hugged Jillie who scurried over to greet her. Despite her stern self-admonishment, questions pounded like hammers inside her head.

Alex and Gail appeared instantly. She returned to the desk where she resumed her paperwork.

"Have you folks met Gail?" Alex asked Mort and Maggie. Introductions and casual chatter passed back and forth.

Victoria stood by like a smiling mannequin.

"Gail just started yesterday," Alex said. "I'm delighted she's here! She'll be working several hours each day, unless things get really busy. Then I'll have to twist her arm and bring her on full time." From the expression on Gail's face, it appeared her arm would remain safely in its socket.

Ice crept around Victoria's emotions while her parents congratulated Gail on her new position, chatted with Jillie, and clucked and cooed over the baby. Finally, they escaped. Back on the street, Victoria said woodenly, "Let's stop by Larson's Grocery and pick up a few things for our dinner and then head home. I think we've toured enough of Prairie Rose for one day." Mort and Maggie exchanged a private look and murmured assent.

Luke came to the front of the store, beaming broadly when he saw them. Having worked together for an evening at the Meadowlark Trail Center, Luke and Mort now fell into easy conversation while Victoria and Maggie pushed a cart through the produce and meat aisles. As they were leaving, Luke said, "If you can spare the time, I'd like to invite you all for dinner some evening."

Maggie accepted instantly; Victoria smiled weakly and nodded when they suggested Friday night. Maggie chattered happily all the way home, "What a friendly town! I don't know when I've enjoyed a morning more, do you, Mort?"

Victoria trudged one step behind them like a dark funnel cloud. *Yeah. We're definitely friendly. On your mark, get set, go, bachelors of Prairie Rose: Ask the single minister and her parents to dinner.*

Mort and Maggie headed to their room for an afternoon nap, giving Victoria time to stabilize her mood. *Just because Gail is working in Alex's office is no reason for me to fall apart. It's great he was able to give her a job.* She flung her leg over the arm of the couch and glared at the ceiling, waiting for these rational thoughts to win over the nagging feelings deep inside her.

While they folded worship bulletins for the two churches' Sunday services, Victoria told her parents about the men who would be their dinner hosts. "We're very content with being friends. Luke and I are working together a lot on the Meadowlark Trail, and we enjoy going to games and concerts and plays at the high school."

"That's nice, Honey," Maggie said evenly.

"Alex and I have similar roles in town. We both frequently work with people who have come on hard times of one kind or another." *Body and soul.* She finished in a rush, "And we are deeply concerned about Gail. She's having a rough go of it, I'm afraid. I'm so glad that Alex has found a way to help her out."

Three people in the room heard those words. Not one believed them.

Victoria eyed Alex's table suspiciously the next evening: a perfectly browned roast with garlic, carrots, potatoes and onions cozied up beside it on one of Grandma Johanson's finest platters; as if he had remembered Mort and Maggie's passion all these years—spring-green stalks of buttered asparagus sprinkled with sage and crushed croutons. *That took some doing—I haven't seen fresh asparagus at Larson's Grocery.*

Alex watched Victoria's face from the head of the table as she said with bright enthusiasm, "You've outdone yourself, Alex. You'll have to share your secrets." Victoria's unspoken *From pancakes to pot roasts?* traveled the same rail as the innocent-sounding compliment. Alex laughed spontaneously and said nothing in response.

Victoria felt like a spectator at a tennis meet watching her parents and Alex bounce conversation back and forth. He regaled them with stories of the Meadowlark Trail, and offered to show them the nearly-ready Main Street banners kept in the temporary workshop at Milt Browning's ballroom.

Mort and Maggie were full of questions about Alex's practice and were impressed with his special research project on pediatric farm accidents. "What I don't understand is why the accidents happen," Maggie said with a shudder. "They're just children."

"The parents are busy and tired, and the children are often either playing near the work site since child care is a problem in rural areas, or some children are even helping with the chores and get hurt on the job, so to speak."

Mort frowned, "Why aren't the machines safer?"

"Sometimes the farmers are still using machinery made before regulations took over, and with the later models, the safety mechanisms have often been removed for one reason or another. That's one area where I hope to educate the parents; I also speak out against using children for adult work."

"Do you feel you've made progress?" Mort asked.

Alex paused. "I'm confident that the kids are better informed; I'm less certain about the parents believing me. They listen, but after all, I'm a non-farmer and a non-parent, a suspect combination for someone advising them to modify their ways of farming. If I had children and farm experience, they might take me more seriously."

Victoria interjected, "But Alex, your talks at the Parent-Teacher group and your interviews with those parents whose children have been injured have been well received." She turned to her parents and then dropped her eyes, following their gaze to her hand resting ever so lightly on Alex's sleeve.

"Time will tell. Just like all the past six months have shown: Your daughter is doing a terrific job with the two churches. She's even got me coming to church faithfully, and not just to admire her standing up there like a regal princess in red-headed splendor!"

Victoria purposely misinterpreted his remarks, "I think the shock or uniqueness of having a female minister is finally wearing off in Prairie Rose. I was actually introduced as "our minister," not "our lady minister" last week. Whoever their next pastor is, I hope that I've helped calm their natural fears of the unknown."

"If I didn't know better," Alex said with a wicked grin, "I'd say your daughter is digging in her roots here in Prairie Rose. It may be hard for a big city church to uproot her even with all their enticements!"

Before her parents could do more than wonder, Victoria jumped in with, "Alex and I have a running debate on the merits of staying in Prairie Rose. Just because his grandfather's shingle says 'Prairie Rose' in burned-on letters, he feels that I'm shirking my duties if I even suggest that I'll eventually move on. I, on the other hand, hammer away at what I believe is his dearth of ambition to match his abilities."

"As her parents," Alex challenged with a wide smile, "do you have any thoughts on your daughter's career?"

"Your mother and I are both very, very proud of you, Kiddo," Mort said, wisely not choosing sides. "At the game the other night, the fellow who runs the General Store—what's his name?—said Prairie Rose can't believe its good fortune."

Alex met Victoria's eyes as they remembered that game.

Victoria clenched her fists in her lap. *He was with Gail, holding Jillie's hand, carrying little Alex. Laughing, his head thrown back, helping Gail up the bleacher steps, just like he always helped me.*

Alex gripped his fork. *She was with Luke. He bought her a large cola and a bag of popcorn. I would have known to specify no ice and light on the butter. They held hands, something she doesn't let me get away with in public.*

"And your parents must be very proud of you, too, Alex," Maggie was saying when they tuned back into the conversation.

Over dessert—raisin bread pudding with rum sauce and real whipped cream—Victoria kept the talk centered safely on Rachel's historical project of identifying the stories of old buildings in town. "The high school English and art classes are writing and illustrating the descriptive posters that incorporate the Prairie Rose design. The teachers have really supported this idea whole-heartedly."

They chatted a while longer and then Alex suggested, "Let's head into the living room. There's no way I can wait until Rudolph-with-the-red-honker hits my roof to open the present I saw you sneak in! I'm opening *that* present tonight." Laughing, Mort and Maggie chose the two armchairs, leaving the couch for the younger pair.

"That was a delicious meal, Alex," Maggie said, leaning back with a contented sigh.

Alex grinned and puffed up his chest. "Yeah, I agree! And I can, since Gail helped me prepare it! When I told her I was having you all over, she offered her skills. I guess I've fed her pancakes once too often for her to believe I could handle it all alone."

"Well, isn't that nice of her," Mort said cheerfully.

"How's Gail working out?" Victoria asked with surface-calmness when Alex returned from putting left-overs away in the kitchen.

Obviously quite well, if she's been working in your kitchen. Just how many times have you fed her pancakes?

"Just fine. You know, it dawned on me after you had left my office that I had never mentioned to you that she would be starting to work for me. You must have been surprised to see her there!"

Surprised? Don't be silly. Try stunned, shocked. "I did remember you saying you needed someone out at the reception desk." *But why Gail? Why the one woman in town who is lonely, the one who named her son after you?*

"The day you had your Christmas party, she came in for little Alex's check-up. She intimated that she needed a job that would pay enough, after child care, to live on."

Maggie's eyes lit up, "Alex, you're a genius! What a perfect set-up you've given her. That's wonderful. But enough chatter; open those presents!"

Alex needed no urging. With quick, precise motions, he slid his finger along a line of tape and let the paper fall away from a set of cherry-wood bookends with the Prairie Rose symbol engraved on each. He let out a low whistle, "These are beautiful, Tori! Who crafted them?"

"Carl and Sigrid Williams. He does the woodworking, she does the painting."

"Carl from the gas station? I didn't know we have such talent in this town." He caressed the wood with a gentleness that left Victoria longing for his touch.

"Maggie, slide Alex's package over to Victoria. I'm dying to see what's in a package that shape," This year was no different from any in Victoria's memory; Mort got as excited as any child at Christmas.

The foil wrapping sparkled like snow under moonlight with the lights from the Christmas tree. Victoria wondered if Alex, in his silence, was also remembering how similar their world had looked from her porch swing on Thanksgiving Night.

When the paper fell away, she held a large framed photograph. "Is this Prairie Rose, Zan?" she asked, wide-eyed.

Alex nodded, delighted by her surprise, neither of them noting her parents' startled faces as the name slipped out from long-buried memories. "A fellow from Minot owns a twin engine plane. On one of your Indian Hills office days, he took me up and I shot the picture from the air. I was amazed how much detail I picked up, and even more surprised that no one mentioned the plane-over-town episode. I let Cate know that I'd appreciate everybody's help in keeping the secret, and it worked!"

"I had no idea! This is a special gift. Thanks..." Her voice trailed off as she noticed the signature under glass, *May all our dreams come true, Tori. Ever, Zan.* "I'll hang it up where I'll see it often," she said softly.

That night, with the picture hung carefully in place on her bedroom wall by Mort, Victoria was lulled to sleep, as she had been often while growing up, by the low rumble of her parents' voices in their room down the hall. Then, as now, she knew full well what they were discussing. *Zan and Tori, then. Alex and Victoria, now.*

CHAPTER EIGHT

The first Tuesday in January was blustery and gray. Victoria's parent had left the day before. She stayed home with a heating pad to ease cramps, finding comfort beneath a woolen afghan. She made a pot of tea and burrowed in with Cino sticking close by her side for a day of reading, napping, and music to chase away misery.

About noon, a splattering of loose snow hit the window beside the couch. Cino came to life and made a dash for the back yard. Victoria pulled back the lacy curtains and saw Alex knee-deep in a snowdrift outside looking altogether like an arctic explorer in his down-filled jacket.

Victoria saw Cino round the corner of the house with his favorite bleach bottle held by the handle in his mouth. She grinned when Alex convinced Cino to release the bottle and then tossed it to a far corner of the yard. Cino plowed through the snow drifts in a doggy-frenzy of joy to retrieve his toy and came bounding back to Alex. Once more, Alex threw the bottle, sending it skimming along the crusty surface of the snow. Then he turned and signaled that he wanted to come in and she waved a welcome.

An invigorating rush of cold, fresh air accompanied him; his nose was like an ice cube when he nuzzled her cheek in greeting; Right on his heels, Cino blazed in through the dog-door, bringing a flurry of snow along with him.

"I bring special brown-bag love from Cate," he said, dropping a package on her lap. "Check it out. Nope, not for you, Cino—it's Tori's treat."

She peered inside and inhaled deeply. "Muffins, I'll bet. Thanks for the curb service! I'm glad to see you. And so is Cino—thanks for playing with him. He hasn't had much fun with me today."

His unrelenting appraisal of her was unnerving. "Are you a model for Afghans-R-Us?"

"Not yet. I thought I'd practice all day, just in case they need one, though." She stretched her legs out; his eyes roamed up and down the hills and valleys her body made.

"This is a day made for afghans, if there ever were one," he said agreeably. "Either afghans or Berners. Cali does a fine job of playing heating pad for cold feet in my waiting room."

Victoria looked out the window at the dismal sky where a storm was brewing. She opened her mouth, ready with a comment on the weather, but stopped when she saw Alex's look.

"How do you feel, Tori? And 'fine' isn't one of the choices," he warned.

She pursed her lips and moved them in and out thoughtfully. "Like something you really should wipe off your feet before coming in the house. You know, those little doggie-gifts we have no trouble finding in our yards." Wrinkling her nose playfully, she added, "That's my edited version. Cate would undoubtedly be more succinct."

His eyes hid his secret thoughts like a misty sea. "No doubt. Can we dispense with the small talk now?"

Good plan. Her fingers tightened on the edge of the couch. "Uh, I've been thinking about your, um, offer on Thanksgiving, Alex. Do you remember saying…"

"Distinctly." With one fluid motion he left the chair and hunkered down beside the couch. "Talk to me." One hand pressed lightly against her stomach, the other caressed her forehead with tender strokes.

"I can't get relief any more from the pain." She touched his hand on her abdomen. "I'm afraid to take more aspirin."

"That's smart. How's your menstrual flow?"

"Ridiculous. Thank goodness Mom replenished my supplies from home when they came at Christmas because I'm not sure I would have the nerve to buy any more 'feminine stuff' locally this week." She twisted strands of the afghan's fringe around her finger. "It's at times like this when I wonder how much longer I can stay in a town that is so isolated. If I ever started hemorrhaging like I did in college, I don't know what would happen."

He looked grim. "These are personal questions, but answer them anyway, okay, Tori?" She nodded and responded honestly to his queries about excessive menstrual periods, mid-cycle pain, unpredictable spotting throughout the month, and backaches that lurked and lunged like giant terrors.

He pushed up from the floor and stood above her. "From what I know about endometriosis—and that's more than I knew a few months ago thanks to on-line references, and my long-distance OB-GYN colleagues, and the Internet—and from all you've told me, there's no doubt that you're in an advanced stage of the disease. I'm sure that's not news to you." He reached down and tipped her chin up, "Tori, it's time you think seriously about surgical procedures. There are options even under the general heading of surgery, you know."

"It's like giving up any hope."

"Not always." His Adam's apple bobbed, the only visible crack in his professionalism. "You've had a laparoscopy?"

She nodded, "Many years ago when they made the official diagnosis. It showed tissue adhering to several other organs, even then. They suggested drug therapy because 'a hysterectomy is too severe a remedy for a single woman,'" she mimicked sarcastically.

A soft groan escaped Alex's tight lips. "That's probably because they looked at you and could only see a vibrant, breath-taking woman. Did anyone suggest laser surgery?"

"Several times, but never when I could take the time—usually, they wanted me to drop everything the week before I began an internship or precisely when I had a major presentation due, so I just kinda blew them off. Dumb, huh?" She looked up at him sheepishly.

He pulled a chair up close to the couch and proceeded to give her a concise description of the process, ending with the positive benefits, "The way it works is that the laser destroys the offending tissue. Lasers are often the treatment of choice because there is less risk of infection. The surgeon has more control, and the results allow for future pregnancies. Another nice thing, laser surgery has a much shorter recovery time."

"But if endometriosis started in the first place, can't it start again?"

"Yes," he said frankly. "Depending on any woman's specific condition, she and her physician may opt for a hysterectomy, in which case the disease is cured. Laser surgery isn't a cure; it's only a very effective treatment."

Victoria mulled his words over carefully. "I'd like to see a specialist and talk it over. Any suggestions for someone up here in our corner of the world?"

Alex nodded, "Good. That's what I have wanted to hear. I've been putting out some general feelers, but now I'll do some serious checking for you. Meanwhile, I'll prescribe a pain killer that will do you a little more good than aspirin and you keep taking that hormone they gave you last time. May I have your permission to call the gynecologist you choose and talk over some things?"

"Sure. Alex, thanks for everything."

He bent and kissed her on the lips, drawing passion from the tips of her toes as he followed the lingering caress with quick butterfly kisses. "No wonder your practice is doing so well, if you finish all your house calls with that kind of medicine!" she teased with a quivering voice.

"That's the technique I reserve for the women who reject my proposals. It's meant to drive them crazy until they see the error of their ways!" He left and the room felt lifeless.

She was almost glad when the doorbell interrupted her listless dozing. It was Luke. He was sitting in the big overstuffed chair, a safe distance from Victoria when Alex returned with the promised prescription. The men greeted each other civilly, Luke adding, "I guess doctors can't worry about catching these bugs, can you?"

Alex caught Victoria's frantic eye signals and said easily, "She's not contagious, but I heartily approve of Tori kicking back and taking it easy. Those look like good oranges you brought her." Unobtrusively, he dropped the little white bag of pills on an end table.

Victoria snuggled beneath the afghan while she watched the two men making stabs at friendly conversation. Luke, the more reserved, handsome with graying hair and muscular build. Alex, life bursting from every pore, unaffected by women's responses to his ruggedness and mesmerizing eyes. A story-line for the scene would have read: Two bucks pace the forest as the doe watches from the thicket.

After Alex said his farewells a second time, Luke stared at her silently for a minute. "Why do you let him call you 'Tori'? Your full name is so beautiful. Victoria." The word rolled off his tongue. "Doesn't it bother you to have him be so familiar with you?" His tone promised knight-in-shining armor action to change this, if she so desired.

Victoria lacked a suitable answer for Luke. *Better to accept the informal name than the kind of familiarity Zan really wants. Trust me; I know.* She offered a reassuring smile, murmuring noncommittal noises. Somewhat appeased, Luke left after a few more minutes of chit-chat.

A storm descended with the evening shadows. By midnight, the howling wind was whipping icy snow against the house. Victoria stood in her darkened bedroom, hands wrapped around a comforting cup of cocoa, watching the snow-laden branches of the huge trees bend and twist like saplings. Cino's trips to the backyard made furrows in the snow which were soon blown over, giving the yard a sculptured artistry.

It was a fierce, awe-inspiring storm. A drift formed from a bush to the peak of the garage roof, creating a sparkling crusty ramp for a stray leaf that fluttered helplessly. She pulled her robe closer around her body and traced patterns on the frosted windowpane with her fingernail.

Her phone rang. She let the curtains fall back in place. "Hello?" The luminous bedside clock read almost midnight.

"Hello, Love. Just wanted to check on my patient. Are you cozy and warm?"

She nodded as if the motion could be transmitted through the phone to him, "Ummhmm." She lifted the bedspread and crept into bed, shivering as the heavy quilts pinned her against the flannel sheets.

Tucking the blankets under her chin, she anchored the phone against the pillow and curled into a ball. She patted the bed beside her, and Cino hit the spot without a moment's delay, delighted by this rare invitation to move from his sentry post beside the bed. Instantly, his warmth worked its way through the bedclothes.

"Pretty rough weather out there tonight. Just wanted to be sure you've got all the hatches buttoned down."

"I'm sure I do, whatever they are."

"How come you're up so late? Can't you sleep?"

"What makes you think I'm up?" she teased.

Silence. Then, "If Protestants had to make confession, I'd have to be at the head of the line tonight. I'd have to do penance and admit that I want nothing more than to be there beside you on nights like this when the cold winds howl."

"I'm toasty warm. Cino's filling the bill tonight." *You'd have to stand in line behind me at the confessional, Zan.*

"And on nights in October, I would scatter our bed-sheets with autumn leaves in all those vibrant shades that candlelight brings out in your hair."

She unfurled her legs in search of coolness as heat radiated from his voice in her ear throughout her body. "Sounds messy, and noisy."

"And on hot summer nights, I would spray your body with mist from a chilled bottle."

Breathe, Victoria, breathe!

"Whatever the season, I wish I were there."

"Zan, call Cali. You're lonely! Or maybe frozen—let heating-pad Cali warm you up."

"That's your ministerial counsel, Reverend? Dog breeders must do a booming business in your parish. Here I am, a love-sick bachelor, calling my pastor for advice, and what do I hear? 'Call your dog.'"

Victoria smiled. "This is a love-sick bachelor? I thought this was my doctor calling!"

"It is; I'm yours forever. You can claim me anytime."

"I'm burrowed in for a long winter nap. The all-night kind. So I won't be out-and-about to claim anything tonight."

"Have it your way. Oh, I talked with your yet-unseen gynecologist; we agreed it might be good for you to try out a new drug treatment for a few months. Stop by my office soon and we'll talk over your options. The snow might be pretty high by morning. If I see drifts covering your door, I'll tunnel in and rescue you. Sleep tight, Love."

"Good night," she said softly.

In response, his soft kiss whispered into her ear. Thoughts of Zan in her bed, winter, spring, summer, and fall lulled Victoria to sleep at last.

* * *

The next week, a jug appeared in Cate's Café. News of it blew along Main Street like an out-of-season tumbleweed. Victoria chuckled along with all who read the sign: "Give spare change to the Meadowlark Trail fund if Cate doesn't swear while you're here." The label showed a caricature of Cate with tape over her mouth, surrounded by piles of money. After the first day, the bottom of the jug was barely visible through the accumulated coins; the bank account for the Meadowlark Trail would show steady profits if Cate succeeded.

One morning when the campaign had been in operation for a few days, Cate ground her teeth and growled to Victoria, "I don't know how you do it. Not swearing, I mean. You minister types have it tough. Don't you ever get mad?"

"You bet. Try substitution. I've got my own list of words for those times I could turn the air blue."

"Huh?" Cate stared blankly at her friend.

"Try one of my favorites: 'Beavers.' It's a very good word. You can say it with intense emotion and it's the perfect choice 'cuz beavers build dams. Isn't 'damn' one of your taboo words?"

"Yeah," Cate said, cautiously. "Beavers." Then, she grinned and slapped the table. "Beavers!"

Victoria nodded. "Works, huh? It won't be long until the jug is loaded!"

Cate chortled. "Imagine, a minister teaching me how to swear creatively." They grinned conspiratorially.

Later that week Cate invited Luke, Alex, and Victoria for a late supper at her house. As anyone would expect from the town's most visible cook, the kitchen was a focal point in her home. One floor-to-ceiling bookcase brimmed over with well-used cookbooks, with canning jars of various dry beans serving as bookends on every shelf. Sundry kitchen appliances and gadgets created a practical decor.

Juxtaposed against this impressive display, it was a simple meal with a huge pot of homemade chili, a pan of cornbread fresh from the oven and golden butter mixed with honey. Seated around the four sides of table covered with a red-checkered tablecloth, the friends talked, laughed and ate with gusto.

With spoons licked clean of the last bites of caramelized custard, Cate mused, "What we need is a Valentine's shindig. People are getting sick of winter, even with all the doings for the Meadowlark Trail."

"How 'bout renting an old romantic movie and showing it at the high school?" Luke suggested.

Victoria nodded with approval. "Hey, that could jibe with something I've been mulling over since my idea certainly can't provide for everyone in town. Ever since Marie Waters told me the story of how Don and she met, I've wanted to mix the long-time-marrieds and the yet-to-be-marrieds. No better time than around Valentine's Day."

"Hot…beavers! I'll cater, if you'd like," offered Cate.

Victoria couldn't help laughing at the bewildered expressions on the two men's faces. "It can be at the Rectory," she said, refusing to enlighten them as to the meaning, origin, or intent of Cate's new-found phrase.

"All right, Victoria, Cate won't say, so will you *please* explain what the heck this 'beaver' business is all about," Luke demanded. "Everyone in town is wondering."

Relenting, Cate pledged the guys to secrecy and then offered the explanation of her so-far successful venture of life without swearing. Hilarity was in full swing and cemented the four-way camaraderie firmly in place. Victoria rejoiced inwardly over the first signs that the long-shattered friendship between Luke and Cate could heal and be more than civility.

* * *

By the weekend before Valentine's Day, Victoria, who began the new medication against her better instincts, had added a few pounds that wouldn't budge off her hips. "I knew it!" she wailed, looking in the mirror. She monitored her calories even more than usual and added an extra mile to her daily walks with Cino, but her clothes felt like she dressed out of a skinny stranger's closet.

She began avoiding the mirror, hating what she saw. But even so, she knew people eyed her; realizing that others were observing her misery made it all the harder to accept. Only the fact that the medicine was alleviating some of the long-endured symptoms of endometriosis kept her going.

Before she could face welcoming ten couples to the Rectory to enjoy a traditionally romantic evening, she had to resurrect some semblance of femininity. Desperate, she called on the local seamstress, Mrs. O'Dell, who had previously sewn several ensembles for her, gladly paying extra to get a dress ready in time despite the short deadline.

Sadie O'Dell, lips tightly clamped over an army of straight pins, nodded approvingly when Victoria showed her the filmy red material she had purchased. With practiced hands, Sadie draped the material over Victoria's body, adjusted it, tucked, pulled, and stepped back to scrutinize her efforts. "Not many red-heads would dare to wear that color, but you pull it off magnificently."

Victoria waited for her to choke on straight pins, ready to dial Alex's office in a second. "Thanks. I felt like something bright and shimmery."

"I'll just need to adjust your measurements since your last fitting."

Victoria flushed and subjected herself to the brutal truth of the tape measure. *No wonder nothing fit right anymore. Half an inch here, half an inch there...I'll be living in my ministerial robe if this keeps up.*

Sadie finished her notations, they agreed on a fitting date, and Victoria left the seamstress' house feeling more depressed than ever. This dark cloud hung over her until she returned for the first fitting. The dress caressed her body like a dream. Even the solemn seamstress smiled while Victoria pirouetted before the mirrors and pronounced it perfect.

The day of the dinner, Victoria picked up the finished dress and practically skimmed along the icy street back to the Rectory. She pulled her hair up in a splendid cinnamon crown, leaving wisps loose around her face. Delight shimmered through her body as the dress slid into place over the lacy lingerie that was Mort and Maggie's Valentine present. Feeling wholly feminine once again, she hummed and floated through the house making a final check before her guests arrived.

Each woman guest received a single red rose wrist corsage, each man, a boutonniere. The younger couples were paired with older couples and all found their designated places at the table. From heart-shaped succulent ham steaks all the way to the towering chocolate wonder Cate had ferried across town, the meal capped a festive evening.

Featured entertainment was each older couple telling a brief version of their courtship. With the blushes that rose to wrinkled cheeks when romantic beginnings were relived, no one could doubt that love had not diminished over the years. Don Waters then brought out his mandolin and played the songs that had won Marie's heart so many years ago. The group needed little urging to sing or hum along, several learning the words of age-old love songs that they sang.

After the last couple had headed out into the crisp night air, Luke and Alex presented two tissue-wrapped bundles of red roses. "Happy Valentine's Day to the best ladies in town!"

"Well, I'll be…" Cate jumped up and loudly smacked first Luke, then Alex, on their cheeks. "Thanks, guys!"

Victoria smiled into Alex's blue eyes and Luke's gray eyes. "Thanks. You are special friends." She wiped the heart-shaped smudges from Cate's lipstick from the astonished faces of the two men.

* * *

Though calendars were stuck on frozen February, Prairie Rose was alive. With temperatures well below zero, wind-chill factor reports that defied belief, and snow crunching under every foot, anticipation stayed high for the spring opening of the Meadowlark Trail. Even though the project's name had been voted in by the Senior Citizens club, people of all ages claimed credit for the success of the dream coming true.

The week's *Prairie Rose Chronicle* headline gave birth to a new motto: We're Proud of Prairie Rose! It captured the truth in black ink.

One noon at Cate's Café over soup and salad, Victoria challenged her friend, "We need a food stand for the walkers. Think you could handle the extra work?"

Puckering her lips, Cate stared thoughtfully in to space. "Hmm, snacks, soft drinks, bottled water. Or how about shaved ice with natural fruit juices? Interesting idea! I'd have to come up with a stand, somehow," and Victoria knew the wheels already turning in Cate's mind would produce the very thing needed.

Cate's Canopy Café, painted sky blue with the Prairie Rose banner design on each side, was almost finished when the parents filed through the wood-working shop during winter Parent-Teacher conferences. Several classes had taken on the challenge. The result was motivation for others to initiate their Meadowlark Trail ideas into full-fledged projects. Each week, the *Prairie Rose Chronicle* highlighted new advances, adding significantly to the heightening enthusiasm with each issue.

The High School Art Club toured Main Street and offered to decorate front display windows. Soon, each store sported new advertising, fresh paint inside, and new merchandise destined to entice both visitors and locals. From her spot at the hub of activities, Victoria realized all this pulsating town pride needed an outlet before spring.

She requested a place on the next town council agenda and presented an idea for an indoor winter flea market. Milt Browning quickly offered to heat the seldom-used ballroom, and Victoria promised to head up the advertising herself. The next morning, she recruited Gail to draw several dozen posters in exchange for supplies, and prepared a couple of camera-ready newspaper ads on the computer, all followed by several productive phone calls that netted a few more volunteers.

The day finally arrived. An overnight snow had filled the crevices of buildings, clinging to the walls of stores and houses, as if inviting an artist's paintbrush to capture the raw beauty. Wind swooped across the open stretches, whipping snow into breath-taking drifts against fences. Cold had chalked faces with frozen expressions of endurance. Prairie Rose was ripe for diversion.

Cabin fever had raged through the Northwest corner of North Dakota, claiming victims every mile. But the war to win back life was on. The people came, armed with wallets and an eagerness for mid-winter entertainment, even though many had to leave their vehicles running to ensure their homebound trip in the numbing 40°-below wind-chill.

Citizens manned tables filled with items they had scrounged from attics and basements. Prairie Rose reverberated with visitors from every town within a hundred-mile radius according to the checks they cashed. The ballroom rocked with toe-tapping, foot-stomping music furnished by the high school pep band and the Gray-Haired Ladies' Kitchen Band. Shoppers dickered over old teakettles, creaking rocking chairs, and hand-knitted mittens and scarves.

Bryce and Richard manned a picnic table with a simple sign on the wall behind it: *Register to win this picnic table and the ROMEOs could visit your backyard! Tickets: $1.50—All proceeds for Meadowlark Trail Fund.* Clustered around them were three ladies digging into their coin purses. Victoria caught Bryce's eye and gave him a thumbs-up signal and called out, "Good idea, Bryce! Where are the rest of your select group?"

"Thanks—check out the next table!"

Victoria's grin changed to an instantaneous chortle. A lattice-work screen against the wall held a dozen or so T-shirts sporting two available logos: *The ROMEOs visited my backyard!* featuring a picnic table, or *The ROMEOs stole my flowers!* depicting a flower pot denuded of flowers. "I guess I need one of those!" Victoria said and pointed to the ivory shirt that told her story.

"Wear it with pride!" said Mitchell as he shook open a bag and Lewis accepted her payment.

Enterprising cheerleaders ran a children's carnival in the nearby school gymnasium, the proceeds in their coffers adding to the Meadowlark Trail fund. Throughout the day, local folks mingled with out-of-towners and goods exchanged hands at a dizzy pace. Lured by announcements Victoria had called in to several radio stations and area newspapers, four eager reporters and their accompanying photographers burst into town, interviewing stunned natives, and capturing the bazaar's festive mood. The population of Prairie Rose tripled—if only for one day—around noon.

"Will this be an annual event?" one reporter asked Victoria, his microphone ready for her reply.

"Stay tuned!" she hedged as flashbulbs blinded her.

Mid-afternoon, Luke found Victoria helping bag purchases at one table and enticed her to join him on a bench along the wall for a home-made doughnut and cup of hot cider. "Bless you, Luke! Where did this come from?"

"The Catholic Women's Guild. They're doing a booming snack business, and our church's bake sale is none too shabby, either. It looks like everybody and his brother is here at the ballroom, and the whole town is hopping! Father Donovan sent this food over to you and said you should be crowned Queen for the Day! He'd have come himself, but when I dropped off a case of groceries at the Catholic hall where they're serving lunch, he was up to his elbows in doughnuts!"

Victoria's eyes shone. "I think it's a hit, don't you?"

Luke nodded happily while he tried to absorb everything happening in the jam-packed ballroom. "How many tables are set up in here, anyway? It looks like everyone came through who said they were interested."

"At least four dozen. The best part is that when they were offered the option, every single table-holder agreed to donate a hefty percentage of their earnings to the fund!" She slid her hand through Luke's arm and squeezed it excitedly.

They leaned back to people-watch on an island of relative peace in the din around them. "Well, I'd better get back to the store," Luke said, reluctantly. "Dave's there, and Dad and Mom are helping out for the day, but I don't want them to get overwhelmed. Everyone's stopping by to stock up before they head home which has made for a steady crowd all day. I just had to get out and make the rounds to see how everything's going."

"Let me get my coat. I need some fresh air." Parked on a strategic corner, Cate's Canopy Café—where space heaters kept down-jacketed teens warm enough to count back change—enticed customers with cups of steaming coffee or cocoa, giant cookies, and bags brimming with buttered popcorn. A sign above the canopy read, "Coming this spring! Hawaiian shaved ice in 14 flavors!"

Several days after the flea market, the four friends got together at Luke's for supper. "The town is still jazzed!" Alex said. "This Meadowlark Trail is hot stuff."

"I did a tremendous business," Luke said, "The new display in the store window really moved the fruit and deli items. And I can't believe my supply of steaks and chops and chicken was nearly wiped out! If I do this much business when the Trail opens, I'll need more help."

"Same here," agreed Cate. "I staffed the Canopy with high school kids for most of the day and ran back and forth between there and the café all day. Lucy's sister, Gladys, came up from Iowa for the 'big doin's,' as she called them and offered to work the same hours as Lucy. Luckily, I took her up on her offer. She put her hairnet on and hit the deck running. We served 68 people for lunch alone! It was one of my best business days in years," she said happily, "even after paying my crews and the electric bill for running those heaters non-stop all day."

Victoria caught a hint of quiet pleasure in Luke's response to Cate's joy. *Hmmm. Is interest growing between these two again? Nah, we're all too comfortable just being friends to mess it up.*

"Gail says dozens of people signed in for the office tour. Can you believe it? Advertising the free blood pressure clinic brought people in, and everyone was impressed with the walking tips brochure we handed out. I think Mattie enjoyed coming out of retirement to be our nurse-for-the-day to take blood pressures with what she calls 'That newfangled thing-a-majig!' What a day, thanks to our red-headed heroine. She's quite the wheeler and dealer, eh, Luke?" Alex teased.

"She's that, all right," Luke agreed. Victoria realized that he wasn't looking at her and wondered again if maybe there *was* a smoldering spark between Luke and Cate. *Interesting. But Cate isn't a red-head.*

✳ ✳ ✳

Several nights each week, lights burned in the old furniture store, which by now was known officially as the Meadowlark Trail Center, or just plain Trail Center to the regulars. Workers of all ages volunteered to wield paint brushes and hammers.

With little Alex sleeping in a basket and Jillie playing with other children, Gail created a mural so lifelike the birds seemed to flutter their wings above the waving wheat fields. Alex was always close by to hand her a clean rag, or freshen her coffee, or entertain little Alex if he fussed while she painted, working steadily himself on whatever the current project was.

But, even with the activity at the South end of Main Street, it did not go unnoticed that Harvey Thompson had begun disappearing—always with armloads of mysterious boxes—into the deserted building on the opposite end of the street. The front windows covered with butcher paper and the sounds of hammers and saws all created quite a stir of speculation.

Victoria heard the talk and one morning knocked on the back door of the much-discussed building. Harvey opened the door a crack and shyly showed her in.

Carefully constructed shelving lined the walls and formed two-sided displays down the center of the large room. Cream-colored walls gleamed beneath a fresh coat of paint. Empty casing waited in paper-shrouded windows. The vinyl flooring shone from a recent scrubbing and waxing. Boxes, stacked in neat piles throughout the room, stood like soldiers guarding the secret Harvey kept.

Victoria absorbed the details and then studied Harvey's expression-less face. "This is for your collection, isn't it?"

"Yup. It's my contribution to the Meadowlark Trail, like a museum." He rubbed his whiskered chin. Suddenly self-conscious, he asked gruffly, "It's okay, isn't it? Do you think anyone will come?"

"I think it's a wonderful plan, Harvey. I'll bet there's nothing like it in the whole country. You've done a tremendous job of getting this place ready." Embarrassed, he fiddled with a pocketful of nails as she continued. "Charging admission would be a good idea; you wouldn't have to ask for much, but people will be delighted to see this collection. You know, it's human nature to respect something a little more if you have to pay to see it."

He chewed his cold pipe in silence. "Fred Becker's gonna print up a flier—he swore he wouldn't tell nobody. Doc's lady drew the pictures for it—she'll keep quiet, too."

"The flier's a very good idea," she said evenly. *Doc's lady, indeed.* "Have you thought about having a special open house for the town—kind of like a preview? The more people know about what's going on in here, the more support and free publicity you'll get."

Harvey pondered this, nodding as the mental light bulbs clicked on. "Then maybe Bertha would see I haven't been crazy all these years."

"That's a very good possibility," Victoria agreed, matching his solemnity. "Let me know if you need any help." *Or ask the doctor and his lady.* Good will toward men suddenly ran dry; Victoria strode along the street leading home in a growing ugly funk.

The Prairie Rose Chronicle had enjoyed an unusual year of hot headlines. From the coming of both a new lady minister and a young doctor, followed by the newsworthy Meadowlark Trail, the newspaper generated enough conversation per square column inch to give the editors of larger cities' papers a fit of envy. But the bold headline beneath the masthead of the mid-March edition set loose an avalanche of intrigue unprecedented in its impact: *Harvey Thompson Unveils 12-year Secret!*

CHAPTER NINE

Sundays at the Prairie Rose and Indian Hills churches drew record crowds, despite the harsh weather North Dakota tossed out. An almost holiday atmosphere permeated every service beyond any designated calendar events. Victoria received approval from church leaders at the monthly meetings; the church members responded well to her sermons, ideas and leadership style.

Only Luke seemed quiet about her successes at church, "I hope," he told her one evening, walking her home from a planning meeting, "you realize how much a part of Prairie Rose you've become. Like everyone else who leaves, you would really be missed."

"Don't start planning any farewell, yet, Luke!"

"Then, let's burn those packing boxes down in your basement," he challenged lightly. "If they were gone, it wouldn't be so easy to think of moving on." He fell silent.

Not knowing what to say, Victoria tucked her hand in his arm for the last block. *Why do moving boxes in the Rectory basement bother him? He surely realizes that ministers rarely begin and end their careers in the same church. Good grief, what is it with him and Alex? Why can't they understand that everyone's hopes and dreams don't revolve around Prairie Rose?* She flashed him a dazzling smile in an attempt to banish his gloom.

From friends around town, Victoria earned teasing. "It's getting so," Frank complained good-naturedly one morning as they sat in Wilson's

Clip and Curl, "we don't know whether to look for Luke or Alex beside you, or Alex with Gail...the social scene in Prairie Rose sure changed when you and Doctor Alex rolled into town!"

"Yeah," chimed in Al who waited his turn beneath Frank's scissors, "you're making it rough on us married guys! It actually started with those dang ROMEOs, and now all this activity. Our wives can't expect us to keep up with you young couples! Joy informed me just this morning, 'Tuesday night we're helping Alex and Victoria paint picnic tables, and Thursday night we stuff envelopes with Victoria and Luke.' Lighten up, woman! I can't stand all this sociality, if that's even a word."

Helen spun Victoria around in the chair for a final look at the fresh cut, and winked broadly over her shoulder in the mirror. "From what Joy told me, you've been filling in your share of the squares on the kitchen calendar pretty well, too! Father Casey is pleased as can be that you're helping out with the kids at church, and Milt Browning dropped a hint that you might be running for city council—that's more than this town has seen out of you in ten years, Al! Sounds like all that 'sociality' has got you pretty revved up!"

Al mumbled something under his breath and left without waiting for his change.

One evening, Gail invited Victoria for a light supper. Victoria's heart fluttered when she came in view of the front yard. "For Sale. Contact Milt Browning Realty." The sign was new and proud beside the driveway. "What's that sign in your yard all about?" she asked as she handed her coat to Gail.

"It's too hard for me to keep this place going."

"Where will you live?" Victoria asked, mentally stomping out thoughts of one particular three bed-room house in town with only one bachelor and his pretty little Berner—who would dearly love to have kids to play with and protect—roaming around in it.

Gail shrugged. "Maybe an apartment over a store downtown, we'll have to see. Milt says it will take time to sell, so I'm not worried. Alex says he'll help me fix up a place in time to move in." Fear washed all the starch out of Victoria and left her limp for the rest of the evening.

Unaware of the lingering inner anguish Gail's news had caused, Casey Donovan teased Victoria good-naturedly the next day as they drove back from Indian Hills together. "I say, whatever you're doing in your two churches, keep it up! My congregation even seems more interested in church life since you came to town."

Victoria shrugged, "I'm glad, though I doubt my presence has much to do with it. Don't you find that people find it easier to worship God with their neighbors and friends when they feel good about themselves?"

Casey pondered this. "Town pride is at an all-time high these days. People are working together, and having fun—it's good." He contemplated his colleague. "How are you doing these days? Personally, I mean."

"Fine. Why do you ask?" Even in her denial, Victoria knew she wasn't convincing.

"Just wondered if I've missed any midnight concerts lately. So everything's fine?"

"You and Rachel! Such concern from the two of you!"

Casey laughed. "I guess we both want to make sure that, while you're helping everyone else out, you're doing okay, too."

"Thanks, Casey. I am. And you?" She pulled up along the curb by Casey's home and they parted, having each assured the other of no need for concern. She mused as she headed back to the office where sermon notes waited her full attention. *It's best to leave Alex to Gail and Luke to Cate. All I need is friends, and they abound here, and will wherever I go next.*

She patted her pocket where she had stuck the day's mail which included a letter from a church facing the retirement in eighteen months of their current minister. It matched all her goals for size, challenge, location, and the time frame was perfect. Carefully, she reread the letter and then filed it away to answer later.

Her studies were interrupted by Alex's phone call. "Tori, you gave me permission to find you a specialist, remember?" Without waiting for her response, he continued. "I had checked with the OB/GYN guy you'd seen before, and he agrees that you need someone closer at hand than the Twin Cities or Duluth. So I checked my alumni directory and there's a gynecologist who trained with me who has a practice in Fargo. I called her last night and had a good talk—she's had positive results in working with other patients with endometriosis. Could you get away for a check-up?"

Victoria frowned at her calendar. Fargo was across the state and just getting there would consume a major chunk of time. Harvey's open house was coming up. She had a funeral in Indian Hills in two days. Every free minute of personal time had a Meadowlark Trail notation beside it pushing at the edges of the full schedule that kept her juggling hours like a circus performer tossing flaming hoops. "Uh, sure, no time is going to be perfect. How soon?"

"Take down this number and give her a call to set up something. Unless it's when I'm gone to this weekend's medical convention, Cino can come to my place at night. Cali will think she died and all *her* dreams came true. So there's nothing standing in your way, is there?"

"I guess not." Victoria stared at her yellow legal pad where a telephone number lurked in the margin of her next sermon outline. She stared at the phone for a full minute before punching the numbers that could change the whole pattern of her life. Fifteen minutes later, she called Alex. "I'll leave in three days," she said without preamble.

He whistled. "That's my gal!"

"I know this overlaps with your trip, but Dave will stay at my place with Cino and when you leave, just bring Cali over here. Dave's happy to take on both of them."

"There'll be no living' with my dog once she's tasted life on the other side of the street!" Alex said with a smile in his voice.

That night she went to a basketball game with Luke. She saw his eyes move up and down her body as he helped her into her coat but he made no comment or gave her any reason to feel that he found her less attractive now with the extra ten pounds blatantly in view. *That stinking' hormone.*

On their walk to the gymnasium, she mentioned casually that she would be leaving town in a couple of days for some vacation. He asked no questions, commenting only that no one deserved some time off more than she, but he seemed unusually quiet while they watched the Prairie Rose Pioneers pound their way across the court to a close-call victory.

As points added up for the home team, Victoria felt the closeness she and Luke shared sliding away. It was as if she had built a wall to hedge any disappointment she could suffer from the new doctor's assessment. And like any wall, once it went up, it shut out strangers and friends alike. Luke responded to her withdrawal by retreating himself. It made for a very quiet evening.

After the game with the crowd milling around, he seemed more like the Luke she knew. "May I squire you home, m'lady? If you don't mind a walk, there's hot chocolate at my place and then I'll escort you back to your place," Luke offered.

"Yes, I'd like that." She pulled on gloves. "We may be hoping to meet a brandy-toting Saint Bernard if it's gotten any colder! The two Bernese Mountain Dogs in town have yet to demonstrate that usefulness, despite their Swiss heritage!"

"Are you dressed warm enough?" Luke asked with concern when the first gust of the wind whipped past their knees to slam the gymnasium door behind them. "Here, let me check you over." He spun Victoria to face him and clucked like a disapproving mother hen; he quickly wound her long woolen scarf around her neck and tugged her brimmed felt hat firmly over her ears. "There. *That's* the way to dress for a North Dakota winter." He tapped her nose with one finger.

"Aye, aye!" She felt like a snowsuit-clad kid again as she took his arm.

"Are you going to be looking over another parish when you're out of town?" His unusually bold question stunned her.

"Oh, Luke, no! It's just a few days off. Personal time." He expelled a sigh of relief beneath his fur-lined parka and pulled her closer.

"You sure you're not freezing?" he asked when they reached the church corner, their shoulders hunched against the cold. "We can go right to your house instead."

"Nah, I'm tough." The scarf muffled her response. Within minutes they stomped snow off their boots on Luke's porch.

Marshmallows formed a soft moustache on Victoria's upper lip; she licked it off after each swallow. Only one lamp lit the living room where they faced each other from opposite ends of the couch. Contentedly, they stretched out their legs until their stockinged toes met midway. "Amazing! You've got warm feet after that walk!"

"That's because men's socks aren't chosen only to go with our out-fits!" He ran a toe up and down her royal blue stocking that did, indeed, match her angora sweater.

Victoria's hands drew warmth from her cup, circling it with entwined fingers.

"Sorry I was so quiet tonight at the game," Luke said.

Surprised, Victoria said, "That's okay, Luke. Everyone's entitled to quiet times."

He twisted his lips to one side; dimples flitted from cheek to cheek. "I guess I was wallowing in some pretty immature pouting. When you said you were going to take a few days off, it caught me off guard, and then I started thinking that you might be leaving us. It serves me right, making plans without checking with you."

"What kind of plans?"

Embarrassed, Luke looked away as he said, "I'd made some prelim-inary arrangements for a dinner in Minot next Friday night. A nice dinner to say thanks for all you've done for Prairie Rose. I was going to tell you about it tonight. Should have asked first and then arranged," he admitted.

"Don't cancel it, just postpone it for a week or so!"

Luke smiled with an appealing sadness, "When you said you were leaving town, I told myself that we could still pull it off; I'd just take a few days off and go with you. But then, during the game, I realized that was pretty presumptuous, especially if you were going off in search of another church. So I acted like a jerk. Sorry."

He looked so glum that Victoria smiled. "Hey, Luke, that's okay. You planned a special surprise and I wrecked it."

As her words hung in the air, the lamp in the corner flickered and went out, throwing them into instant blackness. "Hey! What's going on?" Luke demanded.

"Could the wind be so strong it knocked the electricity out?"

"Yeah; it almost blew us into the next county when we were out there." His voice was an island of familiarity in a strange sea of darkness. Victoria's eyes followed his silhouette as he moved to the window and stood looking out. "Lights are out all over town. It's eerie."

He shifted to one side when she joined him at the window. "No light in sight. Do you have a flashlight?"

"Out in the garage," he said. "Wait here and I'll get candles from the buffet." Within minutes, a tall taper flared in a brass holder that he set on the end table. Instinctively, Victoria reached out like a delicate moth drawn to a flame. Luke's hand met hers in a spontaneous gesture that made her catch her breath.

For a long moment they stayed linked, without physical movement but with racing thoughts. The flickering light of the candle highlighted their hands linked as one.

Man and woman.

No words were exchanged; none were needed. There had been other moments of affection and their friendship had grown on a solid foundation. But tonight was different; both knew it. Luke met her unsteady gaze and held it.

Beginnings unfolding like a new crocus bursting through the snow. Life and hope amidst frozen dreams. It was all there in promise-form.

Gently, he leaned toward her and brushed her neck with a kiss that left her shivering beneath his uneven breath on her skin. In that crystal-clear moment, they could both see the exact point where the safe plateau of their friendship brushed up against the slippery precipice of the next stage in their relationship on this blustery, wintry night.

Before this night of unanticipated closeness, Luke's eyes had frequently communicated interest, even after their earlier decision to remain friends. He awaited her decision on what could be a tantalizing prelude to a rhapsody unlike any that she heard in her mind when she sat at a piano.

Before this night of unanticipated intimacy, Victoria's mind had kept Luke classified as a special friend; now in the aura of a candlelit room, her heart sensed Luke wanted more. His whispered words confirmed her woman's instinct.

"I know we agreed to be friends, but tonight when I thought I could lose you, I realized I don't want that to happen."

The dim light of a candle in the midst of a blinding snowstorm cut through the fog in Victoria's mind. Suddenly, it was blindingly clear that it was up to her to map out the difficult course ahead. As she searched for a response, the moment zoomed into focus for both of them.

Luke dropped his head in obvious torment. "I know, Victoria. We have had something between us that shouldn't be destroyed by my forcing a level of intimacy that neither of would feel is right in broad daylight. You're my friend, but still my pastor."

Victoria's fingers rested on his arm for a moment. "Luke, maybe tonight was inevitable, given the comfortable level of friendship and the amazing working relationship that have developed between us. I really like you—no, make that love you—more like male-female friends than lovers, perhaps, but who knows? What I feel for you right now is too close to analyze."

He pulled her close and she felt him exhale. "Victoria, is it possible we reached out to each other, when we each really were reaching out to someone else?" Victoria sucked in her breath. Had Luke also felt the shadows of an unseen friend? She was quiet for so long that Luke ducked his head to look into her face. "Hmmm?"

She nodded with tears springing to her eyes.

"We can remember tonight," Luke whispered and lightly grazed her hair with his chin, "as a happy memory between friends, or we can let it wreck everything. Personally, I vote for the first."

"I do, too, Luke," she said fervently. "I'd hate to lose what we've had."

"Someday when the time is right, the right thing will happen, won't it?"

Someday, when the time is right, we'll both be honest with the people who need to know we love them.

They allowed the mood to adjust itself to reality again. The candlelight toyed with their unspent emotions. Luke smiled gently and rested his wrists on her shoulders, his fingers playing with her curls. "Thank goodness the lights don't go out all that often," he said wryly. He carried the candle to the front entryway. Just as Victoria bent to pull on her boots, the power returned. In the stark light, they met each other's eyes awkwardly.

Truth enveloped Victoria in the brightness. *This night has made me realize that, despite what I've told both Alex and Luke, I need love, and I want loving. Not just a friendship, but loving.*

Luke held her coat for her as his thoughts roamed free. *What is it about redheads with me? Raw passion almost took over and could have made life in this town unbearable.*

They let the wind propel them along the deserted sidewalk to the Rectory. An anxious snow-covered Cino met her at the gate, and she laughed, "My four-legged roommate will see me to the door, Luke! Head back home before you freeze."

She had finished towel-drying Cino after his guard duty and just crawled into bed when the phone rang. Without preamble Luke said, "Before you start any recriminations against yourself for tonight, I want you to know I think it's best that it ended the way it did. It's never wise to allow candlelight to shape our dreams for us. I just wish it didn't take a freezing walk home to an empty house to help me be so rational."

Without warning, Cate's voice echoed, *Fifteen years ago Luke Larson loved someone. Me. Cate Jones.* "Dreams have a way of crowding a room, don't they?" she asked softly.

Crackles on the telephone line preceded Luke's soft words, "Yes." She could hear him swallow. "Good night, my friend. Have a good trip, but don't stay away from Prairie Rose too long."

In the darkness she watched the shadows on the wall made by the wind blowing stark branches every which way in the night. Uneven shards of light coming through the frosted window pane illuminated Alex's Christmas gift. *May all our dreams come true.*

* * *

Victoria welcomed her normal schedule the next day, cramming the preparations for her time away into the cracks between studying, meetings, appointments, and phone calls. By evening, she knew that the level of nervous energy that had carried her through the day wouldn't allow much sleep that night. All day, warring thoughts of Alex and Luke had created skirmishes in her mind, sharing the battlefield with the unrelenting pain she lived with these days.

If Luke could hold Cate in his arms, would he let that dream come true? Has their love for each other weathered the years well enough to bridge the hurts and let them try again?

How dare Alex invade my time with Luke, even if that invasion is only in my mind? Will it happen as long as we're in the same town? Maybe I need to start packing those boxes.

She roamed restlessly around the house, rechecked the list for her trip, and eventually bundled up in full winter gear and headed out into the bright moonlit night. Grabbing a shovel, she tackled the drifts the wind had piled along the front sidewalk. Cino romped like an idiot, undoing much of her hard work. Finally finished, and before she could change her mind, she strode down the sidewalk leaving a confused Cino behind the Rectory fence.

Like a ship beckoned by a lighthouse, she gravitated toward Alex's house; it stood silent and dark, though she recognized Cali's on-guard voice and knew that meant Alex was not at home. She spun on her heel; snow crunched beneath her, each foot-fall beating out a steady rhythm between the waist-high wall the snowplow had formed along each side of the street.

Light from Alex's office window danced on the wide Main Street sidewalk and confirmed his presence there. She punched the bell impatiently. "Tori!" He pulled her inside before she could stomp snow off her boots. Icy crystals glistened on the tip of her nose. "Whatever possessed you to be out on a night like this?"

"I'm restless and need entertainment!" she retorted, sniffing unceremoniously.

"So, my sign now says the doctor also entertains any restless young maidens who ring his bell?" he asked, chuckling suggestively, and ushered her into his office.

"I hope not just *any*, but aren't you the guy who once told me I was always on his mind?" she taunted impishly. A desk lamp cast a golden circle over papers he had fanned out across the desk, and the computer screen's eerie light cast a shadow across his empty chair. "Oops, I've caught you in the middle of something that looks important."

"Pffft! Sit. I'll reward you for the interruption with the last cup of coffee, unless it has turned to muck." He unplugged the coffee maker, handed a half-full mug to her and perched on the edge of the desk. "Here. I don't pretend to make coffee as good as Cate's, but give me ten minutes and we'll walk off all your restless energy."

"You're on. The meter's running, so get cracking'. I'll only wait so long."

"Hey, that's my line, Tori."

She stuck out her tongue as she moved toward the door, letting the slightest wiggle of her hips propel her out of his view.

She roamed the waiting room. *Plants are doing fine, and the magazines are even new.* She flipped through the top pages of one glossy issue and then continued her tour. Head tipped, she scrutinized an old-time village street scene on the wall and leaned across a couch to straighten its frame. Humming, she meandered toward Gail's desk.

Dropping into the chair, she rolled and spun around a couple of times and then grabbed a pencil out of the Garfield mug and stuck it into the electric sharpener that buzzed it to a needle point. Pleased, she blew off the tip and bent to admire a dual picture in a gold frame. *Jillie's a cute kid.* She studied the baby, trying to conjure up an image of the father from the infant's toothless grin.

In Alex's familiar scrawl, a sheet from a "To Do" pad instructed Gail: *Please call the architect next week to set up an appointment re: addition.* Her temper flared—he was adding on to his clinic? His feet would be set in the cement, for sure, once that got done. She battled against the temptation to ball-up the message and swallow it. *Alex is beyond hope— let him stagnant here. He'll regret it someday.*

A greeting card leaning against a potted fern caught her eye and she read the cartoon message on the outside and flipped it open. The familiar scrawl, *Don't know what I'd do without you. Alex* yanked her attention right past the humorous ending inside.

Dazed, she positioned the card precisely as she had found it and shoved away from the desk as if burned. Slowly she rolled the chair back into place and stood behind it, unable to rip her eyes away from the card.

It used to be me he couldn't do without. She drove her fingers through her tousled curls and rocked back on her heels. *It's an innocent message, Victoria. Gail's a newly widowed woman, and Alex's a respectable doctor. And he's her boss. But he's single. With racing hormones.*

She jammed her hands into the back pockets of her jeans. *He could have chosen a plain old card with flowers and used a standard "Thanks for all your help" kind of sign-off message. Unless he means what I think he means.*

Adrenaline pumping, she paced the reception area. A draft of cold air from under one closed door circled her ankles. She opened the door and instantly saw why. *No wonder—some fool left the window open!* Striding across the room, she had one hand on the window before she became aware of her surroundings. The hospital bed was a jumble of twisted covers and flattened pillows. On the bedside stand there was a vase with a single rose. Victoria slammed the window down with a vengeance and fled the room. *Good Lord!*

She grabbed a handful of pencils and rammed them one by one into the pencil sharpener in rapid succession. *As close as you came to a window-fogging scene at Luke's, you're hardly the person to point fingers, you know, if Alex and Gail have developed their own kind of magic.*

She glared at the card-shaped weapon of destruction that had slashed a life-threatening gash in her heart. Only Alex's repeated whistle from the doorway pulled her eyes to where he stood, her coat slung over his arm. Passions of disparate natures warred in her heart. Anger. Sorrow. Jealousy. Self-rebuke. Longing.

He was enticing in a woolen cable-knit sweater and the inevitable jeans. Tonight, his eyes beckoned like the depths off the Mendocino shoreline. She could certainly understand if Gail was helpless against the tug of that undercurrent.

"Hey, Tori—give it a rest! If that pencil isn't sharp now, it never will be!" He crossed the room with his familiar long-legged stride and helped her into her coat. "Ready for a birds-eye view of Prairie Rose?"

"Huh?"

In reply, he merely captured her hand and pulled her along behind him. When the first cold blast rushed in the open door, he muttered, "On a night like this, she's restless. Women!" He locked the door and linked her hand through his arm.

"Going for a walk was your idea!" she retorted.

"I'm going to take you someplace I can guarantee you've never been." He wiggled his eyebrows suggestively.

This was the old Alex. Not someone who sent roses and love notes to other women. Just Alex. Crazy, unpredictable, lovable Zan. *Remember, you hold him at a distance, so it's only natural he's seeking warmth by someone else's fire.*

Their footsteps drummed a cadence in the night air. One lone car made its way along Main Street, horn tooting in greeting. At the bottom of the steps leading into the Catholic church, Victoria turned. "You're taking me to church? That's hardly something new, Alex."

"I'm going to show you Prairie Rose from the highest spot in town. Unless you would rather climb the water tower?"

The moon moved between clouds. "Okay," she said cautiously, "presuming we don't have to walk along the roof to get to the bell tower."

"Fear not!" He led the way up the steps and into the dark, still sanctuary.

"How come you know about this?" Victoria asked.

"Casey took me up one day." He opened a door and motioned for her to follow him; darkness swallowed them up in a narrow hallway. They climbed steep curving steps, coming to an abrupt halt at the top.

Victoria waited, gratified to note that Alex's rasping breath matched her own after their climb. He felt along the top of the door frame in front of them. "Good; Casey said the key is always above this door, and here it is." She heard the scrap of metal on metal as the key sought the lock. A rush of cold air assailed them when the door creaked open.

Three more steps up, and then one step down. Ominous, gray bell-shaped forms hung from the curved ceiling of the open tower. On the circular half-walls, stick-figure bird footprints on a snow-covered bench identified the most frequent visitors to the tower.

The moon and stars sparkled above them and street lights blinked below. Alex and Victoria surveyed the quiet landscape of their town from this secret center vantage point.

Caught up in the moment, Alex whispered, "Pretty incredible, huh?"

Victoria nodded, no words necessary. She flicked snow away and knelt on the bench, resting her elbows on the wall, and drank in the magnificence of a quiet, mystical landscape.

Alex moved behind her, his chin rested on her head. "Are you scared about tomorrow?"

"A little." *The guy reads me like a book.*

"I thought maybe seeing a bigger picture would help. The 'God's-in-His-heaven-all's-right-with-the-world' view of things."

A comfortable silence enveloped them. "You're full of surprises, Alex."

"I wish I could go with you."

"It's better that I go alone."

"Ah, yes, propriety!" His gentle laugh rumbled through his chin and vibrated in her head. "Don't forget, I'll be heading off to a medical convention in Chicago for several days and need to leave before you get back. You'll just have to remember everything to report later. Our dogs will be fine with Dave at your house. If you need to reach me, you can call Gail. I'll be checking in with her everyday."

Wind whipped around the bells; a faint musical tone wafted from the cold metal shapes and Victoria shivered. He responded by dropping his arms around her shoulders as they looked out at the sleeping town; their bodies formed one silhouette amidst the bells.

"When you have scared thoughts about your appointment, just remember what it leads to: enjoying life more than you've probably ever dared to dream."

Contrasts loomed. In the dizzy heights of the bell tower, she felt at home nestled in Alex's arms. With winter's demon cold inching its way between skin and clothing, love's blaze heated her best intentions to a white-hot danger zone. She turned to face him and placed a kiss on his surprised lips. Even as it held their hearts with the steadfastness of the North Star, the threat to destroy sanity and resolution was real.

Two haunting questions in her mind tormented her. *If my mind was making decisions, instead of my body and my heart, would I set aside my ministry goals to stay in Prairie Rose with Alex? Is resurrected love strong enough to make Alex leave Prairie Rose with me?*

Victoria leaned into Alex's chest; his hands pulled her even closer. "You need to get to sleep. You've got a big day ahead." With Alex making the tough decision tonight, she suddenly knew what Luke must have felt the night the lights went out. The person on the other end of *that* teeter-totter usually hits the ground with a bang. She led the way down the steps, feeling the jolt of hard facts against her ragged emotions.

They walked quickly along the street with their mittened hands swinging between them. Outside her house, he moved her to a hidden spot beneath the overhanging cottonwood branches, heavy with snow.

Shoving his mittens into his pockets, he slid his hands into the back pockets of her jeans; instinctively, she moved closer. *Just like always. The before-Prairie-Rose-and-Gail always.* His breath hung like a wispy cloud between them. He arched back at the waist just as a miniature snow drift fell from a branch overhead, cresting at the spot where their bodies blended into one shadow.

She knew that like a river moves to meet the sea even beneath a crust of ice the torrents inside them were testing the limits of their control. "Everything stops right there, doesn't it, Tori? Right at the corner of what is passion and what is prudent."

"Or you could call it the intersection of memories and now." she said softly, hating to separate them, but knowing she needed to make the necessary move this time or morning's first light would find them locked in a frozen embrace. The snow lodged in the crevice between their bodies now fell softly to the ground as they shifted.

"Are you still convinced that we're not good for each other, or is Luke going to reach the finish line first in the race for your heart?"

"There's no race, Alex." Flushed with the memory of her lights-out encounter with Luke, she bit back the question that hammered in her head. *What about Gail?*

"Then why am I running so hard? And why do I keep eating Luke's dust?"

"North Dakota can be a very dusty state," she said lightly. "Unless, of course, it's winter and then dust hibernates."

"When is spring?" he whispered hoarsely.

"North Dakotans say you never know."

"Maybe tomorrow," Alex whispered. It could have been an answer, or it could have been a prayer. Victoria wondered if even Alex knew which it really was.

CHAPTER TEN

The days Victoria spent away ended like they had begun, with the sight of seven silo sentries on the edge of town, spotlights illuminating the letters P-R-A-I-R-I-E R-O-S-E in the dusk. In her heart, it felt like she was coming home—after the past few days, she craved something familiar and comforting.

"Got your sermon ready, or are you going to be burning the midnight oil?" asked Luke when she called him to let him know she was back.

"Unbelievably, it's ready. You can judge from your pew whether it's ready for prime time or whether your pastor shouldn't be allowed to take vacations!"

Luke, she realized only after hanging up, hadn't asked how her time away had been.

Standing in the pulpit the next morning, Victoria got the first whiff of trouble. Where there were usually smiles of anticipation from the pews, today she faced cool, unreadable expressions. She missed Alex's ready, steady smile from his row, but since this weekend conference was one of the first times he had missed church, she could hardly be critical.

At the door she greeted her parishioners, but their responses seemed distant and impersonal. She assured Harvey Thompson that she would be in place at his open house that afternoon. *Odd that he didn't seem more relieved that I hadn't forgotten.*

The Indian Hills service seemed more normal and she attributed her concerns over the first service to tiredness on her part after the hectic and emotion-laden trip to Fargo.

But as she mingled with dozens of people at Harvey's Open House, doubts flared up again. She wasn't imagining things; from her spot beside a display, she stood like an island in the sea. Alone. *It appears that I'm getting the cold shoulder treatment. What's going on?*

Across the room, Luke nodded briefly with a smile that stopped just short of reaching his eyes and then turned back to talk with someone as they examined a fur-lined hat from Europe. Any other time he would have waved her over to join them.

Victoria had never missed Alex more.

She took refuge in Cate. Accepting a glass of punch, she whispered to her friend, "Is something going on that I don't know about? I'd told Harvey I would help hand out fliers, but he's got several others doing that. I feel like I'm being punished for some unknown misdemeanor."

Cate shrugged, but didn't meet her eyes. "Maybe you've just gotten out of the small-town groove, Victoria. That's what you get for leaving town. Everything will go back to normal once you swing by the General store, or stop at the Café, or work with the troops at the Trail Center. You couldn't be expected to know that Prairie Rose would go through withdrawals without your vivacious presence—even for three or four days!"

That answer reassured her until the next morning when she came into Cate's Café. All eyes followed her to the counter. Just like her first weeks in town, only with less friendliness. Then, everyone had been wanting to talk with her; today, she sensed they were talking about her.

Cate called across the room cheerfully, "Something for you, Stranger? Good to have you back with us at the old watering hole!"

"Thanks. Cut me a piece of whatever smells so good."

"Swedish Coffeecake. Find a spot for two; I'm ready to take a break."

Only when Cate slid on to a stool beside her did the normal hum of conversation resume. Cate pulled a creased paper from her apron pocket and announced, "I finally heard from that company about the Hawaiian shaved-ice flavors. What do you think?" She spread open the glossy brochure between them.

"Wow, they've got a prize-winning photographer, don't they? How many flavors would you get?"

"Why not all fourteen of 'em? Then we could order what was most popular the second time around." They finished their coffee and talked idly a while longer between customers. Rejuvenated, Victoria returned to the church, eager to resume her self-imposed regimen of studying.

Tuesday morning at Cate's Café, she watched Jillie skip across the street holding Alex's hand. While Alex collected two cups of coffee and three bottled juices to take back to the Clinic, Jillie spotted Victoria and headed straight over.

"Hi, River-ant Victoria! We came to get Mommy a cup of coffee 'cuz she's sleepy."

"Has your little brother been keeping her awake at night?"

"No, but she said she's tired of him poopin' his pants so I guess that's why."

Victoria smothered a chuckle and caught Alex's amused look over Jillie's head. "Well, I have to agree, that could get old pretty quick!"

"Thanks for taking Cali and all her stuff home, Tori. It was wonderful to have her there to greet me."

"You're welcome. Gail said you were due back pretty late, and I figured your house would seem pretty empty without her there to greet you. I took her over there right before I went to bed, so she wasn't alone long"

"She did fine. I'll catch up with you later."

After offering her cheek for a quick kiss, Jillie spun off after Alex. A stab of envy took Victoria's breath away as she watched them make their way back to the waiting Gail.

With relatively few phone calls in the evening, she accomplished many long-avoided tasks: clipping Cino's toenails and brushing his teeth, ironing, and polishing woodwork.

Victoria's trip over icy roads on Wednesday to visit Indian Hills parishioners was the most exhilarating episode of the week except for a most unusual edition of the newspaper. She whistled as she read it, wondering if Prairie Rose was ready for this.

Fred Becker, in a flash of editorial vigor, centered the week's edition of the *Prairie Rose Chronicle* around a theme. For the first time in weeks, the darkest ink went not to some facet of the Meadowlark Trail, but to headlines on abortion clinic picketers, and included a story—complete with web-site information—on a woman who crusaded for the unborn via the Internet. Victoria read the paper with interest, wondering what kind of conversations this bold deviation from local news to political and moral issues would produce at tables in Cate's Café.

Oddly enough, though several asked whether she had read the article, no one stayed around to express their opinions once she said she had. *I guess Fred Becker's considerable efforts to raise the town's consciousness haven't been entirely effective if no one has an opinion worth sharing.*

Friday, craving friendship, she decided to host a post-game supper. But five phone calls bagged no takers, so, she felt justified in turning to her friends.

Cate, however, was up to her eyeballs in preparations for catering a golden wedding anniversary celebration at the Catholic church on Sunday afternoon. Luke begged off saying he needed to hang around the store waiting for a shipment that had been delayed by icy roads. Alex faced an evening of returning phone calls. Victoria assured him that things had gone well in Fargo with the specialist and promised to tell him all about it when they both had more time.

"Well, I bet I could entice high-school kids with junk food after the game," she said to Cino. "You'd like that, wouldn't you? They always sneak you treats!" She promptly issued ten invitations. Never had so many phone calls reaped so little success. Other post-games parties, pressing homework assignments, headaches, and babysitting jobs were offered by teens whose voices betrayed their thinly disguised and blatant lies.

Something Luke had said during the past couple of days now zoomed into focus: "You sure set the town in an uproar, leaving without telling anyone where you were going." *Is this an uproar, or is it the retaliation that it feels like for some unknown offense I've committed?*

Victoria drew long angry lightning bolts on the cover of the telephone directory and grumbled, "What do they expect from me? I rarely leave town, and loyally spend most of my money only in Prairie Rose, which is more than I can say for most people. How dare they get in such a snit just 'cuz I take off for a few days?" The pencil broke and she tossed the pieces into the waste basket.

Head held high, she headed off to the game and cheered wildly from her regular, although lonely, spot on the sidelines. At one point she thought she saw Luke's familiar head in the crowds around the refreshment stand, but doubted very much if he would come after telling her he couldn't get away.

The following week's *Prairie Rose Chronicle* featured a new column called "Ask the doctor." Not surprisingly, Alex's face grinned out at her from its place above the dropped-cap letter of the first paragraph. The question featured in the first column knocked the wind right out of Victoria: "What is endometriosis?"

Alex offered the classic textbook definition: Most common cause of infertility in women over age twenty-five...severe menstrual cramps, causing heavy, irregular bleeding...painful sexual activity...in the introductory segment of the column. Then, in the remaining paragraphs, he expanded on that foundation: It is often called the career woman's syndrome, since it seems to affect women who have put off pregnancy until a later age, or allowed an extended time to elapse between a very early pregnancy and their later child-bearing years. He ended with giving the Web site address for a national organization and invited readers to submit questions for future columns.

If nothing else, the column got people talking about something beside abortion.

The highlight of the week was fitting into her favorite suit again, having dropped a few pounds after getting off the medication she had been taking since February. She wore the suit to Amber Larson's students' piano recital. Each set of parents looked at her and then exchanged unreadable glances with each other. Even Luke's mother seemed less than enthused to see her. Amber smiled politely at Victoria and then moved amongst the parents before the recital began, never coming over to speak with her at all. Victoria sat through the recital with a smile pasted in place and left with none of the euphoria she usually experienced when she heard young musicians perform as well as these children did.

The weather on Sunday was typical of a late-March day in North Dakota. But quite a few of the same people she had seen the day before—managing to brave the chill to shop at stores along Main Street—didn't show up for church. She stared out at the sparsely populated pews and reminded herself of the sage advice of a seminary professor, "A minister, like any chef of renown, willingly feeds as many as come to the table."

She thought her sermon reflected this wisdom, but the music didn't echo in her heart, the smiles were sparse in response to her carefully chosen humorous illustration, and the few handshakes at the door were limp and brief.

For the first time in Victoria's tenure, Luke left church without saying a word to her. She had watched dismally as Alex, seated beside Gail and the two children, slipped out early, apparently in response to his beeper. She had hoped to invite him over that afternoon to discuss the fine points of her appointment in Fargo, but if he was called out of church, it meant someone must be pretty sick.

The next hour she faced an Indian Hills' congregation cut from the same lifeless pattern as the group in Prairie Rose. A gray cloud of despair hung over her when she made the drive back home. "If this is what happens when a minister takes a vacation, I swear I'll never leave town again." But in her heart, the heaviness said it was more than just leaving town; she didn't know the answer to her haunting question, *What is it, then?*

Back in town, she drove down Main Street and jammed on the brakes at the sight of two familiar forms moving along the street. *Luke and Cate. Together.* They didn't even notice her car's familiar VW-buzz as they walked toward the Meadowlark Trail. *Well, I had hoped that they could get a chance to talk. Glad something gave Luke the courage to seek her out.*

Despite her magnanimous thoughts, she felt alone. She turned the corner and noticed that a light still burned in the church vestibule. Fussing over the inability of deacons to take care of such a simple detail as turning off the lights, she pulled into her garage and returned on foot to the empty church.

In the martyred mood she was in, she couldn't quit with just flicking the light switch. Muttering all the while, she wandered between pews to straighten hymnbooks in the racks or pick up left-behind mementos of the service.

That's when she noticed a stray worship folder under a pew.

As she bent down to retrieve it, the penciled words along the margin leaped off the page, *She should wear a scarlet letter, not that minister's robe.* Stunned, she crushed the paper and sank to the pew, reading the words over and over until they made no sense at all, searching for a clue that simply wasn't there.

She sorted through memories of her months in Prairie Rose and scrutinized each of them closely, searching for any possible basis for this accusation. To the best of her judgment, her actions with each man in town had been pure. Even with Luke and Alex. What had spawned such an unfair indictment as—even her thoughts stumbled over the word—*adultery*?

"Oh Luke," she groaned, "is this ridiculous lie why you've been so remote since I got back? Surely, you don't believe I'd be different with any other man, knowing how I've behaved toward you." She jammed the paper into her pocket, blinked back sudden tears, and rebuked herself, "Will you quit acting so hormonal? You read one anonymous note and decide you're unjustly accused not only by the writer of the note, but the rest of the town. Get a grip!"

The phone in her office rang; she raced across the sanctuary and flung open the door. "Prairie Rose Community Church," she said, "This is Pastor Victoria."

"Victoria? This is Gail. Could I come over and talk to you this afternoon? I need some advice."

"Of course," she said automatically. "I can't promise much advice, but I'm a willing listener. What time?"

"The kids are down for their naps now. Maybe in an hour?"

"I'll see you then. Come to the house and we'll have coffee while we talk." She knew her voice was lifeless despite the offer she had made of friendship and solace.

She borrowed a few toys and children's books from the church nursery and hurried home to eat a quick lunch that she hardly tasted standing over her kitchen sink.

Gail and the children arrived. With the baby settled in and Jillie playing close by them, Victoria motioned Gail to a comfortable chair in the living room. "Thanks for letting me come on such short notice."

"You couldn't have picked a better time, Gail. I welcome your company."

"Doctor Alex said I could always talk with you if I ever needed a woman's viewpoint. It's about Buzz." She twisted her wedding ring on her finger. "And about the house."

Victoria nodded silently, watching grief darken Gail's eyes. "Are you having second thoughts about selling it?"

"It's hard living there with the memories, but I know I will miss it, too. Milt brought the first prospective buyers over last night. He said they really liked it."

"And it hit you, then, didn't it?"

Gail nodded. "I have to get over Buzz, but why is it taking so long?"

"It's hard to command our emotions, isn't it?" Victoria said gently. "Don't try to rush through the grieving process. You need time to heal and grow, Gail. It will come, just like spring."

Tears trickled down the young widow's cheeks. "Your open house was the best part of Christmas. If it weren't for my job at Doctor Alex's office, I don't know if I could stand it."

"Alex sure appreciates you, Gail." As she said the words, a spasm of guilt twisted her heart. "So does Prairie Rose. All your artwork around town is getting rave reviews." She spoke quickly, pulling a mental shade across the memory of the haunting card and the suspect tangled bed-sheets in the Clinic's hospital room.

Gail smiled tremulously through her tears. "I'm so happy for a chance to draw. It's become such a good way for me to unwind at the end of a day." Jillie trudged in, pushing a gurgling little Alex in the stroller. Soon the baby nursed contentedly and Jillie returned to her toys. "Is there something wrong with my head, Victoria? Even though he's gone, I still love Buzz. Does that make any sense? Doesn't love ever die?"

Doesn't love ever die, doesn't love ever die, doesn't love ever die? The question ricocheted off the walls like a pep-band cymbal's crash. "I think I know the answer to that question, Gail," Victoria said slowly. "Buzz was a special man—your husband, the father of your children, your friend. He'll always have a spot in your heart and memories, no matter how much time goes by. In that sense, no, love never dies."

Her voice sounded like a child's cry in the storm inside her head. *Alex seems to think our love should be picked up right where we left it over ten years ago, despite all the pain that surrounds that time. Luke kisses me, but must still love Cate—does love ever die? What do I really know and believe about that?*

Softly, Gail said, "I didn't mean to make you sad. I'm sorry to barge in on you; you have, uh, your own problems, I know."

For Pete's sake, did Alex leave notes around his office about my Fargo trip?

"Small towns can be real cruel sometimes, I know."

Bewildered by this seemingly incongruous remark, Victoria asked, "*What?* What do you mean?"

Anger sharpened Gail's halting words, "You must know what the gossips are saying about why you left town." Harsh emotions chiseled Gail's jawline to a razor's point.

Ho-boy.

"It makes me so mad," Gail continued, "I won't let anyone say a word about it around me. I know you would never, uh, have an abortion. I've seen how you are with kids, and so has everyone. All they have to do is think back to Jenny Guddman's christening."

"Abortion?" *The scarlet letter that someone thinks I should be wearing is an* A *for abortion, not for adultery?* Victoria sagged in her chair, stunned, as dizziness attacked without warning.

"Oh, Victoria! I'm sorry; I thought you knew. They're saying you, uh, had it done when you left town." Gail's voice dropped to a whisper. "I feel like such a trouble-maker—I really thought you knew." Jillie's laughter and the baby's responsive cooing from his mother's arms contrasted starkly to the misery in the living room.

Any relief she felt in discovering that Gail did not buy into the rumor was sucked up by the gaping new chasm that threatened her life. Each breath Victoria took ripped the jagged hole in her self-possession a little longer, a little deeper. She hardly recognized her own voice asking, "Just who is supposed to be the father?"

Gail's words were almost too faint to hear. "Some say Doctor Alex, others say Luke." The rest of Gail's visit was a blur.

When the door closed behind her guests, Victoria dropped down close to the fireplace clutching her knees to her chin. The crackling flames failed to melt the iceberg inside her even though her face stung from their heat. Cino paced restlessly around her, nuzzling her, whimpering his concern and finally plopped down beside her with his head wedged between her chest and her knees.

She tried to pray, but couldn't break through the wall she felt closing in on her. Clinging to Cino—the only thing that seemed stable in her tilting world—she let her tears soak his coat.

The irony of her dread that anyone would discover the truth about her past relationship with Zan mocked her. *What a fool I was to worry over ancient history.* This town didn't need to dig up dirty laundry to kick around; they created a new disgrace that would do more damage than anything she had ever feared.

"Come on, Cino. We're out of here." Within minutes, they were heading out of town toward any place that didn't know her face. Miles and miles of roads cut across the wide-open prairie and disappeared beneath them, and still they drove on.

At some point in the afternoon, she came to a fork in a mental road and pulled over to the side of the bumpy country road. "You know," she informed the uncaring world outside her car, "it is very tempting to head for the border and send a truck back to pack up my life in Prairie Rose." Though an enticing idea, she knew it was not an option. Leaving Prairie Rose to wallow in its quagmire of conjecture was what she most wanted to do right now.

She opened the door to let Cino roam in the ditch for a few moments. Business completed, he quickly made tracks to her side again. In the brief time he had taken, she had made a conscious choice and turned the car back toward the town full of people she had mistaken for friends.

Only Cino exhibited any thrill at seeing Main Street again.

Back home, she drifted through the Rectory, moving through her home like a weather vane at the mercy of the wind. Upstairs, she migrated from window-to-window, measuring her life by their compass points.

South. Prairie Rose Community Church. They had broken with tradition to call a single woman as their pastor. Would that spark of courage survive, now, until the truth could be told? Would the time-honored tenet of *Innocent until proven guilty* be victorious on her behalf?

East. Her eyes sought out Alex's house. Alex, who had loved—and still loved—her so much and yet hadn't denied her Luke's friendship. *Does love ever die?* Ironically, and despite caution and good intentions, she apparently was linked with Alex, and possibly Luke, in a scandal far worse than she could ever have imagined.

In the darkness she bumped against the lamp on the table and set it swaying. As she reached out to steady it, she could hear Alex's voice. *One flash means I love you, two means I want you.* A sob choked her and she left the room.

North. The silos around the Grain Elevator rose like silent watchmen—sentries guarding the bits and pieces of contributions she had made to Prairie Rose. Was this welcome now exposed as a fraud? Unwilling to let her mind conjure up any more real or imagined slights, she firmly closed the door to silence the lying silos.

West. The pink-tinged sunset formed a canvas for the barren branches of the elm trees along the street between the Rectory and Luke's house. *He must be devastated to be named in this mess, especially since I rejected his advances like a virgin.* Luke: the man who now must believe she had given Alex privileges that went far beyond calling her 'Tori.'

The week loomed before her. Each day moved like a tumbleweed in a ghost-town, somehow frightening in its purposeless flight and empty silence. She executed robot motions of pastoral duties. Each night she fell into bed exhausted but unable to sleep, pursued by the nightmare, mocked by Alex's framed wish, *May all our dreams come true* on the bedroom wall. The strain took its toll on her.

In Larson's Grocery one day, two women in a huddle by the fresh fruit aisle developed guilty crimson blushes when Victoria pushed her cart past them. She left the cart mid-aisle and stormed to the counter where she announced in a voice that could curl winter hay, "I need to discuss beef roasts, Luke. Now. In the meat locker." Head held high, she strode past the gawking women and flung open the heavy steel door to the walk-in freezer.

Luke caught the door before it slammed shut and stood facing her in the sub-zero cavity. "Can't we talk about whatever out where it's warmer?" he asked.

"Don't be ridiculous, Luke," she snapped, "that was an excuse; I refuse to talk about anything even remotely personal within the range of those two biddy-hen gossips."

"Oh."

Victoria stomped her feet to keep warm. Luke shifted, only an arm's length away, but didn't move closer. "Seems the whole town thinks I've had an abortion. I'm sure you've heard that it's a toss-up as to whether the father is you or Alex."

Luke's face was a study in control. Only his eyes betrayed him in the silence.

"I never figured it would be necessary to tell anyone this, but I have endometriosis and probably will never even get pregnant at this stage of my life, so how could I have just had an abortion?" She hiccuped on a rush of swallowed tears. "It just doesn't seem fair that people, I mean, I really love kids," she inhaled icy air and barreled on, "and I know Alex does, so it makes sense for him to be with Gail even though it hurts so much. And I would never lead you on. I think you belong with Cate, because love never dies, does it?" Gasping sobs finally silenced her jumble of words.

Luke reached out and she flew into his arms to bury her face against his flannel shirt. His chest rumbled with low, unintelligible sounds of comfort.

Finally she lifted her head and sniffed loudly, "Sorry, Luke. I cried all over your shirt. And I'm sorry for exploding at you, too. After the hell I've been through in the past couple of weeks, my self-control isn't what it should be."

Luke's voice was gentle, "In your sermon last week you said faith needs to be a decision. I told myself that I would believe whatever you told me. I have to admit this whole thing has rocked me, but I know what you're like with me so I believe that you're the same with Alex. And every man. I didn't understand half of what you just said, but I want you to know that I believe you. I'm just sorry you had to come to me, rather than me being man enough to come to you when you needed someone."

"Thank you. I'm sorry your name is being dragged through the mud with mine. After all, this is your town. You have to live and work here. I don't." Eyes straight ahead, she pulled away without pausing for a response.

Luke stepped aside quickly while Victoria brushed past him back into the store where the two women waited at the counter. The door jangled behind her as she made her escape without a sideways glance.

Minutes later, she dialed a familiar number and heaved a sigh of relief when Luke, not Dave, answered. "Luke? Next time I come in, remind me to finish shopping before I storm out, will you?"

He chuckled, "If you go to your door in about three minutes, you'll find Dave there with the groceries you left in your cart. You can pay next time."

She gave the surprised Dave a five-dollar tip.

Doggedly, she followed her normal routine; it was as if the release she had found in Luke's meat locker gave her the will to go on.

Simple things assumed great proportions. Rachel's casual invitation to come for tea brightened a dull afternoon; Cate's spontaneous laughter over one of Victoria's stories seemed golden; Jillie's young voice calling a happy greeting across the street soothed her heart like a carillon; even the weekly *Prairie Rose Chronicle* provided a measure of human contact, if only on a printed page.

But these things didn't fill the hollowness inside her heart. She missed Alex; she missed Luke. Each, in his way, had filled her life with pleasure. But this week both men, according to Cate, were spending every free hour with the crew building benches for the Meadowlark Trail. Ironically, the project that had given the town a sense of togetherness now left Victoria alone. She walked over to the Trail Center and watched the men pound nails and saw boards, but didn't interrupt the evident male bonding.

Torn between defending herself and riding out the storm in silence, she clutched her work around her like a shroud. She found herself weighing each greeting for sincerity or hidden meanings. When she visited the shut-ins, part of her actively listened and communicated, and part wondered about all that wasn't being said.

Even in her study she couldn't escape the incongruity of such a damning charge. The framed diplomas offered verification that she was well trained, and silently proclaimed the confidence experts had in her abilities. *But what good are these credentials if people believe a lie about me?*

The crammed bookshelves held information and wisdom, and evidenced the solid foundation for her education and her lively quest for knowledge. *But all the facts in the world can't change a person's heart or mind unless they are balanced by trust. Will people give me a chance?*

Even the inviting, comfortable office furniture was a visible illustration of her desire to bring hope and encouragement to the people as they sought her counsel. *Will anyone ever sit in this room again and let me listen to their problems—especially if their main problem is the minister they believe has violated the sanctity of her calling? Will any church ever be interested in having me as their minister when they hear of how my first pastorate ended?*

The hardest thing she had ever accomplished was earning back her parents' trust when she was a teenager. She didn't know if she had the ability, will-power, or desire to win back a whole town.

Victoria took extra care with Sunday's sermon. She detoured on her way home from Indian Hills on Thursday to buy a vivid array of potted plants from a countryside greenhouse. These she arranged in an arc on the altar and offered a silent prayer that she, as Noah of old, would see their rainbow of beauty and know that the future would be brighter.

If they affected no one else, her special efforts lifted her spirits during Sunday's service. Her voice rang out in confidence as she read words of hope from the Psalms that had brought encouragement to generations of people who had watched dreams and visions crumble at their feet:

Lord, You have been our dwelling place throughout all generations. Before the mountains were born or You brought forth the earth and the world, from everlasting to everlasting You are God...He who dwells in the shelter of the Most High will rest in the shadow of the Almighty. I will say of the Lord, He is my refuge and my fortress, my God, in whom I trust.

In her office, as she gathered up materials before leaving for the service at Indian Hills, she overheard the church treasurer say to Luke after having counted the morning's collection, "Too many more weeks like this, and we'll have to dip into the church savings to pay the bills." She heard the timbre of Luke's voice, but missed the content of his response; she closed the door softly.

Whereas up to now she had maintained a normal schedule, the next week, she withdrew. It became too much to face accusing stares or wounded silence in any room she entered. One night she stood for a long time staring at the mound of moving boxes in her basement as Cino sniffed around, delighted to explore this level of the house that was usually off-limits to him. *It wouldn't take long to pack up and disap-pear into the night.*

The emotional pain that plagued her continuously was harder, by far, to deal with than the physical pain she had endured through the years with endometriosis. Since her appointment with the specialist and the resulting treatment, she was relatively released from debilitating physi-cal pain, but she could find no reprieve from this recent emotional tor-ment. She almost wished she could exchange the new for the known.

Victoria and Alex finally got a chance to talk in a corner of the Trail Center while they painted trim. In low voices, they talked about the sug-gestions the specialist had made. "Did she say anything about additional laser surgery?"

"Yes, she was very honest about it."

"What's your prognosis?"

Victoria shrugged and studiously wiped a smudge of paint that had dribbled below the taped line.

"Well?" The repeated question rose above a whisper and turned a few heads in their direction. Victoria glared at Alex and they worked in silence for a few minutes as the gynecologist's voice echoed in her mind.

"Victoria, do you have any plans to marry soon, or any desire to conceive?"

"I don't mean to be rude, Doctor, but what difference does that make?"

"Endometriosis is often successfully treated by pregnancy. In fact, if you conceived, that would be the treatment of choice, rather than either drugs or additional surgical treatments."

"And if I don't get married? Or what if I were unable to get pregnant? That is a distinct possibility, isn't it? Do I continue with extremely painful menstrual cycles in punishment for choosing not to have a child?"

"If pregnancy is not an option for you, then we will proceed with the best treatment we can provide. Either way, I want you to see there is a light at the end of the tunnel."

The woman's kind voice faded into memory with Alex's words, "Do you plan to tell me, or am I supposed to play twenty questions?"

She just had time to hiss, "Alex, she's a wonderful doctor, but she's not God, okay?" before someone called for a break and the workers stopped their various tasks and all attacked banana bread and hot cider. An hour later, Alex helped Rachel bundle up her kids and the four of them left, Alex holding a squirming little Alex against his shoulder, quite content in the role of surrogate father.

Victoria walked home alone.

The aspect of life in Prairie Rose that had brought Victoria the most joy was meaningful relationships. Their past richness now contrasted cruelly against her current black hole of loneliness. Townsfolk watched her every move like vultures. She imposed new stringent limits on her visits to Rachel so as not to cling like a leech to the one person whose behavior seemed unchanged.

She was almost tempted to turn to Casey Donovan for counsel but didn't want to drag him into her personal slough of despair. Instead, Victoria relied on Cino for comfort, companionship, and unconditional love.

But even Cino couldn't fill the void. She was jolted one night by his forbidden in-the-house woofing and she stomped downstairs to tell him off, only to find him patiently sitting beside the closet that held his dog food. "Oh, Cino! Oh, no—when did I last feed you?" It could have been this morning, but it was equally possible it was yesterday.

Shivering, she stood over him as he ate, watched numbly as he lapped up fresh water. When he finished, contented at last, she knelt and hugged his head. "I'm losing my mind, Cino. *How* could I forget to feed you?" It was a scary feeling.

One Tuesday afternoon when it was too muddy to enjoy a walk outside with Cino and his huge hairy paws, she holed up in her living room with a news magazine for entertainment on her day off. The doorbell startled her. "Cate!"

"Glad to know you still recognize me," Cate chided with gentle sarcasm. "When one of my most faithful customers isn't in her spot at my

café for a solid week, I figure somebody else must be doing a rival cof-
feepot business in town. Give me names and locations!" She brandished
a thermos bottle over her head. "I'll drive my competition out of town!"

Victoria grinned. "Peel off your war paint, but first let me rescue
whatever smells so tempting in this box!"

Cate slid off her coat and tossed it on a hook, "Pie. Nothing better on
a looking-up-to-see-the-bottom kind of day than a pie. Did you ever
eat half a pie before?"

"Noooo, can't say I have, but who's minding the store?"

Cate snorted over her shoulder, kicked off her boots and led the way
to the kitchen table, "Things are worse than I'd imagined: you've even
forgotten that Lucy frequently handles it while I'm gone. You're in bad
shape! Get forks, cuz time's a-wasting' while you're talking, Kiddo."

Cate expertly sliced the pie in half. "See this line? Cross over it and
you're a dead woman. Now dig in."

The tinkle of forks on the pie plate centered between them was background music for a companionable silence. "Sheer decadence," Victoria
sighed, chasing a tempting hunk of apple with her fork.

"But fun, huh?" Cate added.

"Yup. Good stuff—apple pie with cheese rolled right into the crust,
huh? Never heard of it before."

Cate dropped her fork and puffed out her cheeks. "I bet I've got a
story you've never heard, either. Wanna hear it?"

"Huh?"

"I didn't come bearing the only apple pie left at the café just to lead
you down the path of gluttony, you know."

"Oh."

"Once upon a time…"

"You weren't kidding! I hope it's one of Grimm's Fairy Tales; they're
my favorites…" Victoria felt giddy with the sudden dose of friendship.

"Hush! Once upon a time there was a good Catholic girl with pretty
red curls and a great body. She lived in a little town that was the best

place she could imagine to live, probably so because of a certain tall bas-ketball-playing fellow who had liked the girl ever since he stole a swing from her in first grade. Handsome dude, he was."

"Do these kids have names?"

"No. Oh awright, they have names, uh, Susie and Johnny."

"That's original," Victoria said dryly.

"If I may continue," Cate rebuked with an exaggerated frown, "our hero and heroine spent lots of time together, probably more than was wise. One starry night Johnny and Susie created a baby, using the tech-niques they had perfected over months of practice."

Cate pushed her chair back from the table and stretched her legs out, ankles crossed; she was relaxation personified, unless one watched her hands. Tense, restless hands plucked at nubbins on her vivid green sweater sleeve.

"When Susie told Johnny she was pregnant, he fell apart. In youth's optimism they decided that they would tell no one, finish high school, leave town, get married, and return later with a beautiful, 'premature', baby. Everyone would live happily ever after."

Lost in thought, Cate picked up Victoria's fork and licked it clean. Victoria barely noticed.

"Problem was, Susie started showing faster than their plan had allowed for, and Johnny's grades suffered. He was in real serious danger of losing the college scholarship that figured so heavily in their escape plans. To top it off, both sets of parents decided the kids were spending far too much time together and joined forces to set up stiff regulations that ended that."

The story hung in the room like a tangible presence while Cate auto-matically refilled their cups from the thermos. "After a long week of iso-lation with only one secretive phone call, Susie and Johnny climbed out their respective bedroom windows and met to talk about revised plans. Later that week, they told their parents they wanted to get married; then their parents fell apart. Pieces everywhere." She rolled her eyes dramatically over the rim of her mug.

"Susie and Johnny," she went on, staring at a place beyond Victoria's head as she talked softly, "weren't dumb kids. They knew that if their parents were against a marriage, they would be really, uh, powerfully upset, about a baby coming. So, they collected all their money on the sly and split one Saturday morning, heading for a place that locker-room rumors said did safe abortions. It was a beautiful morning in early May, but Susie cried the whole trip. Johnny tried to comfort her, but he had the added worry of strange rattles coming from under the hood of his ancient car."

Victoria's body shook like a sapling in the wind as she took her first deep breath since Cate's story had begun.

"Susie had entrusted a taped-up box of prize possessions—including her diary—to her best friend for safe-keeping until she could pick them up after the abortion, figuring she might not be real welcome back at home. Little did she dream that friend would have the power to wreck her life even further: she opened the box and read the diary."

The only sound in the room was the hum of the refrigerator until Cate continued, "That was followed by a second offense: the snoop became blabbermouth and concocted a half-true, half-lie story for Susie's parents: She informed them that Susie and Johnny had left town for an abortion and then planned to elope. What followed should be punishable by hanging: She spread the rumor among school friends in a whirlwind of phone calls that probably tied up every line in town for several hours. When Johnny and Susie landed back to town late that night, everyone knew that fabricated version of their lives."

"Are you okay?" Victoria asked softly after a long pause.

Cate nodded; her eyes glistened with unshed tears, "What the town didn't know was that with all the trauma, Susie did not lose the baby on that trip. Susie and Johnny were two scared kids. All their money disappeared for gas and snacks along the way and then the unanticipated car repairs, leaving nothing for the abortion. Plus, the closer they got, the more Susie had realized she couldn't do it. She chickened out and got Johnny to agree that they would think of something once they got home.

Cate let a shoe drop to the floor and pulled the foot up beneath her. "They then both faced a town's accusations—accusations of something that had never happened, and something they thought no one knew about—and their families' judgments against them. Susie and Johnny were grounded for the rest of the school year. The only time they talked privately after that weekend, Johnny told Susie he doubted he would have been able to let her go through with an abortion."

The stillness in the Rectory was suffocating.

"A trip to the town doctor managed to convince their families that no abortion had occurred, but as far as their parents were concerned, they were in as much trouble as if it had. Most people decided that the abortion *had* occurred, holding tight to that misguided opinion until it became visibly impossible to believe. The rest of the folks in town couldn't handle even the illegitimate pregnancy, let alone an abortion, so they pretty much crucified Susie and Johnny anyway."

She pivoted her shoulders, stretching her back before continuing. "Our heroine and hero did finish their senior year, but it was pretty grim. Susie had the distinction of being the first girl to graduate from Small Town USA High School who felt a baby's kick as she marched in during the processional. And Johnny is possibly the first valedictorian in the school's history to have won his awards without any applause from the audience, many of whom believed he should have been denied the honor."

Cate twisted a strand of snowy hair. "*I started turning white in my senior year of high school.*" Remembering, Victoria sucked in her breath as Cate went on, "Johnny stayed out of college for one year, working for his father in the family grocery store; Susie worked at her old job, in her dad's Café, growing bigger day by day, until their child was born and put up for adoption. Johnny and Susie drifted apart, two kids with big problems and no one to turn to, especially in a town that had so little experience with anything like the scandal Susie and Johnny had dumped in their lap."

"What happened to their relationships with their families?"

Cate laughed harshly. "There's actually another blotch on Susie's character as far as most people are concerned that certainly took the attention off the pregnancy and resulting child. You see, when Johnny and Susie drifted apart, she was so desperate for friends that she snagged Johnny's bad-boy brother and managed to destroy that family once again. Susie and the "Rowdy One" were in the car together, both drunker than skunks and only a month after Susie gave birth, when the car crashed going around a curve just outside of town. Susie survived much to her disgust, but Johnny's brother wasn't so lucky." The biting sarcasm in Cate's voice made Victoria shiver.

"To this day, the three-part scandal is not discussed around these parts. Anywhere. And Susie and Johnny, who run into each other almost every day, have learned lots about prejudice and forgiveness and pain."

"I hurt, too, for all your pain, Susie."

Cate attempted a flippant retort, "Now, what makes you so sure I'm Susie?"

"Because you're here in my kitchen when I need a friend. And because I've never forgotten the look on your face that day when you told me that Luke had once loved you. 'That's another story,' you said then. I think I just heard it."

Cate's jaw tightened. "Yeah, Susie's sitting' right here with you, but not soon enough. For the one person in town who should know what it's like to be a woman on the sharp end of a small town's scorn, it sure took long enough for me to get over here. I guess I've grown tough over the past fifteen years, and I'm not proud of it."

"I don't think you're tough; if anything, I think the last couple of weeks have been as awful for you as for me. You've been reliving the past and suffering through the present. And I think Luke has, too."

"What can I do to help you, Victoria?"

"Erase the last few weeks?" Victoria's eyebrows arched above an ironic smile. "I just wish someone could tell me what the town expects me to do." She flung her left hand in the air, "Am I supposed to act like nothing's happened and kill the rumor, or should I resign?" Her right hand lifted. "But then if I resign, won't that seem a confession that, yes, I have broken people's trust in me? Nobody's holding up any cue cards for me, so I don't know my lines in this drama." Both hands dropped to her lap.

"One reason I stayed away from you at the beginning," Cate said, "was the fear that if I spoke too loudly in your defense, it would do more harm than good. I'm sure there are still some people who remember in vivid detail all the bits and pieces of hell that surfaced that weekend all those many springs ago and floated for years. You could have been condemned by your association with me. Birds-of-a-feather sort of thing."

Victoria stared across the pie plate. "So you don't think I've had an abortion?"

Cate's jaw dropped, "You?" she said incredulously. "No way! I would swear to it on a stack of Bibles, in fact."

"Why are you so sure?"

"I know you, I know Luke, and I know Alex." She ticked off each name with a finger. "As for you, there's one thing that is very important to you: your ministry. The fact you've preached two weeks in a row to the same people who are treating you like dirt affirmed all I know about you. For the first time in my life, I'm seeing 'turning the other cheek' being lived out."

"Well, don't give me too much credit. The first week I was ignorant; last Sunday, stubborn. Either way, I'm hardly worthy of sainthood," Victoria protested.

Cate ignored her. "And I know Luke; he's hurting now, but it's from memories, not guilt. Remember, I know him pretty well. We've both made our way back into the town's good graces—I mean, the guy has a leadership position at your church, and we both do a pretty good business on our opposite sides of Main Street. But he remembers when that would never have been believed possible. And then there's Alex; Alex would love to sweep you out of town to elope with you, but he would never have let you destroy a child of your love, and I get the feeling that he knows where you went. How's that for an unsolicited, unprofessional psychiatric analysis?"

"It's so impressive that you could change your sign to 'Cate's Café and Counseling," Victoria lifted her mug in a silent tribute. "Actually, Cate, you're both right and wrong. I did not have an abortion when I made that suspect trip out of Prairie Rose."

She took a deep cleansing breath and barreled on. "But back in high school, I made the opposite decision of Susie. Another difference is that my Johnny didn't even know about the pregnancy, let alone the abortion."

Cate bent to pet Cino, taking a long moment to marshal her thoughts. "You didn't have to tell me that, but thanks for trusting me."

"It's all that I've been thinking about lately. It needed to be said. And I know you're someone who can be trusted."

Cate nodded, "I have plenty of faults, but blabbing isn't one of them. My heart goes out to you; the only thing that kept Susie and Johnny sane was knowing that someone else in the world knew how desperately afraid and adrift they each felt. I can't imagine going through that hell all alone, Victoria. And I'm willing to bet big money that you've had your share of not-so-happy family memories, too."

"You've met my folks. They are wonderful people and we are very close, but it took a long time to get to back to where we are today."

"Will you ever tell Doc, uh, your Johnny? Don't look so surprised; I've wondered about the electricity between the two of you and now it makes sense. So, what will you do?"

"I don't know, Cate. Now hardly seems the time to bring up old pains or involve the person who has been kept in the dark all these years, especially when the current rumor is technically false, but actually true. The only difference between truth and rumor is the question of when it all happened."

"I've had an unrequested front row seat at the café during this event. Walking my beat, as it were, I've seen interesting things emerge. I'm sure you think people are against you."

"Hey now, where would I get that goofy idea?" Victoria asked in a flare of sarcasm.

Cate held up a cautionary hand. "The folks who were the most vocal against me years ago are completely silent about you. They come into the café and just sit there, thinking. I keep their cups filled and give them lots of time to sort this whole thing out."

"If they're not talking, who's keeping the rumor alive?"

"People who don't remember how damaging their words and actions were before. The ones who don't realize that, despite our activities fifteen years ago, today Luke and I pulled our lives back together in their full view and now are vital parts of Prairie Rose. Or, the blaze is being fanned by the ones who weren't around then and think this is the first sin to rock the town."

Cate absentmindedly chewed on a thumbnail. "But I dare say, when you look out from the pulpit, what you see isn't accusation turned toward you as much as it is toward themselves. Many feel guilty about how they are treating you, or maybe just unable to cope with really loving a pastor when they suspect or believe she is guilty."

A sudden thought stopped Victoria cold. "Cate, that *Prairie Rose Chronicle* article on abortions was for my benefit, wasn't it? No wonder people kept checking to be sure I had read it."

"Yeah. I cornered Fred and told him I knew what he was doing and that he had better make sure of his facts before printing any more such stuff."

Victoria jammed her hands into jeans pockets and rocked back in her chair. "Do I resign so the church can call a pastor who isn't linked to a scandal? Congregations shouldn't need to deal with something like this in their spiritual leaders. And what if the truth about that long-ago abortion would surface after I regain their trust now? That would pretty much cork it, wouldn't you think?"

"No one, *no one*, will hear it from me, but stranger things have happened. Maybe congregations should learn to accept their pastors as flesh-and-blood kind of people. Or doesn't the Golden Rule go both ways across a pulpit?" Cate asked with a sardonic grin. "Maybe your role now needs to be one of teaching them to weigh issues and make responsible judgments and decisions. If you leave, aren't you reinforcing the idea that if one of their daughters gets pregnant, she loses her place and rights in the church? Is there any room in the church for a woman who may have had an abortion, or an illegitimate child?"

"Oh, Cate—if I have one goal, that's it: to make sure that any church I pastor is the safest place for the deepest hurts. But one thing I really believe, Cate, is that church leaders are accountable to their parishioners. We don't live by different rules, but we accept different expectations once we assume our positions of spiritual leadership. I know I'm living a lie by not telling the whole truth, but I haven't settled in my mind just how much of that truth needs to be told—or if it even needs to be told—and, if so, to which people."

Cate looked grim. "It's not often that a lapsed-Catholic girl gets to tell Protestant clergy what to do, but I want you to know that Cate Jones would miss Victoria Dahlmann very much if she left Prairie Rose. Think about that before you start packing. You have helped me more than you'll ever know. In fact, hearing your sermons second-hand every Monday morning from your parishioners almost makes me want to drop in on one first-hand sometime. Now wouldn't *that* set the town on its collective ear?"

She checked her watch, frowning. "Time to roll or Lucy will be swamped by herself. Promise me you'll chant loudly and resolutely, 'I'd be a fool to leave Prairie Rose' and keep chanting until you believe it." They paused in the open door to share a quick hug. "Tomorrow. Cate's Café. You've used up your excused absences, so be there. Aloha. Come taste the fourteen flavors of Paradise. It will take your mind off Prairie Hell."

Rinsing off their dishes, Victoria stared at the water swirling down the drain and smiled. "Thanks, Cate," she toasted her absent friend with a dripping mug, "and thanks, Susie. And thank you, Lord, for sending a friend when I needed one."

CHAPTER ELEVEN

The following Tuesday morning when Victoria was in the laundry room rinsing out stained bed-sheets that had soaked overnight in bleach, the phone rang. Since no calls lately had been pleasant, she debated ruining her day with yet another person feeling perfectly free to express their opinions on her character or lack thereof. Against her better judgment, she trudged up the steps to the closest telephone.

"Hey, preacher-woman! Would the world skid to a stop if you and I skipped town for a couple of hours? I've got to make a run to Minot to drop off some specimens and pick up some supplies that I can't wait to have delivered on Friday. Here's my deal: you go along, I buy lunch."

It was like an answer to her prayer-without-words: if only she could sprout wings and fly away. Cali shared her back seat with Cino, each claiming a window, and Victoria felt the weight of the world fly off her shoulders as the town disappeared behind the four of them. With a simple invitation, Alex had performed the Herculean task of setting the world back on its axis, if only for a few hours.

Yellow lines on the highway pointed the way to a morning of blessed anonymity. Victoria waited in the car with the dogs while Alex dropped off the specimens at the hospital's laboratory, but when he headed for the medical supply store, she—as spokesperson for his three passengers—elected to spend the half-hour he would need in a city park.

Cino and Cali propelled Victoria around the bushes, willingly stopping for frequent squealing children to pet, prod, and poke them. Victoria gave the dogs the full length that their leashes allowed and followed their mindless lead. She delighted in their antics and basked in the luxury of no one knowing or caring who she was—the dogs got all the attention from passers-by.

Lunch, as promised, was on Alex. He chose a quiet, delightful deli off the beaten track. "Don't tell Cate, but this is one fine place to eat—we'll have to come again," Victoria said as she dusted away the crumbs of their three-cheese-and-sprouts sandwiches.

They ambled back to the car, satiated both by lunch and each other's company. Two dogs were rocking the car with their enthusiasm and the windows were a mess of doggy nose-prints. "I think these guys need another romp. Shall we hit that park again?"

"Sure."

Each on the business end of a dog's leash, Alex and Victoria alternately strolled and jogged allowing the dogs to call the shots for a while. It was on a bench Alex spotted off-trail that he pricked her balloon of blissfulness.

"Remember when you told me I could talk with your specialist? Well, I did, and she said something that that got me curious. In layman's terms, it translates into 'even though you have been pregnant, your endometriosis persists.' At first, I thought she was mixing up your record in her mind with another patient's so I didn't challenge her on it. But, I think we need to talk, Love."

Victoria felt both light-headed and nauseous and would have gladly welcomed any diversion at this point. None came. She gripped her knees in silence.

"Tori, where did you disappear to after our high school graduation?"

Her pulse felt like a metronome gone wild in her neck.

"Please talk to me."

"Chicago." Her cheek twitched with a nervous tic.

"Were you pregnant?"

She managed only a hint of a nod.

"It was our baby, wasn't it?"

"Yes." Her lips formed the word, but her response was soundless. He pulled her closer on the bench as her breath caught on the sharp edges of the memory, "I was almost three months along when we graduated. My folks—Mom, especially—were suspicious and when I 'fessed-up," she paused in retrospection, "they made arrangements for me to stay with my godparents in Chicago until after the baby was born—mostly to get me away from you, Zan. We were both so young and they were justifiable concerned that we would mess up our lives even more if we stayed together."

Tears pooled in his eyes and a sigh shuddered through him.

"I loved you so much, Zan. I didn't want to have the baby if I couldn't have you, so I took charge of my life in a most frightening way. Once I landed in Chicago, I made it my mission to find a place that would do abortions, no questions asked." She bit her lip, stiffened her shoulders and looked at Zan through a haze of tears.

"I went back to my godparents' house after the abortion, knowing they would be at work. But I realized it was pretty dumb to think I could still stay there without my parents eventually finding out I was no longer pregnant. So I ran away, and ended up living with a girl I had met during my abortion-search."

A moan escaped Alex unchecked. "Oh, Tori." He could not form his thoughts into words.

But for Victoria it would have been easier to recapture hair spray in a bottle than hold back this long-dormant conversation. "I called my folks that night to tell them I was okay, even though I wouldn't tell them where I was or about the abortion. I promised—and kept my word—to call them every week."

"How did you live?" Alex asked softly.

"I found a low-pay, bad-hours job at a convenience store and somehow muddled through the next months. When enough time had passed for the baby to have been born, I showed up again at home in Duluth thinking I had pulled it off."

Alex said, "By that time we had moved—*that* was the traumatic event that followed *my* Senior year: I had to *give up* the only place I'd ever called home. I punished my folks for the great injustice of making me move by changing my plans and going away to college. I didn't come home even for Christmas that whole first year."

"We were something else, weren't we? My parents have always been smarter than I give them credit for being."

"Same here. But what happened to you then?"

"Mom had me in a doctor's office the very next day. That's when the gig was up at the Dahlmann house. There's little point of trying to hide a messy abortion from a doctor—and that was the caliber of the one I'd had: effective, but sloppy."

"Did that butcher do irreparable damage?"

"No, in fact, something good came out of it. The repairs I needed enabled the doctor to diagnose the endometriosis. Throughout puberty, I had thought I was going crazy with symptoms that no one else my age had until I finally learned that it had a name."

"It's pretty amazing you were able to get pregnant, isn't it?"

"Yeah. Chalk it up to youth—on both our parts. Not to be crude, Alex, but your little guys really knew how to swim! Ironically, the doctor told me that since I had had the abortion so early in the pregnancy, it wouldn't be enough to halt the progress of the disease like a full-term pregnancy could have. So I live day-to-day with yet another reminder of how a solitary decision can truly shape the rest of life."

Cino and Cali had nuzzled up to each other for a nap in the sun and joggers moved rhythmically along a path several yards away. On the park bench, Alex and Victoria reached for each other's hands.

"Oh, Tori, I wish I would have stood up to your parents and made them tell me where you were. I tried several times, but they told me in no uncertain terms that you were off-limits to me, to get on with my life and let you get on with yours. And I buckled. *Why* did I buy the story they fed me that you were off spending the summer with friends, like it was a pleasure trip for you?"

"Because they were protecting their young. Their minds were made up. They had sensed for months that we were destined for trouble but we were two cocky, defiant, deviant teenagers. My pregnancy proved that all their fears were justified. For some reason, I kept my word to them that I would not try to contact you. I wrote you zillions of letters, but ripped them all to shreds. Just the act of writing those letters kept me sane, Zan."

"I wish I could have gotten just one," he said sadly. "How do you get along with your parents these days?"

"I love my parents dearly now, but back then? You're right: they were tough. We've come through some rocky times, and I had to earn their trust again. That's why this whole situation sickens me. If Mom and Dad catch wind of this latest scandal, it will hurt them immensely."

He gave her a tight, lingering squeeze and pushed himself up to his feet and moved around behind her where he rested his hands on her shoulders.

"I finally understand how you must have felt when you saw me for the first time in Prairie Rose, and why you have been so insistent that we are not 'back together again.' If I were you, I'm sure I would find it just as impossible to welcome someone back into my life who has been part-and-parcel of—but not there to help shoulder—so much hurt."

"I bear no hard feelings against you for that, Alex. My parents made sure we stayed apart, and I knew that was what had happened. I wanted you and missed you desperately, and usually dreamed that somehow, somewhere we would look across a room and see each other and head off into the sunset together. But I didn't blame you for disappearing."

Alex ran his fingers through his hair and expelled a puff of pent-up air. "The past years have been so different for each of us; I had no idea just how different."

"I know our parents had many conversations about what to do with us while we were still in school, but we were so headstrong that it took something pretty dramatic to shake us up. Looking back, if we had gotten our way and kept on the same track without getting side-lined by a baby, I doubt if you would have ever ended up in medical school or that God would have had a chance to talk sense to me about where my life was headed."

"How did you get from there to here? Why isn't Tori Dahlmann bitter against God?"

"I credit a college roommate with sharing her faith with me—and making me want what she had when I saw the difference it made in her. She didn't say a lot, but the way she lived got through to me. How about you?"

"Much of the change in me has come from sitting in a pew in Prairie Rose, North Dakota. But before then, a guy who gave me a ride when I was hitch-hiking home from college told me that God answers prayer. At that point, I was willing to try anything, so I started praying. That's when I made the deal with God about you and me."

Victoria nodded thoughtfully. "It was a truly awful time, but life has turned out to be good for both of us." *If you don't count what's going on right now back at Reality-ville.*

He came back around and turned her to face him on the bench. "Tori, even though I have often wondered over the years about that summer, I wasn't as prepared as I thought I would be to hear the truth. You've come through it all with flying colors. I feel like I got in the path of a steam-roller."

She smiled crookedly. "Right now, I think I'm black and blue, emotionally."

He gripped her hand. "You've grown in ways I will never understand, and I respect you. No, don't look at me like that—I do not, *do not*, think less of you because of any decisions you made. I should have been there during the hard times like I was during the times we were so brazen about 'what we're doing is our business, no one will get hurt.' I ache inside to realize how many people have been brutally affected by our actions, especially you."

"I've always wished you knew or—since coming to Prairie Rose—that I could just come clean and tell you, but after burying something so deep for so long, the effort required to dig it up has been more than I could handle. It's like all those cliches rolled into one: No use crying over spilt milk, water under the bridge, and Humpty-Dumpty."

"I'd like to be one of 'all the king's men' who tries to put you back together again," Alex said softly. "After all, I've been waiting all these years for you, and finally believed in God again when I saw the answer to my countless prayers standing in the pulpit last September."

Like thunder in her ears, she heard his words from that Sunday at his house: *Sometime I'll tell you about my personal decision. I made it over ten years ago and reaffirmed it sitting in the pew at Prairie Rose Community Church this past Sunday morning.* Stunned, she whispered, "You mean I'm the only one you've…?"

"I considered that the most important promise of my life: to be faithful to you, even if you never knew I was. When I lost you, I started praying—but as time went by and we didn't get back together again, my conversations with God were usually quite enraged on my part, and silent on His."

'But surely in college or med school you had girlfriends."

"I dated several times, but it wasn't a huge success—it's amazing how few women are interested in hearing how wonderful another woman—especially one from high school—is! As far as going beyond movies and dinner, nope. I could usually tell they were aiming for much more than I wanted to give. So I buried my nose in my books, got a terrific grade-point average, developed a reputation—according to my roommates—as being snooty, and decided that if God wasn't going to answer my prayers, I would still honor my memory of you by keeping my vow to you."

"That is so unbelievable. There must be frustrated women from coast-to-coast calling you unimaginable names."

He shrugged. "It really wasn't hard—you made such an impression on me that no one could come close to tempting me. I must say, it's good to have you back in my day-to-day life. And now I have an addendum to that earlier promise: I will never leave you in the lurch again." His smile was lop-sided as he added, "You're still the only one for me, Tori. Ready to go home?"

All the way back to Prairie Rose they held hands like two drowning sailors with just one life-jacket between them and a churning sea.

* * *

Victoria called her parents one evening and Mort answered the phone. "Your mother will be upset that she missed talking to you, but she's over at the library helping prepare for the Friends of the Library book sale. But I'm glad to get a chance to talk with my favorite daughter all by myself!"

"Well your favorite one-and-only daughter is mighty glad, too."

"So how's Cino doing?"

"Fine, as always. Of course, he wouldn't be upset if he and I lived in our car. With Prairie Rose being so walkable, he doesn't get nearly as many rides as he thinks he deserves!"

"And how's Alex?"

Victoria swallowed a lump the size of Rhode Island and leaned back against her chair. "Fine." *Ask him, Victoria. This is your big chance.* "Dad, can I ask you something?"

"Sure, Kiddo. What's on your mind?"

"Quite a bit, actually."

"Sounds serious."

"It's about Alex…and me."

"Ah."

"How is it that you and Mom have been able to swing from one side of the wall to the other where Alex is concerned? I mean, when I was in high school you did everything within your power to separate the two of us. Quite successfully. But now, when Alex and I end up unwittingly in the same small town in a remote corner of North Dakota, the two of you act like this is just wonderful. What made you change your mind so drastically?"

Mort paused a moment. "Back then, we had distinct responsibilities to guide you along the path of life. We knew you were involved in some things that weren't part of how we had raised you—which alarmed us. It made us sit up and take notice as to just how powerful peer pressure is. You and Zan were besotted with each other, Kiddo—and it led to pretty serious consequences. While we weren't able to prevent some things, we had an obligation as your parents to continue to try to help you see how the future would be if you continued down the path you were on. That responsibility lasted as long as you were under our roof."

It was Victoria's turn to be silent. "And now?"

"It is different parenting. Like this phone call, adult-to-adult, with a relationship that makes honesty a requisite. Now, you and Zan—Alex—are adults. We never doubted that the two of you loved each other back in high school. If we had believed it was just infatuation, we wouldn't have had to take such drastic steps. And the first time your mother and I saw you together in Prairie Rose, we had no doubt that that love still existed."

"But it didn't worry you," Victoria said, not as a question but as a statement.

"Nope. You're both single. You've both made excellent career choices and are enjoying the successes of those decisions, and obviously you love each other—though it is equally obvious that you, Victoria, are holding back for some reason. But if you and Alex were to get together again, you would certainly have our blessing."

"This is such an incredible conversation, Dad. You never cease to amaze me. What's your secret for making the leap over the wall with such dignity?"

Mort chuckled. "Well, I read a quote from Shimon Peres—remember him? He's the fellow who won the 1994 Nobel Peace Prize—the quote was something along the lines of how if something has a solution, it can be considered a problem and you should work to solve it. That was how we needed to view you and Zan. However, Peres says, if a situation arises which doesn't have a solution, then you should view it as a fact. You don't solve facts, you either cope with them or accept them and go on with your life."

"And that's how you see Alex and me now."

"Right. When we were the parents of high-school Victoria, we had to solve a problem. Now as parents of adult Victoria, we look at the facts and accept them. Happily, I might add."

"You could win a prize yourself, Dad, in parenting."

"Well, your mother's no slouch herself."

"I'll nominate you both!"

"So, how's Alex?" Mort asked casually. "I don't believe I got an answer the first time I asked."

"He's fine, Dad. He's really mighty fine."

"I thought so."

"I've just got some deciding to do—what's a problem, and what's a fact."

"Ahh, I see ol' Peres has got another Dahlmann thinking. That's what I like about those Nobel Prize winners—they are dandy folks."

Victoria hung up smiling and opened up her laptop. Just a few minutes surfing the Internet produced the very Peres quotation Mort had paraphrased so well. She unfolded her Pros and Cons list and bracketed

Con #3 *[Too much negative history. We'd always have our past hanging over our heads—especially with our families]* and added *Think about Dad and Shimon Peres—when you can't solve it, accept it!*

She whistled for Cino. "Let's go for a walk, Big Boy. I've got plenty to mull over after that phone call."

The agenda for the town council appeared in the *Prairie Rose Chronicle* and sparked interest like no previous meeting had ever generated. Four speakers were scheduled, covering four aspects of the Meadowlark Trail.

Luke was slated to present items still needed, including rest area equipment, safety features and sanitation facilities. Alex's presentation would cover services to be offered to walkers—both recreational and medical, if needed. Victoria's area would touch on staffing needs at the Trail Center, and additional entertainment to provide for their visitors, highlighting the historical project Rachel had nearly completed. The Mayor would address publicity, opening ceremonies, project evaluation, and future plans.

Hearing the talk around town, Milt Browning knew that a larger space than the town hall would be needed to accommodate the crowd. Signs appeared announcing an unprecedented change in location for the meeting that was traditionally poorly attended. The hour arrived; the high school gymnasium churned with excitement as friends and neighbors called greetings to each other.

The lively conversations on every side could almost make Victoria forget that these were the people who believed a lie about her. She watched the bleachers fill and waved across the room to Casey Donovan who viewed the crowd with amazement. He took a deep breath and plunged into the fray until he reached her side and queried, "*This* is a town meeting?"

Resolutely, she banished all dismal thoughts with a toss of her head. When Casey turned to talk with one of his parishioners, she leaned over and asked Milt who had joined them, "Who's running the refreshment stand tonight?"

He chuckled, "High school kids. They've learned—and I'd be willing to bet on who their teacher was—that no opportunity to earn money for the Meadowlark Trail fund should ever go unexploited!"

She nodded with approval at all the popcorn boxes and soft drinks visible everywhere from the platform. "Good for them!"

After the scheduled talks were given, lines formed around the designated tables as the citizens surged forward to sign up for landscaping crews, the remaining building projects, and other tasks that welcomed volunteers.

Milt had announced that golf course and tennis court plans which had been tabled by the city council several years ago would be reconsidered if enough interest was generated. Victoria moved to Milt's side and pointed at one long line, "Looks like the golf course is back in business! When you were speaking, I got an idea for the opening day of the golf course that I'd like to talk over with you. I know a pro golfer I just may be able to persuade to come our way for the event."

"Is there no end to the ideas you can come up with?" Sparkling eyes robbed his dramatic sigh of its punch. "Okay, come by tomorrow and bend my ear." *Almost like old times.* Victoria squeezed her eyes closed in a quick and silent prayer of gratitude.

Conversations around tables at Cate's Café changed overnight. So many rough sketches of corner flower patches, bush arrangements, and rock gardens used up the napkin supply that Cate, grumbling good-naturedly, kept each table supplied with a scratch pad and pencils tucked in-between the condiments and napkin holders.

The Meadowlark Trail account at the bank, fed by everything from Cate's successful Anti-Swearing Fund to kids' pilfered piggy banks to the pancake breakfast, now showed a hefty balance. "Enough for shrubs, flowers, paint, materials needed to complete safety projects, and funds for newspaper ads in several surrounding communities," Victoria crowed to Luke one day when he weighed out a pound of hamburger for her. The spontaneous smile he returned made her heart soar.

Encouraged by the renewed enthusiasm evident in Prairie Rose, Victoria presented an idea at the monthly church leaders' meeting that seemed destined for success. "During the children's Sunday School activities, I'd like to offer the adults something to challenge them to explore new ideas. In my planning notes, I've referred to it as Adult Forum. I see it developing into discussions, lectures, panels, or small groups that would cover a variety of topics."

Wilbert, holding true to form, asked cautiously, "What topics did you have in mind?"

"Understand that I'm just tossing out ideas here, but things like parenting or marriage, ethics in daily living, aging gracefully, money management, health topics—we could plan a month's worth of topics, and then poll those who have attended for their interests for future seminars. I think it would be a way to help people learn how to apply what they hear on Sunday mornings to their everyday lives."

The group discussed the idea at length and finally nominated Luke to work with Victoria to plan and advertise four Adult Forum programs. Balancing Wilbert's expected resistance to any changes, their general willingness to try new ideas encouraged Victoria and fueled her commitment to continue doing her best as their pastor.

Luke and Victoria began planning the Forums the next morning over coffee at Cate's, and looked at each other with surprise when each pulled out a small notebook labeled "Adult Forums." "We're two of a kind, Victoria," Luke laughed, "I guess that's why the earth shakes when we get our heads together over a project."

"If Adult Forums take off like the Meadowlark Trail did, Prairie Rose may chain us at opposite ends of Main Street to prevent any further collaboration!"

The ideas flowed as freely as the coffee. Within half an hour, they had expanded the list of possible ideas and potential speakers to six. They divided up the responsibilities and left the café proud of the hour's work. "Have notebook—will plan, right, Victoria?"

"Hey, Luke, what will we do if all six of our possibilities say 'yes'?" Victoria asked as they made their way down Main Street.

"Personally, I'll cheer. It will just mean that we've planned more than anyone thought we could."

"Just so they don't think we're overstepping the guidelines they gave us," Victoria said with a frown. With things going so well again, she hated to stir up trouble.

"Fret not! Four wasn't a limit; they meant it as a goal they were sure we would never achieve." With that, he disappeared into his store adding a parting shot, "Last one to get their speakers lined up cooks dinner!"

Victoria tucked her notebook away; her sermon preparation came first. As much as she enjoyed the discipline of studying and sermon preparation, it was a lot like writing a term paper and presenting it orally each week—without knowing the grade for the last one—and knowing the whole time that another one was due in seven days.

In rubbing shoulders with her congregation on a daily basis, Victoria learned what their struggles were, how they wrestled with faith and doubt. The more she realized this, the more she enjoyed all levels of participation in their lives—socially, emotionally, and spiritually. The dearth of involvement now with so many pulling back both saddened and worried her. She cherished each positive encounter more than ever before.

As she faced her notes for the upcoming sermon now, she realized that the past weeks had given her personal insight into human nature and foibles that, if used correctly, could improve her sermons. She halted her studies and prayed that God would remind her of all she had learned whenever she started to forget.

* * *

One weekend when spring was temptingly close, Rachel issued a dinner invitation that pulled Victoria, Alex, Luke and Cate together for the first time in weeks around her dining room table. Casey Donovan had arrived earlier and met them at the door with a booming welcome and a crisp frilly apron tied around his waist that he wore without embarrassment.

When twelve hands linked in a circle around the table, tears fogged Victoria's eyes; Casey's simple words expressed her feelings so well: "With the blessings of food, loving friends, and work to do, we feel rich and offer You our heartfelt thanks. Amen."

The baked lemon-chicken was perfection on a platter, but the friendship satisfied Victoria's inner hunger even more. She let the kind words and smiles renew her battle-worn spirit. While they digested a two-berry meringue torte, they pushed back their chairs and enjoyed refilled coffee cups and flowing conversation. Rachel wisely didn't interrupt them just to insist they move into the living room. The night was young, the mood too precious to disrupt.

"My parents are planning to come up for the Meadowlark Trail opening ceremonies," Alex announced, "and if my Grandfather's health stays steady, they plan to bring him, too. He's been eager to come back to Prairie Rose ever since I started my practice, but he didn't want to come too soon."

Cate and Luke broke into excited responses; Victoria caught a special look flitting between Rachel and Casey and sensed the powerful feelings that Alex's news had released in the older woman's heart.

Rachel's happy reply gave no clues, "Splendid! I'm delighted Alexander will be back in Prairie Rose. I'll keep my fingers crossed that things will go well."

Talk moved to other things; Victoria saw Rachel delicately wipe invisible crumbs from her lips and noticed the napkin slip a little higher to pat away a wetness around her eyes.

"What's this Adult Forum that was advertised in the *Chronicle* going to be like, Victoria? I need to know because once this begins, I'm sure to be bombarded with requests for the Catholic equivalent!" Casey said.

"You'll have to ask Luke about this week's since he's planned the first one." Victoria responded, noting a wistful smile that remained on Rachel's face as the conversation shifted.

"Oooh! The pressure's on!" Cate said, jiggling Luke's elbow. "Can you produce, Luke?"

Luke tossed his head and blew out a derisive puff of air, "Pffft! You'll all stand in awe after the booming success of the first one. Actually, the pressure's not on me at all. It's all on Alex, our first speaker!"

Rachel laughed, "Wise choice, Luke, with Alex's growing fame as a public speaker over the past few months. What's the topic for this crucial first week, Alex?"

"People are probably expecting me to jump on my soapbox and spout off about kids and farm-related injuries, but I'll refrain. Luke offered to gather questions on the topic 'When private health concerns become public crises' so I'll just wait and see what I draw."

Rachel's nod was one of thoughtful approval. "I can see the possibilities: AIDS, diseases related to drug abuse or mistreatment of children, conditions that come from our lack of self-control. It sounds very interesting!" Conversation bubbled, and Rachel eventually urged her guests to find more comfortable seats.

Luke suggested a game of Dictionary. Casey chose the first word, *Karst*. Alex received no votes for his made-up definition of "a rhinoceros." As if in defiance of such blatant snubbing, for the next three words there was always one slip of paper with the definition "a rhinoceros" repeated, despite how remote the possibility seemed.

When the proposed definitions were read for the fifth word and "a rhinoceros" showed up again, pencils and wadded up papers flew across the room, all aimed at Alex. "Hey, the law of averages ought to come into play here pretty soon! There has to be some word out there that means 'a rhinoceros'! And when that word shows up, I'll be right!" Alex protested.

At last it was his turn to pick a word. "Keitloa. A noun. K-e-i-t-l-o-a."

Chewing pencils thoughtfully, the others manufactured noun-sounding, dictionary-type definitions. Erasing several attempts, Cate said, "I almost feel obligated to use 'rhinoceros' for my definition since we've gotten so used to hearing it as one choice!" She glared sternly at Alex and promptly joined in the laughter.

Alex collected all the papers, read through them silently, and then aloud. "Keitloa. A limestone region." He scanned the room. No votes.

"Keitloa," he continued. "Closely woven cloth from Africa." No votes.

"Keitloa. A game involving chance." A few studious frowns, but no votes.

"Keitloa. A large ancient sailing vessel." Casey's hand signaled his vote. Alex nodded and marked the record.

He resumed, "Keitloa. Edible seed from the sunflower family." No votes.

"I hold in my hand the final sheet, folks." His eyes moved from person to person. "Keitloa. A rhinoceros."

"Alex!" Victoria practically yelped. "Or do we yell at Cate?"

"Hey! I was kidding," Cate protested. "That's not from me!"

"Punch Alex for me, Victoria, you're closest!" This came from sweet gentle Rachel.

Alex threw back his head and laughed all the louder as the barrage of voices attacked him. "Since five of you didn't vote for any definition, one through five, am I to assume that you all chose number six, the infamous 'a rhinoceros'?"

"No way, Alex. Read 'em again. I'll choose seeds or sailing vessels before that," Victoria said defiantly.

Solemnly, Alex reread the definitions; everyone voted, mumbling the whole time. He returned each sheet. "Congratulations, Luke, you got two votes with your 'closely woven cloth.' Rachel, I believe this is Casey's handwriting—he liked your 'ancient sailing vessel.' Sorry, Cate, no one bit on your 'edible seed,' but good job. Tori, you got a vote for 'a game involving chance,' and Casey, one vote for your 'limestone region.'"

He returned to his seat and beamed smugly around the room. It took a few seconds before the realization hit that no votes had been correct.

"You mean Keitloa *is* a rhinoceros?" Luke asked incredulously.

"You've got to be kidding!" Rachel chortled.

"Kick him, Victoria," Casey boomed, "you're still closest!"

Cate rose from her chair. "I demand to see the dictionary!"

Alex did a victory dance around the room, whooping wildly while pencils and wads of paper pelted him. "I did it! I suckered all of you! Let's hear you chant your new vocabulary word, class!"

Rachel said, "Alex, you're just like your grandfather. I should have caught on when 'rhinoceros' showed up in the list you read! I must admit, I assumed Cate had used it." The harsh ring of the telephone in the kitchen interrupted their chatter. Cate was sitting closest and sprang up to answer it.

She returned to the living room with a puzzled look and said, "It's for you, Luke. Beats me how he found you here, but I think it's Wilbert Windsor from your church."

The living room grew quiet; Luke's voice wafted in from the kitchen. "Yes?" The leftover smiles faded on five faces when Luke's voice sharpened without warning, "This has gone far enough. I won't be party to anything like this. Listen, Wilbert, you're being impossible."

Those in the living room stared at each other with an unnamed fear. Luke continued harshly, "This is not right. You know it, everyone knows it. There is a proper way to handle things and this isn't it."

Everyone in the living room jumped as if the unseen telephone receiver had slammed in their ears, not Wilbert's. Casey shot a look at Rachel and went out to join Luke. Their voices were a low rumble.

The four remaining resembled a still life painting of children playing statue. Abruptly, Cate jumped to her feet and attacked the wads of paper around Alex's chair, collecting all the pencils and slamming the dictionary back on the shelf.

"Thank you, Cate," Rachel said.

The looks the others gave their hostess held as much surprise as if she had burst into an operatic aria. So focused had they been on the hum of voices in the next room that ordinary conversation seemed as startling as Gabriel's trumpet.

"Forgive me, Rachel," Luke said from the doorway. He held his coat. "I've disrupted the evening. I must leave." But he didn't move.

Rachel's voice was soothing, "You need not apologize." Luke moved to the guest closet by the front door and then returned like a zombie to his empty chair. He rolled his coat into a ball on his lap.

Victoria plunged into deep conversational waters, "Is there any way we can help, Luke? There are about as many friends in this room as you're likely to find anywhere."

Startled, Luke looked at her. Victoria caught his quick look at Casey, and Casey's slight nod in return. Luke moistened his lips. Once. Again. His chest filled with air and deflated. For a man whose posture usually could win awards, his shoulders now sagged, his head hung down disconsolately.

"The church leaders met tonight, without me since they felt I would hardly be impartial," he choked on his next words, "to ask for your resignation, Victoria. They want me to show up now so I can make an official announcement tomorrow." Something snapped inside him. "Oh, I'll show up all right!"

Suddenly, Victoria knew. She gripped the arms of her chair. "Does this relate to my alleged abortion?"

Luke nodded and lifted grief-ravaged eyes to meet hers.

"Damn," Cate said.

Alex asked softly, "What will you do, Luke?"

Luke raised his head and looked his friend squarely in the eye. His voice rang out clearly, "Fight. Every step of the way."

"Is it a closed meeting?" Alex asked.

"Beats me. I've been playing dictionary while Rome burns."

It was the first time Victoria had ever heard sarcasm from Luke's lips. She swallowed hard. "Where is the meeting?"

"Wilbert's." His knuckles whitened as he clenched a fistful of his forgotten coat. "On his own," Luke's tone sharpened, "Wilbert has already contacted the Indian Hills families and told them that there will be only one service this week, here in Prairie Rose. That way, all can hear the damning sentence at once."

Rachel looked at Cate's bowed head and said sadly, "Somehow I had hoped such vindictive behavior had run its course years ago."

Luke suddenly stood and shook out his coat. "I'd rather face hungry lions like Daniel did, but God only knows what those blinking idiots will do if I don't get there to reclaim my position as Chair from Wilbert. Victoria, like you said about this room, remember, you have lots of friends in Prairie Rose."

"The best of whom are sitting right here tonight." Victoria expelled built-up tension with one breath. "I know, Luke. Thanks, Rachel, for bringing us together tonight." She brushed her friend's cheek with a kiss.

When she stood straight again, she backed into a human wall. Luke, Cate and Alex circled her with their arms. The foursome swayed, locked together like an impenetrable fortress, until Victoria puckered her lips and aimed a playful kiss at each person.

"Don't leave me out of this kissing stuff!" protested Casey.

Victoria sprung free from the circle and threw her arms around her colleague. "This could start a doozy of a rumor, huh?" she asked between planting loud smacks on each ruddy cheek. "Next week's headlines will read: 'Local clergy linked in bizarre kissing ritual. Town shocked.' That's a good story for the *Chronicle*, huh?" They all laughed a bit too heartily to be convincing.

Alex slung a bracing arm around Luke's shoulders. "I'll walk Victoria home. If you need us, we be at her place. Just call. In fact, call anyway once you get home."

"And I'll see our Cate home, Luke," Casey called out.

Luke nodded grimly and disappeared into the night.

Beside the Rectory's porch steps, Victoria turned to Alex. "I'll be fine, you know. You don't have to stay."

"And if I can't think of a single place I'd rather be?"

Their eyes locked and held. With a feathery touch, Victoria traced Alex's eyebrows, the ridges of his cheek, his decisive chin. He sucked in his breath like a man tormented. "Thanks, Zan," she whispered. Their lips met in a kiss that mined passion from their depths, piercing a dark cavern with light like a torch.

Her voice quavered, "No matter how this mess turns out, Alex, these past seven months have been the best of my life. You said once that you saw that I'm doing what I was meant to do. I believe that with all my heart. If they ask me to leave, I'll just open shop somewhere down the road. Sadder, but wiser, like the old song says."

Those eyes that rivaled the stars for their untold mysteries glistened with unshed tears. "Please, God, don't let that happen."

Conversation was a low priority. They alternately paced the living room and sought comfort in each other's arms. The phone rang. They stared at it and then looked back at each other. A second ring stabbed the silence. Victoria slowly reached across the arm of the couch and lifted the receiver.

"Victoria? Can you and Alex come to Wilbert's?"

"Of course."

"May I talk to Alex for a minute?"

Silently, she handed the receiver to Alex.

He tucked it under his ear. "Yeah? Oh, right. Sure, no problem. Is it open? Okay. Gotcha. See you in a few minutes. Hang in there." He turned and said tersely, "Ready when you are, Love. Luke wants me to stop by his place and pick up something. Can we take your car to save time?"

At Luke's house; Alex ran up the steps and returned quickly with a bag and no explanations. Within minutes, Luke was opening Wilbert's front door and escorting them into the living room where the church leaders waited. Tension permeated the room like a cheap perfume.

Victoria chose a side seat opposite Luke and refused an offer of coffee or tea from Wilbert's wife, Mildred, who fluttered nervously around the latest arrivals. Luke addressed them with unsmiling formality, "When I got here, I reminded this group of the special rules for meetings— adopted several years ago, thank God—which say all members must be informed of every meeting, whether they can attend or not."

Except for Wilbert, who stared sullenly at Luke, the other leaders shifted uncomfortably in their seats. "Victoria, you and I were not informed of the meeting, so any business conducted prior to our coming is invalid. Wilbert will speak first, now that all are here." He nodded curtly in the man's direction.

Wilbert pulled a paper from an envelope in his notebook and dramatically unfolded it. After searching for his glasses in an inside jacket pocket, he anchored them in place with nerve-wracking precision and coughed dryly before he read, "On behalf of many of our members, I seek the resignation of the Reverend Victoria Dahlmann."

"On what grounds?" Luke prompted.

Wilbert frowned. Obviously, he had planned to drop the bombshell, nothing more. "Uh, on the basis of whatchacallit—conduct unbecoming a minister."

Cal Westhaver, with all the presence that had carried him through forty years of teaching, dropped his foot to the floor with window-rattling force. "I sat quietly when you spread filth pretty deep and thick the first time around, Wilbert, partly because I couldn't believe my ears, but if I don't hear some solid evidence to substantiate this inflammatory charge, I will move to adjourn this meeting. *Evidence,*" he clapped his hands and everyone jumped as if shot, "that our pastor has conducted herself in an unseemly manner or, by God, let's beg her forgiveness and let this town and our churches get back to normal."

Luke spoke in a voice that was eerily calm, "Thank you, Cal. The floor is open for a response." His eye swept around the room. "Wilbert, I hear no one, so it's up to you to answer Cal."

Now Wilbert shuffled nervously. "Well, there's the matter about her, uh, absence from town a few weeks ago. She was gone for almost several days, and without explanation to any of us."

Luke silenced Wilbert's ramblings with a steel-cold voice, "I don't recall that our pastors, past or present, have ever had restrictions on how they spend their vacation time, nor are they required to inform us where they go."

"No, no, I didn't mean that."

"Since you're having trouble wording your complaint, Wilbert, let me expedite things. Isn't the reason this meeting was called because of an ugly rumor that Victoria Dahlmann had an abortion during her absence from Prairie Rose?"

"That's the truth," Wilbert mumbled.

"I believe you mean: that's the rumor." Luke's unreadable gaze now turned on the others in the room. "The floor is open to anyone who can substantiate this claim."

Silence.

"These are serious charges. If you know them to be true, you must speak now or we will entertain Cal Westhaver's motion for adjournment and two things will happen. One, there will not be a second meeting tomorrow, and two, Reverend Victoria Dahlmann will continue as our pastor with full restoration of our united support. Do I make myself clear? *United support.* From now on. If there comes a time we cannot offer that support, we will meet with Victoria in the proper manner and deal with it."

Silence.

"Is someone ready to speak?"

Wilbert ran his hands across his thinning hair and chewed on a toothpick he pulled from his pocket in lieu of his usual cigar. "All I know is the Reverend is a bad example to our young people." For the first time, he met Victoria's eyes with an almost palpable animosity.

"All right, I'll speak," Victoria was not the only one stunned to hear Sadie O'Dell speak from the living room door; behind her, Mildred wrung her hands helplessly. "I called Wilbert when I had some concerns about the Rev'rend's morals and I've been waiting in the kitchen tonight to be sure action is taken."

The room reeled like an amusement park ride around a nauseous Victoria.

Widow O'Dell's voice sounded above the hubbub her presence and announcement had created. "We're a small town, kind of backwards compared to the *Big Cities*," her voice rising in emphasis of key points, "our *Pastor* here is used to, but we have *Morals* and *Standards* for clergy. When a *Single* woman—a *Minister*, mind you—spends too much time *Alone* with *Men*, and then gains so much *Weight* that I needed to *Alter Patterns* for her, and when she *Loses* that weight after a *Mysterious* trip out of town, I see *Red*."

Victoria choked. *So do I. I see the red Valentine's dress that made me feel like a woman again when nothing else could.* She fought against tears, determined not to let this misguided woman get the top hand.

Luke regained control of the meeting in the only way he could: by pounding his fist on an end table and bellowing, "Silence!" Startled, all complied. "I would like to call on the one person everyone seems to have forgotten in this whole discussion. Victoria?"

No! Please, Luke, don't make me do this. She met Luke's eyes and soaked up the strength and courage she needed from his steady gaze.

Luke's voice grew gentle, "Victoria, I have just one question."

A pen dropped from someone's hand and echoed like a cannon in a valley. "No, I'll answer without you needing to ask. I was not pregnant when I left town, therefore I did not have an abortion." Her voice was low, but the words carried throughout the room.

"Thank you. Does anyone hold verifiable information to the contrary?" He looked around the room slowly. "Then we will assume the charges made are without foundation and will accept the statement our pastor has made. Cal, I believe we can entertain your motion for adjournment at this time."

Victoria did not feel the burden lift from her shoulders that should have accompanied freedom from false accusations. In fact, she felt so weighed down that even standing seemed a colossal task. Dazed "ayes" echoed around her, but no one rose to leave.

"Luke?" Alex nudged everyone back to the present. "I realize it's irregular to ask permission to speak after adjournment, but may I?"

"Unless anyone objects, you've got the floor."

"Thank you. I'll be brief. Since tomorrow is our first Adult Forum, Luke suggested when he called me and Victoria to come over that perhaps I should give the church leadership a preview of tomorrow's question and answer session. Luke has already collected specific questions on the general topic," he opened the bag he had carried out of Luke's house as he spoke, "'When private health concerns become public crises.' I'll select one of those questions tonight to give you all an idea of how it will work."

Appearing oblivious to the justifiably confused faces around him, he pulled a fishbowl stuffed with folded papers out of the bag and shook it dramatically before selecting one slip. He scanned the question with maddening thoroughness before he nodded and commented, almost as if to himself, "Hmmm, I guess my column in the *Chronicle* got someone thinking." Shifting slightly in his chair, he read aloud from the slip of paper he held, "How does a Christian respond to medical advances that are steadily conquering diseases, such as endometriosis, which have historically kept population growth in check?"

The room spun around Victoria. Her brain locked in on the one word, endometriosis, and ceased to function. *Who…? How…? What…? As if the newspaper column weren't enough, now this?*

Alex was unruffled. "I may be reading between the lines, but I think this question addresses a valid concern for us in a world that sees problems like overcrowding and hunger, to name two, in the news almost every day. In some respects, diseases like endometriosis are physical—as opposed to drug-induced—forms of birth control that…"

An Indian Hills representative broke in, "Doc, it's getting late and I don't even know what this endo-something-or-other is. I hope this Adult Forum idea is going to be more understandable and practical than that."

Alex was unflappable. "Good point. I'll need to remember to clarify my terms and show how things tie together tomorrow. For those who may not have read the column or who may not recall, endometriosis is…" He smoothly reviewed the brief expansion on the classic textbook definition he had given in the newspaper column as all listened in bewildered silence.

But the point that snapped Victoria back to attention followed quickly: "If we balance one fact—that being that these intelligent, contributing women often postpone marriage and then may find they can no longer conceive—against the world problems that accompany population explosion, we see the dilemma and we see the point at which our discussion tomorrow can get interesting. If such women *were* able to conceive, their gene pools indicate their children would likely be marvelous additions to society: possibly the thinkers and doers who could solve the very world problems our question addressed."

I'm going to faint in a heap on the floor. She looked up, drawn to meet Luke's gray eyes. *This is his question. The meat locker. Of all I rattled on about, how is it possible he remembered 'endometriosis'?*

Wilbert harrumphed loudly, interrupting Alex. "Look Doc, I'm sure this Forum thing will work out just fine, but it beats me why we have to sit around here tonight listening to all this female stuff when what's on everyone's mind is how our pastor destroyed our trust."

Alex wadded up the paper and jammed it in his pocket.

Victoria could stand it no longer. "Wilbert, I'm a very private person. If it weren't for the newspaper column and what Alex has told you tonight, I doubt if anyone in Prairie Rose would have ever heard of endometriosis. Not many of the millions of women who live with the disease will talk about it. It's too painful, too personal. I know. I'm part of the statistics."

As her words sunk in, responses varied. Sadie O'Dell said in a strangled voice, "You mean, there's no way you could have been pregnant? You've got this, this disease-thing?"

Victoria met her troubled gaze with steady eyes and nodded. "At this point in my life and with all my symptoms, it is unlikely I will ever get pregnant. Which means I did not leave town to have an abortion."

Wilbert swallowed hard, "Uh, Pastor, I...uh, we...had no idea."

One of the woman who had been silent, now interrupted, "And we lacked proof. Every woman's weight fluctuates sometimes. We turned this very private matter into a public lynching—and for our pastor. I feel sick about this whole mess."

Only Wilbert's wheezing broke the stillness. From the couch, a pleading voice asked, "Can you forgive us?"

Victoria nodded slowly. "On a personal level, it hurts a lot to have been suspected and condemned without a chance to answer my accusers; I ask for your prayers as I work through this. On a professional level, I'm glad my congregation is willing to back up their beliefs. We can work together to rebuild the bridges."

Wilbert stammered, "Luke, uh, we, uh, owe you an apology, too. I'll tell it plain: we were all set to kick you out of church leadership."

Luke's face was an unreadable mask. "I'm not as quick to forgive as Victoria, but I'll admit, I'm a lot happier going out of this meeting than I was coming in. It's late; we need to get to our homes now. I'll make an announcement in church to set things straight. I'll excuse our guests, but I would like the church leadership to stay a few minutes to get that announcement into the Minutes."

"If you need any help, call on Doctor Alex" suggested Cal gruffly. "He's pretty good at clearing things up, even though I didn't know why he insisted on pulling out that fishbowl." The unofficial meeting ended with strained smiles and awkward handshakes all-around.

Victoria dropped Alex off and made a U-turn that took her home to the waiting Cino. As she got out of the car, she spotted the fishbowl bag on the backseat floor and took it into the house to ensure that it would make it over to church with her in the morning.

She ran a tub of water, liberally poured in bath oil, and anchored her hair in a heap on top of her head. Exhausted, she lowered herself into the tub and willed each tense muscle to relax. She felt like a battle-worn soldier and found it difficult to unwind. Suddenly, she jerked up, grabbed a towel, and skidded wetly with Cino at her heels all the way to the kitchen counter where she had tossed the fishbowl bag.

Shivering, she dug down into the folded sheets and chose one randomly. Slowly, she smoothed it open in the palm of her hand and read it. Tossing it on the counter, she quickly chose another, and another, reading them all while a puddle of bath water formed at her feet. She dumped out the remaining papers, lining them up. Twenty-three creased papers, all in Luke's handwriting, all saying, *Make up some question about endometriosis and answer it.*

CHAPTER TWELVE

Looking out over her combined congregations gathered under the stately arches of the Prairie Rose Community Church, Victoria wondered idly just how far down the street the overflow from the parking lot had spilled. The place was packed. She had told Luke she wanted his announcement to be made at the end of the service; she always hated to interrupt the flow of the service, but felt it was especially important today.

Everything was in place. Pulpit Bible open, notes ready for today's message. From a procedural standpoint, it was all systems ready-set-go; from her emotional precipice, it was like trying to swim in tapioca pudding. The years of training, the hours of preparation, the innate understanding of how clergy conduct services of worship all failed miserably this morning.

I have nothing to say. I'm drained.

She moistened her lips and slowly surveyed the crowd, wondering just how one proceeded to end a service without a sermon. There was only one empty corner in the church today—back where Casey had sat that long-ago night when the darkness had offered him a place to pray and her a place to cry.

She could almost hear his voice saying *Thanks, Victoria, I needed that...* The answer to her current dilemma came from the empty seat; she knew what to do.

"We all came expecting a sermon today. While hopefully that will still happen, the message may come to each of us in a different way. I ask your indulgence as I change *how* you may have expected to hear from God." With quiet dignity, she walked from the pulpit to the gleaming grand piano.

Sending an inaudible prayer heavenward, she let her hands seek out their place on the familiar keyboard; one crystal note sounded and took its place in a chord; the timeless wonders of music moved across the sanctuary with the haunting, calming, penetrating power that simple, blended notes possess.

She began with the well-known hymns of the church, not wanting anyone sitting in the sanctuary to miss a chance to worship God in this unusual way, knowing that familiar words flowing through the minds and hearts of her congregation—even with hymnbooks closed—would lift their spirits as they did hers.

It was an eclectic mix of music—few worship services include "Swing Low, Sweet Chariot" tucked between "The Battle Hymn of the Republic," and "Amazing Grace" followed by the contemporary "Bless the Lord, Oh My Soul," but Victoria was playing from her heart and this was the repertoire she found in its depths.

Fifteen minutes later, the echoes of an anthem's resonating bass-roll rose upward as it had in cathedrals and open-air services around the world throughout the centuries. Victoria let her hands slip off the ivories. A slight movement on the pew next to the piano caught her eye.

There—a giant pink bow perched precariously atop her curls—sat Jillie, eyes wide-open and feet swinging. The child had probably not known a word of any of the hymns or recognized a single melody, but she had been part of the crowd on this day—a small, but significant part.

Oh, Jillie. You're growing up in a world that isn't always going to make sense, or be kind, or work out all right. How will you make it, how do any of us make it, if we don't see the world from God's perspective?

She met the young girl's unfaltering gaze and smiled. She sent the opening chords of a tender, familiar song on their way to the child's heart. Jillie's eyes brightened in recognition and slid off the pew to come closer to her trusted friend, River-ant Victoria.

Victoria began the song again, humming softly as she nodded encouragingly. Jillie's innocent voice picked up the melody and wrapped itself around Victoria's heart. *Jesus loves me, this I know.* Like a lone bird in a sun-streaked sky, the child's voice lifted the simple Sunday School song with its words of confidence-in-a-world-gone-awry sending them out to every heart. *Yes, Jesus loves me!*

When the last note faded, Victoria took Jillie's hand and they moved past crowded pews to the back of the sanctuary. Victoria raised her hand in benediction: *Go in peace, confident that His love surrounds us* rang out in evidence that her own heart had received a message from God today.

No one moved; the organist didn't begin the postlude, the people didn't rise from their seats. Seeing this, and realizing that Luke was among those still seated, Victoria retraced her steps along the center aisle and turned to face the congregation. "At this time, Luke Larson has asked to make an announcement."

Luke covered the distance between them in confident strides. "The first Adult Forum will begin in fifteen minutes, but first I wish to inform you of a decision made at the leadership meeting held last evening. I am reading from the secretary's official Minutes, 'We announce that, effective immediately, Reverend Victoria Dahlmann will be given a ten-percent raise in appreciation for her fine work among us, both in the church and the community. It is hoped that this will demonstrate the congregation's sincere desire for her to continue among us for many years to come.'"

A young voice jolted everyone. "I'm glad 'cuz' I really like the way Pastor Dahlmann always lets us kids eat all her popcorn and stuff. Now she won't go broke."

It was as if a dam had broken, releasing a flood. Weak-kneed, Victoria dropped to the front pew as adulation bombarded her from every direction.

"I sure am glad she came to town and got us all feeling like Prairie Rose is some place special again," was followed by "Pastor Victoria always makes me feel like anything I can do counts" and "She started Mom's Morning Out and I feel like being a Mom isn't a life sentence, anymore" came on the heels of "Her sermons make sense and she's got me reading the Bible again" which was followed by "I like the way she makes church interesting for us young couples who wouldn't always find time for church before she came here."

In the midst of the hubbub, a pocket of silence opened up and a child's voice said wistfully, "I just wish I had pretty hair like Rev'rend Victoria." Without missing a beat, a man's bass voice responded plaintively, "I just wish I had hair."

Luke joined in the spontaneous laughter and then, suddenly solemn, turned to Victoria. "Victoria, your people have spoken. Please forgive us for the grief we have caused you, either by speaking out against you, or by waiting until today to speak out for you. Please know that this raise is not an attempt to cancel the debt we owe you—we just felt it was important to put our treasure where our heart is: we want to invest in you. Over the next few days and weeks, you'll be hearing from a lot of us with personal apologies and sincere regret."

Victoria nodded mutely. As Luke turned back to the congregation for a few closing remarks, she crept away and secreted herself in the office, resting her head against the loveseat cushions.

Soon Alex would be dipping his hand into the fishbowl for the first question in the Fellowship Hall. He had truly shown his capabilities when he created a believable question from Luke's scribblings last night. She knew he'd do equally well fabricating something when he read any one of the new two dozen slips she had substituted for the original twenty-four, all saying, *There are three eligible women in Prairie Rose. Upstairs, one waits for you.*

She listened as the hubbub that accompanied people leaving the sanctuary faded away. Soon, she heard rapid footsteps that came to a halt just outside the office. Alex flung open the door. "Tori, I saw you come here from the sanctuary, and when I read the first question..." He straddled the coffee table and pulled her to her feet. "We can't be alone together in here, or I'll be doing some not-very-churchy things any minute." He flung open the door and pulled her out into the deserted sanctuary.

"What's happening in the Fellowship Hall without you?" she whispered. *Don't leave me, though, no matter what.*

"When I pulled out the first slip of paper, I fabricated something about the role persons with handicaps have in the community, and Rachel—thank God she came today—bless her, she knew something was going on, and came to my rescue. The only thing on my mind was finding you."

"What if it hadn't been me? It could have been Gail or Cate waiting for you, you know. They're eligible."

"I know your handwriting. And God knows who I wanted to be in this room making that kind of promise."

They reached the altar of the church; Alex stopped and lifted his hands to rest lightly on Victoria's shoulders; she covered them with her own. "All I care about is you," she whispered and felt the flutter of love's wings in her heart with the long-denied admission finally freed from its prison.

His eyes were deep pools of surging emotion. "Like a friend?"

She pursed her lips and tipped her head thoughtfully, "Yes."

"Oh."

"I think it's important for a wife to love her husband like a friend, don't you?"

His lips twitched. "Are you proposing to me?"

"That would be superfluous, wouldn't it? Your last proposal to me is still hanging in the air. Noooo, I'm not proposing, or accepting. Let's just say I'm reopening negotiations. Or have you rescinded your proposal to me?"

"Hmmm. It would appear that the Reverend Victoria Dahlmann is flirting with Doctor Alexander Johanson. Or is she rambling, like a certain Tori Dahlmann used to do around Zan Johanson when she was flustered?"

"Well, there always was one sure way to shut off the flow." She puckered her lips seductively.

A disapproving frown grew beneath periwinkle eyes. "Here? Have some dignity! We're in church." Remembering that, he pulled his hands away from her body as if burned.

Victoria grinned and glanced around, taking in the now-empty pews and the lofty beams. "It's okay. God approves of love," she tossed back at him in a stage whisper.

Alex stuck a thumb in a belt loop and rocked back on his heels. Lightly, he traced her lips with one finger. She sucked in her breath like a swimmer seeking the last gulps of air before an overwhelming ocean wave strikes

She felt his lips, once on her forehead, once on her nose, once on each cheek. In ecstatic anticipation, she ran her tongue quickly across her lips.

Seconds passed.

She opened her eyes and met his steady gaze. "The next time I kiss those lips, we'll both know what it means. No doubts, no wondering, no turning back. Negotiations over. We each have issues to deal with." Thoughts raced back and forth on the fragile wire that linked two hearts beating in unison.

She needs to settle the matter of whether she can live in Prairie Rose.
He needs to understand how scared I am of loving—and loving him.
She needs to decide about Luke.

He needs to decide about Gail.

Outside, a car engine revved to life. Laughter rang out in a corridor nearby. Quickly, Alex and Victoria exited through the church's side door, both unwilling to allow intrusions into their new and private world. With a lingering touch, they parted.

Victoria straddled the first chair she found in her kitchen, propped her chin on the back, hooked her feet on the rungs, and stared at the floor. *You took a chance, Victoria, and may have lost. You took the bull by the horns, which is always risky business. There is no guarantee Alex is going to come running back to you just because you write cute little come-ons and stick them in fishbowls. He made it perfectly clear that he has issues, too.*

When the phone rang, her arms had fallen asleep. It rang again, and a third time. Cino looked at her, confused. "I know, I hear it." She moved to halt the annoying buzz, shaking her arms back to life.

It was Cate. "Can you meet me at the Café? I just got an order for more cookies than one person could ever produce. Help! I know it's Sunday and you're probably exhausted, but I'm calling in all my chips today."

The fog lifted. Amazed, she realized over an hour had passed. Under her original plans, she should have been part of the Adult Forum just now ending. But Zan Johanson had pretty much blown those plans out of the water.

She arched her back and protested, "Me? You're crazy, woman. Just think back to my Christmas party." But Cate was persistent. Victoria hung up the phone and groaned, heading off to change clothes. "Cino, I'm an idiot, but I'm going off to bake. If I don't survive, jump the fence and go live with Cali and Alex, okay?"

Cate and Victoria baked ginger snaps.

And consumed a pot of coffee.

They baked crunchy chocolate chip cookies.

And talked endlessly of everything except Luke and Alex. And drank coffee.

They baked lemon drops.

And, switching to decaf, talked only of Luke and Alex.

They baked oatmeal-pecan-raisin cookies.

And, coffee forgotten, they wiped tears on floury aprons as they talked of tough and tender things neither woman had shared with anyone else for years.

Better friends after an afternoon of confidences and cookies than ever before, they cleaned up the café kitchen when the sun went down and stowed memories of the special time away in their hearts.

The smell of cookies lingered in Victoria's mind the next morning when she pulled her chair up close to her desk and powered up her computer. It had been a strange weekend, to say the least, with the exhilaration of the dinner at Rachel's, closely followed by the intensity of the church leader's meeting, mingled with the Alex-scene at the altar, and ending with the closeness of a new level of friendship in Cate's Café's stainless steel kitchen.

Between the exhausting pace of the cookie marathon and the sleepless night's furtive trips between her basement and Luke's burn barrel out behind the grocery store with armloads of moving boxes, she was one exhausted heap of bones. Finally, she let her head sink into her arms for a moment's rest, and Cino flopped over with a heart-felt sigh beside her.

No wonder the words just sat on the screen and stared back at her this morning; she was wiped out. She lifted her head only when she heard footsteps and then a knock on the door. "Come in," she invited.

"Victoria," Luke began, and then choked, unable to continue.

She rolled back her desk chair and crossed the room, arms outstretched to meet her half-way. He grasped her elbows. "Dave just told me there's not room for even two measly produce boxes in my burn barrel this morning. Care to tell me why I found it full of a certain somebody's cardboard dreams?"

She pulled back; Luke's eyes were riveted on her face. "Because that's exactly what those moving boxes in the basement were. Flimsy cardboard hopes and dreams. Life should be built on more."

Luke pulled her down on the loveseat. "Wasn't that a hard decision to make? Especially after all this town put you through?"

Victoria paused for a moment. "It was hard, but things that count usually are."

Luke exhaled slowly. "You're right," he said, eventually. "I think it's time I took better care of a few of my dreams, too."

"Cate?"

The single syllable jolted him. "Is it that obvious?"

"We've never named our secrets to each other, but we've known, haven't we? Ever since the night the lights went out."

"I've been a fool too long. It's time to light a fire to my foolish pride along with your boxes."

Victoria watched through the window as he strode across the lawn back to the store. Soon, wispy gray smoke circled above the trees behind the grocery store, mingling with the clouds. She turned back to her desk, knowing a major burden was literally going up in smoke.

So deep was her concentration that she heard nothing until the briefest knock preceded the words, "Can you come with me?" Alex stood in the open door, watching her. He was in his office clothes.

"Is someone sick?" She hit *save* on the computer, and grabbed a light jacket off the coat rack.

"Nope. I want to show you something." He held her jacket while she slipped into it. She turned off the light and urged a reluctant Cino toward the gate that would mean he didn't get to go along.

Alex's car was parked by the curb. "We're driving?" she asked, surprised. "Wow, how far are we going?"

He shrugged and opened the passenger door. They talked of inconsequential things as they headed South, past City Park, past fields where farmers had begun to till their fields. After a few miles, he turned in a long dusty driveway marked *Private.*

A grove of trees hid a house. "Who lives here, Alex?"

"No one, now. It's the home-place of one of my grandparents' friends. Grandpa borrowed money from the man when he started his practice in Prairie Rose. The man traveled a lot, having made his money on the railroad during its heigh-day. Grandpa often cared for the place when the man was away."

Suddenly, Victoria knew. She looked at Alex and then back at the spacious, overgrown yard. "This is the 'special secret spot on a country estate,' that Rachel told us about, isn't it?"

Alex nodded and casually reached into his pocket and pulled out a bag. "Want a cookie?" He chose one and offered the other to her.

"Thanks, Alex, but I'm not exactly hungry right now." Food was the last thing on her mind as she looked past Alex toward the house and overgrown but still enchanting yard.

His voice was insistent, "Come on, just one bite."

"These look familiar."

"Uh, yeah. I talked Cate into selling me some"

"Well, I'll share. I've had my fill of cookies lately," she hedged and broke one into two jagged pieces, only to gasp and stare at the chunk she held in her hands. It held a shining gold wedding band amidst the crumbs.

Not a diamond, but a wide band like the one Tori Dahlmann had described at great length in exquisite detail to Zan Johanson many years ago and told him she wanted one just like it someday.

"I've got the matching one in my pocket."

The cookie crumbled into bird-feed in her hands.

Trembling, she looked from the ring to azure eyes. He pushed open his door; her eyes followed him as he circled to her side and flung open her car door. Then, he reached for her hand and she stumbled after him.

With long strides he led her to a low backless bench beneath an ancient tree. Straddling it, he gently pulled her down beside him. She tucked one leg up beneath her and faced him; his closeness overpowered her senses. Heart pounding, she looked at him and knew they were both struggling to get their bearings in a dizzy world.

His first touch traced her lips. "I love you, Tori. I know Rachel will forgive me for stealing her line, but you're the only one whose name is love for me."

"I love you, too, Zan." she whispered, her eyes riveted to his face.

But her words didn't penetrate, and he continued. "Somehow, I'd hoped you would figure it out for yourself, but you've got to stop using Luke as a shield against me. He loves Cate."

"I know. And she loves him. And I love you."

"I almost don't want you to say that unless you are willing to marry me. I can't live without you."

"What about Gail?"

That got his attention; he looked blankly at her. "Gail?"

She nodded, "Gail. The one who named her son after you, the one who works side-by-side with you, the one who cooks roast beef dinners for you to feed my parents, the one who...you don't know what you'd do without..."

"Oh, you mean *Gail*...the one who kicked me out of the office today and said 'Doctor Alex, if you don't quit mooning around here and go propose once-and-for-all to that woman, I will march into her living room and tell her myself that, no, love doesn't ever die...' whatever *that's* all about. That Gail?"

"You mean...you and she aren't...lovers?"

Alex's hands cupped her cheeks and held her head steady as he looked into her eyes. "Gail is the only person in town, beside Rachel, who knows for a fact that I've loved you for all these years, and not just since we landed in town. Gail needed a friend, and since you've been so stubborn, I've had plenty of time to be that friend, but lovers? Never. She can work in my office, and I'll tuck her kids in for their naps in the big hospital bed in the back room at the office just like their Daddy would do at their house if he were still alive, but nobody but you has ever been—nor ever will be—my lover. I told you my vow and I've kept it."

"Oh, Zan, what an idiot I've been."

His body trembled like a quake line. "If we drive straight to Minot to the marriage license place, Casey will perform a ceremony for us this afternoon and we can make love all night," he said softly.

She rose, but his arm circled her legs and held her; he buried his face against her breasts. She ran her fingers through his hair, twisting a strand around one finger. Then, she tipped his face up; his hands were warm against her thighs, radiating heat through her clothing as she showered hungry kisses on his eager lips.

Her senses reeled as she sank at last to his lap, their lips still exploring. With a ragged moan she pushed herself up away from him and staggered toward the car.

His voice was hoarse, "Tori, Love, where are you going?"

"Minot."

Alex covered the distance between the bench and the car before she could open the door. He nuzzled her hair with his chin while they clung to each other, panting like race-weary runners.

"Alex, I'm scared. Believe it or not, the last few days have helped me resolve the issue of living in Prairie Rose. Back in September, I made a Pros-and-Cons list that I revisited several nights lately. Wanna see it?"

His eyebrows shot upwards. "Now? You carry it around with you? Wow. Sure."

She reached into a hip pocket and pulled out the tattered page from a legal pad, opened it and handed it to him. "When I knock something off a list, I bracket it."

Alex read with great care:

Cons

1) [I don't agree with his goals.] He's had his feet on solid ground all along. I'm the one with distorted goals.

2) [I doubt that he is husband-material for a minister.] Give the guy a break—and a standing ovation. Think Gail—when she needed help, who really gave it?

3) [Too much negative history. We'd always have our past hanging over our heads, especially with our families.] Think about Dad and Shimon Peres—when you can't solve it, accept it!

Alex arched an eyebrow and paused in his reading. "Peres?"

"Keep Reading; I'll explain later. Believe me, it's powerful!"

4) [He thinks we can just pick up where we left off. Maybe he can; I can't.] Love never dies!

5) [What would happen if the truth, the whole truth and nothing but the truth were told? Picking up with him again would require total honesty on my part.] Done that now, been there, and nothing but good to show for it!

Pros

1) No surprises with his personality; no getting-to-know-you time required

2) There's lots to like about him. He's fun, good with people, loves adventure. He's got a Berner!

3) He can handle my having a career. Our careers are compatible

4) I used to love him, so falling in love again wouldn't take much

Alex looked up from the list in stunned silence. He scanned it once again, emitting a low whistle. "That's a pretty powerful Cons list, Tori. I'm glad you didn't scratch it out beyond readability. I was up against some serious issues."

"I try to do more than cross something off one side or the other—I make myself explain why it moves to the other side. Everything—absolutely each item—on the original left column moved over to the Pros side in the past few days. Several of them should have moved long ago, but I was too stubborn to admit it that I have no valid reasons to turn you away. I'm not looking to marry just anyone—I want it to be you. And I can't imagine you being anywhere but here in Prairie Rose—and I can't fathom ever leaving you again."

"You're willing to live in a small town even after the way this one has treated you lately?"

"If that's the worst episode I face in my career, I'll be fortunate. How can I turn my back on the people who need me to help them build something positive for their own lives out of the experience? That's what pastors do. If I'm really up to snuff, I won't run at the first sign of trouble."

"Tori, you're quite a woman. I hope these people come to realize that."

She shook her head absentmindedly. "You know, I'm not all that convinced that the fact this is a small town has much to do with it. The issue is really just people—people living and working and building relationships with other people. When trust is broken, it hurts and we lash out. It makes no difference if we live in a small town, work with an intimate group of people, get to know a group of neighbors—anytime we trust someone, there's a risk for hurting another person and being hurt. It's the cost of doing business as a human being."

Alex nodded. "Even so, it takes a special person to face up to it all and love again." He peppered her face with a rash of kisses.

Suddenly, she pulled back and looked him straight in the eye. "There is one thing, Zan, that all this kissing won't let me forget. On that first Sunday with the pancakes, we talked about those busy hormones coursing through your veins. I'm not sure I'm ready to handle that much sexual expectation." She dropped her head and fiddled with a button on his shirt.

"Listen to me," he commanded, grasping her shoulders. When she met his eyes again, he released his grip; one thumb traced circles on her chin. "What did you preach on that first Sunday?" he asked in a softened voice.

She stared at him. "Huh? Something from the Gospel of Matthew?"

He offered a lop-sided grin and said, "Pretty good guess, especially since you're still in Matthew all these months later! Even if you don't remember your text that September morning's sermon, I do. You challenged us to step out in faith."

"You listened. And remembered. I'm impressed."

He absentmindedly pushed back her hair. "And you listened to me about seeing a specialist. I know I don't want to make the mistake of letting you get away again. So I had to step out in faith—which is something I've listened to you about—and hope God would put us back together again in spite of the mess we made of the first time we spun around through love together."

"Then ask me to stay. Just one more time."

"Tori, will you marry me and be my only love forever?"

"Yes," she whispered and his lips sealed their promise.

Three hours later, rings and the license in hand, Alex held open the heavy door leading to the hallway that ended in Casey's office. Once inside, away from the town's view, Alex stopped and turned to Victoria. "Any second thoughts?"

Victoria rolled her eyes dramatically. "Now he asks! After I buy this dress," she ran her hands along the silken lines of the new two-piece ivory dress, "and spend three times what I would have had to pay Sadie O'Dell to make it!"

He straightened his shoulders beneath a crisp ecru suit. "Spanking-new clothes aside, any doubts?"

"I only wish our families could be here, but we agreed, this is just the legal part; a church ceremony will come later. Thanks for thinking of Casey, Alex. He's such a wonderful choice instead of some unknown Justice of the Peace."

"Let's go get married, Tori."

With that, he knocked lightly on the door to Casey's office. The door opened and Victoria faltered as Alex caught her. She looked up at him, her lips open in a wordless question. He smiled and said, "Do I know how to elope, or what?"

Mort and Maggie Dahlmann, Charles and Jessica Johanson, and Alex's grandfather sat in chairs around the room with a glowing Rachel Lindquist as their hostess. Victoria was swept up in hugs. A babble of voices, laughter, and joyous tears formed a cocoon around the room. Casey unobtrusively made a couple of telephone calls and within minutes, there was another knock at the door. Luke and Cate entered, with Cino and Cali on their leashes for the event.

"*How* did you pull this off, Alex?" Victoria asked.

"I would have married you in blue jeans, but we needed the couple of hours we took shopping for everyone to assemble here. Our families were coming anyway for the Meadowlark Trail Grand Opening, so I just asked them to come a few days early!"

"But…"

"Once I gave Cate the ring and instructions to keep you busy baking cookies, I spent Sunday afternoon on the telephone."

"Rather confident, weren't you," she chided playfully.

"Let's just say I read between the lines of your fishbowl message!"

She pulled his face down for a kiss.

"It appears that these two want to get married!" Casey's brogue rippled through the room. Everyone clapped and someone whistled while Victoria blushed happily.

With Cate and Luke on either side, Victoria and Alex stood before Father Donovan. Their voices rang out confidently in their vows.

When the simple, moving ceremony was finished, Cate slipped away briefly and then rolled a cart inside the room. "Let the reception begin!" she called out.

Cookies. Ginger snaps. Crunchy chocolate chip. Lemon drops. Oatmeal-pecan-raisin. Cookies galore.

Victoria circled Cate's waist with one arm and whispered, "Hmmm, how on earth did you come up with so many kinds of cookies with such short notice?"

"A true friend helped," Cate responded with a hug. "Happiness always!"

After toasts all around and plenty of cookies for all, Victoria and Alex slipped away. "The troops—including both dogs—are staying at my place for the next couple of nights," Alex began.

Victoria interrupted, "We'll have enough decisions without picking a motel. Let's go to my place."

Alex grinned. "I was hoping you would say that! If everything is proceeding according to Hoyle, my suitcase should be up in your bedroom right now!"

"How…? Never mind! With everything else you've achieved behind the scenes lately, getting your suitcase into my bedroom is no accomplishment, at all!"

"The whole thing hinged on you not questioning why we didn't go to Williston instead of Minot for our license!"

"I hate to ask, but don't you have patients who will wonder where you are?"

He grinned. "Gail made up a sign that is hanging on the office door. It says, 'Gone Hunting,' which she figured covered it pretty well! I've switched the phone over to her place and she'll field calls and send people to Williston just like they used to do before I got here. I'm on my honeymoon, and I mean to spend it wickedly well!"

The Rectory stood dark that evening since the light of the glowing taper didn't go beyond the bed. Alex's eyes followed the long lace-clouded lines of Victoria's body. A shooting flame of passion melted her fears.

"Beautiful…" he breathed softly. He clasped her hand and lifted it to his lips while he brought her closer, closer. She shivered in anticipation. Adonis lived and breathed in one bedroom in this amazing corner of North Dakota.

Alex's jagged breathing filled her ears like the roar of the Mendocino surf. Waves of desire lapped against every cell in their bodies.

"My bride," he whispered. "I love you, Tori. Every inch of you." Whitecaps of pleasure crashed against her inner shores beneath his touch. "Love, we have all our lives to enjoy each other."

"Let's begin tonight," she whispered shakily and bent toward him, her hair falling around them in a copper cloud.

In ways as fresh as their reborn love, each delighted the other. Beneath the same moon that drifted above Mendocino and tonight lit the North Dakota skies, in one house two lovers, with an urgency that had extended beyond a decade, became one.

When they finally stirred, Alex whispered, "Well, my sea-breeze, meadow-grasses, sandy-beaches lover." Victoria smiled and nuzzled his shoulder, basking in the sweetness she found there.

"Are you okay?" he asked softly.

She nodded.

"I'll fill the bathtub for you if you'd like."

She silenced him with a finger on his kiss-bruised lips. "I'm fine. God bless lasers." She couldn't finish. Who could with all that followed, leaving mere words pale?

When the first rays of sun lit the sky Tuesday morning, Alex opened his eyes and looked at the woman in the circle of his arm. He smiled. Gently he kissed her earlobe, the tip of her chin, the creamy skin of her shoulder. She sighed in her sleep and snuggled closer.

Tenderly, he brushed back a vivid lock of hair that hid one side of her face. He reveled in the sight of his lover and knowing all the tangled bed-sheet covered.

"So that's where you hung that picture," Alex said with a smile.

She followed his eyes to the wall where his Christmas gift hung. "'May all our dreams come true,'" she recited.

"I think they have, Love," he responded and reached for her again.

* * *

The long-awaited Grand Opening Weekend for the Meadowlark Trail had finally arrived. In the intervening four days, Alex and Victoria had conducted lives as close to normal as possible, having decided to announce their marriage in a manner they would always remember. They were never more than a few feet apart, unless they were at their separate offices, but considering the dizzy pace at which folks approached the weekend festivities, their marriage remained a secret shared by only the wedding guests.

The various planning committees for the Grand Opening met for a picnic early Friday evening. Alex and Victoria, Luke and Cate, Rachel and dozens more who had worked long and strenuous hours together laughed and joked together, consuming an impressive variety and prodigious quantities of food. The Senior Dahlmanns and Johansons staffed the food tables, enabling the workers all to eat together rather than serving each other.

When church bells struck seven, picnic baskets were stowed away and all headed to the school for the evening's program. It was an event that rivaled any occasion Prairie Rose had previously hosted or dared to dream. Victoria looked up from reading her program in a front-row seat just as Lauren—"the designer of the Prairie Rose symbol" as the program designated her—approached Milt Browning who would serve as Master of Ceremonies. She whispered something next to his ear, he nodded and with an unstoppable grin, stepped off the low platform to follow her a short distance away from the stage.

Surrounded by the Dahlmanns and Johansons, Victoria watched Milt and Lauren's spirited conversation. Lauren could no longer be considered shy; she had developed into quite a confident, capable person. Happy for any small part she had had in Lauren's remarkable transformation, Victoria watched Milt return to his seat to gather up his notes. The din lessened to shuffling and scattered coughing when he took his place behind the podium.

"Welcome!" His voice over the loudspeaker stilled the last noises. "I am pleased to see such a good crowd. It speaks well for your interest in the Meadowlark Trail." Wild applause interrupted even his few introductory words several times. He concluded with, "We are delighted so many are here to share in the official beginning of this event. A special interest group will begin our program." He nodded discretely to his left.

A group of four teenagers moved quickly from the front row of bleachers to the podium, led by Lauren who adjusted the microphone to her height. "Good evening. On behalf of the youth of Prairie Rose, we want to honor several who have changed our town radically over the past months. Please come to stand beside me as I call your names."

A hum of anticipation moved through the audience. "Mr. Luke Larson." Luke was directed to a spot on the stage. "Reverend Victoria Dahlmann." Mort squeezed his daughter's shoulder excitedly and she moved to stand at Luke's right. "Doctor Alex Johanson." Alex came up beside Victoria and winked at her.

Lauren read from prepared cards, "These special people took the first steps that sent our town on its most exciting journey. Through the various stages of developing the Meadowlark Trail, we have seen a growth in civic pride and watched citizens and businesses work together toward a common goal."

Victoria's practiced eye scanned the crowd. Lauren's well-delivered speech was receiving encouraging nods and approving smiles. "The Meadowlark Trail officially opens tomorrow, but we have already seen changes. As Freshmen, Sophomore, Junior, and Senior representatives, we give tribute to these leaders." She moved back from the podium and led what grew to a thunderous ovation.

The Freshman girl pinned a corsage on Victoria and boutonnieres on Luke and Alex. The Sophomore boy draped ribbons with gold letters proclaiming "Honored Citizen" around their necks. The Junior representative shook their hands solemnly and presented each of them with a framed certificate.

At some undetected signal, the high school band burst through the door—in full uniform with instruments gleaming in the bright lights—sending a rousing Sousa march into the highest tier of bleachers. The crowd clapped and stomped in sync with the drums. Lauren led Luke,

Victoria and Alex to the front of the band and they led an impromptu parade around the gymnasium several times. Each grade-school class then marched in loose formation around the perimeter of the room after awards were given to them for their contributions: planting trees, painting signs, cleaning up the ball field, distributing fliers and posters—everyone had participated.

As nothing else could have, the high schoolers' roles in the program set the mood for the evening. Rachel received special recognition and a bouquet of peach-tipped roses for her considerable contributions to the historical buildings project. The woman's tremulous smile aimed straight into the bleachers and brought tears of joy to Victoria's eyes when she saw where it landed: squarely with the Senior Doctor Johanson.

Victoria watched those two steady gazes locked together. Oblivious to the cheers, Rachel tipped her bouquet in her old friend's direction and they shared a secret island of memories in the crowded room.

The various special committees awarded enthusiastic members for jobs well done. The Golden Shovel Award, given to the man who had dug deep holes for bushes—in the exact location where, two days earlier, the Garden Club had carefully planted hundreds of choice bulbs—brought down the house. He bowed lavishly, basking in this moment of dubious fame, knowing he would receive his share of comments along Main Street the next morning.

The high school photography class had created a classic video to capture the past months' activities: the new sign, designed by Gail, hanging over Harvey Thompson's special museum; Rachel's poster stories in windows along the historical tour; flowers blooming in new stone-rimmed beds on Meadowlark Trail; from garages and wood shops all around town, the handymen's winter work: freshly painted picnic tables and new benches that awaited weary walkers at strategic points.

Ripples of sheer delight spread throughout the auditorium as neighbors and friends spotted candid shots of homeowners throughout

Prairie Rose working together at the Trail Center, or spending their evenings raking yards, sweeping up the debris of winter, or spit-shining the town in anticipation of the weekend visitors.

Main Street had been cleaned by the local Scout troop and now, at the end of the program, barricades diverted traffic around the two-block area cordoned off for a street dance. Long after the official ceremonies ended in the gymnasium, dancers of all ages dipped and whirled beneath a brilliant moon to the tunes from Prairie Rose's own Prairie Pluckers.

Cate's Canopy supplied parched dancers with cool drinks. After one such break, Alex disappeared into the crowd and returned with a bow to Victoria. He led her to the center of the street. When the first chords moved from the loudspeakers through her body, they moved into each other's arms, totally oblivious to the rest of the world, while "Georgia On My Mind" spun a web between past, present, and future.

Among the last to leave Main Street, Victoria and Alex walked home under an umbrella of darkness. With their families arriving early, the extra activity around their two houses and throughout the town with last-minute preparations for the Grand Opening in full swing, they had no qualms that they would be discovered by unsuspecting locals. They spent each night locked in each other's arms in joyous abandon.

"What a weekend!" Victoria smiled as they climbed the Rectory steps on Friday night. "So much has happened in town, and in our lives. It's all beyond my wildest dreams!"

"Do you think Prairie Rose will be able hold your interest, Tori?" Alex asked, pulling her against him in the dark entryway.

"Hmmm," she said, willingly matching the rhythm of the dance his hips were beginning. "If it dims from time to time, I think there's something else that will manage to entice me!"

"Something like this?" He knew exactly how to make her forgot everything about Prairie Rose except its doctor who had staked his claim on her heart.

By early Saturday morning it was evident that word had spread throughout the state about Prairie Rose's venture. Just like a sale always brings people hours before the announced opening, a steady stream of cars drove into Prairie Rose on the coattails of a vibrant sunrise, spilling their occupants out along Main Street. Victoria had warned that this would happen, so the first shift crew was in place to welcome those who zeroed in on Meadowlark Trail Center.

Soon, armed with maps and brimming with enthusiasm, some visitors fanned out along the marked and gleaming Meadowlark Trail while others roamed Main Street or followed the trail of the Historical Buildings' tour, picking up a snack from Cate's Canopy or Larson's Grocery along the way and making note of the time Harvey's museum opened.

Walking across the lawn to her office before breakfast, Victoria saw a family—already wearing new T-shirts imprinted "You Are Here: Prairie Rose" with a star marking the proper place on a North Dakota map—sitting on a specially placed bench facing the Rectory. She grinned when she watched them point out the garrets on her home while reading segments of the brochure aloud. She opened the office door to begin her final review of Sunday's sermon before joining her parents and newly minted in-laws for breakfast at Alex's house.

Just in time to snag the traditional early risers who were winding their way to Cate's Café for coffee, Fred Becker delivered the first copies of a special edition of the *Prairie Rose Chronicle* to the box outside the Post Office. Fred didn't just deliver the paper, he did so with a flourish and strut: he had been let in on the secret of the year, and could finally let it out.

News spread quickly. From Alex's office window, the newlyweds watched a line form; when the box emptied, the growing stream of people snaked its way to the *Chronicle* office where Fred handed out papers and collected quarters with an unquenchable grin. Within minutes,

Prairie Rose was buzzing over the headline: "Meadowlark Trail Opens to the Sound of Wedding Bells" and the accompanying detailed story.

Mid-morning, Victoria and Alex made their first walk down Main Street as an openly acknowledged couple only to be besieged by best wishes, hugs, and handshakes. The rest of the day was a blur of smiling people, floats and high school marching bands in the parade, and dozens of visitors all planning their return trip to "Prairie Rose: the little town that dared to dream big" as Victoria heard one reporter say into his microphone.

By the end of the day, Victoria was sure she had tasted all fourteen flavors of Cate's new Hawaiian Fruit Ices what with all the cups that were offered as congratulatory toasts from dozens of well-wishers throughout the day. In a variation of the spoon-tapping that at wedding receptions guarantees kisses, Alex happily swept his new bride into his arms each time someone waved a copy of the newspaper.

"I told you the *Prairie Rose Chronicle* would have fun with our wedding!" he whispered in her ear before he released her after one lingering kiss.

"At least the account mentions our names!"

Saturday night ended with a wedding reception in City Park, hosted by the senior Johansons and Dahlmanns. Cate had somehow managed, midst all the bustle of the past six days, to create a towering wedding cake. Tables sagged beneath punch bowls, coffee pots, and plates heaped with finger sandwiches and special cookies. The bride and groom popped bites of cookies into each other's mouths while cameras flashed.

Then, when the youngest children were fighting to keep their eyes open, Milt Browning invited Alex and Victoria to join him at the microphone on the parade master's stand. "Victoria and Alex, you've surprised us beyond our wildest dreams. What a weekend! On the heels of the Grand Opening, this wonderful celebration. We'd like to hear a few words from you before we all head home."

Alex accepted the microphone. "Thank you all for making this a day we'll never forget. I'd like to take this opportunity to answer a question that we've heard all day: What are we going to do with two houses?"

A laugh rippled through the crowd seated on blankets and lawn chairs around the park. He continued, "We hope our plan will meet with your approval. My wife will tell you about it!" He handed her the microphone while whistles and cheers rose to the treetops.

She scanned the faces around her and sensed their excitement. It's hard to believe these are the same people who had once thought the state's centennial celebration was their last hurrah. "In just a few weeks, Prairie Rose will be host to yet another Grand Opening." She waited while Charles Johanson walked to the platform and handed his son a package. Everyone watched Alex carefully unwrap a sign and turn it so all could read, "The Johanson House. Bed and Breakfast Inn. Prairie Rose, North Dakota."

Victoria's words rode the crest of the excitement, "Following remodeling, Gail Harker will move into the Johanson House as its resident hostess. The Inn is our joint business venture with Luke Larson who first had the dream. Alex and I will make our home in the Rectory for as long as the Prairie Rose Community Church and the Indian Hills United Church wish me to be their pastor."

On Sunday morning, Victoria woke Alex with a toe-tingling kiss. Sneaking a peak, he grinned and pulled her into the crook of his arm. "Don't start something you don't plan to finish, woman!" he growled.

"Hmmm, that sounds tempting," she said, nuzzling his neck. "But there's something going on outside I thought you might want to see before everyone else shows up for church." She pulled back the sheet.

He lifted one eyelid and groaned melodramatically. "Wouldn't you rather start the day with heavy breathing exercises?"

She hid a smile. "If we do much more heavy breathing, we'll need to install oxygen tanks in the Rectory. Explain *that* to the town!"

Hastily clad in jeans and sweatshirts, Victoria led Alex around the front corner of the church. The early morning sun reflected wildly off the opened glass door of the church sign. Sitting cross-legged on the ground in front of the sign, Gail wiped a paintbrush and looked up over her shoulder at the two who walked up behind her.

Alex's eyes were glued to the bottom line of the sign where it read in Gail's inimitable calligraphy, *Pastor: The Reverend Tori Johanson*. A pile of discarded sticky letters lay nearby.

"I may not remember my text from that September Sunday, but I do recall hearing that I'll only be Tori to you." The rest of what she planned to say was lost in an embrace that rocked her off her feet.

* * *

Monday morning, Cate's Café was packed stem-to-stern, keeping both Cate and Lucy hopping. It had been a weekend brimming with conversation topics and everyone had something to say. The Grand Opening had been a booming success. The secret wedding had sent romance rocketing into a place of prominence. Today, Prairie Rose was alive, humming and kicking up its heels.

In the whirlwind of chatter, no one paid much notice to Cate. She looked up as Luke walked in. Their eyes locked and held as he moved from the door to the counter where he straddled a just-vacated stool. He ignored the filled coffee cup she automatically put within his reach.

Heads turned and the babble of voices dropped to a bewildered hush when, just seconds later, Luke set his seat a-spinning and made a beeline after Cate through the swinging doors into the kitchen.

Those doors were hardly soundproof. Around the now-quiet tables and counter stools, everyone could hear the unmistakable sounds of kissing.

Lots of kissing. Long, loud, lustful kisses.

Everyone listened—embarrassed to be eavesdropping, but frozen in place. Then, in a rush of collective propriety, they shot wordless glances at each other, dropped coins and bills on the tables and left Cate's Café. Each witness to the unseen event wondered *What next?* as all scurried along Main Street of the North Dakota town.

AFTERWORD

Hats off to the thousands of women around the world who, like Victoria Dahlmann in *Uncharted Territory*, live day-to-day with endometriosis. This is a novel, not a medical publication, so I do not pretend to have presented all the facts of this condition. Those interested in knowing more about this disease and medical advancements not covered in these pages may wish to contact:

The Endometriosis Association International Headquarters

8585 North 76th Place

Milwaukee, WI 53223 USA

Phone: (414) 355-2200. In North America & the Caribbean: (800) 992-3636. Fax: (414) 355-6065. E-mail: endo@endometriosisassn.org.

Their web site address says a lot: www.killercramps.org. Check it out.
Hadley Hoover

ABOUT THE AUTHOR

Hadley Hoover and her husband of 22 years enjoy country auctions, Saturday morning breakfasts at small-town cafés near their Rochester MN home, and the daily antics of their nine-year-old male Bernese Dog. Hadley welcomes e-mail at: hadleyhoover@chartermi.net. She is currently working on her third novel, *Rough Terrain*.